CONJECTRIX

Other Books by Candace J. Thomas:

Vivatera
(Book 1 in the *Vivatera* Series)

CONJECTRIX

CANDACE J. THOMAS

Xchyler Publishing ,
an imprint of Hamilton Springs Press, LLC
Penny Freeman, Editor-in-chief
www.xchylerpublishing.com

Paperback Edition: April, 2014

Cover and Interior Design by D. Robert Pease, walkingstickbooks.com
Map created by Beth Ipson
Edited by Elizabeth Gilliland and Terri Wagner

Published in the United States of America
Xchyler Publishing

To my sister Becka, for simply being invincible.

Parbraven

Ignis Mountains

Netherfields

Tristus R.

The Willows

Sharlot

Musungu
Marshes

Southwick

Northern Crest
N
W
E
S
Linnonbury
Mt. Ibis
Durundun
The Caelin
Lake Kolintur
Ravian R.
Echoes
Eastern Mountains
Davonport
Salt Dunes
Sister Elm
Springs of Sephar
Tapoof
Butterfly Islands

Take me winds...

and seas...

and oceans...

Back to the grass and the earth so deep.

For my soul is restless and longs for a bed

In the peace of dreamless sleep...

—Song of the Damned

PROLOGUE

The city shimmered in the night like gold. Near the top of the palace, one could see over the wall to the sea, the marsh, the jungle, and beyond. Parbraven looked peaceful, though nothing could be further than the truth.

After so many years away from that place, Taren once again found himself in the den of the devil.

"Son of Lockwood." The voice woke his senses back to the moment. He turned and faced the king of Southwick, a man he'd never known or honored.

"You are the son of our captain, are you not?"

Taren reserved his speech for the one who mattered.

King Reinoh stood near the end of the long hallway, where tall guards flanked the exit. "A son of a captain has honor among my court."

Taren moved from the window and chose a seat on a bench near a bowl of ornamental knickknacks. He picked up a sharp crystal and held it out in front of him, examining the images in the sliced glass. "Where is my father? I came to see him, not you."

The king came forward, visibly irritated with his arrogance. "We are splitting our efforts to track the stones."

"You mean *his* efforts."

1

CONJECTRIX

Reinoh stood tall before Taren, looking every bit the king, playing the part well, even as his strings were being pulled by an elegant master.

"Your time is coming, Reinoh." Taren stared at the king's hard expression. "Sharrod is using you. He'll dispose of you as soon as you're no longer useful."

The stern creases in the older man's face deepened as he analyzed Taren's comment. "My loyalty lies here. Where do yours?"

"This isn't about loyalty. It's about greed." Taren tilted his head, asking directly, "What do you want from me?"

Reinoh sneered. "You can read magic."

"I don't—"

"The Oracle has seen what you can do."

Taren's eyes stayed on the king, betraying no hint of his suspicions. "I don't know anything about an oracle. I think you're grasping at any straw in front of you—"

"Silence, firebrand!" Reinoh ordered. "We know all about your adventures in the Echoes, but since that night, the girl Harrow sought has vanished."

The glass crystal in Taren's hand grew hot and he threw it across the room, shattering it into tiny shards. "Don't you have others willing to carry out your plan? I'm not interested."

"We have located a few of Prolius' daughters. It's just a matter of time until we can reclaim them."

"Then why do you need me?"

"The girl."

Taren knew where this was leading. "I already did what I could."

"And Sharrod noticed." The king snapped his fingers and the two guards left them alone. Bending low, he whispered, "The girl didn't die . . . and you *knew* she wouldn't."

Taren felt the accusation flare through him like a rush of heat. The memory pierced his vision—the knife hot in his hand; driving it deliberately through Naomi's flesh, right to her heart where the magic lived. His magic may have guided his decision, but he was the one to act. He didn't move, facing his accuser still as a statue. "You know nothing."

Reinoh glared at him suspiciously. Taren stood to meet his challenge.

Suddenly, the atmosphere changed as if time had stopped. A tall man—or what Taren presumed was a man—entered the room, surrounded by crackling energy. There were horns on each side of his head, marks of a demon. The magic that accompanied him was unlike the complicated stain of a soul, but rather of pure power, dangerously strong.

"Do not attempt to read me." Sharrod's voice felt like an echo from the grave. "I do not mask my power. I wear it with honor."

Taren stood, trying to look braver than he felt. "You don't need me."

"You are wrong." Sharrod moved to him, smooth as a snake. "The circle cannot be complete as long as she lives."

"But she can't—"

"Find her!" His voice echoed around the walls. "Lure her to Ignis. The souls will take her. There she can be destroyed."

Taren felt hatred bubbling up inside. "If I do, what will you do for me?"

A wicked laugh sounded through the hall. "I'll give you what you want."

"You don't know what I want."

Sharrod turned. "I can release you from the dark magic that holds you captive." They now stood face-to-face, his voice a whispered hiss. "I own you."

CONJECTRIX

Taren didn't move but stared at the demon, contemplating his decision. The last thing he wanted was to face Naomi again, but freedom was within his grasp. He breathed deep, knowing what his choice would be.

The magic needed to be stopped.

CHAPTER ONE
INSIDE THE CAELIA

Naomi stared at the strange crisscross patterns flitting around the walls of the chamber. Rippling water reflected aquamarine light from the bottom of a shallow pool, relaxing and calming her mind with the rhythmic lapping of the water. This spot had brought her much comfort over the past few months. How unusual and lovely to see that light in such darkness. Here she found a safe haven away from her troubles. Here she found peace.

Spotswood had created his home in an unusual way. He called it Durundin, his refuge, hidden deep within the earth, all hint of it on the surface concealed with exposed roots and tangles of undergrowth. Tunnels branched out in confusing patterns, designed to trap uninvited guests, though Naomi had learned how to navigate them, and grew to love the smell of the earth and minerals in a strange, intangible way.

Before long, Spotswood had brought her to a cave under the lake, the Caelia, where air was held trapped by the surrounding rock. The cavern walls were lined with bluish green crystals, the color of the sea. Monstrous stalactites and stalagmites lifted upward through the water and downward from the ceiling, reaching for their missing brothers in the cavern. Light filtered in through crystal pockets like windows of sunshine, gently coloring the walls.

It was her favorite place.

The Caelia had a remarkable, even miraculous effect upon her, healing her body from the wound sustained in the Echoes. Veins spiraled near the healing scar—the Vivatera, resting within her skin. The sight regurgitated a painful memory of Taren standing over her, the dagger in his hand, wearing a tortured look on his face, like he had no choice but to kill her.

The magic inside her panicked at the recollection, so Naomi took a deep breath and pushed the memory back again. Although she felt strong enough to resume her normal activities, her state of mind was fragile.

And Reynolds had left without saying a word.

Her body may have healed, but her spirit had changed. Naomi no longer had any lingering doubt about identity, though she wished she had never found out the truth. She just wanted to be Naomi, not a daughter of the great King Prolius, who had cursed the world by exposing rare magic and sentencing his daughters to die for his mistakes. Just Naomi, barefoot and carefree. As she sat in the Caelia watching the water ripple, she was reminded again of her own significance, but she could not feel more worthless.

The Vivatera had saved her life, but at a great cost. The life-giving medallion that so many had sought for now rested inside her chest, living and moving in her veins, a life force of its own. She could feel the power course through her striving to get out, pulsing with an uncontrollable strength. It made her feel restless and scared. The magic felt stronger than she. She wondered how long it would rest here inside her, dormant, before it searched for a way to escape and destroy her.

Maybe Reynolds knew it would destroy her and didn't want to stay to watch.

Spotswood endeavored to help her understand the Histories—the legends and mysteries of Parbraven. "The Histories are of time and of beginning," he told her. "Force and magnetism attracted the fibers together, binding and creating the world we know. The great chemistry of life expanding within the frame of creation, every strand pulling toward a new structure—creating life."

He talked over her head most of the time. "So everything is connected?"

"They are here." He pulled up the sleeve of his robe to reveal the many purplish veins pulsing in rhythm. "And here." He took her hands and placed them palm to palm. A warm sensation came over her, like a stranger's touch. "And here." He moved her hand again to the top of his chest. She felt the rhythm thump again and again. "We are the same. Everything knows the sensations. When it wakes in you, you are home. It is safe. That is the danger."

Naomi's brain tried desperately to wrap around Spotswood's words. She spent many hours reading about the different cultures, wars, traditions, births, and deaths in Parbraven. There were the early years, when Parbraven was called Paresia, before the conquering by Ravenmoor, the southern tribe that was seduced by the richness of the land and the first establishments of the king. She stopped at the name and laughed to herself, wondering if her friend Katia could be a relative to the ancient tribe.

She also read very sad tales of betrayal; of Princess Asjahliere, married to a powerful commander whose lust for a ring made from Camisium drove her to suicide; and the records of triplets born without sight, who could prophesy of future events.

CONJECTRIX

With each history, Naomi's heart grew heavier. The lingering thread through every story was the elements—the singular connection to everything. The last page revealed a small prophecy written on ancient text. On the side, small notes were written in Spotswood's handwriting. Looking over the words, she sighed. *I am one of the tragic tales.*

Birth of a marked child, Spotswood's writings stated, *seventh of all.*

The complexity of the situation overwhelmed Naomi—sisters whom she never met now linked with her in fate, all hunted by Sharrod, demon of the underworld, who sought to destroy them and take their stones. One sister, Ymber, had suffered the consequence of separation from her stone: death. Each of her sisters knew of her role in the destiny their father had created for them, and accepted it.

But Naomi's fate had come at the hand of Reynolds.

For those reasons, Naomi kept returning to the Caelia where she could ponder. There had to be a different way. She felt tremendous guilt, as if all of it were her fault, this essential part she played in a crisis with broad ramifications; and though she now held a central role in this unique family, she had never felt more alone in her life.

"Hey." She felt a gentle nudge as Ferra appeared next to her. The girl had believed herself the youngest of the six daughters of King Prolius, until they discovered Naomi was the seventh. Ferra's warm personality had helped Naomi accept the truth of her own heritage—a hidden princess, sealed to a terrible fate. "You okay?"

Naomi continued to stare. "I think so. I'm alive."

"And that's the best part." Ferra winked and gave her a small shoulder squeeze. "Come on. Spill it. What's going on with you?"

Naomi just shrugged. "I'm distracted."

"I wish you would stop thinking so much. I need someone to have fun with."

8

"What about Landon?" Naomi had witnessed how Ferra had flirted with the boy over the past few weeks in the Durundin.

"He's fun, you know?" Ferra shrugged, grinning. "I'm glad to have him down here with us. He makes things bearable." Her smile faded. "Katia sure is a sour grape though. She doesn't take to joking very well."

Naomi did smile at that. Fiery, red-headed Katia, though clever and spirited, did seem to have daggers out for Ferra. Landon had acted tenderly toward Katia after her fall in the Echoes when she had shattered both hips, but soon it became clear that Ferra and Landon had similar personalities, the same sense of humor and zeal for life.

"I wouldn't worry about him," Ferra spoke up.

Naomi stilled. "Are we still talking about Landon?"

"Of course not."

Naomi knew who she was referencing but tried her best to concentrate on other things. A lingering fear remained that he would not return.

The few days after Naomi woke Reynolds had stayed away, the confession of his guilt reading like a book on his face. Then, without a word to her, he disappeared. Spotswood said he'd gone to find more secrets in the outside world, though she didn't believe it. Deep down she knew he'd left to get away from her. Now everything felt complicated. As much as she ached for his return, she feared it as well.

"Do you want to practice again?" Ferra asked. She was helping deepen Naomi's understanding of magic—to learn the fibers and how they functioned in harmonious control.

Naomi nodded. It would change the subject and help her focus on something else. Ferra's abilities were limited underground, but she taught Naomi how to recognize the sensations created by her magic. "How about we work with the water?"

CONJECTRIX

"Okay." Naomi rubbed the palms of her hands to get the blood circulating. She closed her eyes and the magic danced round her eyelids. Fiery pink and purple tendrils flared excitedly—the Vivatera's power inside her, just waiting to get out.

"We are here. . . ." it whispered, an echoing refrain.

Naomi opened her eyes and cupped some water from the lake in her hand, feeling the coolness between her fingers. As she hummed, sweet wind exited her mouth. She blew on her hands. The water loved the sound and pushed out of her palms, cascading down the back of her hands and spiraling in beautiful falling arches.

Ferra looked awestruck. "Amazing."

Naomi changed her breath to a whistle and the water contorted into the shape of a ball. It moved closer to Ferra, who stared, engrossed in the magic. As it floated up above her head, the whistling stopped—

—and the water came splashing down on her face.

"Nice." Ferra wiped the water from her eyes and nose. "Fine way to treat your sister."

Naomi cracked a smile.

Through the tunnel, different voices echoed her name.

Ferra turned. "Who's that?"

"He's back." Naomi whispered. An uncomfortable knot pitted in her stomach. For weeks she'd worried and wondered what Reynolds was doing. Now, within moments she would see him again. The Vivatera reacted with a warm thumping in her chest.

Reynolds entered the Caelia with Landon behind. He looked tired, weathered, and wet, but still Naomi couldn't help but stare.

"Oh, good," he said with hardly a glance at her. "Glad we found you."

Naomi couldn't hide her smile, but the look on Reynolds' face made it fade altogether. "What's happened?"

"Come." He helped Naomi to her feet, his hands icy cold. "We need to leave."

"Now?"

"As soon as possible."

"But we're not prepared!" Ferra pulled herself up. "We have no plans, no provisions . . ."

Within moments everyone, including Katia, Micah, and Spotswood, gathered together in an earthy room with a trickling spring.

Micah pulled out a large cloth map with a small portion ripped away—the same cloth he had shown them back in the camp so long ago.

"We have identified where Naomi's sisters and the stones could be," Spotswood explained. "To the west, past the drying land of Hope, lie the Ignis Mountains, and in the middle of these mountains sleeps Lux Lucis—the fire-breathing mountain. Caminus is there."

"Caminus?" Naomi asked.

"Sera," Ferra whispered next to her.

"And down here," Spotswood trailed his finger to the edge near Southwick, "in the Musungu swamps, we find Nox."

"Vespa is down there," Ferra whispered again.

Reynolds nudged Naomi. "We think the prince and your Zander will head there according to this dream." He pointed to a rough parchment stacked together where the vision had been recorded.

"I suggest Ferra and I travel down to Southwick to find them," Landon spoke up.

"Sounds fun," Ferra added with a wink.

"Not so hasty, young one," Spotswood interjected, pointing to the other corner, down by the islands. "This is where Aquos is, far by the water's edge. We have a lot of traveling ahead of us."

11

CONJECTRIX

"Those are only three of the stones," Reynolds added. "We have the others. Ferra's—"

Ferra reached down, grabbed the chain holding her precious medallion, and rang it like a bell. "And Silexa's in Southwick."

"And that leaves—"

"Ymber's," Ferra sighed, lowering her stone. "Sharrod has it. How are we going to get that?"

"Courage is not planned," said the enigmatic Spotswood.

Naomi felt the weight of the daunting task before them. "This is going to split us up, isn't it?"

Spotswood nodded. "Strength can come from separation. The watchful *eye* can only observe us one at a time."

CHAPTER TWO
DEPARTURE

"M e?" Landon exclaimed. "Why me?"

"You roamed with the gypsies," Reynolds explained. "You're familiar with the area—Naomi said you're from the Springs."

"Well, yes, but that doesn't mean I want to return."

"Me, neither," Katia spoke up, watching Landon from the corner of her eye. "I don't want to go back."

Reynolds attempted to calm himself. This should have been the easiest part of tonight. "This is a logical decision. We need Ferra to go to Southwick; she has an idea where to find her sister there. And Naomi needs to stay as far away from Southwick as possible—"

"You don't know what it's like down there," Katia interrupted, silencing him. "I can't relive those nightmares."

Landon leaned in toward Reynolds' ear. "If you were me, you wouldn't want to return to the Springs, I promise."

Reynolds clasped his shoulder. "Honestly, I'd switch with you any day." He tried to smile. "It will be an adventure."

Ferra smirked at Landon from across the table. "Reynolds says 'adventure', but he means boring. Fontine is, by far, the least fun of my sisters."

"I'm sure she would be a lot more fun if you found her," Landon teased.

Ferra laughed. "I'm the reckless one, remember? She'd never agree to go anywhere with me, even if my father got involved."

"I have gifts to give for the journey." Spotswood grabbed a few things from a shelf in the hollowed-out wall. "Special, special . . ." he muttered. "Here we go. For the Trickster and the Ice princess"—he looked to Katia and Landon—"I have the Phasm Stones. Makes illusions." He handed Landon two round steel marbles. "Roll them in your palm and the magic ignites."

Landon looked closely. The stones rubbed against each other and started to move.

"Not now, Trickster," Spotswood warned.

Landon placed them in his pocket.

"And lovely, for the Ice Princess." Katia smiled at the nickname. "The Everstar." He handed her an old, worn cloth with the insignia of the same interweaving star on the back of Naomi's neck.

"A scarf?"

"The Everstar will bring luck and protection. It is not just cloth; it is a shield."

Katia took it in her fingers, rolled it around, and then muttered something under her breath.

"For lovely Effrenus, the Venia guides by the winds and will point you where you need to go." He took down a small wooden cup, placed it under the drizzling waterfall next to the wall, and handed it to her. Ferra peered into the water and saw the shadow of a needle pointing downward in the gentle ripple.

"Thank you," she said graciously and stepped back to look at it with Micah.

Spotswood turned to Naomi.

Reynolds' eyes widened. He knew what Spotswood would give her, but would it work? That remained a mystery.

"I don't want anything, Spotswood," Naomi told him.

"Want is not need."

"What could I possibly need?"

Spotswood had nothing in his hands, but with a quick twirl of his wrists, a fist-sized purple ball appeared. Reynolds knew exactly what it was. It had once belonged to Jeanus.

Naomi looked confused. "I know this." Her eyes met Reynolds', remembering their first meeting. "From the cellar?"

He nodded. She looked to Spotswood.

"You're giving me this?"

"This is the Conjectrix," Spotswood explained. "Out there, it will be very dangerous for you to use your dreams. The world knows you now and every secret you keep must be hidden."

As Naomi reflected on her dreams, Reynolds brooded. Each was a prophetic insight to her magical connection to the world. But she couldn't control them, however dangerous. "But what does it do?"

"The Conjectrix is an interpreter. It will help you see without seeking."

"See without seeking?" Naomi repeated.

Reynolds, standing near the doorway, saw her confusion. "That's how Jeanus used it. She couldn't see the outside world, only the magical. This stone helped her see the danger."

Naomi's mouth turned up in a smile, charming him again. "Did it also help her travel?"

"We'll see," he murmured, forcing himself to look away. "I also asked Spotswood to make something for you."

CONJECTRIX

Spotswood pulled out a beautiful new cloak made of Shadesilk. "Spun from my own worms." The design moved like fluid in cloth form.

"Wow," Katia breathed. "Can I get one of those?"

"My worms are very small, my dear."

Katia pouted.

Suddenly, footsteps sounded above. Small particles of dirt fell from the top of the ceiling and landed on Spotswood's dusty spectacles.

Reynolds' fears appeared well-founded. He grabbed Naomi's arm. "Come on."

Both Spotswood and Micah turned and touched the dirt wall, feeling and listening to the rock and what it had to say.

"They have found the tunnel," Micah interpreted. "They have bruised the rock and entered."

Reynolds swore. "I knew they were following me. My medallion is broken—it doesn't conceal my passage anymore." He slammed bits of crusted metal onto the table, leftovers from the magical item he'd worn in the Echoes to disguise his appearance. "Everyone, it's time to go."

He grabbed a couple of provision packs and wrapped the cloak around Naomi, who still looked in shock, frozen in fear. "I know a way out." He turned toward Landon. "There's a tunnel to the south. Micah will lead you."

"But what about us?" Naomi asked.

"Still trust me?" He smirked, but the smile did not reach his eyes as he grabbed her arm once more.

"Wait," she pulled against him. "Wait, I need to say goodbye."

"No time."

As another rumble shook the ground overhead, he dragged Naomi away.

❄ ❄ ❄

The tunnel before them was bathed in shadows. Landon glanced back, checking for anything that might appear from the dark. A loud rumble shook the tunnel and sent everyone tumbling down, dirt showering their heads. The ground felt wet and slimy, making a muddy paste that smelled of dead fish and rotting seaweed. The further they moved down the tunnel, the darker and murkier it became.

Micah kept pressing his palms into the dirt.

"What are you doing?" Landon asked in a harsh whisper.

"Listening for information," Micah returned, touching the walls. "There is a lot of movement above us."

"So where do we go?"

"Do you trust me?"

"I guess."

Micah rushed off. Landon and the others held onto the walls to find a way down.

"Micah, come back. We don't all have night vision!"

"I do." Ferra stepped forward, taking her green stone from around her neck and placing it before them. An emerald hue lit the path.

"Well, I'm glad *someone* is helpful."

A quick jab from Katia forestalled any further comment.

Micah's small outline appeared in the distance. "Come. I've found something."

The tunnel began to narrow. "What now?" Landon dusted the dirt off where his head scraped the low ceiling.

"A choice needs to be made," Micah explained. "We need to avoid the mountain. Harrow is there within the crumbling."

"But I thought Harrow disappeared?"

"Someone as powerful as Harrow won't just disappear," Ferra

chimed in. "His boundaries of banishment might have altered. I think it's best to avoid it altogether."

"This tunnel leads to the plains on the southern shore of the lake," Micah continued. "If we exit here, it will lead us directly into the army's encampment." He listened again to the walls. "There are many men with horses, many tents, waiting for orders—"

"Horses you say?" Ferra piped up. "That's easy."

Katia looked suspicious. "What do you mean?"

Ferra smiled in the faint green light as she lifted up the stone around her neck. "Horses are my favorite. Come on, Kat." She grabbed Katia's arm and headed down the tunnel, oblivious to the other girl's glare.

Landon followed them through the dark path with Micah close behind, all the while feeling the warmth in his pocket generated by the steel marbles given to him by Spotswood. He tried to imagine what they could be used for but came up blank.

The path got smaller and muddier. Rain saturated the ground. They pulled and lifted every footstep with difficulty, and Landon almost lost his boot in the muck. Some outside light began to filter in, a sign that the end was near, but the tunnel shrank until he had to crawl on all fours.

"This is awful," Katia muttered from up ahead.

"I agree." Ferra lifted her arms, covered with a film of slimy, stinking filth.

"I don't mind getting dirty," Katia grumbled, "but this is beyond my tolerance."

Landon struggled with the mud. His weight made him press down deeper into the muck than the rest, getting an up-close and personal view of the stagnant refuse flowing on the water. "We won't need to use any magic. Our stench should frighten anyone away."

Fifty feet or so down the tunnel, the water got deeper and opened at last to the outside. Sweet, fresh air swept across the lake, filling the tunnel with the fragrance of rain. A thick overhang of grass and mud hid a small cove near the entrance. Sticks and debris cluttered the opening, which had prevented the water from circulating.

Ferra was the first to reach the edge and took in a deep breath of the fresh, crisp air outside. Katia followed, lunging forward with an awkward splash in the knee-deep cove. The eerie half-light reflecting off the water indicated the clouds had not parted and a gloom still loomed over the horizon. The passage of time down in the Durundin blurred together, but the sight of the sky reassured that time still continued to pass on, with or without them.

Micah swam to reach Katia at the opening as Landon struggled behind. "Above us," he whispered, pointing toward the sky.

Ferra took the initiative to see what they were near.

"What are you—" Landon tried to say, but Katia quickly covered his mouth with her muddy, wet hand. He was too disgusted to respond.

Anticipation covered Ferra's face. She grabbed the overhang and pulled herself up, then disappeared.

She came back in only a moment.

"Lots of tents," she whispered, her face reflecting her surprise. "Hundreds. The insignia of the Monarch army is on everything. I thought it would be around twenty."

"There's no way your little marbles will create an illusion for that many," Katia murmured to Landon.

"Why do you always doubt me?" he snapped. "You're always doubting my magic."

"Because your magic is so stupid."

"Well, I'm not the great Ice Queen, but it is useful—"

CONJECTRIX

All at once, without warning, Ferra pulled herself back up and took off running.

Stunned, Landon scrambled up behind her and watched Ferra move, quick and nimble, up the muddy slope to the nearest tent. A few moments later she returned, carrying something.

"Here." Ferra dropped a bundle of clothes before him. "I'm tired of you two sitting around picking at each other."

Landon looked through the pack and saw the insignia covering the robes. "You're a genius."

Suddenly, voices drew near. Landon and Ferra hurried behind the nearest tent.

"Shut up, okay?" one of the voices said in a harsh whisper. "I swear I saw something. If you don't believe me, you can return to the fire."

"If it's that bear again, I'm outta here."

Landon saw a smile creep across Ferra's face at the mention of Paolo, her giant bear—and her truest friend over these past years.

The footsteps passed the tent and headed toward the water. Two men, dressed in full battle gear with their hands on their swords, stepped closer and closer to the water's edge.

"Down there," the first said. "I saw something move."

"I ain't lookin'."

"Fine." The first man began to lean over the side.

Ferra sprinted toward them.

Landon panicked. *What is she doing?* He took off after her.

Ferra reached the soldiers in a heartbeat. She took her staff and walloped the second man on the head, knocking him off-balance. The first heard the movement and stood to face her but then suddenly fell to the ground.

Katia stood behind him with a large rock in her hand, breathing heavy. "Close one." Micah climbed up next to her.

"Thanks." Ferra returned, then noticed Katia's face was completely covered in mud. "You okay?"

Katia glared at Landon, bracing herself.

"Looks like you slipped."

"I knew you would make jokes."

"Quickly," Ferra interrupted, drawing them back into the moment, "put on their clothes. I only found two robes in the tent."

"They'll never fit Micah," Katia pointed out.

"I will use my medallion." Micah motioned to the stone he held in his hand, slipping it on. As Spotswood had explained earlier, they would still be able to see him, but others could not unless he wanted them to.

"Katia, you'll have to wear the robes," Landon told her.

"Forget it. I'm not undressing this soldier."

"Stay here and die then. I don't care."

Katia huffed and started taking off some of the unconscious soldier's gear.

They moved quickly before the soldiers woke, pulling the uniforms over their dirty clothes.

Once everyone was ready, Ferra called them forward.

"March like a soldier," Landon reminded Katia, who was still slinking around like a predator. "The point is to blend in."

"I don't know how to blend in."

"You look enough like a boy. Just act like a boy."

Katia placed the warrior mask over her face to hide her features. She extended her posture and started walking with a swagger.

Landon laughed under his breath but said nothing. He would have to figure out a way to save her once she was discovered. It was not an *if* but a *when*.

CONJECTRIX

Ferra led the way through the tents, toward the horses. She slowed and moved over to Landon.

"They're close. I need to find horses that will be willing to help us. Give me a few minutes. Then use your magic."

Landon nodded and watched as she left, alone.

"Do you know what you're doing?" Katia asked.

"Not a clue."

Fires burned near the edge of the tent ring where they stood. The warmth coming from that direction felt very enticing, especially to Landon's cold, wet, muddy body. But he knew it was best to stay in the shadows, listening to the hub of talk that mixed with the night air. The few minutes of waiting put his nerves on edge. Then, a commotion rose among the soldiers.

"Don't do it," Katia whispered. But Landon quickly hushed her, trying to listen to the shouting.

". . . has come back. I saw him."

". . . by the lake. Got two . . ."

"Grab your swords, men!" the loudest voice shouted.

Katia changed her mind. She quickly moved behind Landon for protection. "Do it."

Landon stiffened. "But, I don't know what—"

The soldiers moved past them, toward the water, and Landon and Katia quickly fell in at the rear. The wafting smell of smoke and sweat from the men masked any stench of the muddy lake. The talk and clanging of weapons rattled as they marched.

"I'm gonna kill'm," said the leader at the front. "That werebear is mine."

Shouts of excitement came from the others, so Landon punched the air, trying to blend in.

As they neared the lake, a few men ran ahead. Katia grabbed Landon's arm as the group came upon the unconscious soldiers, but he shook her off.

"That werebear was definitely here," someone said. "Maybe appearing as a human again."

"They do that?" asked another.

"I've heard they can take human form," Landon added. The discussion stopped as the men turned to look at him.

"And who are you, knowing about werebears?" the large leader asked.

Landon turned on his charm, leaving Katia behind him. "I've seen them. But there are worse creatures close by than just werebears. There are people who will drink your blood and change into women to seduce you."

There were a few groans from the crowd, but the large leader laughed. "Into women? Young man, I have never heard such a legend."

"Well, I've seen it." Landon was beginning to feel more confident about his decision to speak. He just needed time—a distraction. His hand fiddled with the stones in his pocket. "Not far from here. I saw a girl around here, too. She's friends with the bear—a big, brown werebear. But she's not a girl at all. Just a disguise to lure men out. In fact, she's a werebear herself."

"Ridiculous!" The leader moved from the unconscious bodies toward him. "I've never heard such things."

A rumbling of whinnies came from the right of the tents. The soldiers all raised their guard.

"What is that?" the leader shouted.

"The horses, sir."

"The werebear is there!"

23

"Nonsense! Go check what it is," he barked at a few men near the edge, then turned to Landon. "And you? I don't recognize you. Are you one of Rennick's men?"

"Yes," Landon returned confidently.

"Rennick was a fool to go get himself killed. He should've never insulted my mother."

Wrong answer. "I am Ungerman," Landon returned. "And I do not follow his ways."

"That's a good lad," the large one returned. "But what about your friend?" He motioned to Katia.

"Um . . . he's not my friend. I don't know him."

All eyes turned to Katia. Landon could see the panic on her face.

"It's a girl!" someone shouted. A soldier near her yanked off the helmet, revealing her red hair.

"She's the werebear!"

Katia glared at Landon, her face reddened with anger. He saw frost starting at her fingertips.

"Get her!" the leader shouted as all hands converged on her.

Katia's defenses went up. She crossed her arms in front of her as webs of ice spread out protectively. She grabbed the closest soldier, who screamed from the burn of her frozen touch.

Landon clutched the silver marbles in his hand and began to twirl them round his palm. A long, loud moan emanated from the stones.

The soldiers covered their ears. Confusion rose among them.

Then came the tramping of horses, stomping uncontrollably.

The men, taken by surprise, were caught in the stampede. Those who tried to calm the beasts got stepped on or kicked for their efforts.

Landon silenced the marbles and ran toward Katia. "Come on!" he shouted, trying to grab her still-frozen hand and immediately shrinking back. "Ow!"

"I hate you, you know that?" she snapped.

"Of course."

"They're in on this!" the large soldier shouted. "Don't let them escape!"

Landon and Katia ran as fast as they could toward the picket lines. Katia was faster than Landon and sped ahead of him. Close to the edge of the forest at the furthest tent stood two horses, calm and ready to ride.

"Only two?" Landon huffed as he ran. "Where's Micah?"

"Landon! Watch out!"

Landon turned to see a large soldier right on his heel. A blow hit his head, knocking him to the ground. Stinging, searing pain covered the right side of his face. His vision blurred. He forced his eyes to focus, just in time to see the large soldier readying his club to take another swing.

He pulled out the stone again and rubbed as hard as he could.

An ear-piercing scream came out of the stone and stopped all the men in their pursuit. A strange mist emanated from his palm and crept over the soldiers, ghost-like and ominous. Many of them yelled and ran; others tried to fight the mist.

Landon scrambled back to his feet. His head spun uncontrollably, his vision dulling as the sounds muffled together.

Galloping.

"Come on," came a shout. He felt a tugging and his body moving upward.

Then he heard a long, ferocious roar . . .

. . . right before he blacked out.

CHAPTER THREE
WATERKIND

A shower of dirt hit Naomi's head. Somewhere a pounding continued its rhythm, shaking loose the dirt around the Durundin. She dusted it off and continued running.

Reynolds grabbed her wrist and pulled her forward, all the while mumbling to himself. Naomi wanted to talk, to ask him questions, but the words never formed in her mouth.

The maze of tunnels wrapped around each other in confusing patterns, the original worm track still evident on the walls. The entrance in and out of the paths disoriented her and she began to feel dizzy. Reynolds' tight grip on her wrist started to hurt with the constant pulling. She made two strides to each one of his.

There were only a few ways to get out of the Durundin. Micah would lead the others through the cave that ran beneath the armies, but she didn't know where Reynolds would lead them. Would he take the tunnel down to the top of the lake on the side of the mountain, away from the intruding army?

Reynolds turned down a tunnel and found it blocked. Huge boulders and earth crumbled down. He scrambled up the pile, excavating what he could.

"What are you doing?"

Reynolds continued to pick through the dirt but didn't answer.

"What is that rumbling?"

"Could you ask later? Now's not the best time." He heaved a heavy boulder out of the way. "You know, you could help a little?"

"Do you want me to talk to the rock?"

"No!" Reynolds paused. "Sorry. I didn't mean to yell. No. No magic. I don't want to risk it."

Naomi frowned. "But I could move this. We could get out—"

As Reynolds pushed another large boulder out of the way, more rocks fell, covering the hole he had just created. He spit out words under his breath that Naomi couldn't hear and thought it best that she didn't. "Oh, come on," he sighed in defeat. He looked at Naomi as another rumble shook the already unstable ground. "They might have a troll . . . or two."

Naomi knew what he spoke of. "Like those beasts from the Blackwoods?" The experience had been one of the most terrifying in her life. The tall, thick monsters roared in her mind, the memories so fresh. Warlock trolls could smell her magic and wanted her blood. If the army had two of those creatures, they could easily sniff her out.

She panicked. "What do we do?"

Reynolds searched the fallen rock for a way through. "I don't know."

"They'll smell my magic."

"Yes, I'm aware of that," Reynolds returned dryly. Finally giving up on the tunnel, he pulled Naomi away.

A louder rumble followed, showering them with dirt. It felt like the entire Durundin might collapse. The low rumble became more of a growl.

"I have to calm the dirt." Naomi moved to lean her palm against the wall.

Conjectrix

"No!" Reynolds shouted again and grabbed her right hand before she could touch it.

"Reynolds. We'll die! I have to do something."

Reynolds began to run again down the dark paths, away from the growl. Naomi struggled against his tight grip. Seconds later, a green flash lit up behind them. She turned to try and see what was going on, but it was too dark.

"Spotswood," Reynolds answered her unspoken question.

Naomi didn't like it at all. His tight grip on her wrist pulled her forward, but she had to get away. She relaxed her hand and her tiny wrist slipped right through his fingers. With the loss of propulsion, she slowed.

"Naomi!" Reynolds shouted. "I know what you want to do, but we can't go back for him."

"I have . . . an idea," she said through uneven breaths.

There was another flash, this one much brighter. As they ran closer, the sounds of fighting came nearer. But before they reached the battle, Naomi turned left down a different path. She headed toward the Caelia.

Reynolds ran right behind her. "Naomi. This is a dead end. There's no escape."

Naomi slowed as she approached the cave. "But we could use the Conjectrix." She remembered the way Jeanus had used it to escape the guards in Sharlot at her first meeting with Reynolds.

"I wish it worked like that, but the Durundin is too protected."

"Then I have to use my magic," Naomi insisted. "There is no other way."

Reynolds leaned his hands against the cave wall. "No, it's too powerful. The trolls will tear you to pieces."

A thought struck her. "Will they smell me underwater?"

Reynolds blinked. "Underwater? Are you suggesting we swim?"

"No. I'm suggesting we walk."

"Walk underwater?" He laughed.

Naomi liked the idea more and more. "Yes. I know it will work until we can use the Conjectrix to take us out."

A huge growl filled up the room, so loud Naomi covered her ears.

Reynolds pulled out his sword and stood guard at the entrance. "They will find us, you know that."

Naomi barely heard him as she connected to her magic. She could feel the energy in her veins fueled by the excitement of the Vivatera. It needed to escape and wanted to rush out, but Naomi stayed calm.

The magic waited patiently at her fingertips. With a soft, swirling motion, she began to move the water. A tiny whirlpool formed, sending curling fountains moving right and left. The vortex grew as the water around them deepened, slowly pushing its way up from the bottom. The ground became visible, still moist from the years of saturation.

Reynolds seemed momentarily distracted by the fantastic spectacle, but when a loud crash came, he readied his sword as two trolls pushed their way through the opening. Large, crumbling rock tumbled down near his feet. The trolls looked hungry, long strands of drool hanging from their giant jaws. He lunged forward, hitting the front of the first troll's leg. The slice hardly did anything but anger the troll who flung out his arm at Reynolds, hitting him on the side and slamming him back to the wall.

Two soldiers followed the trolls and Reynolds took action, slashing and stabbing as best he could. "Naomi! Naomi, go!"

Naomi lost concentration and moved under the watery archway. She turned and saw the trolls at the edge of the water. The sight of them was more terrifying in the light of the Caelia than in the dark forest.

Their eyes looked possessed by the magic. She could see their deep lust for it in their bulging pupils and gaunt expressions.

"Reynolds!"

"GO!" she heard in the distance, but she was not about to leave without him. Not again.

Reynolds ran around the edge of the Caelia until he stood between the trolls and Naomi, slashing both of them with his blade as he moved back, protecting her as much as he could.

She knew the time had come to trust her magic. The water pushed up and over in a beautiful arch, safely separating her and Reynolds from the lumbering beasts.

With it, the trance of the magic disappeared and the warlock trolls became enraged. Both began hurtling themselves through the water.

Naomi lost the connection. Terror filled her, and the whirlpool began to fall.

"Focus!" Reynolds yelled as he was hit with a splash of water. He forced his way to her. "You can do this!"

Naomi moved backward and touched the water again. *Please, help me. Please.*

The water again rose above them with incredible force, like a huge wave commanding the sea, taking prisoners in its anger. In the torrent of furious spinning, the trolls were swept up, struggling for breath, but eventually they had none and slowly sunk to the bottom of the lake.

The wicked crashing of the whirlpool waves were replaced by a harmony of gentle swirling. Reynolds and Naomi stood under a protective bubble created completely out of water.

Reynolds eyed the water arching over his head and then looked back at Naomi. "No more magic," he said as they walked together at the bottom of the lake. "And . . . thank you."

CHAPTER FOUR

SOUTHBOUND

Landon stirred awake. A cold hand held a cloth to his head. As his focus returned he saw Katia kneeling next to him in a dark, stony place. He heard rain coming from beyond the darkness.

He sat up too quickly, a stab of pain shooting across his forehead.

"Lay back down," Katia ordered.

"What happened?" Landon grabbed his head. "Where are we?"

"Blizzard needed to rest, so we're near the foothills."

"Blizzard?"

"Well, the horse needed some kind of name. Blizzard seemed appropriate with his white color and me as the rider. I was so mad when we left, I thought it might have looked like a little snow storm riding across the valley."

"You're still freezing." Landon touched her hand again.

Her shoulders slumped. "And I can't start a fire."

Landon felt in his pockets. "Guess it can be tricky without sunsparks. Let me see what I can do."

"You really should lie down."

"And let us freeze to death? No thanks." He looked around. It was night and everything around them was wet.

31

"A fire might alert attention though."

Landon huffed, but he knew she was right. "Come here." He tried to put his arm around her.

"What are you doing?"

"I'm trying to get us warm," he returned. "Your insides are as icy as your exterior. Now will you come here?"

Katia hesitated.

"Kat, I promise. I'm a gentleman." Which was true, though he privately liked to watch her squirm. "We need to get you warm and I'm the warmest thing here."

She gave in and drew near him.

Landon could tell she felt awkward but wrapped himself around her, moving his arms on her back to help with circulation. "Now, can you tell me what happened?"

Katia lifted her head. "I didn't see Micah at all. I don't know where he is."

"He'll be fine. Go on."

"Right when I reached the horses, Ferra rode out on a bear. I had never seen such an amazing animal before. The soldiers had the right to be afraid of him. He was enormous! Anyway, he had been waiting for Ferra to return, I guess. She galloped straight for the soldier who knocked you down and sent them all running." She was quiet for a moment. "How did you know about the bear?"

"Ferra told me," he returned. "I thought he might be around, but I really didn't know what to say. It just came to me."

"But what if he wasn't there? You pointed me out as the enemy."

"Yeah, but that was just to get you mad." Katia tried to move away, but Landon held her fast. "It was just to get your magic out. I wasn't afraid. You took out two guys without my help."

"True," Katia returned smugly. She moved back against Landon's chest, seeming a little more accepting of his warmth.

"So where are we now?"

"I rode as fast as I could for as long as I could, but I really don't know if we're in the right place."

"I guess we'll find out tomorrow." Landon rested his still-throbbing head against the dirt wall of the foothill and fell asleep.

❊ ❊ ❊

Landon woke to a strange sensation on his face: wet slime brushing over and over. Blizzard was licking the dirt and salt off his forehead. His first impulse was to yell at the animal, but Katia still lay curled next to him, so he simply kept pushing it away with his hand.

"Get away, you mangy beast," he muttered.

The horse moved his attention to the grass next to them.

Landon slipped away from Katia, removing her hands from his chest, placing them back by her side, and resting her head on a soft patch of grass underneath. She stirred a little but remained asleep.

The day had only begun from what Landon could tell. The sun sat behind clouds like usual, but the warmth colored the morning on the eastern horizon. The strange purplish glow around the peaks gave life to the dreariness. He climbed up the muddy slopes to a platform above the alcove. With the light behind him, he had a great view of the valley. At one time he had known these plains very well, but with time and growth, the landscape had changed. It surprised him that they were still near the edge of the lake. To the south, he could see groves of trees where the settlements were laid out, but mist covered everything else to the west.

Landon looked again to the south and felt the knots in his stomach. The last place he wanted to return to was the south of Parbraven. There were memories buried there, very deep and undisturbed. Now he felt they might claw their way to the surface, shattering his cool façade.

And Katia was with him, which could easily turn this excursion into a nightmare for both of them. He had demons in his past, but nothing like Katia's. His mother hadn't committed suicide or killed his baby brother like hers had. His story seemed rather tame compared to all that drama. He took a deep breath and made the decision not to speak about such things if possible, and to try to keep Katia far away from the Salt Dunes.

Landon picked through the grass and found some edible roots and wild berries for breakfast. When he returned, Katia was sitting, trying to wash herself off with large damp leaves. She was still very muddy from the fall the night before.

"Hungry?"

"A little." Katia eyed the roots in Landon's hand. "Did you sleep well?"

"Well, I slept, how's that?"

"As well as one would expect. Your head okay?"

Landon had forgotten about his bump. "Yeah, I guess."

"Tell me, what did you see on the top of the rock?"

"That we have a longer journey than I thought. We're weeks away from anything. Plus, the army could be after us."

"Why chase us when there's a bear to be hunted?" Katia reminded him.

"I'd rather not chance it. How are your legs?"

"Sore." Katia thought about it. "I'm not a fan of horses."

"Sorry to hear that." Landon offered a hand to pull her to her feet. "Blizzard and I have grown attached to each other. Haven't we?" He patted the horse's side, and Blizzard gave a whinny. "Besides, if we take the horse, we'll shorten our time considerably."

"I like that idea. The shorter, the better."

Within minutes, they were travelling down the hillside towards the forest floor, Landon guiding the horse and Katia wrapped tightly around him. They rode close to the river. Landon knew the Ravian well, having traveled it many times as a boy.

Lake Kolinhur split into two rivers—Ravian and Tristus. The Tristus ran down the center of Parbraven, while the Ravian traveled to the east and south, a main support to the fishing villages on the eastern side of the city. The two rivers met back at the Springs of Sephar, creating an amazing waterfall. That was the supposed hiding place of Naomi's sister. Landon hoped the river would hide their tracks, and if they rode along its side it might guide them directly to the sister.

The large rocks, loosened earth, and exposed stumps slowed their progress, but Landon did his best directing Blizzard through it. They rode much of the day, only stopping briefly to rest the horse. Near sundown Katia had had enough and asked to stop for the night.

She slid off the horse and held onto her legs. "My legs are burning," she complained, hobbling bow-legged to find a rock to support her.

"Good boy." Landon patted the horse as he dismounted. "That was quite the run today. I think Blizzard liked it."

"Do you know where we are?"

"Good question." Landon took a drink from the river and rinsed off his face. "I think we're on the right track."

"I don't know if I can do another day like this," Katia mumbled. "I wasn't prepared to flee so fast."

"None of us were."

"Do you think we could find shelter?"

Landon thought about it. "Too risky. Not to mention we have no money and nothing to trade if we happen upon weary travelers."

"I'm sore and tired and cold."

"Do you want to cuddle again tonight?"

Katia laughed. "I think I would rather sleep with a rock. It has more emotions, so Micah would tell me. I'll take my chances, Landon Rhees."

"I think I'll sleep next to Blizzard anyway. He'll be nice and warm." Landon lay down near the animal. Blizzard was warm to the touch and his slow, steady breathing felt comforting as it rose and fell.

"I'll *cuddle* on this side, if you don't mind." She moved over to the soft patch of ground where the horse lay and curled up next to the white stallion just opposite of Landon. She gently stroked the horse with her hand. "You have a way with animals."

"I don't really," Landon returned. "But Ferra certainly does. I've never known a horse to be so understanding and loyal."

"I'm not talking about her," she snapped. "But I think this horse likes you." Katia listened in the quiet for him to respond. She peered over to see Landon asleep and grumbled as she lay back down.

Landon softly smiled. He loved getting under her skin.

❄ ❄ ❄

Blizzard stirred and quickly jumped up, knocking Katia off him.

Landon hushed the horse and patted him gently to calm him down.

"What is it?" Katia asked as she scrambled away from the hooves of the animal.

"Someone is close."

Katia sat up and listened. A noisy clatter came from the forest—not just a few, but many voices.

Landon calmed the animal and tethered him to a tree near the river. "Let's go check it out."

"Are you crazy?"

"Do you always have to argue with me?"

Katia shrugged but otherwise didn't answer. She followed behind him anyway.

Landon led her down through the trees, being careful to stay on the damp foliage of the forest floor to mask their sounds. The light of a fire began to illuminate through the trunks. Loud laughter and mumbled talk disturbed the night calm.

Landon stopped and, using his instincts, hid behind a large tree. Katia followed in the shadows, when the noise suddenly ceased. There was shuffling around.

"What is going on?" Katia mouthed the words.

Landon peered around the trunk of the tree to get a better look, but the camp now looked abandoned. Then he felt the cold steel blade of a large knife at his throat.

"Well, look who we have here," a familiar but unwelcome voice resounded in the darkness. "I never thought I would see the day when you would come back this way, Landon Rhees . . ."

CHAPTER FIVE
THE TRAVELERS

Katia froze. A man held Landon at knifepoint.

Landon stood very still. "I must say, Lionel, I never expected you to hold a knife to my throat."

Lionel? Katia thought. Before she could process anything, the big man turned and embraced Landon, kissing him heavily on the cheek. Others came around the corners of the wagons and tents, laughing heartily at the display.

"What in the world?" Lionel scratched his head. "I assumed you dead. Out of all the misfits, never in my dreams would I figure findin' you."

"In my nightmares, I never imagined myself back."

A roar of celebration erupted from the others as Lionel grabbed Landon around the neck and rubbed his head.

"Hey, look everyone! It's the rat that ran away from his home!"

There was a large "Yeah!" from the others.

"And who is this?" Lionel spotted Katia's shadowy figure hiding behind a tree. He moved closer to her with a curious look.

Katia side-stepped away from the tree and gritted her teeth into a hesitant smile.

Landon grabbed her arm and pulled her awkwardly close. "Lionel Pipkin, this is Kat," —he took a deep breath—". . . my wife."

Katia gasped. She tried to protest, but Landon jabbed her in the stomach with his elbow.

"Well now, Landon my boy," Lionel said with wonder. "This is a pleasure." He took a long look at Katia. "Now I am surprised. You're so young, and with your charms and all."

"Married. Yes. We are."

"Well, bless the stars. The wife of Landon Rhees!" Lionel stuck out his hand in greeting.

Katia took it, feeling the rough calluses of a hard-working life.

"Come! Sit with us." Lionel walked back down from the tree line to the fire.

Landon slipped his hand into Katia's.

She leaned in. "Married?" she whispered, indignant.

"I have my reasons," he whispered back. "You have to trust me here. I know these people. Gypsies can never be trusted with the truth."

They walked hand in hand down the dirt path and took a place near the fire, the warmth inviting to their frozen bodies. Katia let go of Landon and stood next to the flame to warm her hands. A large, sweet-faced woman came forward with broth for them both.

Katia took the bowl. "Thank you." She sipped slowly. The warm, heavenly sensation went directly through her body.

She took in the scene around them. The wagons from the caravan wrapped around the fire in a circle, giving a feeling of security. There looked to be around two dozen people of varying age and size, some with babies in their arms, others with missing teeth and deep scars or pocked scabs—all smelling of chicken fat and sweat, with grease stains streaking the fronts of their clothes.

CONJECTRIX

"Landon Rhees," Lionel said again in disbelief. "This is an honor, truly. You must tell us where you have been all this time. You were one of the best, and then you were gone like smoke."

Landon laughed. "Now if I tell you that, then where is the mystery?"

"How in this world did you end up here?" Lionel asked again.

"Before I get to that, you must tell me what has been happening with the Pipkins."

Lionel's face fell. "Hard times, hard times."

"Sorry to hear that." Landon looked around. "Where's Tania?"

"Dead."

"What?" Landon's face changed immediately with this news.

Katia stopped sipping her soup and looked at Landon. An unfamiliar feeling came over her, jealousy mixed with concern for her friend.

"She and Little Rolfy both dead."

"How?"

"Creatures went wild over the taste of magic."

Katia choked. Landon quickly patted her back.

"Magic? What do you mean?" he asked.

"Something awakened the madness. Poor Tania didn't have a chance. We could only figure it was her magic, since no one else was harmed but Little Rolfy. She had been dosed with magic as a child, but hid her song from others. But I had heard it. She shared it with me."

"And me," Landon added, a look of sadness on his face. Almost to himself, he uttered, "Really sorry to hear that."

"The magic is dangerous," Lionel continued. "Our shows are not threatening, but others do not want to see them now. The world is changing and people are scared. We have sworn off magic ever since that night." He looked directly at Landon. "You still dabbling in card tricks?"

"Not really."

"Good. I wouldn't want you harmed." The crowd again laughed with him.

Landon also laughed.

Katia didn't laugh at all.

Lionel changed the subject. "So, tell me about your good wife here."

Katia stiffened. "Me?"

"Kat?"

"Oh, yes, we could use a good story." The others sitting in the circle agreed.

"Oh, sure. Kat? You want to tell them?" Landon asked dumbly.

"But you're such a good storyteller, dear. I think it should come from you," Katia smirked. She couldn't wait to hear him crawl out of this one.

Landon cracked his knuckles. "Okay." He took in a quick breath. "Have you ever heard of the town of Shellcomb?" Many shook their heads. "It's high in the Eastern Mountains, where there is always snow and never summer. The village had a leader whose name was Vladnir. His wife died in childbirth, leaving a daughter. And he named her Katarina." Landon motioned to Katia. "Now, what made the people of Shellcomb so unusual was their fair heads. The entire village had the lightest hair you had ever seen. Have you ever seen a blond head?"

A few in the circle nodded, but the children didn't know what he was referring to. "Their hair is so light that it looks like the sun has kissed it and made it shine. It's a remarkable sight."

The kids seemed awed at the idea of it.

"But when Katarina was born she had beautiful coppery red hair, which was so unusual in this land of the fair head. Vladnir thought it a sign of good fortune, stained with the blood of the sacrifice of his wife. And because of the good fortune, he never cut her hair. In time, Vladnir

41

grew more wealthy and powerful. Katarina had never traveled outside of the town because her father forbade it, thinking selfishly that his fortune would disappear.

"But when Katarina turned sixteen, she had the chance to travel outside the village to the tip of the eastern range with her nursemaid, Elnora. I happened to be in the village performing card tricks in a traveling carnival. And when I saw her"—Landon turned and looked at Kat, who was completely mesmerized by his telling—"When I saw her, I never wanted anything more in the whole world." He took her hand and kissed it.

Around the circle came sighs and murmurings.

"So what did you do?" a little girl asked from her mother's lap.

"Well, I showed her a magic trick like this." He walked over to the girl and pulled a flower from behind her ear. "And she thought it was beautiful. For days I did the same trick until she finally asked me my name. We started to talk, and I learned that she would be leaving to go back to her home within a few days. By then, I had made up my mind. I couldn't let her leave me or I might never see her again. I persuaded her to run away with me. We found a mystic in the village to marry us and left a note for her father with the nursemaid—to return along with a long lock of hair."

"So that is where your hair went?" the girl asked Katia. "You cut your long hair for him?"

Katia watched him, just as surprised. "Yes," she returned, almost wiping her eyes. "He was more important to me."

"We knew her father would try to find us, so we cut all her hair off and have been running ever since," Landon finished.

"Did that make you sad?" the girl asked Katia.

Katia thought for a moment, looking at Landon, then back to the girl. "There are things that I miss about my old life. There are things that you will always miss, but there are better things in my new life that make up for the loss."

Landon smiled, impressed.

"So how long have you been together?" an older woman asked.

"Only a few months. We stole a horse from the village, and we're trying to get as far south as possible."

"Well, travel with us, my boy." Lionel slapped Landon on the back. "We have the room and have a place for your horse here. Bertha! Do we have a tent for the two lovebirds?"

The large sweet-faced woman who'd handed out the broth stood at the prompt. "Oh, yes. I'll fetch it." And she went off to rummage through a cargo wagon.

"Excellent!" Landon placed his hand on Katia's knee and shook it. "We've got a place to stay, sweetie, just like you asked."

Katia grinned, but it was more of a grimace.

"Come, Landon, where is this blasted horse you speak of?" Lionel asked, and together they marched back to the river.

Katia sat alone, watching Landon leave. All the eyes in the circle kept staring and smiling at her. She tried to smile back but couldn't wait for Landon to return. Minutes of uncomfortable silence passed until finally she saw Landon approach with Lionel and the beautiful stallion.

"What do you call it?" a little girl asked, petting the animal.

"Blizzard," Katia answered.

"In honor of where you came from?"

"Uh, yes," Katia smiled uncomfortably. "And what do they call you?"

"Lottie, ma'am."

"Well, I'm glad to meet you," Katia returned.

CONJECTRIX

※ ※ ※

A small, round tent stood a short distance from the caravan and was filled with thick blankets and animal skins. Katia lay by herself, a wave of exhaustion hitting her as she stared with dreamy eyes at nothing, not knowing when she closed them.

"Hey, princess," came a whisper in the dark.

She opened her eyes to see Landon's outline hovering over her. Turning, she propped herself up on her elbows.

"Stay on your side," she whispered.

Landon put up his hands without protest and moved to his side of the tent. "Not that there's much of a side. Everyone is heading for bed. A few of the men take turns keeping watch. I volunteered to help, but Lionel said I should see to my wife."

Katia fluffed her pillow unnecessarily, avoiding his eyes. "Why lie to these people? They seem so genuine."

"Genuine, sure." Landon smoothed his hands through his hair. "But Travelers are very wary of strangers." He bent down closer to her, but she shoved his chest. "Hey, I'm saving us. I'm one of them. With us married, your acceptance is guaranteed. Without, we would be separated, and they'd probably sell you because of your lack of usefulness."

"I'm useful," Katia said defensively.

"But you can't use your"—he mouthed the word 'magic'—"here."

Katia sank her head back against the blankets. "How did you come up with that story?"

"That was something, right?" Landon answered smugly.

"You amazed me."

"And you said I don't have any talent."

Katia leaned forward on her crossed arms. "Did you use a charm? Did you charm me?"

"Sure, but that wasn't the ingenious part," Landon continued animatedly. "I not only charmed everyone listening, I set up a story so well-woven that instead of looking past you, which they'd do in a heartbeat, they admire you. Travelers only care what you're worth to them. I've given them a stolen princess. You're as valuable to them as gold."

Katia smiled, shaking her head. "They'll be mad when we leave."

"Maybe, but we can't stay with them."

"How long then?"

"Just a few days, I think. I don't want any of them to get suspicious, but our cover is pretty good. These people have no other connections, especially with the monarchy or the daughters of Prolius. They have no love for government."

"I'll tell you what I love—these blankets." She pulled one over her legs. "Can I ask a question?"

"Of course."

Katia couldn't rest until she knew. "Who's Tania?"

Landon huffed. "What? Is my wife jealous?"

"What? No." Katia turned her head. "I'm just curious."

Landon's smile faded. "Tania was the closest friend I had as a Traveler. She shared her gift with me the night I decided to leave. When she sang, the winds changed. I tried persuading her to leave with me, but she refused to leave her family." He looked as if he would continue, but then stood to exit. "I'm going to help watch. I'll be back later."

Katia watched the tent flap close behind him. She sank into her covers, thinking about the forgotten girl, and fell asleep.

CHAPTER SIX

RASMUSSEN

The glow from outside lit the water with a warm, sweet blue. An ethereal glow surrounded Naomi and Reynolds as they traveled along the bottom of the lake. It seemed unreal, like walking in an unknown world. Every so often, a ray of glittering sun hit the water and lit the small particles around them, dazzling to the eye.

They had walked for hours. Naomi didn't talk much, but her mind kept active, thinking things it would be better not to think. Reynolds strode alongside her, lost in his own thoughts.

She wanted to speak to him but didn't know what to say. Her tongue felt swollen in her mouth, too tight to talk. His presence sent a wave of intimidation through her. As Naomi's mind processed his actions, she couldn't explain away her fear of failure and disappointment.

When the light began to fall, she knew she had to say something. She thought about it several times before it came out. "Reynolds?" Just saying his name relieved the pressure.

He stopped and turned to look at her. His gaze sent her mind spinning and she almost forgot what to say.

"What do we do now?"

Reynolds sighed and looked around. "Well, I don't want to swim."

The joke surprised her, and Naomi laughed.

"Well," he said more seriously, "I guess we could try to use the Conjectrix. I think we're far enough from the Durundin." He softened his voice. "By the way, I need to say thank you—you know, for saving us back there."

Naomi's cheeks flushed red with embarrassment. "It's the only thing I could think of."

"Well, it worked."

"But you don't think I should use my magic."

Reynolds rubbed his face with his hands. "I need to hide you."

"What do you mean?"

"When your—"—he coughed a little but recovered—"when Taren attacked you, something changed. Your blood . . ." He stopped, seemingly lost for words.

"Just like the water knows my touch," Naomi muttered as she moved her hand back through the ripples. He didn't need to say it; she understood. When her blood spilled on the cave floor, it had exposed the magic.

"Can I see the Conjectrix?"

Naomi sorted through her pack and found the strange object. It looked as though all the light had been sucked into the stone and was reflecting it back out in luminous pictures. Naomi held it, mesmerized, before handing it over to Reynolds.

"What are those pictures?"

Reynolds lifted it up in his palm to show her. "The Conjectrix holds memories. It can travel to places it knows. Unfortunately, where we're going is too far for its memory. It's never been there. But I see a place within it we could portal to."

"Where?"

CONJECTRIX

"I don't know exactly," he returned. "A town far from anything in the east. I recognize the culture as western Parbraven."

"I don't even know how to use this," she admitted.

"There will be time for that." Reynolds placed it in his palm. "It's a long journey."

He moved his hand over the smooth, round ball again and again. Images flashed past. He stopped on one and swirled his finger around it. "I think I've found it. Hold on to me tight."

Naomi remembered something. "Wait." She moved back one of her hands to the water. "Thank you."

The water rippled rapidly in reaction, like a tiny giggle of gratitude.

She replaced her hand on Reynolds' arm. "Okay, I'm ready."

He focused on the image, closed his eyes, and formed a tight fist around the Conjectrix.

Suddenly there was a bright flash, and Naomi felt the water around her. She lost her grip, her arms flailing helplessly. *It didn't work.* She swam toward the surface of the water, faster and faster, pushing to reach it. Pressure built up in her lungs. Her magic couldn't help her; she needed to reach the surface.

Finally, she took in a deep breath as the outside breeze cooled her wet cheeks and hair.

Naomi wiped the water from her eyes and looked around, surprised. She was not in a lake but a country pond near a farm house. Her toes touched soft marsh underneath and she stood up. Tall, yellowing grass surrounded her, with different paths worn down, like it was used as a watering hole for animals.

Something splashed near her feet. Reynolds sat in the pond next to her, wiping away the cat tails and snake reed. He bent down his head and shook out the water like a wet dog.

"What did you do?" Naomi asked, pulling herself away from the mud.

"I didn't do it on purpose." Reynolds spit grass from his mouth. "I didn't know how it would take us." He still held the Conjectrix in his hand but tossed it back to her. "You can keep it."

Naomi dove to catch it, but her feet got stuck and she fell face-first in the water.

Reynolds began to laugh. He stood and tried to move over to her. "Sorry," he said, offering his hand.

Naomi looked at him with wet grass dripping from her nose. She wanted to be mad but couldn't hold the frown. "Thank you," she returned as he lifted her out.

Reynolds looked at her a long moment. "Here." He removed the scarf from her neck and rung out all the water.

Naomi was surprised by the kindness. Reynolds always had a motive behind his actions, usually something she never understood until later.

He moved her hair out of the way and slid the scarf back over her scar. "There." He noticed the expression on her face. "What?"

Naomi didn't say anything but gave a faint smile.

Reynolds stopped and moved away. He started to say something but instead replaced his hands in his pockets.

It would have been perplexing if she hadn't expected as much.

"Come on." Reynolds stepped out of the pond and extended his hand to help her up.

The sun set beyond the western horizon, taking the warmth with it. Naomi shivered in her wet clothes. The pack filled with goods was saturated and nearly useless. Her cloak no longer hung around her neck, proving too heavy to stay on her shoulders and unable provide

CONJECTRIX

much warmth as wet as it was. She looked up at the farmhouse. There had to be help in there.

"Good idea," Reynolds spoke up as if he'd read her thoughts.

Naomi looked over at him, confused at his clear clairvoyance.

Slam!

A noise came from somewhere near the farmhouse. Reynolds moved quickly and hid Naomi behind a small henhouse. The back door opened. In the growing darkness, all that could be seen was the silhouette of a man with a brimmed hat.

"Who's out here?" a rough, powerful voice yelled from the entry.

Naomi shivered while Reynolds arched over her as a shield.

"I know you're out here!"

Whispering filled the wind, then silence. Naomi craned to hear more, but Reynolds held her back. The henhouse creaked as if a chicken had jumped to the roof. Naomi glanced up and found herself face-to-face with a pair of bright orange eyes.

She squealed and jerked away as the animal let out a scratchy howl. Reynolds grabbed her by the arm and pulled her to run but stopped at the blade of a sword aimed right at his chest.

"You thought you would be sneaky, eh?" The long, silver sword reflected the orange eyes of the animal. "Running off my farm without saying a word. Not even a hello."

"We mean you no harm," Reynolds spoke up.

"Of course you do or you wouldn't be here."

"No, it's not like that. We're just trying to find our way."

A snicker. "Lies, lies. Your tales won't fool me. What do you call yourself?"

"I'm Hawk, and this is Goldie."

The sword wobbled, moving so it glinted on Reynolds' face. "Hawk? A bit pretentious, don't you think?"

Reynolds remained still, revealing nothing.

The sword lowered, and the man leaned on it casually. "Come on, Nobbs. These people aren't a threat to us."

The little creature moved over to his shoulder. It was hard to tell what kind of animal it was, but the eyes, filled with an eerie longing, haunted Naomi. Its long, bushy tail wrapped around the man's neck like a scarf.

The shadow of the man turned to leave but stopped. "I'm glad to have met you, Goldie, even if you're running around with this riff-raff."

"Who are you?" Reynolds asked.

"You used to know me," the man returned. "Or was that too long ago?"

Naomi tugged on his arm, confused. Reynolds remained silent.

"Listen . . ." The man scratched his face, thinking. "The ball brought you here, right?" The brim of his hat cast shadows against his face. "So, why do you figure it has memory of here?"

Naomi didn't know what to think.

"Why don't you come in and get warm?" He gestured toward the farmhouse. "Or stay there and be wet and cold. I don't care." He moved his sword back up to his shoulders and walked away. "It's your decision, Reyn."

After the door shut, Reynolds kicked the side of the henhouse. A few disruptive clucks broke the silence.

Naomi moved to his arm. "Reyn? He called you Reyn. He knows you?"

"I don't like this." Reynolds shook his head. "This could get us in worse trouble." Clearly agitated, he clenched his hands into fists, ready to expel the energy built up inside.

"What's going on, Reynolds?"

CONJECTRIX

He began pacing. "Jeanus knew. She knew this and left it for me to find out. Oh, that sneak. How is that fair?"

Naomi moved in front of him and pushed his chest. "Hey! Sorry if this upsets you, but I'm freezing and I don't care what kind of person this man is. He has a warm house and hot food and that's all I care about."

She started walking to the house, but Reynolds caught her by the arm. "Sorry. You're right. Of course you're right. This is the last thing I expected and I don't like to be surprised. If I could hide this part of my life I would have."

"Surprised by what?"

"My brother."

❄   ❄   ❄

Inside the farmhouse, a fire blazed in the hearth. A few blankets hung over an arm of a chair, warming for the two guests.

Reynolds' brother pulled out some clothes that might fit, as they were similarly built. He then handed Naomi a long shirt for her to change into.

"Glad you came to your senses," he muttered to Reynolds as he handed over the clothing.

Naomi looked around the small farmhouse, but there wasn't much to it, just a square box with no other rooms attached. Near the corner sat a pile of blankets for a bed and a washtub cluttered with different tools for gardening and farming. The ring of dirt caking it suggested that it had not been used in a long time.

"We'll give you some privacy." Reynolds nudged his brother towards the door.

"Just turn around," Naomi suggested. They did as she requested, and she quickly removed her wet clothes and put on the shirt. When she finished, she wrapped her shoulders in the warmest thing she could find: the sheepskin hanging closest to the fire. "Thank you." She began hanging her clothes to dry before sitting in front of the fire.

The men turned around again. Reynolds had replaced his shirt but excused himself to the darkness outside to finish changing.

The room became very still for a moment, the silence awkward. Reynolds' brother moved closer to the fire. "So, you're Naomi." He poked the coals with a stick. "I'm Rasmussen, but you can call me Arie, if you like."

"Arie?"

"Yes, Rasmussen Errol," he explained. "Rasmussen was rather long for the chaps growing up, and they shortened it to R.E., my initials."

Naomi didn't mean to, but she found herself staring at Rasmussen. In one moment, he had told her more about himself than Reynolds had ever divulged. The difference was surprising, and refreshing. His features were highlighted in the firelight. She noticed the same sharp nose and smart chin as Reynolds. His hair was hidden under his hat, but she could see bits of unruly, light brown pushed near his forehead. He had the same tan skin and unshaven face, but there was a light in his eyes that was absent from his brother's. Even in the dim cabin, she could see the activity and life in Arie's, while Reynolds' seemed filled with regret and burden.

"What are you doing?" Arie gazed at her. "You're doing something."

"I don't know what you mean." Naomi gazed back toward the fire.

Arie sat up. "Wow, you are something. You enchanted me. I felt it. I can see why Reynolds has a problem with you."

Naomi stared at him, confused. "A problem?"

"Sorry, I didn't mean *problem*." Arie stumbled over his words. "You're something. That's all. I didn't mean anything by it." He poked a big log that had crumbled down to embers before he turned to her. "You were analyzing me—examining me. Why?"

"I didn't know Reynolds had a brother."

He laughed. "That doesn't surprise me. Reyn keeps things from everyone—even me. But look, I'm not the best representative of the Fairborne name. Not the best older brother either. Well, I'm only a half-brother, so I can't blame everything on my father." His stick was now glowing at the end, but he just moved it around the ashes to cool it down. "I think Reynolds wanted it that way, don't you?"

Naomi looked at the fire. "Reynolds always thinks he's doing the best for me, but—"

The door opened and Reynolds returned. He seemed to know he'd interrupted the conversation but didn't care. "What are you telling her?"

"I'm not saying anything," Arie returned defensively. "Why do you assume I'm up to something?"

"You usually are."

"He was telling me he is only your half-brother," Naomi interjected.

"Ah, yes. Same fantastic Fairborne father, different mothers." The way Arie said 'father' sounded like acid on his tongue.

Reynolds moved closer to his brother. "Father did his best for us. You can't blame him for your bad decisions."

Arie laughed in his face. "Might be true, but it's more fun."

Anger flitted through Reynolds' expression. He stood abruptly and went to the door. "No. I'm not doing this. I won't get tangled up in your messy life again, and I'm not exposing Naomi to it. We're leaving."

"And where are you going to go?" The brothers stood eye to eye, no difference in height or build—a fair match. "Go ahead and go if you don't care. But let me ask you. Why are you here? Did you ever think of that?"

Reynolds' face went hard.

Naomi quickly placed herself between them both. This time, she used her charm deliberately. "Talk to me. I want to know why we're here. Tell me. Help me understand why the Conjectrix brought us here and why you're here. Please."

The atmosphere calmed at her question, Reynolds and Arie both softening.

"Why *are* we here?" Reynolds reiterated. "Who found you?"

Arie pondered, taking in a few breaths. "I think you better have a seat. I have a lot to say." He took off his hat, his shaggy hair falling in his face in sweaty curls. At first impression, it looked enough like Reynolds' but wilder, which was hard to believe. But his hair had so much more gold in it. She found herself staring again and felt her cheeks flush.

"Jeanus found me," Arie continued. "I should be invisible to her sight—I had been for years—so it's still baffling how she did. But I was far up north in a town called Heartridge. She found me drunk and face down in the snow. When I became coherent, she asked me to do something for her. I owed her so much that I had to say yes. That was when she brought me here and told me to wait for you."

He pointed to Reynolds. "She said you would come here, but I didn't know when. I figured you would come sooner than now, but she never lies and I knew you would eventually. Nobbs here is hers." He gestured to the now-sleeping animal with the bushy tail. "He's been fun, also very helpful."

Naomi studied the creature. "What kind of animal is he?"

"No idea," Arie returned. "But he has warned me of dangers around here. This isn't the safest country."

"Did Jeanus give you any idea why we would come?" Reynolds asked.

"She said you would tell me."

Reynolds shook his head. "Then we don't need your help."

Arie furrowed his brow. "Hold on. Before you go along this untamed country by yourself, remember she wanted me to help you, and I will do as she asked."

"What makes her different? You never did anything for Father."

"Hey, that's not fair." Arie's guard raised. "Cornelius never gave me a chance to prove myself. He enlisted me in the army and then wound up dead before I could do anything."

Naomi processed the conversation, not liking the tone of it. "Where have you been since then?"

"Running. I had nowhere to go. If I stayed in Southwick, I would have died or become a brainless puppet like the others. There wasn't anything keeping me there. My father was dead. Reyn disappeared. So I got out of there."

"Why didn't you go to the camp?" Naomi asked.

Arie stared at the fire without answering.

"Because he doesn't have magic," Reynolds answered her.

Naomi felt foolish for thinking the question. "I'm sorry. I didn't know."

"Nothing to apologize for. While Reyn was out playing with things he shouldn't, I was in a war I had nothing to do with."

Arie turned back to face them. "So, now you're here. Just like Jeanus said you would be. She's the closest thing I have to a grandparent and there is nothing I wouldn't do for her. I'm ready, I'm healthy, and I'm anxious to get out of this farmhouse. So could you fill me on what we have to do?"

Reynolds looked hard at his brother. "We have to travel to the Ignis Mountains."

For a long moment, Arie didn't say anything; didn't even blink. "Ignis Mountains?" He swallowed hard. "Sorry, not going there."

"But you said you would help us."

"Well, the Ignis Mountains are a deal breaker." He moved over to a bottle he had near the chair and took a quick swig of the liquid inside. "Ignis? Really? You're mad. Do you know what you're facing?"

Naomi shook her head.

"Fire beasts. Dragons. The souls of the dead feast on the bellies of those beasts."

"But we have no choice," Naomi explained. "I have to go."

Arie pointed a finger right at her. "You have a choice. Don't go."

Reynolds stepped between them. "This is what we're doing. Naomi is right—she has no choice, and I'm going with her."

"Great. You can both die together."

As Arie went to drink again, a strange thing happened. His bottle dropped and shattered on the ground, the fire went out, and the orange eyes of Nobbs floated near Naomi's shoulder, a small growling coming from his throat. It wasn't threatening, but instructional.

Arie sighed as if the creature had spoken to him. "All right." The growling ended and the fire returned.

The furry creature curled close to Naomi's shoulder, trying again to fall asleep.

"I'm not going in the mountains, understand?" Arie reinforced. "But I will guide you there. That I can do." He turned to Reynolds. "Here's some advice: keep her away from the river."

"What river?" Naomi asked.

"The river that will lead you to the crack in the earth, the crack that will swallow your soul."

"I don't understand." She turned to Reynolds.

CONJECTRIX

Reynolds nodded to his brother and looked down to answer her. "A volcano in the Ignis Mountains opened up a gateway long ago. A crack." His chest heaved. "It's the entrance to Hell."

CHAPTER SEVEN
Lottie's Secret

The morning brought heavy rain. The small company had plans to break camp and head for the town of Davenport, where they could replenish their supplies, sell goods, and perform to make money. The rain made everything hard. Packing the wet tents and soaked gear proved more difficult than Katia and Landon had anticipated. After strenuous effort, Lionel and the others decided to wait for better weather.

The rain didn't lighten for three days, and throughout that time Landon and Katia did their best to pretend to be in love.

At first, Katia was uncomfortable. Affection of any kind felt foreign, and even the simple act of holding hands made her uneasy. Landon would do things on purpose to annoy her, like calling her sweet names in front of the little children who would get disgusted by the thought of love. Through all the play-acting, it became easier, and soon a level of trust formed between them. And though many times the children asked him to kiss her, he never did.

By morning on the third day, the wagons were rolling toward Davenport, where they would arrive in the afternoon. Katia walked near a wagon while Landon took Blizzard ahead to talk with Lionel.

"May I walk with you?" Lottie asked Katia. The little girl had become a favorite of hers over the past three days. She was an orphan, found abandoned near the river by a mute woman as a baby. Lottie called her Sweet-mum out of respect.

"Hello Lottie," Katia returned to the freckle-faced girl. "Where is Sweet-mum?"

"She's helping with the mules." Lottie quietly slipped her hand in Katia's. The touch felt strange but warm, and she accepted it with a gentle squeeze. They walked in silence for a while before Lottie spoke again. "Can I ask you a few questions?"

"Okay." Though Katia didn't want to appear nervous, she was.

"Are you going to grow your hair back?"

Katia laughed a little. "Oh, yes, I think that would be nice."

"You're pretty with short hair, too. I was just wondering." Another quiet minute passed. "Landon is really handsome, right?"

"Yes, don't you think so?"

Lottie shifted her gaze to Landon walking in full stride, helping guide Blizzard through the mud. "I've never met anyone like him. He is very clean and tan, but he is really silly sometimes."

"I agree." Katia smiled. "He can also be quite difficult. Sometimes we have very different ideas about things. He knows how to get me mad."

Lottie turned her head, thinking. "That's not such a bad thing sometimes."

"Why do you say that?"

"Oh, I like to feel emotions sometimes, to remember how much I like things."

Katia loved hearing this little girl talk. She sounded so smart for a seven-year-old. "I guess you have a point."

"What are you going to do when you get to Davenport?"

Katia didn't know how to answer. "I'm not sure."

"Are you going to stay with us? You could, if you like."

"It might be too dangerous."

"Will your papa find you?"

Katia clutched her hand again. "I don't know what is going to happen, but we'll think about it, okay?"

Lottie smiled again. "I miss the sun. Why is it never out?"

Katia looked up again at the dark clouds and wished for the same thing.

"Can I tell you a secret?" Lottie's voice took on a serious tone.

"All right."

"Sweet-mum cannot talk, but she can tell me things."

"How?"

"With her hands. She cannot read or write anything either, but she will tell me things and I can understand them."

Katia was amused. "Like what?"

"I know how her tongue got cut out."

The conversation had just become very interesting. "Really?"

"Yes, but nobody talks about it."

Katia looked around to see if anyone else was near enough to hear. "I swear I will keep it secret."

"Okay." Lottie seemed like she was just bursting to tell. "Well, before I was born, there was this woman and a girl who traveled with the caravan. I think the girl was my age, I guess, and she had golden hair like in the story Landon told about your village."

Katia stopped walking and fell silent. She bent down to face Lottie to make sure she understood what the girl was saying. "What happened, Lottie?"

Conjectrix

"Well, Sweet-mum saw something on the girl's neck, I guess—like a strange scar—and asked her about it, but by the next night they had vanished." Lottie's hands went up to her face as she made an extravagant vanishing action—very over-dramatic.

She continued. "One day when the caravan was in Southwick, guards stopped her and asked her about the woman. She didn't want to tell them anything, but they tortured her until she told them."

"Told them what?"

"Where they were hiding."

Katia furrowed her brow. "But how did she know where they were?"

"Sweet-mum can read the cards," Lottie said. "They made her tell them, and just so she wouldn't tell anyone what happened, they cut out her tongue." She made a swift motion like a knife cutting.

"Oh, no," Katia gasped. How could she have forgotten? These Travelers knew Naomi also. Some might even remember her. Landon had said these were dangerous people, and she started to see how.

She began to walk again. Her mind mulled over the details of the story. How could Lottie piece together so much of it? She wished she could talk to Naomi. Maybe it would help in some way. "That story is very detailed. Even for a little girl."

"I'm not so little. I am seven, you know."

A small laugh escaped Katia. "Yes. You're right. But you're such a good storyteller to make it sound so real. Without Sweet-mum's voice to tell you, I just wonder how you understood."

"I told you, with her hands."

Katia looked at her, confused.

Lottie's face beamed. "When I touch people, I know their secrets."

Katia stopped and looked at her in shock. "Secrets?"

"Yep." Lottie's eyes told her everything: this girl knew the truth about her and Landon. She knew about the mission, she knew about the lying, and she knew about the magic.

"Lottie?" she asked, mouth dry. "Why are you telling me?"

"Let me come with you. Let me come and I won't tell."

Katia couldn't respond. She was speechless.

"When we get to Davenport," Lottie continued. "I can help you."

"Give me some time to think about this, Lottie." Katia let go of her hand. "Can you do that?"

The girl smiled her sweet smile and skipped on ahead.

Katia made her way to Landon and out of impulse grabbed his hand. He immediately knew something was wrong. "Are you okay?"

She wasn't sure anymore. She was more terrified than ever.

❁ ❁ ❁

The small fishing village of Davenport sat on the very edge of the Ibis Mountains. The long cliffs of slick rock stood tall on the eastern side of the river. On the west side, stone homes fitted tightly together lined the bank, with each facing the water. Down toward the south end of the town, a few wooden homes stood on stilts, connected by a long bridge fastened with pontoons. A tall tower, possibly belonging to a church, loomed over the square. The caravan would trade there.

The entire town smelled of rotting fish guts smeared with mud, and as the caravan got closer, the smell became more pungent.

"Smell that?" Landon said to Katia. "That's the smell I love."

"Fresh salt fish from the boat smells much better than rotting corpse fish."

"This is where we must differ." Landon sighed, satisfied. "I miss this town. I think I did my best thieving here."

"Don't you think it will be dangerous coming back?"

"I doubt anyone will remember me here. But personally, I wouldn't care if they did."

"I just want to get away," Katia muttered to herself. She had not left Landon's side since Lottie had talked to her. She had kept so quiet that her jaw hurt from clenching it so long.

"What's going on" he asked. "You're ice cold."

"I know. I just need to get out of this weather."

"That's not what I'm talking about."

"Landon, what do we do now?" Katia turned to him. "Why are we still with the Travelers? We have to get away from here. Can't we just go on our way?"

"It's not that simple, Ice Princess." Landon sighed again, not happily this time. "The Travelers are not as generous as they appear. With their kindness they expect payment. A lot of the hard work we've done over the last few days has helped, but it doesn't entirely make up for what we've used. Lionel already asked us to repay him in full before leaving."

"How are we going to do that?"

Landon grinned. "Steal it."

"Oh, you idiot." Katia slugged him in the arm. "We can't do that. And what if the army is looking for us?"

"Why would they?"

Katia pointed to the approaching town, complete with the conspicuous blue cloaks of Southwick guards. "What if those are the same guards from Durundin? What if they see Blizzard and recognize him?"

"Blizzard *is* a magnificent horse. We should probably leave tonight."

Lionel approached, ending their conversation.

"We're riding the wagons to the north port, and that is where we'll stay. Not much in this town to speak of, but we will start trading tomorrow morning. I expect to have my payment like we agreed."

"Understood." Landon stuck out his hand and they shook on it.

Lionel headed back to the front to help guide the others through the gate.

Once out of earshot, Katia turned. "And if we don't?" she whispered.

Landon almost laughed aloud. "He said he would tell our secret to your father."

"And if he knew our real secret?"

Landon frowned, trying to decipher what she was telling him. "He would most likely kill us. Travelers don't like to be tricked—they liked to be the one tricking you. The safest way for us is to pay off the debt, and they can forget we ever existed."

Katia bit her lip. "I think we have a problem then."

A guardsman helping some of the Travelers eyed Landon and Katia. "You!" he shouted to them.

Landon started forward with Blizzard at his side. "Yes, what do you need?"

"The horse will need to go to the eastside stables."

Landon smiled back at Katia before he turned and walked with Blizzard to the opposite side and out of sight.

Katia watched for a moment, then walked with the others to the designated camp. She made herself busy and useful, trying to help where she could. Every once in a while, she would see Lottie out of the corner of her eye and worried about what the little girl might say.

Time passed and Landon had not returned.

Katia's nerves controlled her thoughts, and she couldn't help but worry. He was caught—she knew it. The soldiers had him and were torturing him. He would have his tongue cut out like Sweet-mum, and his magic would be useless. She would be on her own. If he was being tortured, could she do anything? How would she get him out of this mess?

CONJECTRIX

Those years in the Willows had taught her nothing but envy and contempt. She didn't know how to pick locks or earn money. She only had her ice magic. If she had to fend for herself, she might as well become a Traveler and be enslaved by their rules.

Katia helped the Travelers set up tents and kitchens, organized supplies, and helped with dinner, all just to keep her mind occupied. When all was done that she could do, she set up her own dome tent, isolated from the other group. It was a nice retreat from her thoughts.

She looked through the packs Spotswood had fitted her and Landon with. There were supplies of all kinds: cutlery, roots, bread, and cheese for eating, a couple of medical herbs for healing, strips of cloth for bandaging, and at the bottom lay the small strip of cloth with the Everstar on it. She saw it and her hope renewed. She could do this.

Something rolled around at the bottom of her bag. It was a small purple marble. The mist inside swirled around as she moved it back and forth in her hand.

"What is that?" a voice shattered the silence and rattled Katia's nerves.

She looked up to see Lottie's silhouette at the tent opening. "Oh, you scared me. I wasn't expecting anyone."

"It's getting late," Lottie said. "Landon isn't back."

The painful reality returned. "I know that." The thought pitted in her stomach, to the point it made her sick.

Lottie came back over and looked at the marble closer. "May I see it?"

Katia placed the marble into her palm and watched as the girl rolled it back and forth.

"It's pretty," she said. "Can I keep it?"

"I don't know what it does."

66

"It looks like a pearl or something." She smiled at the object. "Should I see my own face in it?"

"Can you?" Katia looked at the marble again. The mist formed a small mirror and reflected very small images of the two of them. "Well, that is pretty. If you want, I'll give it to you."

"Thanks." Lottie played with the object as she thought. "I will keep it forever with my other treasures."

"What kind of treasures?"

Lottie pulled out a little leather pouch tied on a string she wore around her neck. She emptied it into her hand.

Katia's eyes widened. There were a few random pieces of paper and a string or two, but the one that caught her attention was a ring with the clearest stone. It caught reflections of light as it tumbled out of the bag and onto the blankets. "Where did you get that?"

"I don't think you want to know. It wasn't a good thing."

Katia winked. "We can keep secrets, can't we?"

Lottie smiled. "I stole it from some lady. She was so rich I didn't think she would miss it."

"Would you part with it?"

Lottie quickly took her items and swept them back in the pouch. "No. This is all I have in the world."

"Sorry." Katia immediately felt selfish. She'd thought of using it to repay the debt to Lionel.

"I think we should get out of here."

Katia turned. "Why do you say that?"

Lottie looked into her eyes with a deep understanding beyond her years. "Landon is in trouble."

"Landon is very capable of handling himself."

"Then why are you so worried?"

67

CONJECTRIX

This girl could sense so much. It wasn't just about Landon—it was everything. Without a second thought, she reached for Lottie's hand. Her icy touch reflected her emotions. She felt bad holding the little girl's hand so tightly, but her thoughts melted as Lottie deciphered her secrets.

And then the little girl smiled. "I understand now. If I use my ring to pay your debt, can I come with you?"

Katia knew there wasn't another option. "Yes, Lottie."

Her grin increased. "Lionel won't like that I took it."

"We'll leave it for him and he'll never know." Katia began throwing things in her rucksack. "We'll leave tonight after everyone has gone to bed."

"But what about Landon?"

"We'll need him also, but I think it's too risky to try to find him until later. We'll also need another horse. We all can't fit on Blizzard."

"Oh, but I'm very small, even for my age."

Katia smiled. "True, but you'll need food and a blanket. Can you get that?"

"Yes."

Katia grabbed her hand again tightly. "If you are good at keeping secrets, you must keep this very deep. No one must know."

Lottie nodded her head and exited the tent.

Katia sank on the blankets, the only sound her heart hammering away in her chest. Landon should be here. He needed to be here. Her courage rose and flared with anger towards him.

"Shades, Landon," she whispered to herself. "Where are you?"

❅ ❅ ❅

When darkness covered the camp and the last of the fires disappeared, Katia emerged with her traveling cloak and a pack on her back.

Lottie trailed right behind and slipped her hand in Katia's. The ring Lottie had carried as a treasure lay in a small handkerchief with a note.

Thank you, Lionel, for your kindness. Lottie is with us. She will be safe and well taken care of. This is for you. The debt is well paid.

Short and to the point. If she explained any further there might be suspicion, and Katia wanted to avoid any more trouble with the Travelers.

The two crept through the camp, disappearing in the shadows between street lamps. Lottie tugged her forward, leading the way to the east side. The horses were kept there, away from the town center. In time, a long stable appeared by the gate. Many horses were tethered to latch posts and others behind gates. Even in the dark, Katia could tell that Blizzard would not be picketed with the other horses. Quietly they moved through the aisles to the back stables.

There were five stalls with padlocks. A small whinny came from the last one. Blizzard. Katia rushed over. Landon must be in real danger. Why else would they padlock him if they hadn't suspected Landon of something?

She sighed as she looked at the heavy lock.

"I don't know how—" she started, but before she could say anything else Lottie had already reached in her pouch and pulled out thin wire. Within seconds, the little Traveler had picked the lock.

Katia looked at her, impressed. "Can you read animals, too?" she asked in a low whisper.

"Never tried." Lottie placed her hand near the horse's belly, trying to figure out what the animal could tell her about Landon. "Dark cloaks. That's all he saw."

"Can you find another horse?" Katia whispered. "Meet me outside the gate. If I don't come, then something's happened and you'll need return to Lionel, understand?"

69

Lottie nodded.

Katia crept out of the stables and into the town. She wandered near many stone buildings, all quiet and still. There were few lights shining, but a tavern looked open for weary travelers. She pulled her hood up close to her and went inside.

Only a few scruffy locals occupied the place. She walked up to the bartender. "Excuse me."

The bartender eyed her wearily. He finished wiping his glass and came closer. "Have ya lost your way? Someone so young shouldn't be out so late."

"I'm looking for a friend."

"Don't know yer friend." He went back to wiping tables.

"He's—he's with the guards."

"Lost cause."

"Please." Katia raised her voice a little in desperation. "Please, I need to know where they are."

The bartender scowled. "Well, your neck, I guess. What do I care? They took housing in Sly Otter's."

"Thank you." She exited back into the darkness. Outside the tavern, she moved in the shadows as much as possible, working her way down the small street.

The post for the Sly Otter swung high at the corner near an open canal. Tiny light reflections shimmered on the water's surface. She could hear loud, drunken laughter toward the back of the building. She followed the voices and listened.

It was the guardsmen from the lake, no mistake. She recognized the large leader's growly voice. Their conversation made little sense until she heard them mention Landon. Her heart pounded hard within her chest. They'd found Landon and taken him.

". . . do you think he's conscious yet? That was some blow you gave him."

"He deserved it," the gruff leader laughed. "Trying to charm me. I knows that magic when I sees it."

The others laughed.

"Go check," the leader ordered. Someone moved, and a light passed into a room at the very end of the building. Katia crouched under the window in the back. She couldn't hear any talking coming from the room, and soon the light left.

"I kicked him just in case he was dead," the voice returned. "He stirred a little, so you'll still have the pleasure tomorrow."

There was more laughter.

She had found him, but the situation was more horrible than she thought. What was she going to do? Katia could feel her emotions take over. She closed her eyes and connected with her magic. The white light waited like shimmering snowflakes, ready to play.

Katia opened her eyes, sensing her magic close on her fingertips.

She looked at the window. It was locked on the other side. Pressing her finger against the steel on the latch, she froze it. With a few tugs, the latch snapped and she slipped inside.

The door to the other room was still open a crack, creating a slit of light in the room. Landon lay in the corner, tied and gagged. He had a deep purple eye and blood on the side of his face.

Katia gripped the rope until it was frozen solid, then snapped it in half. Landon stirred. After a few pulls, his gag came loose.

Now what? He was still unconscious. She placed her hands on his face, hoping the cold would help wake him. He moved a little. She moved her hands down his neck to his chest.

"Careful." His eyes opened wide.

Katia's cheeks flushed with embarrassment. But the thought that he was alive overwhelmed her, so much so that she leaned in and kissed his cheek. "Sorry. Let's get you out of here."

Landon nodded.

She struggled to help him up. Landon slipped against the wall, making a loud thump.

A moment later, the guards entered with their weapons drawn.

"You!" the leader shouted, recognizing Katia from the lake.

Katia's magic moved instinctively and slammed her hands to the floor. Branches of ice ran rapidly down the wooden planks. The approaching guards stepped on the slick surface, freezing their feet in place. They swung their weapons wildly, nearly slicing Katia as she helped Landon to his feet. Another swing caught her off guard, and she pushed Landon toward the open window.

He fumbled around and fell.

The leader smacked the ice with his sword, freeing his feet. He came right at her, slicing through her cloak and cutting into her arm.

Katia staggered back and quickly put up her hands. Ice wrapped around each finger, forming a shield, protecting her. She latched onto the leader's arm, the cold moving from her fingers up his arm and to his body.

Astonishment seized the leader's face. He was about to yell when the ice froze his throat, choking off the sound.

Katia turned to the others. "I wouldn't," she warned, waving her icy palms toward them. The other two men stopped struggling with their boots and dropped their swords.

She crawled out the window. Landon lay in a crumpled heap on the dirty street. Katia quickly wrapped her arm around him. The magic flowed rapidly, taking much of the weight as she tried to drag him to safety.

About halfway up the street, she heard a whistle. Her pace quickened as she headed for the gate. Running footsteps clipped on the streets behind them. She glanced back and saw more than a dozen guards approaching.

As they reached the gate, she saw the brilliant white horse accompanied by a brown mare with Lottie on top.

Katia used magic to lift Landon up on the horse. She grabbed the reins and steadied herself behind him. "Okay, Blizzard, live up to your name."

The horse whinnied with excitement and raced away.

CHAPTER EIGHT
THE BLACK WOLF

Ferra raced down the countryside from the army and far from the Durundin. Paolo, her bear and protector, could not run as fast as she needed, so she'd found Stargate, a mare she'd persuaded to help them travel to Southwick. She was a captain's horse, the best and fastest to be found. Behind her, Micah held on tightly, burying his head against the wind.

The escape was dangerous and the ride hard, but by the break of morning, they were past the lake and into the hills of Mendleford near central Parbraven. Wet grass, jutting rocks, and clumps of trees dotted the landscape.

Dawn crested near a town of very little consequence, and Ferra found shelter in an abandoned barn. Stargate needed the rest, and her own legs ached from a long ride. She took first watch, but after a while she couldn't stay awake anymore and fell asleep, too.

Stargate neighed and awoke the two sleeping humans. It was dusk, and the day had gone by without incident.

"I'm sorry for falling asleep," she apologized. "I push myself all the time and never drift off like that."

Micah smiled. "What a weakness is sleep."

Ferra stood and dusted herself off, looking around. "Well, maybe I was wrong. Maybe no one is following us."

Micah placed his hand on the ground and listened.

"The river isn't far from here," she informed him. "The water could hide our tracks."

"I am not as worried about the army as I am something else."

Ferra sighed. "I knew it. Something is following us. You think it's an animal?"

"Yes."

"Come on." She rose to her feet. "Let's get to the river, just in case."

They traveled a few miles further. A haunting feeling overcame her; they were definitely being followed.

As they approached the Tristus River, the roar of the cascades filled the night air, accompanied by the whistling reeds near the lips of the bank. Small groves of trees sprang up in families near the shore, giving a feeling of security. Everything was dark except for a few fireflies buzzing around the tree trunks.

Ferra wanted to cross the river quickly and get farther away from whatever tracked them, but Stargate hesitated to move across the slippery rocks.

"Come on." She pulled, but to no avail.

Something splashed in the water upriver.

Ferra whipped her head around, scouring for any sign of movement, but couldn't see anything in the blackness. "Micah, can you see it?" she whispered.

He peered toward the sound. "A black wolf."

She saw the outlines of the dark mass with its intense, flashing red eyes.

CONJECTRIX

Stargate reared up at the threat. Ferra held tightly to the reins, but Micah slipped and fell with a splash into the water.

"Micah!" Without a thought, she leapt from the horse to find him, but he had already been swept away.

The black wolf growled and stepped forward. The horse reared wildly and broke free. Ferra struggled to grab the reins, but it was no use. She tumbled back into the water as her beloved Stargate disappeared into the trees.

Fighting the current, Ferra finally stood, only to find the wolf just a few feet away. Its matted fur told of an unpleasant journey. Ferra reached for her neck and pulled out her medallion, but her stone kept cold in her hand. It would not work for this creature. This was not an animal at all.

Ferra's heart hammered in her chest. She looked deep into its eyes, searching for a clearer understanding, but the wolf responded with another growl. Slowly, she began to back away, afraid to break eye contact. She continued walking backwards across the river with the wolf's eyes following closely.

Wild splashing came from behind her and she knew Micah was in trouble. Ferra turned her back to the wolf and ran toward the sound. A little hand frantically sprang up through the water. Ferra grabbed hold, but then lost it again in the current.

The distinct smell of wet animal filled her senses. She spread her hands out frantically, trying to find her friend before the beast did.

Then a voice called from the river's edge—not Micah's. "Here! Over here!"

Ferra turned to see the outline of a young woman standing near the bank of the river. She glanced back over her shoulder, but the wolf had disappeared.

Turning back, she saw the woman reach down in the water. "I've got him! Here, help me."

Ferra quickly grabbed onto Micah, and together they lifted him out of the river. The girl laid him face-down in a small clearing. With a few pounds to his back, Micah began to cough and sputter. She turned him onto his back so he could catch his breath.

She turned to this stranger who had just saved Micah's life. "Thanks."

The young woman sat back and looked at Ferra without responding.

As Ferra studied her, there seemed to be something familiar about her. She had long dark braids and haunting eyes. There was no mistaking they had met before. "Are you the black wolf?"

The young woman laughed slightly to herself. "I might be."

"Why were you chasing us?"

"Better question is, why were you running away?"

Ferra frowned at the answer. "I know you're not in the army. Why chase us?"

"To kill you." Her laugh wasn't pleasant. "Guess I ruined my own plans."

Ferra did a quick mental check on where her knife was hidden. "Why didn't you?"

The girl patted Micah again on the back. "Because drowning is a horrible way to die."

This girl was more than puzzling. Ferra tried to pick out her true meaning. "Do you still mean to kill us?"

"The truth is"—the young woman smiled up at her—"I'd like your help."

Seeing Ferra's confusion, she laughed. "I'm Browneyes. Don't you remember me? The very one you fought in that awful cave. All that shaking almost killed me, thank you very much."

CONJECTRIX

The prompt brought instant recognition. A thrill of hatred ran down her spine. "You have some nerve—"

"Pish posh." Browneyes waved her hand, not caring. "Louvings are hard to trust, even each other, so I understand why you're so defensive." She sighed, the sharpness of her voice falling away. "I'll be honest with you, I promise. I need your help, and I think you owe me after I just saved your friend's life."

Ferra hesitated, keeping a careful distance. "What kind of help?"

"I want to go to Southwick."

"Why?"

"We share a similar mission." Browneyes flicked the edge of her knife with her finger, the tip poking through her flesh. She pinched the wound until it dripped blood. "I need to find Reynolds Fairborne."

Ferra's eyes followed her movements closely. "And you think I can help you do that?"

"Most certainly." Browneyes licked her bleeding finger. "Helping you will serve my purpose, I think." There was an odd smile on her face that Ferra couldn't interpret.

"Why Reynolds?"

Browneyes took her knife and stabbed the hard ground. "I'm still in love with him."

❀　❀　❀

Browneyes could not be trusted. Ferra knew this as a simple fact, even though the three of them had now formed a company. The first night had been very long. Ferra wanted to find Stargate, but she couldn't trust leaving Micah alone with the Louving, so she was left with no other option but to travel on foot.

By the following day, Micah had returned to his optimistic morning song, though his voice sounded strained. Ferra did not sleep well but would not let it affect her mood. As for Browneyes, she was not a morning person.

"I think it only fair we leave later in the day." She shifted against the uncomfortable lumps in the grass.

Ferra began putting on her pack. "Or we could just leave you. Then you can sleep all you want."

Browneyes glared but grudgingly leaned up on her elbows.

Ferra helped Micah with his pack and started to move down the hill toward the river, hoping Browneyes wouldn't follow.

The Louving caught up to them as they stopped to pick berries. "You don't need to be so rude, you know. I'm trying to help."

"Chasing away my horse didn't help." Ferra muttered. "Scaring us with your wolf trick. That didn't help."

Browneyes smiled halfway. "So, I'm a little theatrical. No real harm done. I'm trying my best at friendship. Never been a very good one in the past."

"That's sad," Micah said with a berry in his mouth. "I'll be your friend."

"He will not," Ferra spoke over him. "Why not leave? Go find Reynolds yourself?"

"I'll be useful. Trust me." Browneyes grabbed a handful of berries, threw them in her mouth, and walked away.

Micah watched her go. "Different people can make a journey fun, you know."

"It's plenty fun with just the two of us," Ferra returned disdainfully.

On they walked through the day, staying close to the river. Browneyes stayed in the lead. She had better eyes and ears than the others, and it suited Ferra just fine to stay behind her. She evaluated the Louving carefully from a distance. What was she really after?

Browneyes led them along an unsettling trail, and because of the approaching army, they spotted no other person during their journey that day. No one spoke until they stopped for the evening to fish.

"We need to leave the river," Browneyes stated soon after catching a good-sized river trout.

"No," Ferra argued. "The river will give us safety—"

"But Southwick isn't that way." Browneyes pointed down the river. "It's this way." Straightening out her knife, she pointed another direction. "Trust me, we don't want to follow the river. There are a few main ports coming up that are gateways for trade. If you want to stay out of sight, it's best to avoid them."

Ferra had neither the logic nor the energy to argue.

They ate and camped near the river again. Ferra was so exhausted, she immediately collapsed before they had made assignments for watch. She woke to a rustling sound in the middle of the night. Sitting up, she saw Micah fast asleep near her, but there was no sign of Browneyes.

Picking up her staff, she set herself guard. She listened closely to the sound of the rustling. With the Louving around, she couldn't trust her eyes. Ferra wished she could figure out her game. Her magic couldn't help her, either; Louvings had part-demon blood, which corrupted the connection she might have otherwise made. But maybe her magic could help in other ways. It was dangerous to use it, but in this case, it was important.

The magic sat still, waiting for her to communicate. Her stone told her much of the abundance of life the river held within and around it—the fish, the land creatures, and other bigger animals hunted by man. All were at peace.

The stone emitted light as it communicated. She pushed forward with her magic to find any information about the Louving. And then Ferra found her. An aura of black smoke surrounded Browneyes, almost as if it were sucking in the light from around her—trapped colors, with at least twelve captured souls. *So this is how Louvings work.* She focused on Browneyes' magic and searched for the faces of the souls, but the darkness snuffed out the light and she could see nothing.

Ferra opened her eyes and found Browneyes in front of her, holding out a knife. "Trying to use your magic on me?"

"What?" Ferra asked, surprised.

Browneyes made a reproachful noise with her mouth. "Your disdain for me is dripping from your mouth." She held something in her hand that she crunched down on, like an apple. At least, Ferra hoped it was an apple. "What did you see?"

Ferra tried to stay calm. "Nothing."

"Don't lie. You saw something."

Ferra knew she had to be honest with her—it was the only way to gain trust. "You're right. I did see something."

"What?" Browneyes' voice changed to match the sharp edge of her blade.

"I saw the souls in your pocket."

Browneyes crouched down, flipping her knife. "Do you know how easily I could kill you right now?"

"I'm not as easy to kill as you might think."

Browneyes relaxed a little, her smile returning as she lowered her knife. "I believe you. But you shouldn't use your magic. If anyone were around, they could see you bright as day."

"I'm not worried—"

CONJECTRIX

"You should be," Browneyes interrupted. "I've been around a lot of different magic, and yours is very desirable."

Ferra shifted. "I was honest with you; will you be honest with me?"

"I'm always honest."

"How do you know Reynolds?"

A harsh laugh escaped her throat. "Oh, Reyn . . ." She eyed Ferra very carefully before answering. "I don't want to tell you."

"If you don't tell me, I can make up some pretty wild explanations for—"

"Souls," Browneyes cut her off. "I'm a collector, as you claim. You saw all my pretty colors didn't you? Well, you need to know something about Louvings. We're soulless. A soul creates a frame—a sort of cage within the human body. Mine is different . . .empty."

Ferra took a deep breath, her mind racing.

Browneyes moved to sit directly in front of her. "If you think I care about your soul, you're wrong. I care nothing for it. Every soul I've ever taken, I have felt nothing for. That is why we can change and adapt— there's no soul to contradict it. No inner conflict. I might feel a pang of jealously every time I take a soul from someone, but I don't regret what I am." Browneyes sighed. "Reyn is someone for whom I would like a soul." She fell silent, the only sound the trilling of the water down the rocks. "Without a soul, I'm damned. I was born damned, but for a fleeting moment I felt I had a soul and that someone cared for it. It's hard to fool Louvings. It had to be real."

Her hand moved to her lips, her expression reflective. "He doesn't trust me, you know. But I think I'll win him over in the end."

"Why do you say that?"

"Because I'll survive and she will not."

Ferra kept calm. "Do you plan on killing her?"

82

"Of course not. Reyn would never take me if that happened. No, it's just a matter of time." She moved closer to Ferra, like she was a better friend than she was. "So, you and your sisters returning all the stones and whatever you guys are doing—I'm not stupid. Everyone is looking for them, but there can only be one way, and I understand that."

Her voice got really quiet. "But here's the thing I think a lot of people miss, and that girl has everything to do with it. Harrow was very direct on this. That girl is the key. Bringing back the stones might work to take back the magic, but the world won't be fixed until the girl dies."

Ferra's breath stayed cool and even. "I don't think it's easy to kill her either."

Browneyes smiled. "That's where a Louving might understand things where you do not." She went back to crunching whatever she'd been eating before, her words muffled but clear. "Kill the soul. Kill the body."

CHAPTER NINE
RUNAWAY

Silexa glanced across the table and watched Zander as he nibbled on his biscuit half-heartedly. Her own had few bites as well. Nervous energy had replaced her appetite.

Every once in a while a few dwarven men would come in, talk briefly, take something, and leave again. It had happened continuously for days now, but all the preparation came down to today, the day the company left for their mission.

She knew finding her sister might be difficult. The magic surrounding each of the daughters of King Prolius was unique, hers included, and hiding it was not easy. The underground city of UnderElm masked her element as the protector of stone and earth. But her other sisters had been forced to venture far from Southwick to conceal themselves.

Eight scouts were sent out, but only one returned with the vague possibility of knowing one of her sister's whereabouts. The scout described a harrowing escape, barely making it back alive. Prince Bryant was preparing for the worst. His dedication to helping Silexa only increased her adoration for him.

Despite Zander's pleading, Bryant had refused to let him join the search party, saying he had to stay and help protect Silexa. Zander had such a brave heart, one reason she loved him so much. His stutter had improved and he had grown since coming to UnderElm. Mother fed the twelve-year-old boy well. Having four grown sons, she took care of him like one of her own. Silexa could see his legs stretching away from his hemline, and the sight filled her with a sweet pleasure.

Silexa set down her tea cup and placed a hand on his arm. "Are you okay?"

Zander's head dropped and hit the table top. He looked up and met her blue eyes. "Yes."

"Are you worried?"

"No . . . n-not really."

"I am," Silexa confessed. She reached over and rubbed her fingers through his hair. "I'm glad you're here with me."

The burly dwarf, Thornock, oldest son to Mother, came in. "We are ready, your highness."

Both Mother and Silexa stood to wish the company luck, but Zander just sat there.

"Come, Zander," Silexa pleaded. "Bryant will want to see you before he leaves."

Zander shook his head. "I don't . . . want to s-see him."

Silexa frowned, knowing how badly he wanted to go.

Mother grabbed her hand and led her out the door. "They are by the tree. Come now, dearest." She patted Silexa's hand gently, reassurance in every touch.

They walked together down the small cobblestone road. Other dwarves crowded around, families and friends coming to say goodbye to their loved ones.

Conjectrix

The party consisted of Prince Bryant and the Mullgilly brothers—Thornock, Hix, and Brandell—along with a handful of other dwarves Silexa had never formally met, ten all together.

The Elm of UnderElm had changed colors over the last few months. Mother had suggested burying Silexa's sister Ymber on the same grounds, which sent the tree into mourning. The leafy green color turned to a vivid red as if ready to shed its leaves for the winter. But no winter came in UnderElm, nor in Southwick; both were too warm and near the sea. As Silexa looked at the tree, it only reminded her of the enormous task they were about to embark on—the mission to find her sisters.

Looking through the pages of the dream journal Zander carried, the one thing he treasured more than anything, the details of where her other sisters were hiding stood out clearly. Sera wouldn't leave the Ignis Mountains, and Ferra should be near the Echoes. She didn't know for certain where Fontine hid, but knew her dainty sister would never travel into the haunted marshes. But Vespa would. Her stone favored the dark elements. It had to be her. Traveling there caused problems dealing with the terrain.

Silexa reflected on the creator of the journal. She accepted it as truth—never questioning it like others might—that this Naomi, whom Zander loved, must be of some relation; everything about her felt familiar.

Over the last couple of months in UnderElm, Silexa became very familiar with Naomi's writing. It was the journal that had led a scout to search the marshes. When he returned with proof that a sister was indeed hiding there, Bryant prepared the party and Silexa gave thanks for the serendipitous leap of faith.

The city gathered at the tree to wish the company off. Bryant towered over the rest, giving instructions and making sure the packs were secure. A dwarven priest stood by him.

Silexa remained a distance away from the others so as not to attract attention. But the moment Bryant saw her, he cleared a path and grabbed her tight.

"Where is Zan?" he whispered in her ear.

"He didn't want to come," she returned. "I think he is still really hurt."

"He'll get over it." He kissed her on the cheek. "Will you be okay?"

"Just find her." The blue stone blinked between them, feeling the energy as they held each other.

"HO!" shouted Thornock and slammed his axe on the ground. The crowd silenced. Bryant broke away from his love but held her hand securely.

A priest from UnderElm spun his hands in a circle, fluttering his fingers and sparking a glow from the tree. His low hum penetrated deep into her heart. Streams of fairy lights emerged from the tree and crisscrossed each other, dancing around the crowd.

"The fairies have blessed you!" the old priest shouted. "And with this blessing, great power will be given to those here. Power to see through the evils that betray. May you be quick in your thoughts and in your actions. And go with peace."

The fairies sped around, ringing the company with a white glow. Then with a large clap, showers of sparkles rained down on them.

Silexa thrilled at the sight. She wished Zander had come. He would love the splendor of such wonderful magic. She held Bryant's hand so tightly that she could no longer feel her own.

Bryant kissed her. He smiled as he looked upon her again, winking before he turned back to face the others. He motioned to Thornock, who yelled to the others to get into formation.

CONJECTRIX

The small company of dwarves, some with packs, some in cloaks, moved with deliberation down the cobblestone to a tunneled exit that would take them to the edge of the city wall.

Silexa watched them until she could no longer see Bryant's head marching along.

"Come, come, my dear," Mother prompted. "There is still much to do here."

"Yes," Silexa moved slowly away. She took her time going back to the cottage, spending a few special moments to place petals upon Ymber's grave.

She expected to see Zander still sulking at the table, but as she returned, she saw it lay empty except for dried crumbs left from his biscuit.

She turned to Mother, who had entered behind her. "Where's Zander?"

"Oh, I think he might be in his room."

Silexa went upstairs, ducking a little down the hallway. When she reached his room, the closed door felt like a slap in her face. She knew he hurt and that nothing she could say would help.

"Zander? Zander, I know you're upset, but I'm glad you are here with me. It's best."

Nothing.

"Zander?" she called again.

Still no reply.

She opened the door. The small room sat in eerie calm. She looked around. Zander's possessions were gone, the journal, his cloak, his pack . . .

Oh, no. Panic hit her. Silexa quickly moved back downstairs. "Mother!"

"What is it?" Mother answered, responding to the panic in her voice.

"He's gone."

"What?"

"Is there food missing?"

Mother searched. The fruit and biscuits and a few other things were gone.

Silexa sank to the table, her head in her hands. She should have seen it coming. All those cloaks, a perfect camouflage.

Zander had joined the company.

❄   ❄   ❄

Bryant marched at the head of the crew, toward the west exit of UnderElm. The years of neglect filled the tunnel with earthy roots and thick cobwebs. A few swipes of the dwarves' axes cleared a path, but the company weaved in and out of the maze they created.

Bryant took the lead, along with Thornock, hacking and cutting what they could to get the men through. The lack of circulating air constricted the space with thick, dank heat. On and on it went with very little change, but the men did not complain. Bryant actually liked the feeling of the earth around them, sheltering them.

Finally a wall came into view. Long, heavy bricks covered the entrance to the outside world. "Did you expect this?" he asked Thornock.

"Yes, my prince," the dwarf returned in his rough voice. "It is the wall that surrounds the city. We have prepared for it."

He snapped his fingers and his youngest brother, Brandell, came forward with a small pouch.

"I have it here." Brandell steadied the pouch with his hands. A bright light emitted from the opening. As he reached his hand into the pouch, soft words escaped his mouth. "Little Lovely, it is your time now."

CONJECTRIX

Out crawled the tiniest creature Bryant had ever seen—a lacey-winged little fairy, all in white, brilliant as a tiny sun. It curled up on Brandell's thumb as it looked around the darkness. Its delicate wings unfolded and stretched out, fluttering reflexively.

So this was Little Lovely.

Thornock had suggested using fairy magic, but Bryant distrusted fairies and their secrets. One had bitten him as a young boy. He'd never wanted to squish something so much as he did that fairy. "Well, get on with it then."

The men all stared transfixed at the splendid light that came from the fairy. Brandell spoke some gentle words to the creature and it flitted above his hand, a small hum emanating from her wings. The sound increased as her wings beat faster and faster. A ribbon of white light began circling her tiny little body, and with a flash she accelerated directly into the brick wall and disappeared.

Darkness filled the space, a startling contrast to the bright light of the fairy. It took a moment for their sight to adjust to the dim light of Thornock's lantern.

"So what exactly can this fairy do?" Bryant asked.

Brandell smiled. There was no topic he loved more than fairies. "Fairies possess the special attributes from where they were born. Our Little Lovely was hatched from a Highthorn flower in the Musungu Marshes. She is blessed with the power of healing. We are very lucky to have her here. It's hard for her to survive underground."

Bryant pressed his hands to his lips, pondering. "But how is a healing fairy going to help us right now?"

"It's not the healing that she is here for; it's the haunting."

"Haunting?" another dwarf spoke up.

"The Musungu is haunted by Stains. The whole marsh is stained with magic, which is what can make it so dangerous. Highthorn flowers create fairies to help combat the evils of the stains."

Bryant's interest was piqued. "So what can she do? Chew through brick?"

Before Brandell could answer, the lines in between the brick appeared with a white glow that slowly ate away at the layered stones, making the bricks translucent. Soon the company could make out the faint light of a cloudy night before them.

Little Lovely flashed back to Brandell's hand and whispered something. He nodded, satisfied. "There. It's done. She has created an illusion."

"Are you telling me that this wall isn't real?"

Brandell smiled and nodded. "It never was. But Little Lovely put a charm on it for our protection. She broke the charm to get us through. If anyone enters from the outside, the fairies will know and alert the town."

Bryant smiled back at him. "You're a smart man, Brandell. Sorry I gave you a hard time about Fairyspeak." He walked headlong into the brick wall, passing through it easily.

The other men passed as well. Not until everyone had exited did the fairy return the charm, whizzing back and forth until the solid wall appeared visible again.

The fairy returned to Brandell, who gently placed her back into the pouch. "She's rather tired now and needs her rest."

Bryant slapped his shoulder in appreciation.

The party found themselves surrounded by a forest on the edge of the west wall of Southwick. A heavy ceiling of clouds hovered over the orange glow of the city.

"Are we all accounted for?" Bryant asked Thornock, who took a head count.

"There are thirteen, my Lord." Suddenly, Thornock sprang forward, grabbing someone by the throat: a cloaked figure near the back. The others drew their weapons.

Bryant unsheathed his dagger from his side. A circle formed around the scrambling man in the hood, and Bryant approached and placed the blade to his throat. "What kind of spy are you?"

The hooded figure breathed in sharply.

In one quick stroke, Bryant removed the hood to reveal a crop of red hair so vivid it could be seen in the dark.

Anger pulsed through him as he threw the blade to the ground and grabbed the boy by the shoulders. "What are you doing here?"

"I—" Zander tried, but couldn't speak.

"Take him back!" he shouted to Thornock.

"We can't do that without the fairy," Brandell reminded him. "We will have to wait until she is rested."

Bryant let go of the boy and walked toward the trees, swearing as he went.

Thornock fell into place next to him. "We cannot wait. We are losing time. We must move on."

Bryant kicked the ground, then turned back and strode toward the boy. "Does Silexa know you're gone?"

Zander shook his head no.

"Dammit, Zander! I trusted you. I needed you to stay with her, to protect her."

It looked like Zander would cry.

Bryant sighed. "Silexa will kill me if you don't come back alive. Promise me you'll stay by me at all times. Got it?"

Zander nodded.

"Don't make me swear again," Bryant warned him. "I turn into a bear sometimes."

Zander nodded again and walked sheepishly behind him.

CHAPTER TEN
In Stone

Naomi's eyes flitted open. A blurred face looked at her with concern, his voice distant and muffled. Sharp features came into focus as her remembrance of the night before returned in a flash of memory. She slowly sat up, pushing the dream out of her mind.

The little farmhouse looked emptier in the daylight than at night, and all the grime and ruin that had hidden in the shadows cast by the fire were sorely apparent.

Naomi's eyes were drawn toward the morning light coming through the window. The clouds parted, allowing the sun to peek through. Sweet songbirds filled the wind with music. She'd forgotten how beautiful the world could be in the morning.

Reynolds sat with his back against the hearth. He looked nervous.

Naomi massaged her neck to relieve some of the stiffness. "Is everything okay?"

Reynolds just stared at her in silence. Naomi knew his pain came from her. The heartache caused by her brush with death had complicated their relationship. She didn't like seeing him weighed down with such an overwhelming burden. She wished she could see the half-smile displayed on his face when she said something charming, like it had before.

She glanced around, then back to him. "Where's Arie? Has something happened?"

"No." He rubbed his scruffy beard. "Is it possible for you not to dream?"

Naomi blinked. "I don't think so."

"No, really. You can't dream anymore."

"Reynolds, that's ridiculous. I can't stop dreaming." She bit her lip. "How did you know I had a dream?"

"By the way you reacted in your sleep."

Her cheeks flushed. "You watch me sleep?"

"It's not like that." He ran his hand through his hair like he always did when he was frustrated. "Your magic gives you away. That's how the Southwick soldiers knew how to find us."

Naomi looked away. "I don't know if I can control it."

"I have a plan." Reynolds pulled out the beautiful purple ball that had led them there. "I have a theory—mind you it's just a theory—that your magic needs to connect with those you care about, and that's one thing I know the Conjectrix can do. It's driven by emotion, which I found out the hard way. I hope it might help curb your curiosity and keep your heart from wandering."

He reached into his pocket and pulled out the curious purple ball, handing it to her. The Conjectrix flickered to life in her palm, excited and alive with energy.

"So what should I do?"

"Remember the purple marbles Spotswood gave to each of us?" Reynolds asked. "We can use those to direct the Conjectrix, instruct it what to search for."

"It sounds too easy."

Naomi looked down at the ball, rubbing it experimentally. A spark moved inside it, but nothing else happened. "What should I do?"

"Try rolling it around with both hands."

She tried again. The spark returned, and different images flashed through. Finally an image of a fantastic valley appeared. Landon stood alone, looking out over the scene. And then it disappeared, and a swirling mist rested in the ball. "They made it out," she said, closing her eyes with relief. "I'm glad they're safe."

Distant whistling approached from outside. Reynolds snatched it out of her hand and put it back in his pocket. Arie entered, carrying a sack filled with a few different items.

"Good morning," he said pleasantly, a stark contrast to his brother's irrational concern. In the daylight, he looked different—not in a bad way, but Naomi had clearly underestimated his looks in the flickering light of the hearth fire. His sun-streaked hair hung around his face with reddish blond tips. He didn't look much older physically, but some invisible burden had aged his eyes.

His thoughts seemed to be along the same lines. Glancing over at Naomi, he stopped. "Reyn, you told me she was beautiful, but even in the early morning she is radiant."

Reynolds elbowed him in the stomach. "Did you get what I asked for?"

Glaring, he answered. "I think so. I found some onyx root and some red river brush, but I doubt it will work. I mean look at her."

Naomi still felt the flush of color in her cheeks. "What are they used for?"

"Reyn's trying to hide you." Arie placed the bag on the floor.

"What? How?"

"I wanted to try to change your hair color with the onyx root."

Naomi heaved a sigh. "Well, it's already short. I guess coloring it wouldn't hurt me. But I agree with Arie. It won't work."

"The red river brush will stain your skin."

Naomi hunched her shoulders. "What if it turns me orange?"

"It's not permanent. Just while we journey to the west."

Arie snapped off a piece of a dirty carrot into his mouth. "There's no way you can hide her. She radiates life."

"Stop it, Arie," Reynolds snapped. "It may not hide her charm, but I have to do something."

The brothers continued to argue until Naomi had heard enough. "Stop. Just stop." She took the little sack and looked over the roots and grass. "Tell me what to do. Do you need me to roll around with pigs? I'm good at that. I've done it before."

Reynolds expression softened a little. "No need to do that. We need to slice open the root and crush it up into a paste, then smooth it in."

"And this—red brush, you called it? What about that?"

"The seeds will dissolve in a warm bath."

"Oh." Naomi shivered at the thought.

Arie smirked. "Well, I guess I'll clean up all this." He headed to empty the tub.

Naomi struggled with cutting the onyx root. The pit felt hard; the knife slipped as it hit the slimy exterior of the black root.

"Here, let me help." Reynolds took over. A moment later, he handed Naomi a lump of gritty paste. With determination, she scooped a large amount with her fingers and massaged it on to her delicate golden locks. A huge glob slipped down the side of her face and chin. She couldn't help squirming at the sensation, but the movement created more of a mess and the black goop fell onto the floor.

Reynolds tried to salvage what he could and placed it back on her hair.

Naomi tried to be tough, using both of her hands to scrub the black stuff all over her scalp. When she finished, Reynolds' look said it all—still and contemplative. *It must be horrifying.*

The cluttered, dirty tub had been cleaned of all tools and grime. Arie was in the act of filling it, heating some water on the fire. Red river brush leaves floated around like tea, coloring the water a reddish orange.

He finished pouring the water and stared at her hair. "Is it supposed to do that?"

"I don't think so." Reynolds touched her hair with his fingers. "Maybe if we leave it for a moment."

Arie gestured. "Well, your bath awaits. Reyn and I will go gather some food while you soak."

Reynolds nodded and moved toward the door, where he paused. "Leave the onyx on for a while and then rinse it out."

The brothers left. Naomi looked at the bath. Her little finger brushed the tip of the water. The temperature felt perfect, the hot sting dulled by the cool metal of the tub. A bit of excitement rushed through her spine, ignited by the warmth that would soon surround her body. She couldn't remember that last time she'd had a warm bath. The red water looked ominous, but she quickly slipped off her clothes and entered the water.

Naomi looked down at the scar of the Vivatera on her chest above where her heart quietly beat. As scars went, she thought it looked lovely, coupled with the sacrifice and the pain associated with it. Peering closely, she could see the tear marks from where the knife had penetrated her flesh. From Taren, who had tried to kill her. He'd meant for her to die, but she hadn't. Did he even know she survived?

Naomi lifted her arm out of the water. The little red leaves had turned her skin orange instead of the beautiful southern tan she'd imagined, like Katia or Landon or Reynolds.

Reynolds. Her mind drifted back to her scar as she noticed the hawk with his wings spread. The Accipitor symbol was lightly displayed on the pinkish gold marking. She looked closer. The Vivatera looked as if it moved with her, with the rise and fall of her breathing—a part of her skin, her soul.

In that moment, the overwhelming burden she was trying to forget crept back to her memory. Hot tears formed in the corners of her eyes, but she pushed them back. She didn't want to think about it anymore.

The water became tepid as she dunked underneath, rinsing out the black onyx root, turning the water a murky shade. She got out before the water could stain her body purple.

※　※　※

After she dried off and dressed, she went out to visit the chickens and enjoy the beautiful day. It was nice to be outside in the warmth of the sun. The clucking in the pens made her think of Sharlot, her home town, and of Zander and a simpler life, a life she missed.

A growl came from behind the henhouse, startling Naomi. She jumped back to see the same funny creature from the previous night sitting on top of the coop. Naomi had never seen anything like it. Its orange eyes glowed, even in the daylight. It wasn't a cat, but more like a tiny bear with a long, fluffy tail than anything else she could imagine.

Naomi moved closer and it growled again—not threatening, but a warm, round sound in its throat. "Don't be scared of me, little guy."

CONJECTRIX

The creature turned its head, growling again.

"Well, I would agree." Naomi smiled. "I hope my hair doesn't frighten you away."

It blinked at her, somehow managing to make its eyes even more brilliant.

"What is your name? I think it must start with an R, since everyone in Reynolds' family must start with an R—"

The animal growled again, but this time Naomi heard something in the sound: a name.

"Dow. doo. . ." she tried to repeat it.

"Nobbs," a voice said. Arie emerged from behind some trees. "Well, I call him that because it's easier to say."

The creature blinked again in acknowledgement.

Reynolds followed Arie, carrying a basket of berries and fruit, but stopped once he spotted Naomi.

A nervous pit grew in her stomach. She knew she looked different, nothing like she had before—new skin, new hair.

He walked up to her and peered closely. "I don't get it," he muttered to himself.

"Please don't tell me. I know I look awful."

"Awful?" Reynolds took her hand and led her to a pond. "Look."

Naomi hesitated but looked down. Through the wavy currents in the water, she saw what Reynolds had been staring at. She couldn't believe it either. Grabbing a lock of hair, she examined it closer, the gold color radiant in the daylight. It looked livelier than it had been before. The plant didn't diminish it at all, but actually increased its brilliance. She stretched out the curl, disbelieving.

Next, she took a good look at her skin. It now gave off a warm glow like the sun had kissed it from heaven. It looked healthy and warm.

As she ran her fingers through her hair, she found that her hair had miraculously grown by several good inches.

Reynolds sank to the ground. "It's supposed to hide you." Frustrated, he grabbed a stone and skipped it over the surface of the pond.

Arie moved toward the hen house with Nobbs wrapped around his shoulder. "All right, Reyn, time to go. I think we've wasted enough time trying to hide her."

Naomi watched him walk away, then turned to Reynolds. His face was hard and his focus direct. "Are you mad?"

"I'm disappointed," he clarified. "It's not the same." He stood up and dusted himself off. "Why do you make everything so difficult?"

The words stung Naomi, though she knew he hadn't meant them to.

❀ ❀ ❀

After a few hours collecting supplies, they left for the Ignis Mountains. Clouds hovered high around the tops of the range. The wind died down, creating perfect conditions for their passage. Sometimes the sun warmed Naomi's cloak, bringing with it a renewed hope from her memories of sunlight and spring breezes, fresh flowers and bare toes in grass.

Reynolds insisted she wear her hood up, even in the nice sunshine, and battled with her over wearing her boots, a fight she didn't like losing. She hated them out of pure spite.

The lush countryside unfolded in grand scope before them. Hilly valleys hid away between the peaks of the west. Arie explained the township of Heartridge sat near the overhung cliffs in the north, but their path took them far enough from travelers to escape notice.

There were more rocks than trees with lovely hillocks filling in the terrain. A canyon road passed through the mountain range, called the

Shardrin Pass, which led to the Lapis Valley at the foothills of Mount Ignis. Not many passed the Shardrin Canyons, Arie told them, though he didn't explain why.

Near dusk, they found shelter in a cluster of rocks. A trail sloped down between the boulders where Arie made a small fire and roasted a rabbit he had trapped on the way. The evening felt peaceful and tranquil; even the stars came out and twinkled.

Naomi stared, transfixed by the stars she hadn't seen in ages, like reuniting with old friends from years ago. She didn't know the calendar or where the night fit into it. Did it matter that she was now eighteen or that the day had come and gone without her knowledge? A sweet peace entered her mind, one she had only felt in her blessed tree long ago, alone with her thoughts.

"Why would I ever return to the south?" she muttered to no one. "If I had known it was so wonderful up here, I would have left long ago."

Both Arie and Reynolds laughed at her remark.

"Honestly, I feel so at peace here."

"You're at peace when you are with nature," Reynolds corrected.

Naomi couldn't argue that. "What makes you laugh then?"

Arie pulled off the meat from the stick and handed it to her. "This land is haunted."

She accepted the food. "Haunted?"

"Yes." Arie looked around before speaking further. "This may look like a paradise in the day, but at night, the Stains come out. A long time ago, the Lapis Valley was once lush and beautiful and filled with life. It was the great country you believe it to be. But that was before the mountain erupted."

"Erupted?"

"Lux Lucis, there in the distance."

Naomi saw the shadowed outline of the mountain range.

Arie's face grew animated. "An eruption so catastrophic, so violent, so rapid and quick, people couldn't evacuate. The ash was so hot and fast that the villagers basically turned to stone."

Her eyes focused on the valley around them.

Arie motioned, taking a large bite from his rabbit leg. "Look closely at these rocks."

She moved away from the boulder she'd been resting against, smoothed over like a hunched woman. She concentrated at the details in the formation: the lines held together close, like tiny fingers; the draping around the ground like fabric. She squinted in the firelight. A sickened, sad feeling swept through her that turned to horror as she recognized a face looking right at her.

It wasn't just the face, but the eerie sadness behind it—this woman in her final moments of life, huddled over to protect herself against the raging heat. At once, she recognized an entire family frozen in time—a little boy crouched around his father's ankles, a little girl reaching for someone to protect her. It was a terror too overwhelming to comprehend.

She focused on the largest statue, a father with a stern, sad face, the realization that he could not save his family forever imprinted on his features. She ran her finger against his cheek as if wiping his tear from his brave face.

"People are afraid of this place," she thought out loud.

A thick silence followed. "Yes," Reynolds muttered, looking at the fire. He cleared his throat. "The eruption was manmade."

Naomi turned to face him. "You mean somebody caused this to happen? I don't believe it."

"Trust me." Reynolds met her gaze. "You of all people know what the enticement of magic can do to a person."

"Magic? They wanted magic so badly they destroyed this entire area?"

"Well, I doubt they meant to do this." Arie swallowed down his mouthful before continuing. "A lot of people came to mine out the magic from the Ignis Mountains. I heard this was where some old king found the origins for those stones you and Lytte worked on." He pointed toward Reynolds with his empty rabbit leg. "You know, when you were nine or ten."

The words were casually thrown out, but Naomi could see the impact of this in Reynolds' expression.

"These people died because of those stones?" she barely whispered, hardly able to comprehend the words.

"Maybe," Arie returned, going back to his dinner. "No one knows for sure. I'd blame that beast down in Southwick, personally."

Naomi sat down where she stood, overcome with emotion. "I don't know what I'm doing here."

Reynolds and Arie looked at each other as if they'd had this conversation before. "You wonder why I've been so careful," Reynolds murmured to his brother. "This is why."

Arie stretched out on the ground. "And this is why I said to leave her alone."

"You don't understand the danger here."

Arie nearly laughed. "I know this country better than anyone, trust me."

Naomi watched the anger flash in Reynolds' eyes. The air thickened with tense, unresolved brotherly jealousy. "Do these people return at night like other Stains or ghosts?" Naomi changed the subject with calm silk in her voice.

Reynolds shook his head. "I don't know."

"But I thought you knew everything," she teased.

He smiled unexpectedly. "Well, not everything."

Naomi laughed, then sobered. "I think I can help these people."

"Help?" Reynolds' smile faded. "Magic killed these people. They'll be able to recognize it in you."

"Can they harm me?"

Arie kicked him. Reynolds sighed. "I think they will; Arie thinks they won't."

Naomi smiled at how different the brothers were. She could envision their competitive upbringing through their bickering, and it secretly pleased her to know someone could motivate Reynolds when she couldn't.

"Sera should be there protecting the entrance," Reynolds continued.

Arie looked up. "Who told you that?"

"That's what the Shade of Prolius asked her to do."

Arie kept oddly silent.

A lump grew in Naomi's throat. "I don't think I can go there."

"Why don't you get out the Conjectrix and look at the others before you go to sleep? That might help control your dreams."

Liking the idea, Naomi pulled out the warm crystal ball from her pocket. At first she forgot what to do, but Reynolds reached over and helped rub it smooth. Soon she could feel through the different images.

She rested her fingers on the tiny image of Katia's face, bathed in the dark shadow as she talked with Landon, whose smooth face was lit by the light of a fire. She moved on to a different image. The picture went blurry but cleared as she saw Ferra running hard and fast with the wind blowing brown strands of hair around her focused, determined face. Micah was nowhere to be seen. Her worry resolved as she saw a flash of him in the background. Her fingers moved hard

CONJECTRIX

to find Zander, but she couldn't tell what she was seeing. Eventually she gave up.

Reynolds stirred the embers in the remaining fire. "Does that help?"

"I don't know." Naomi curled up, wrapped her cloak tight around her, and rested her head on a soft patch of grass.

She felt Reynolds tuck the cloak around her legs. He didn't say anything, just turned back to poke the fire.

Unexpectedly, little Nobbs moved over to her and nuzzled under her hand, curled his tail, and went to sleep. The soft creature comforted her enough she drifted easily to sleep.

The

    H a n d s

        grab her

f a ces

    hollow

                   and gaunt.

S t a i n s ,

    former lives taken.

She floats . . .

                     Below

                     her body still.

              Below

                     A watchful, weary eye.

    . . . but does not see . . .

The faces surround her f o l l o w i n g her

This is not a dream,

        but a realm.

The hands grab

    they take her.

The mountain beckons her forward.

> *a haunting song*

> *rhythm hum, muffling screams*

> *the rivers*

> *the rivers of fire. . .*

The souls of the lost . . .

> *No.*

> *Struggle to break free.*

> *The grip of the lost. Tighten. Squeeze.*

No . . . . let go . . .

> *She must go back.*

Swallowing p u l l s

> *Force   her*

> *Down   in the mountain.*

The heat!

A scream from her throat!

Scratches . . . she felt the scratches . . .

> *Woman's face full of flame*

> *A screetch!*

> *Thump!*

> *Wet on her cheek.*

> *Tickles on her nose.*

CHAPTER ELEVEN
Wanting Souls

Naomi opened her eyes, her heart still racing. The small boulder refuge had disappeared. She found herself standing in a clear field of yellow grass slowly swaying in illuminated waves. The sky had changed, too, filled with dark pink and purple clouds. Streams of strange light pulsed like lightning, the sky heavy with storm.

The grass felt real, soft and lush. The breeze pressed on her face, sweet as it swept past her ear like music. How did she get here?

Then a soft purr hit her ear and she looked down. Near her feet sat Nobbs with his warm, curious eyes staring at her.

"Are you in my dream?" she asked. He just blinked, but his eyes intensified as if he understood what she spoke. Naomi knelt in the grass near him.

He placed his paw on her heart. The magic within her came alive as he touched the Vivatera resting in her chest.

Dancing light encircled them with ribbons of white swirls, its energy and life pulsing within her.

A figure walked forward, interrupting the blaze of light—someone she had never met, or not that she could remember, but she immediately felt trapped by his penetrating orange gaze.

"Who are you?" her voice quivered.

"My name is Dobbins Foger. I am Nobbs. We are the same."

"I don't understand."

"This is my magic." His voice rang in circles around her. *"My life was taken by a power I had never experienced before in the deep woods near what is known as the Crying River. There were many of us killed—simple Travelers, murdered so long ago I can hardly remember it. The Grumbears happened upon us as we died and kindly took our stains upon them. As animals, they lack the ability for rational thought. We offered them intelligence and organization, and they gave us the ability to move and think. Now we co-exist as one."*

"How am I here?

"You are the sky, Naomi. You are the beautiful earth. Legions will follow you. Others will kill for you. But I . . . I will honor you until I die."

Naomi saw the look on his face. Such a beautiful, gentle face. No malice or deceit. Within that look she recognized a hidden cry for help. He had searched for years for an answer, trapped in a body he did not own and longing for freedom. Without a thought, she reached up to his face and gently stroked it with the back of her hand. The gesture made him cry.

"Please help us," he pled.

"You think I can free you?"

Without answering, his eyes told her yes.

"How?"

"All Stains want to be freed. Living forever is not a life, but hell itself. Our souls are restless. We are not meant to linger around unwanted bodies. Our souls are searching for the Paradise beyond this place."

CONJECTRIX

. . . Paradise. . . . like a whisper of a sweet dream . . .

She knew this paradise—one she would not forget, one that she never wanted to leave, but had been persuaded by her heart to return. She remembered the breeze, the sweet smell of flowers moving under her nose, the purr of the kitten on her lap, an empty meadow, except for the shade of Reynolds' magic persuading her to return.

If she had truly died, there would have been others there with her—thousands.

"I've been to this paradise," Naomi whispered. "I know the ache you feel. I do not fear death if this is where I will finally rest." She turned directly to him, her eyes full of admiration. "I will do whatever I can to help you return there."

"I am but a guardian. But I am not alone. There are others. Some will save you, others will want to possess you. They do not understand the release you will give."

She connected the pieces. "You're talking about my dream. The souls pulling me away."

"That is where we are traveling. The doomed souls are held prisoner in the river of fire."

A swirling, swimming sensation flooded her head, a sudden dizziness she couldn't explain.

Nobbs continued, *"A place called Lux Lucis."*

A piercing scream ran through the air, sudden and sharp, like a quick stab. The magic flurrieed in confusion. Nobbs covered his ears.

Naomi collapsed to the ground, feeling the heaviness in her chest, a pull she couldn't control. Her body slipped from the realm that held her.

❋   ❋   ❋

Naomi gasped and sat up. The scream still rang in her ears. She looked around, panicked. She saw nothing but grass and stars and heard only the sound of the night wind blowing through the straw.

A gentle nudge pushed on her palm. Nobbs sat wide-eyed, looking at her again through his animal body. He spoke to her through his eyes, hypnotic with understanding.

Reynolds grabbed her arm. "What's going on? Were you seen? What happened?"

"Nothing, I promise."

"I couldn't wake you," Reynolds stammered on. "What did you dream of?"

Naomi shook out of his grip. "I'm fine. Everything's fine. I . . . I was just really tired." She eyed Nobbs, then used her charm to help ease the tension.

Reynolds looked through her, trying to find a hint of some untruth, but she held his gaze, daring him to discover the secret. It might be better if he did. She wanted to look deeper, to find his thoughts and read his mind, to understand his fear and calm the storm within him. But his eyes relaxed. She knew he wouldn't find the truth.

He left her alone the rest of the night.

❃   ❃   ❃

Nothing disturbed their journey the next day—no trolls nor bears roaming the valley. She caught sight of random, scavenging animals like highhill coyotes and lemon finches, though they scattered before the company approached.

In the afternoon, rain clouds filled the sky. Naomi took shelter in a small alcove of a large, grassy hillock. After watching the rain for a while, she turned her interest to the dirt on the inside of the mound.

CONJECTRIX

Scraping away some of the mud, she uncovered an old wheel. She glanced around the valley, contemplating the destruction. "Entire villages turned to stone."

Arie took his knife and chipped away more clotted dirt. "Looks that way."

Naomi's stomach sank. The Netherfield hills stretched all the way to the mountains. A peaceful life had been turned almost instantaneously into a buried graveyard. "I don't like it here."

"Nobody does," Arie returned, still uncovering the stone.

"This place makes me feel guilty."

"How is that?"

Reynolds' eyes raised up to meet Naomi's. "I feel the same way," he said before Naomi could answer.

After the initial downpour, they continued, not wasting any daylight. Throughout the day, Nobbs stayed with Arie, curling around the shoulders of his master. Periodically he moved down to check on Naomi. She liked it when he brushed his tail against her leg, understanding the importance of the secret only they shared. Neither Arie nor Reynolds knew the terrors of this place like Nobbs did. And with Nobbs near, she felt safe—safer than with Reynolds.

They arrived near the foothills at dusk. The grass continued up the mountain, even as hard stone sliced the landscape with protruding sharpness. Past the jagged stone lay pockets of hidden caves at the base of the mountain range. Arie squeezed through a tight opening, motioning for Naomi and Reynolds to follow. A narrow passage opened up like a small room concealed from the outside, a tiny bit of light filtering through an opening at the top.

Arie cleared some of the rocks from the ground. "I doubt any troll will try to get in here."

Naomi didn't say it but agreed with him as she sank to the floor, exhausted.

Soon Arie and Reynolds were quietly discussing plans for the mountain passage, but Naomi didn't listen. Her own fear flooded her mind as she lay terrified of the impending darkness. Night would come soon and the need for sleep, and dreaming could bring dangerous consequences.

A wet nose rubbed against her hand as Nobbs settled down next to her, his warm body calming her spirits. She eventually ate some rations from her pack before she lay down on the hard stone watching all the light fade away.

There was no way of tracking time in the dark. She heard someone exit and return, then more talking and arguing. She lay quiet in the still night.

"Naomi?" came a soft whisper in the dark. It was Reynolds.

"Where's Arie?"

"On guard outside the cave. You should rest. Have you looked at the Conjectrix?"

"Yes," she lied.

"Good." She heard him sliding down the wall. "Good."

Naomi watched him closely, trying to make out the details in his face within the dark silhouette. Her restlessness turned to memories of him with her in the paradise she now longed to see. Reynolds talked freely and openly then, not like the sulking, desperate man near her now. He was different; the man she knew and loved had changed. Doubt came back into her mind as it had in the months sitting in the Caelia. He didn't love her at all but felt indebted to her for everything that had happened.

It became a very long night. She rested her eyes for a while but never slept. In the middle of the night, Reynolds left the cave and replaced

Arie at post. It wasn't as comfortable with him near, but soon the slight rattle in his deep throat brought an assurance of his slumber.

In the past, on nights like that, she would travel to her tree or look through her journal. After a deep grunt from Arie's throat, which shook her nerves, Naomi decided to follow Reynolds' advice and find the Conjectrix.

Within moments after stroking the smooth glass, she found Katia sleeping, surrounded by thick furs. Landon was close also, though he looked more restless.

Many forms passed by that she couldn't decipher: glimpses of running and darkness, possibly Ferra or Micah in the images. She pressed hard to find Zander but still could see nothing.

She continued searching, hoping to find a connection somewhere—then stopped. Her face froze. She looked at the sweeping hair, the dark eyes, and blinked a few times before realizing—*Is he looking at me?*

But how could he see her?

Thunk. She dropped the Conjectrix; the image of Taren disappeared as it rolled away. Naomi sat awake, really awake, knowing he had seen her. He knew she'd survived. She snatched the ball back and hid it again, then pushed her way out of the cave.

"Didn't sleep well?" Reynolds asked, perched above the opening.

Naomi nodded.

He rested his head against the rock. "Not surprised."

Naomi climbed until she could sit next to him and see what he saw—the sun rising near the crest of the mountain range, casting a strange light through the shadows and filling the entire valley with a wonderful orange.

"It's been a while since I've witnessed a sunrise," Naomi sighed.

Reynolds looked ahead at the light. "There is a power the sun gives us. It can renew us and strengthen us without really doing anything at all, just shining on us."

Naomi smiled. "What is this power?"

Reynolds slowly turned to her, looking worried and rundown. "Hope," he replied quietly, then returned his gaze to the valley.

Naomi sat with him in silence, taking in the strange rays as the sun moved closer to the peaks. The clouds gathered around the light, warming up the color and eventually breaking to let a ray from beyond the heavens through. It was beautiful.

After a few breathtaking moments, Reynolds sighed. "Well, this is a surprise."

"Surprise?"

"When have you ever been this silent?" He sounded like the Reynolds she remembered their first few days together—in the apple cellar, the cave, the canyon. To her astonishment, Naomi found herself blushing.

"I didn't want to disturb the lovely morning."

"Oh, I wish that were true." Reynolds grabbed a rock and threw it over the edge into nothing. "Tell me what scared you."

"What makes you think I'm scared?"

Reynolds almost laughed but stopped himself. "You don't know much about my magic."

That was true. There were no flames like Taren or dust like Micah or ice like Katia. "I learned early on that you don't like sharing."

He laughed slightly. "What do you think?"

"You're quick and you know when we're close to danger."

Reynolds sat up. "Like you, I can sense magic around me. My own is a good friend to me. He shares with me what he senses and feels and trusts."

CONJECTRIX

Naomi thought it over. "Why are you telling me this now and not before?"

"I think you understand more of my pain than you did before."

Pain. So that was how Reynolds felt his magic. To Naomi it was more like friendship. "So you can sense I'm scared."

"Sort of," he clarified. "My magic responds to yours, and right now it's glowing. It's all around you. Something haunts you, but I can't tell what it is."

She looked down. "I don't like this place."

"Is it the valley?"

Naomi remained silent.

He threw up his hands. "Naomi, I need to know what happened the other night. If your safety is at risk, I'm involved."

She sighed. "It was nothing."

"I won't take you any further. This place is still the calm before the storm, believe it or not, and I won't jeopardize your safety."

"My safety?" she snapped. "As far as I can tell, I'm the most powerful creature in Parbraven. My safety? What about yours? What about Arie's? What about villages and towns—people I've never met—what about their lives?"

Reynolds watched her smolder. "You're right," he said finally. "I'm sorry. I won't ask again. Tell me when you're ready."

Naomi didn't say anything. She felt the distance growing between them, and she wished she hadn't snapped at him. She respected him more than anyone. Her young adolescent crush had disappeared long ago, replaced by the roots of dependency. It felt like energy surrounded them, filling in the space between. As the silence grew, the need to tell him became stronger. *He needs to know.*

Then a deep growling echoed from below. Before Naomi could react, Reynolds whipped out his blade. Another low growl followed, accompanied by a big *crack*.

Two mountain trolls pounded their way into the secluded cave. They heard a scuffle before Arie's heroic battle cry. Reynolds stayed perched above like a hawk.

As the trolls emerged, Reynolds pushed Naomi back behind a rock, but not before she glimpsed Nobbs' brown fluffy tail hanging out of a bag and Arie's unconscious form slung over one of the trolls' backs.

❊ ❊ ❊

Deep inside the caverns, a chasm opened up to lava flow below. Heat waves blurred Taren's line of vision as the molten rock bubbled and popped, releasing a stench that stung the lungs.

Taren stood at a distance, watching, mesmerized by the sheer beauty of the formations in the flow—the churning waves and the star-burst shapes as air escaped from the bubbles. He knew his father wanted his attention, but still he waited, continuing to gaze on the lava. The churning heat mimicked his own anger.

Finally, Lockwood would wait no longer. "I have wasted too much time on this, Taren. If you have news, I must know."

"I found her."

"Where?"

"She's near the valley. I have done what you asked."

His father sneered with satisfaction. "So she survived."

"I think you underestimated her."

Lockwood's voice snapped back, cold and harsh. "I think *you* got too involved."

Taren glared at his father, his expression hard as stone. "Involvement was the idea. Don't pretend otherwise."

Lockwood's hand struck him across the face. Taren felt the anger burn inside him.

"That is another one of your failings. You care too much."

"You talk like this was easy—"

"It should have been. She should be dead! That knife can sear through any magic. For centuries it has done more damage in this world than can be imagined. Entire kingdoms have been crumbled by its power. It was meant for this—for killing *her*."

Taren stood immobile. The smooth hilt of the very knife his father spoke of felt hot in his hand. He envisioned returning the ancient dagger to his father, a prize he loved more than his own son. The knife swiftly plunging into his father's heart, penetrating deep in the soft flesh, Lockwood's fine robes soaked with scarlet blood, his father flailing and screaming as he fell into the running lava . . .

Lockwood's voice interrupted the vision, and Taren saw his father stand before him, unharmed.

"See that you keep an eye on her."

Taren kept his voice cold. "She could be very useful."

A flaming figure rose up out of the lava—a towering spiral of heat with wings formed like delicate butterflies and eyes that seemed to slice through Taren's very soul.

"The girl *will* be very useful, in her own way," Lockwood sneered. "There can only be one with that much power, after all. Best to destroy the girl before she realizes her own significance."

Taren gripped the knife tighter in his hand. This time he would not fail.

CHAPTER TWELVE
GURR

Reynolds swore as the trolls disappeared out of sight through the Shardrin Pass, keeping his eye on the trail.

"What do we—" Naomi began, but he silenced her until he knew the danger had passed.

"This isn't good. Stay here." Reynolds scanned for other signs of the trolls but saw none. He climbed down the rock and looked inside the cave. The trolls had ransacked the supplies. His eyes scanned the ground and found a ruffled bundle stuffed in the corner: Naomi's cloak. He furrowed his brow. The beasts had known where to find them. Naomi glowed like a beacon for creatures who hungered for magic, after all.

He emerged near the ledge, offering Naomi his hand. When she landed, he swiftly handed her cloak over. "I think you forgot this." He tried to keep his voice light, though he couldn't hide his frustration. "I don't want to see you without it again."

"I won't take it off," she promised in a near sheepish whisper.

Reynolds bit his lip, holding himself in check and finally accepting her promise. "Come on, I have an idea where they took him."

119

CONJECTRIX

The Shardrin Pass loomed before them: a tight, slick canyon with various sharp ridgelines where the shale split, surrounded by heaps of scree. Deep into the canyon, the shadows grew longer. The tall mountain passage filled with a tight wind that swept through like a flash of heat, nearly burning their skin.

The arduous travel played tricks on Reynolds' brain. Every little sound put him on edge: the crunch of gravel, the scamper of tiny animals foraging for food. Being extra careful made everything slower. Naomi followed behind him, staying uncomfortably quiet.

The sun disappeared, leaving behind long shadows, and before they knew it darkness covered everything. Reynolds found a thick ledge above the passage, and there they rested. Neither of them were mentally or physically prepared to continue.

Reynolds tried scavenging for food, finding a dinner of crickets, a dirty turnip, and water squeezed from cactus root. Naomi refused the crickets but drank the cactus water in one gulp.

They kept moving through the darkness. Reynolds' night vision helped him find a path, though he needed no heightened senses to detect the stench along the trail. Mountain trolls left a very distinct odor. Unlike the forest trolls in the Blackwoods, mountain trolls' smell had ripened over years of evolution, meant to keep others as far away as possible.

Reynolds kept pushing forward until he heard a thump from behind him. He turned to see Naomi on the ground.

"Naomi?" Reynolds ran to her. "You okay? Come on, wake up." Her pulse still held strong, the magic very alive. He had no choice but to scoop her in his arms and carry her along.

Through the canyon and around the boulders, Reynolds held her, hoping she would wake. His insides twisted with anxiety, his arms burning, pushed to their limit.

Finally, she began to stir. Her eyes flitted opened and she smiled at him sadly. "Zander." Her voice sounded far away.

Relief settled his nerves. He placed her down against a rock. "Are you okay?"

"I dreamt of Zander. I could finally see him. He's in such a dark place."

Reynolds rested his hands on his knees, overcome with exhaustion. "That's good."

"You need rest." He felt the heat of Naomi's analyzing glance—probably because for once he hadn't scolded her about dreaming.

"No." He shook his head. "I need to find Arie." He stood before Naomi could use her charm to persuade him otherwise. "Can you walk?"

Naomi stood and adjusted her cloak. "Yes. I'll be fine." Her sheepish blush only drew him in more. Reynolds took a deep breath to clear his head.

They walked together in silence. The wind accompanied them with bursts of heat as they climbed the side of the mountain. Strange formations of rock surrounded the landscape—tall and arching, contorted by time.

Small, harsh grumblings echoed amongst the rocks.

Reynolds felt his magic shouting.

. . . Move! Fast!

He pushed Naomi, covering her like a shield. A large boulder smashed down next to him—right where she'd been standing.

Another smash sent debris showering around them.

. . . Down!

He grabbed her shoulders and ducked as something hit the monolith next to them, shattering it to pieces. Reynolds dodged this way and that, pulling her toward a light glowing behind the taller rocks. As they reached it, another boulder smashed right above them.

Naomi screamed in surprised. Reynolds covered her mouth, but too late. The echoes careened around the remaining stones.

Reynolds pulled her into the shadows.

All fell silent except for their rapid breathing.

A strong thump shook the rock beneath their feet. Over and over again it kept pounding, as if the earth would crumble, swallowing them whole. A monstrous form came lumbering closer, until it growled, low and angry.

Reynolds kept Naomi behind him, pressing her against the rock. He stood so close to her, he could feel the heat from her magic filtering through. "Naomi," he whispered, "cover up with your cloak. It can sense your mag—"

Naomi shushed him with her finger. "I can hear him."

"What?"

A loud growl reverberated in the rock, the incomprehensible but universal language of hatred. Naomi took hold of the stone walls with her hands.

The beast appeared, blocking their escape. It was a mountain troll, larger than the creature in the Blackwood. Thick, black hair covered every inch of his disproportionate body. His arms alone were longer than a human body and could easily crush them.

Reynolds stepped forward, blade ready. The creature yelled and took a swipe with his claw. Reynolds hopped back on his feet and between the troll and Naomi, who still clung to the wall.

Another swipe. This time, Reynolds angled his blade upward and slashed against its arm. The troll sneered, bearing ugly, black teeth.

"Don't hurt it," Naomi spoke up from behind. "Let me talk to it."

Reynolds turned to argue, but the beast ran forward, knocking him into the wall.

Naomi stepped toward it.

Reynolds watched in horror. "What are you doing? Get back!"

"I know what to do!"

He stumbled to his feet. The creature's limbs stretched out, leaving its chest unprotected. One slice and the raging monster would be dead.

"No!" Naomi ran between them. Before Reynolds could prevent her, she grabbed the blade with her bare hands, screaming as blood appeared on her palms. A thin line appeared in her hand.

Reynolds dropped the sword immediately, shocked, and instinctively tried to cover her precious blood.

"No!" Naomi yelled again.

The troll pulled back its arms, preparing to strike, when Naomi waved her bloodied hands, stopping it in place.

"What are you doing?" Reynolds asked, horrified. He turned to look at the troll. Its nostrils flared open wide, and a grunt of want escaped its mouth.

The beast moved so quickly Reynolds couldn't react as it slammed him to the ground with a strong swipe of his giant hand. It moved directly before Naomi, a growl tearing from its jaws.

To his shock, Naomi took her blood-streaked hand and placed it on the troll's open wound.

The beast roared, the sound morphing into a scream. Its eyes gleamed at Naomi with hatred.

Reynolds scrambled back to Naomi. "Let go of him!"

Naomi ignored him, focusing on the beast's wounds. Reynolds grabbed her around the waist and finally pulled her away. The blood on her hands was no longer fresh red, but mixed with the dark brown coloring of troll blood.

Other shapes appeared, assuming positions near the tall monoliths.

Reynolds wearily picked up his sword and stood. Roars of protest filled the rock around them, the creatures moving in on all sides.

The wounded troll growled in the middle of the chaos, silencing all grumbles from the others. Another growl followed in a lower tone.

Next to Reynolds, Naomi twisted toward the troll to listen.

He growled once more and the others stopped.

Naomi's eyes widened. She tried to step forward, but Reynolds prevented it. "I understand him," she protested. Reynolds didn't care.

Another growl.

"Don't harm him," Naomi said.

"If he comes toward us—"

She shoved him aside.

"Please, Reynolds. He's asking about you." She ducked under his arms and stood before it. Reynolds watched with disbelief as she spoke to the troll. "This man wants to protect me. He is my guardian."

The troll looked over at him and grumbled something else.

"But I can help you," Naomi responded. "I opened your eyes to the magic by healing you. With time, it will help you."

More grumbles.

"I will not hurt you. We will not hurt you anymore if you help us."

Grumbles.

"We would be honored."

Reynolds watched the exchange with a mixture of frustration and amazement.

Naomi turned to him. "His name is Gurr. He's taking us back to their home."

"Where they'll eat us for dinner," Reynolds quipped back.

"No, where they're holding Arie and Nobbs, and where I can explain the magic."

"How is it he can understand you?"

"I'm only talking out loud for your benefit," Naomi clarified. "My magic is in him now."

He sighed. "Do you have any idea how bad that is?"

She smiled. "I understand much more than you. The source is still in me. Everything I touch is affected."

Reynolds stood still, keeping his expression vacant. Of course. He knew that.

Gurr moved forward, gesturing to the right of him. Naomi pulled Reynolds along as they followed the large mountain troll. The others around stood still, watching as they marched past the large rock and through the dark mountain.

They went to the source of the light. The mountain opened up to a huge crater with a large fire in the middle. Lined around the crater wall were pockets of caves, some dark, others containing peering, curious faces. Beside the fire sat a troll larger than Gurr, sitting on a solid rock throne. Gurr stopped right before him.

They started grumbling between each other. Naomi turned to Reynolds and translated.

"Touw is the oldest of the mountain trolls. He's called the Elder Troll. Gurr is explaining the magic to him."

"I don't like this," Reynolds whispered back to her.

"It's the best solution."

"We could have fought our way—"

"Fighting is not the only way," Naomi returned. Reynolds thought about a rebuttal, but she silenced him, listening to the trolls speak. "Oh, no, they're going to chain you up."

"What? Why?"

"They consider you dangerous."

"Because I stabbed him? He threw rocks at us."

Naomi listened. "They're going to put you with the other—he means Arie. Oh, no. They want me to go up there."

Reynolds grabbed her wrist. "Don't do this."

"We don't have a choice." She slipped out of his grip and moved forward until she stood before the one called the Elder Troll.

Every instinct in Reynolds' body told him to run and protect her, but he held still. All he could do was watch and listen.

The two trolls exchanged their strange, garbled language.

Naomi glanced back at Reynolds, desperate for instruction, but he was helpless. She straightened up to speak.

"I am Naomi, the seventh daughter of the great King Prolius of Southwick who died before I was born and whom I never knew." She pointed back to Reynolds, "This is my guardian, Reynolds Fairborne. He acted in defense to save my life."

More grumbling.

Naomi sighed. "I used magic to heal him. It opened his mind to its possibilities, a consequence that I cannot change."

Grumbles.

She looked frazzled by the exchange. "No. It is not in my nature to destroy anyone. I'm here to help."

The Elder Troll stood. He did not look pleased with her response. His outburst filled the surrounding crater with loud, throaty growls. Reynolds gripped his sword at the hilt.

Naomi's head sank. "I don't want to harm anyone. Let me help. I don't know what lives in the mountain, but I know I can protect you from it. I . . . ." She looked back at Reynolds. "I will give my life to protect you."

Reynolds stared at her without comprehension.

The Elder moved toward Gurr and looked him up and down. He grabbed Gurr's arm and felt his body, seeming to be checking for any magic. He placed his large palm upon Gurr's chest. The Elder then turned back to Naomi and spoke, pointing his finger right at her.

She stood, silent. Her voice shook as she answered. "A promise."

Reynolds hated not knowing what she agreed to do. He knew she was trying to protect him, but that was supposed to be his job. The failure of it flooded through his veins.

CHAPTER THIRTEEN
Blood Promise

The trolls separated Naomi from Reynolds, sending him away as a captive and her to a high stone parapet overlooking the rock crater, their prisoner. Despite this, from what she could observe, the mountain trolls were not the mindless animals she'd assumed them to be. They were kind within their race and lived in unity, caring for their families. It was the last thing she'd expected from these so-called beasts. The higher caves were reserved for the women and caring for the young to keep them from threats like fire eaters or other creatures who could bring harm.

She couldn't communicate with anyone but Gurr, her magic translating through his own. She wished desperately she could speak with the others. The trolls watched her with suspicious eyes, threatened by the power she carried. Naomi couldn't contradict them—she was a threat, and the longer she stayed the more dangerous it became.

Days passed without any news of Reynolds or Arie, and dreaming was impossible. The trolls lived at night and slept through the day. After so long in the Durundin, her body needed the sun, but she modified her sleeping habits to spend her nights with Gurr.

He, like many others, rampaged and scavenged for food and helped protect the trolls' sacred mountain. Being the Elder's son, Gurr was known for his vaktra, or courage as a leader. Naomi saw through this façade. Her introduction of magic into his body had created a scared, insecure, intelligent individual searching for understanding of a world he never knew existed.

Naomi tried to experiment with the magic as a connection, much like she did with Katia, but had very little success. Gurr was not a magic user. He couldn't interpret it the same way as Katia had, though it opened his understanding. Now he experienced compassion and felt and reacted to others, a nurturing instinct he'd never had before. Her time spent with him had opened a flood of emotions he didn't understand and couldn't control. Every night, she wondered if she'd made a terrible mistake.

After a week of being there, the Elder granted Naomi permission to see Reynolds and Arie in the underground caves. An overpowering sense of relief ran through her. She needed Reynolds' help, his cunning, his plans for escape.

As they led Naomi down the dark cave, she felt a stifling dread come over her, like the anxiety she'd felt in the Caelia when she heard Reynolds return. She needed him, just him, and the realization hurt.

Knowing he and Arie were safe would ease her mind.

A narrow tunnel led down into the cave. Naomi covered her nose against the overpowering smell of rotting, hot, sweaty trolls. The deeper she traveled, the worse it grew. She finally reached three small cells, each with a surprisingly creative cluster of thistles and briar at the opening. Gurr accompanied her, as he always did, and talked to the guard who opened the first room.

CONJECTRIX

Naomi entered. In the dim torchlight, she saw the sad state of her friends and felt a sharp pang at her heart. Arie rested against a rock, completely knackered, while Reynolds sat propped up against a wall, staring right at her.

"Give us a minute, please," she asked Gurr.

After he left, she sat on the floor before Reynolds' feet, wondering what she should say. He gazed at her, not blinking, waiting for her to speak.

But in the end, it was he who broke the silence. "How is your new protector?"

"I didn't have a choice," Naomi tried to explain, but Reynolds cut her off.

"You could have let me handle it." His voice raised. "Cutting your hands was a stupid thing to do."

She lowered her eyes. "I didn't want anyone to get hurt—"

Something brushed across her legs, startling her. "Nobbs." He gave her a reassuring look, speaking words with his eyes. In an instant, all the frustration disappeared.

As Reynolds continued to stare, burning a hole through her, she looked to Arie. "Is he going to be . . . ?"

"We'll both be fine if we can get out of here."

Naomi stroked the grumbear, thinking. "Gurr needs to come with us."

"No." Reynolds' voice was flat. "No way in hell."

"I have to take him to the River of Souls—"

"This is getting worse and worse."

"The River of Souls?" Arie seemed to have been awakened by the very idea, his tone confused and unbelieving. "Do you know what the river is?"

Naomi glanced down at Nobbs, a moment of understanding passing between them. "I know it's terrifying."

Reynolds shook his head. "Naomi. All we need is your sister. That's it. I'm not risking the River of Souls for a troll. Ignis is dangerous enough without it."

"Don't forget the fire eaters." Arie rolled over on his back, staring at the low dirt ceiling. "I don't know how many live there, but they circle the mountains at night."

Naomi straightened. "I'm not scared of fire eaters."

"Not when you have a big mountain troll as your protector," Reynolds fumed.

"That's not—"

"Would you trust him over me?"

"Of course not."

"Stop badgering her, Reyn." Arie sat up, Nobbs now at his side. "This isn't her idea. The trolls are making her take him."

Reynolds sank back against the wall, sighing. "Is that true?"

Naomi nodded. "The Elder wants to find someone in the River." She swallowed. "I don't think I can do it."

"Can you rescue the dead?" Arie sounded interested.

"I don't know."

"This is suicide," Reynolds informed her gruffly. "Those dead souls will sense your magic. They'll take you—"

"I don't have a choice," Naomi cut him off, her frustration bubbling out.

"Yes, you do. We could leave this place and head to the Ignis Mountains, completely avoid the river and the fire eaters, and find your sister like we planned."

"But I can't do that. You don't understand."

Conjectrix

Reynolds moved forward as far as his chain would reach, stopping directly in front of her. The heat from his body emanated his natural sandalwood scent, flooding her mind with memories of when they first met. "What's there to understand?"

He had a power over her and he knew it. Why else would he move so close to her? She felt compelled to tell him everything. He needed to know the truth.

"They'll kill you," she whispered. She held the tears in her eyes as long as possible. "If I can't find whoever they want me to find, they'll kill you."

Reynolds sat back and sighed. "Ah, shades," he muttered, then without warning wrapped his arms around her. She tried to stay angry but didn't have the fight in her. "Stop worrying about me," he murmured.

"I can't help it," she said into his tunic.

"No, really." Reynolds pulled back. "Stop caring so much about everyone. I wouldn't worry about mountain trolls. Nothing scares me anymore."

Naomi wiped her eyes. "There's a gathering of the Elders tomorrow. They need to do some ritual before we go to the river."

"Ritual?" Reynolds brooded. "That sounds bad. I say forget about the Elders and we figure a way out of here."

Naomi stood up. "I know you want me to forget about caring, but I can't. I can do this the right way and it will work. Trust me."

"I'm trying." Reynolds slid back next to the wall. "But I don't like this kind of bravery—"

"It's not bravery," Naomi said as she turned to leave. "It's integrity."

❀　❀　❀

Naomi traveled back to her cave with Gurr. The argument had frazzled her confidence.

Gurr noticed. *"You are cloudy."*

Naomi didn't understand. "Cloudy?"

"Not clear."

She thought about it. "I'm bothered, for sure."

Gurr tilted his head, trying to understand her.

"Bugged," she tried to clarify. "Bothered, irritated."

Gurr processed the words without comprehension.

"I guess if that makes me cloudy, I'll accept it."

"The man?"

"Man? Ah, yes." She knew he meant Reynolds. "Sometimes he makes me feel stupid."

"Stupid?"

Naomi grabbed her head in frustration and moved to where Gurr sat. She kept forgetting that she needed to explain not only the word but the emotion. Passing her palm over his, she opened their communication.

Gurr processed it the best he could. *"Who is the man to you?"*

"I don't know. I thought I did, but I don't." And she left it at that. With her mind muddled, she moved closer to the cave opening and looked out at the night sky. The warm glow of the fire reflected on the cave wall but did not distract from the clearing in the clouds and the brightness of the stars. Her thoughts went back to her tree and the night before her life changed. "Gurr?" she asked. "Do you understand anything about love?"

Gurr moved behind her. *"Love?"*

Naomi grabbed his palm again, sending through feelings that he might understand: the scent of flowers, the warmth of fire, the soft skin of a baby . . .

Conjectrix

Gurr recoiled his hand back at the last image, his brown, hairy face soft and confused.

"Mother."

"I loved someone once like that," Naomi smiled. "My guardian, Malindra. She gave her life to save mine. I can never repay that sacrifice."

"The Man?" Gurr motioned down.

Naomi understood. "No. Reynolds is different. He's complicated and confusing. I don't think I'm brave enough to admit what I feel. I think I'm a little naïve. I don't know." Her thoughts wandered again, and she became lost in thought.

Gurr said nothing but moved his hand to her shoulder. His magic was small, but she felt the sympathy he shared. *"I can protect you."*

Naomi slowly moved away from him. He meant no harm by it. "Thank you, Gurr. I'd like to be alone now."

Gurr bowed and left the cave.

Naomi sat still, thinking of the mess she'd created. Her friends scattered across the world. At the thought, she pulled out the Conjectrix, which she hadn't touched since Taren's image had flashed in the sphere. A nervous curiosity itched in her fingers as she rubbed the mysterious object.

The ball did not immediately respond to her touch like it had before, but filled with a dull, grayish haze. *Maybe it's broken,* she thought. Reynolds would not be pleased. Her hand pressed harder. "Please," she muttered. An image appeared, but she saw someone she didn't expect: a little girl.

The girl had long braids and dark, hypnotic eyes. Naomi drew closer to the image, looking around to see what she could. Why had the Conjectrix stopped on this little thing? The girl did nothing out of the ordinary, but even with this small glimpse, Naomi formed an attachment to her. She looked frightened, maybe even in danger. Naomi wished she could help her.

"Katia," Naomi whispered, rubbing the smooth surface with her thumb. "Show me Katia."

The Conjectrix did not move, just rotated the focus, and there she sat. They were in a conversation, this little girl and Katia; they were traveling together. Katia looked worried. Something had happened. Where was Landon? There must be trouble. But what could she do from so many miles away?

A thought came to her—a vortex, like she had done before to save Zander. Could she do that now? No. She snapped back to reality. No magic. Reynolds would be furious with her. She had to trust that Katia could make it right. It was useless to think about helping.

Naomi took the Conjectrix and hid it back in her cloak. It hadn't helped clear her mind, just made her thoughts more confused. *What a stupid thing to do.*

She rested her head back, wishing she had never looked.

❀ ❀ ❀

The next night, Gurr led Naomi to the ceremony. The smooth floor curved downward near the edges into a dizzying abyss. The Elders stood in the circle at the center around a huge blazing fire. Gurr called it the Fruvo Ej—the sacred fire.

Naomi glanced at many as she passed. This was not the civilized society she'd imagined after getting to know Gurr. These were brutal, bloodthirsty trolls, much like the Warlock trolls in the forest. Her stomach pitted into knots. Why had she even come here?

Conjectrix

Gurr escorted her to a throne made of stone. At the top sat the Elder, or as Gurr called him, Touw, Great Father. Naomi prepared herself with her cloak fastened around her. She couldn't trust these trolls.

"I don't know what to do. What do I do?"

Gurr looked at her. *"They want magic,"* he admitted. *"Show them magic."*

No magic, she heard Reynolds' voice say. Naomi walked forward, closed her eyes, and found the magic inside her. The magic didn't like them either. It wanted to hurt and destroy the trolls. Naomi couldn't do it.

She opened her eyes, the circle of trolls became more visible. "Gurr, I don't know if I can."

"You must make your promise."

"I have made my promise," Naomi insisted. "What else do they want?"

"A blood promise."

She tried to connect what he meant. "Are they going to kill someone?"

"A blood promise binds you. Seals fate."

Naomi understood. "No. I didn't agree to this."

Gurr moved her forward. *"It is our way."*

She stopped, turning to face him. "Gurr, you promised to protect me."

"Yes. You, I promised. Not the others."

"Others? My friends?" Naomi thought quickly. "The others are part of me, like you are part of me. Killing one will hurt me. You cannot do it. Understand me. What emotion is this?" She pressed her palm on his chest.

Gurr shifted, trying to understand. *"Bad and sad."*

"Fear," she informed him. "Fear is what I feel before something bad happens, when others are in pain, when I'm scared. How can you stop this emotion?"

Moved by the magic, Gurr sunk his head and turned toward the prison, leaving her alone.

Naomi felt the circle of Elders staring. The heat of each eye blazed into her like a searing iron. A tremor of fear traveled down her neck as the trolls conversed in barbaric grunts. She couldn't understand a word. Without Gurr, she felt lost and confused. One shouted angrily and she froze.

Elder Touw stood and silenced the others. His words, like the others', were unrecognizable to Naomi. His arms flailed around and he pointed to the fire. The others cheered at his response. A troll came up behind Naomi and forced her forward. Her shoulder felt the pinch as he shoved her with his sharp claw. Grunts and squeals erupted from the other trolls. They tugged on her arm, pulling her forward until she stumbled to the ground in front of Touw. He took her hand and placed it on his chest, like she had done with Gurr, then threw her arm down and started talking, fast and angry.

Naomi took a few deep breaths to calm herself, calm the magic. Her anxiety grew, wanting out.

Calm, she keep repeating, but her fear rose and her magic intensified.

Two trolls flanked her and dragged her to her feet. Naomi screamed in surprise.

Knife in hand, Touw loomed close to Naomi's face. "Ej undgu wah no pootten." The rest of the trolls went crazy. A rhythmic chant moved through the circle.

A yell echoed around the rock. Naomi turned to see Gurr with the two prisoners, their hands still bound. His grumbled language sounded like the rest, but she could understand him. *"You do not want it!"* he shouted.

The Elder responded with gestures and words.

"The magic is unkind," he implied. *"The magic changes the mind."*

More talking and more shouting. The circle agreed with him.

Gurr moved into the circle, dragging the prisoners.

"A blood promise is not needed."

The great Elders shouted at him in protest.

Touw ran over to the prisoners, straight to Reynolds, lifted his bands, and shouted in his face. Other Elders joined. He pressed the knife close to his neck.

"Stop!" Naomi shouted, still struggling with the magic inside her. "Gurr, what do they want?"

"They want proof."

"I'll give them proof!"

Gurr relayed the message. Touw moved the knife slowly from Reynolds' neck, pointing it now at Naomi as he spoke.

Gurr translated. *"I don't believe you can find her. You do not know anything about her."*

"Gurr, cut your finger," Naomi instructed.

Gurr moved closer to the Elder's blade and stabbed his little finger. Tiny drops of blood formed at the tip. Naomi walked closer to his finger and wiped up the blood in her own hand.

She knew the idea was crazy, like all of her ideas, but she had no doubt it would work. She closed her eyes to find her magic and slowly walked forward.

"Naomi!" she heard Reynolds shout right before the fire consumed her.

Bright white heat enveloped every inch, swallowing her with flame, sucking the air from her lungs and the moisture from her body. The burn moved up her legs with a sharp sting. All consuming heat licked around her delicate skin with searing, unquenchable pain.

Naomi's senses went dead from the shock. She heard a scream but didn't know where it came from—possibly from her own throat. The magic pulsed so fast it stifled her breath. In her blurred vision, she saw her skin bubble with glowing pearls. A hum resonated inside her, waking every particle. The scream in her head magnified until her body failed.

Bright light illuminating
Fantastic white

> *A face moved through the heat. . . a woman.*
> *Flame lifting around a beautiful flame.*
> *She stood tall with her palm outstretched.*
> *No words could she hear.*

She grabbed and felt peace.
Skin bubbling with heat melted to a glow.
Pearling opal magic moved in streams down the arm.
> *Fire moved around them.*
> *Together circling over and over—fast and faster.*
Words appear in her mind.

> *"Come find me."*

> *Flash of an image.*
> *A cave in a mountain, three stones.*

> *"I will keep you."*

❉ ❉ ❉

Reynolds reacted lightning-quick. Within seconds of Naomi disappearing, he circled his bound hands around, jumping through them like a hoop, then grabbed a scimitar from one of the trolls and slashed.

Conjectrix

The trolls, though still shocked by what the girl had done, screamed and howled in protest. He focused. He had to get to the fire. To Naomi.

Flames erupted outward, from fiery red to hot blue, scattering the trolls.

Inside, a trapped Naomi lay collapsed on the ground, cocooned in a large ball of flame. He couldn't reach her; the fire was too intense. His insides screamed in panic.

"Gurr!!" he yelled for the big troll, but there was no need—Gurr and Arie, with Nobbs perched on his shoulder, were now at his side. But it didn't matter. All of them stared, none knowing how to save her.

Nobbs, his eyes bright with the reflection of the blaze, tore down Arie's shoulder, heading directly toward the fire. Arie shouted after him, but it didn't change the grumbear's direction. With a deep huff, he threw his little body into the flame. A scream came from the fire itself, filling the air. Through the blue heat, Reynolds couldn't see a grumbear anymore, but rather a man, tall and stern. He walked through the magical flame, carrying Naomi's body like a feather, his orange eyes still visible as he approached.

Reynolds watched in shock as Naomi was held out from the fire. He took her in his arms, his gaze meeting the strange man's who did not emerge from the flame.

The fire blew out an angry swell then consumed itself, taking the man with it.

Within the smoldering black circle lay the body of a small grumbear, his fur singed and his skin charred—an incomparable sacrifice.

Arie fell to the ground and sobbed.

CHAPTER FOURTEEN
SAFE KEEPING

Zander followed Bryant's lead as he directed the small company of dwarves with deliberation and speed through the thick forests west of Southwick. Bryant's long legs accelerated the journey. For every one of his strides, Zander had to take two. Every so often, the prince grabbed the back of his collar and yanked him forward to keep up with the rest of the company.

When the crest of the morning sun hit the horizon, Bryant ordered a halt. They found shelter in leafy thickets and long-branched trees. Two men kept watch at all times, everyone taking his turn—except Zander.

For days, they journeyed with very little incident. A few times, they came across a Travelers' camp, but quick avoidance meant no problems arose. Bryant assured his men that moving at night played an important role in their success, but Zander had his own thoughts on the matter—no one went where they were heading. No one entered the Musungu, ever.

Through the journey, he heard the others talking about different dwarven legends of the Musungu, but inside each tale were fibers of truth, fragments Zander pieced together. A battle had been fought in those marshlands during the Great Wars. A leader of the tribal people misused magic he did not understand, and with one single act wiped out his entire civilization, including himself. It left the place with a powerful stain of magic, the souls of the people never left and hung around like ghosts. He later found out 'Musungu' was an ancient dwarven word for 'burial.'

Bigger than Zander's worry about spirits was the kind of magic it took to do such a thing, the kind that played tricks on the mind.

Zander tried to join the storytelling, but Bryant forbade him to listen. When the dwarves started talking, Bryant would send Brandell, the youngest son of Mother, to distract him from the evil thoughts that would likely plague his dreams.

Zander formed a friendship with Brandell, sharing both bravery and gentleness. Brandell stayed with him most nights and kept him company during the travel. On a few occasions, he would bring out Little Lovely and let her fly around, which pleased Zander very much.

"Fairies are very special creatures," Brandell explained to him. "To earn their friendship, you need to tell them a secret. Do you have a secret?"

"Yes . . . I-I think so."

"If you tell her a secret, she will keep it forever."

Zander smiled at the idea.

Brandell held out Little Lovely, who sat curled around his thumb. "Just whisper it in her ear."

Zander looked closely at the fairy. She was very small, like a strange firefly. Everything about her was white: her wings, her dress, and her creamy skin—all except the small crop of black hair on the top of her head. She could be mistaken for a Highthorn flower, white with black in the center.

He leaned in closely and whispered, "I hate the color of my hair."

Brandell looked at the fairy, who looked rather uninterested. "Boy, you need to think of a better secret than that. Try again."

Zander thought harder and then whispered. "I-I know about . . . the Everstar."

Little Lovely zipped up and fluttered around Zander's head. Her speed made it difficult to follow the buzzing wings. She landed on his shoulder next to his ear and whispered, "You are my secret," then flew away again.

"What does that mean?"

Brandell laughed. "It means you can now hear Fairyspeak."

Zander liked the idea. It was lovely, like the fairy.

❊ ❊ ❊

On the fourth night traveling through thick, bushy forest, the terrain abruptly changed. The tall evergreen trees morphed into crooked, moss-covered trunks, decayed and rotten. Patchy foliage covered the forest floor, leaving thick, muddy footprints where they walked. The air changed as a mist hovered near the base of the trees, hiding the secrets within, watching as they approached. The Musungu.

Unease crept down Zander's spine, a fear that pushed beyond his skin and sank into his bones. His body froze, refusing to move. Other dwarves stopped as well, sensing the same ominous doom.

"Someone's missing," Thornock stated as he finished a head count. "Where's Helik?"

Helik was one of the older dwarves instructed to stay with Hix and Jarem toward the back of the company. Neither had an answer.

"He was with us at the Crooks," Thornock's brother Hix stated in his rough voice. "I'm sure of it. I asked him to take right."

143

"Then that's where we must go," Bryant spoke up. "Zeth, you stay here with Zander."

"I want to go with you," Zander started, but Bryant shot a quick glance that silenced his request.

"We won't be gone long." Bryant pulled his broad sword from its sheath. He grabbed the knife from his belt and handed it to Zander. "Just in case. Stay hidden."

The knife felt uncomfortable in Zander's hands, the blade clumsily dancing in the air until he got a grip. Very carefully, he slid in into his bootstrap.

Brandell could see his distress. "Here." He grabbed the fairy's pouch from his pack. "Take her. She will help protect you."

"No," Zander protested. "She's yours."

Brandell only smiled and placed the pouch in his hand.

Zander watched as the rest of the men walked back through the trees, abandoning him so near the eerie entrance of the Musungu.

He looked back at Zeth, a large dwarf with a long red beard. He hadn't talked very much during their journey, but Zander felt like he should say something to him.

"Where sh-should I hide?"

Zeth stopped chewing on his stick. "I'd say the trees, if I were small like you." He returned the stick to his mouth and motioned upward.

Zander looked up. He couldn't imagine being tall enough to scale the massive evergreens.

"Here. I'll boost ya." Zeth held out the flat edge of his axe, hoisting Zander far into the trees until he was close enough to grab the closest branch. He scrambled through the prickles, scratching his hands, his legs flailing until he slid close enough to climb in and nestle his shoulders between branches.

Zander sat very still, listening to silence as the light slowly faded. Nothing moved, nothing breathed. Zeth, too, held still as a statue near the base of the tree. Zander could barely make out his boxy outline in the half-light. A crunch nearby startled him, unnerving the quiet. His eyes strained to see Bryant's return.

But it was not Bryant, or the dwarves. Zander could make out the man through the branches, his tall hat elongating his presence, his eyes cold and dead. He'd seen this man in his nightmares. Zander remembered too well the night when he tried to rescue Silexa's sister, Ymber, only to be fooled into a trap. The man standing below had been there, along with the demon Sharrod, ready to kill the both of them. His name was Curtis. Others accompanied him, sleek-bodied archers with cloth hiding everything but their eyes.

Zander tensed as they approached. He glanced down to see Zeth no longer at his post. The archers searched around the area, looking for something or someone. Inside his chest, Zander's heart beat so fast he felt it in his throat. Suddenly, an archer released an arrow, the whizz splitting the air until it hit something, hard. A small grunt came from the bushes.

Zeth stumbled forward, clutching his chest.

Curtis came into view, crouching down next to the wounded dwarf. "Bryant. Where is he?"

Zeth said nothing.

Impatient, Curtis grabbed the arrow and twisted it deeper. Zeth yelled in agony.

"Tell me now and I may spare your life."

For a moment, Zeth looked as if he would speak, but then turned and spat in Curtis's face.

Humiliated, Curtis reached for his knife and stabbed Zeth in the neck.

CONJECTRIX

Zander clamped his hand over his mouth, preventing any sound from escaping.

Curtis cleaned his knife on the dwarf's clothing. "He's not far. Search the area and find the trail. He will lead us right to her, I promise."

Zander sunk deeper in the branches, silently praying he was invisible.

The men scoured the surrounding area, looking for clues. Only Curtis and two other men stayed near the tree, fumbling through the fallen dwarf's pockets. "Why are you here, dwarf?" he muttered to himself. "And why not with the others?"

Zander held as still as possible. Curtis could easily kill him. If he stood, his hat might hit the very branch Zander held onto.

The velvet black pouch wrapped around his wrist swayed slightly with the movement of his breathing. Slowly, he moved his finger toward the opening. Even the slight exertion made the branch swing. He quickly stopped and hid his head.

Curtis stood. His tall hat came near the branches, barely brushing the dangling pouch. He and his men left and Zander listened as the sound of their crunching footsteps moved farther and farther away from him. Zander did not move. His muscles grew stiff and burned with pain.

A crash of thunder boomed beyond the trees. Little droplets of rain slowly began pattering down, barely trickling through the evergreens.

And there Zander sat, all alone. He felt lost and confused, unsure of what he should do. No one knew where he was. He had no food, no shelter. A dangerous man roamed the forest looking for his friend. All hope fading, he silently began to cry.

The wetness on his face mixed with the rain as it began to pour through the trees. He didn't care. His hands were sore and began to itch from the bristly pine needles. A sharp pain jarred him out of his musings and almost made him lose his grip. Glancing down, he saw Little Lovely standing on his right hand. She had bitten him, trying to get his attention.

Zander sat up, shifting to slide his back up against the trunk. He examined his hand and saw the tiny bite between his thumb and knuckle. "Ouch." He scowled at the little thing.

Little Lovely hovered near his ear. "I need your help," she said in her sweet whisper of a voice. Flying to his face, she tried to wipe away his tears with her white flower-petal dress. The gesture made Zander smile.

"What should we do?" he asked her in a whisper. "It was wr . . . ong of me to come."

Little Lovely flitted to sit on his shoulder. "I do not like the rain."

Agreeing silently, Zander looked off in the distance as the reality of his situation filled him with despair. "I don't know where to go."

"We should find her."

"Silexa's sis-ter?"

"Of course."

Zander's tears returned. "I d-don't know where to go."

"I can help you."

"H-how?"

"Trust me."

Little Lovely jumped off his shoulder and spun in the air. Glitter sparkled around her until, in a spurt of magic, she fell down and landed in Zander's hand—a delicate bell-shaped flower.

It was the most amazing, beautiful flower he had ever seen. Gently, he tucked the stem into his leather vest.

Filled with new hope, he covered his head with his cloak and then checked for Curtis and his men before slowly climbing down, dropping lightly on his feet.

CONJECTRIX

Zeth's body lay motionless, his eyes still wide open. Zander stared, a sharp burst of grief coming over him. He reached over and closed his eyes before heading into the thick forest.

Zander stepped cautiously into the darkness, his path lit only by the light from the fairy flower. Terror pierced his heart, which thumped hard and fast. He hadn't a clue of where to go but felt guided, led without conscious thought.

The land began to slope downward as the looming forest morphed to sparse marsh. The large evergreens grew fewer and fewer as the swampland grew deeper. Mist hung around the trunks, revealing eerie patches of crooked trees. Far in the distance, he could see a strange blue glow coming from the marsh.

As soon as he entered the fog, an uneasy feeling crept around his shoulders—the feeling of being watched. Tiny whispers drifted around him, but when he turned, he saw no one. He heard his name, echoing in his head again and again. Someone called to him, a voice he didn't recognize. It was a girl. Naomi? Silexa? He felt confused and disoriented. The fog grew so impossibly thick he could barely see his hands in front of him. His eyes strained, focusing on the bluish hue. Stepping carefully forward, he listened for the little voices he'd thought he heard.

The fog lifted enough for him to see a small lake ahead, so calm and still it looked like glass. An island of thick, crooked marsh grass sat in the middle, lined with tall cattails and rocky banks. The blue light hovered right above the water in cool, slivering patches. Zander blinked. Another trick of the eye. Hollow faces appeared in the gathering mist—not fog at all, but the spirits of ghosts watching him.

He gasped and stepped away from the water, but stumbled into the bush. A hand wrapped around his throat.

CHAPTER FIFTEEN
Almond Eyes

Landon slept a lot, drifting in and out of consciousness. He kept seeing the soldiers in his dreams, feeling the repeated blows. He'd wake in a spell of confusion, finding nothing but desert and sun. His head fell back again, rocked by the gentle motion of the horse as he lay strapped to its back.

Finally, he woke in the gloomy half-light of morning, not remembering anything. "Katia?"

"You're awake," she answered from behind him, sounding tired and irritated. "Finally."

He turned and spotted her leaning against a rock. "Are you okay?"

"Are *you*?"

"My head hurts." He felt the gash at the back of his head. "Where are we?"

"I don't know," Katia admitted.

Landon looked around as best he could, glimpsing overhanging trees and a small pond.

"I remember being with the Travelers. I remember I was winning at cards and . . ." He stopped as his eyes came into focus and he spotted a small girl curled up next to Katia, sleeping soundly. "Who is that?"

149

CONJECTRIX

She spoke quietly so as not to disturb the child. "Lottie."

"Who is she?"

"One of the Travelers."

Landon gaped in absolute disbelief. "You . . . you took one of them?"

"Don't say it like that. I had no choice," Katia snapped. "She helped me save you. She was the one that paid our debt—under one condition: if she could come with us."

"She blackmailed you?" Landon slowly sat up. "I like her already."

"And I like her." Katia stroked the sleeping girl's long hair.

Landon rubbed his temples. This would lead to trouble, he could already tell. "I think you might need to fill me in."

Katia told him about the last several days but couldn't quite hide her irritation with his memory loss. "So, now we're here, in the middle of nowhere, just waiting for you to wake up so we can get out of this place."

Landon smirked. "Well, thanks for caring." He tried to move a little and grunted in pain, rubbing at his ribs. "Geez. I hurt everywhere."

Katia looked a little abashed at her previous snappishness. "I wish I had something for the pain."

"First things first. I need to eat."

Katia automatically went back on the defensive. "Don't blame me if you don't remember eating. I've been feeding you. It might not be the best food, but I've been trying."

Landon gave a weak smile. "I'm sure you did. Right now, I don't even care. I just want to chew on something."

Katia opened her pack, tossing him some stale bread. He ate slowly, satisfied just by the effort.

She watched him, swallowing. "Promise me something, Landon. Don't leave me alone."

"I wish I could make that promise," he returned, crumbs falling from his mouth as he spoke. "But I'll do my best."

Katia sighed, as if a huge weight had been lifted from her shoulders.

Landon stood stiffly and tried to walk, hobbling at first until he stretched the kinks out of his legs.

He disappeared into a grove of trees, gathering together some leafy greens. When he returned, Lottie was standing near the edge of the pond and Katia had dozed off, though she roused as he dropped the pile at her feet.

"Look what I found," he said with enthusiasm. "Burmba plants. Didn't Lytte teach you about these?"

"I don't remember."

"They take pain away." He pulled off one leave and crunched on it. "I can already feel it working."

"I thought you wouldn't eat green things."

"Desperation changes a man." Landon snapped off the end of the leaves, squinting past Lottie to where their two horses stood, nibbling the long grass growing at the edge of the pond. "Nice horse."

Katia followed his gaze. "You mean Blizzard?"

Landon smirked. "No. I know *my* horse perfectly well. I mean the brown one. Not as excellent as Blizzard, but I'm glad you found him a girlfriend."

"Very funny. Stop trying to steal my horse."

Landon shifted, his grin fading. "And thanks for saving me. I should be dead, I know. So, thanks."

Katia gaped at him. "Are you sure your head's okay?"

Ignoring her, Landon stood to meet Blizzard, who had trotted over during their brief conversation. He patted him on his side. "I actually feel pretty good right now."

CONJECTRIX

"You ready to ride?"

"I think so."

"Good." Katia rose and brushed the dirt from her clothes. "I'm ready to get out of here."

❀　❀　❀

Katia held Lottie close to her on Cocoa Flower while Landon took the lead on Blizzard. Streaks of sunlight shone through the thick clouds, but never a drop of rain. Crooked, thorny trees cropped up along the cracked, dry ground. Small patchwork towns were scattered in the distance. Katia thought Landon would head to one of those, but instead he continued in a direction that seemed to lead nowhere.

After a long day of riding, they saw a large town coming into view. Little hills dotted the place, each filled with pink brick homes in circular formations spreading out over the land like spider-webs. Strings connected each house, some lined with laundry, others with decorative seashells gently tinkling in the soft breeze that smelled of salt.

"Do you recognize this area?" Landon asked.

"No. . . Well, maybe." Her early years had been either on a boat or in seaports, or sometimes she'd stayed on the Butterfly Islands with her mother before her brother was born. She tried to remember this place. The style of homes looked familiar. "They have a hole in the middle."

"Huh?"

"The houses have a hole in the roof to let out the smoke," she recalled. "I remember lying on the ground and watching the clouds move. The sun would streak in and leave patches on the walls. And you could redirect the light off a shiny surface. That was how they lit the rooms. So strange I remember that. I was very little."

"Well, that's a start," Landon returned. "We'll find lodging and some food when we get there."

"But we don't have any money."

He smiled, patting his pouch. "The guards didn't find *all* the money I won. Though, the Salt Dunes are notorious for thievery. We'll need to be very careful."

Katia's anxiety lifted a little at the thought that Landon wouldn't need to steal.

A tall stone wall surrounded the entire city. Its large wooden gate was propped open with braces. The streets inside wrapped around in a maze-like pattern, zigging and zagging within the stonework.

"What a funny little place," Lottie remarked with a laugh.

The stone passageways opened up to a large market. Beautiful, colorful tapestries and rugs hung down from the rounding architecture. People bustled from here to there, bartering over market stalls, filling the area with constant noise.

The people of this region looked slightly different than the rest of Parbraven. The dark hair remained, but their almond-shaped eyes were unique. Katia found comfort seeing others like her with her father's almond eyes and her mother's red hair—finally, a place where she could blend in and disappear.

They dismounted and wandered through the maze of streets, pulling the horses behind them. Up one of the hills in a back alleyway, Landon found lodging for the three of them for the night and stables for the horses. The room was furnished with two cots, a small table next to a window that opened to the alleyway, and a washtub in the corner.

All three of them tumbled onto the cots and fell asleep.

Katia woke from her nap with Lottie still curled in her arms. She felt a little blurry-eyed but knew her vision didn't deceive her. Landon stood near the tub, his hair dripping, falling down into his eyes. His bare shoulders bore deep bruises, now greenish yellow.

"What are you doing?" she asked in a harsh whisper.

"Well, contrary to what you think, I don't particularly like smelling like a horse," Landon retorted as he splashed the water around his neck.

"But there are girls here."

"It's not like I'm naked." He motioned to his trousers. "And I didn't think you would mind after living with boys the last five years."

"Well, I'm not a boy," Katia spat. "And I hated being treated like one."

Landon looked back at her with a sly smile. "I've never treated you that way." He looked over at sleeping Lottie. "And if you're trying to protect that little girl's innocence, I wouldn't worry. She's not as pure as you think."

"You have no right to judge, only knowing her a day."

Landon was about to say something but closed his mouth. "Well, I still need to get clean."

Katia sat up, careful not to wake Lottie. "Are you headed to the Fighting Knight? I saw all the pretty girls there."

Landon sighed. "Listen, I'm going there to get some food and information. We don't even know what town we're in. And it might be good to play the tables and get some money."

"Oh." Katia swallowed down her regret. "I just—"

"We're only staying the night." He threw on his tunic and vest. "I don't trust this place. Meet me there when you can."

"Sure." She watched him go.

As soon as he was gone, Lottie sat up straight. "Boy, you guys sure do argue."

Katia silently agreed. She liked to think that he cared for her—for *them*—but it was hard to tell sometimes. She glanced down at the younger girl, whose hair was a mess. "Come on. Let's get cleaned up."

She washed up, then attempted to help Lottie get clean, brushing her long black hair until it was smooth and shiny again.

"Sweet-mum always loved to brush my hair," Lottie sighed. "I hope she isn't mad at me."

Katia stopped brushing. "You didn't tell her you were going?"

"I thought she would be mad at me and not let me go."

"She should have known all the same." Katia wiped a smudge off the girl's face. "Promise me, if you leave, you'll tell me. I won't be mad." Lottie nodded. "Well, let's go. I'm starving."

They walked to the Fighting Knight, a tavern of great size. It was surrounded by stone, with wooden archways. The stone muffled the sounds from the street, providing a more peaceful atmosphere, despite the fact that it was crammed with little round tables filled with people.

Katia searched but could not see Landon anywhere.

A girl in a tight vest with sheer undersleeves moved over to them. "You're looking for the tall, dark gentleman, yes?" Her voice sounded like a whispering snake.

"Yes, his name is Lan—"

"We do not use names here," she interrupted. "He told me to look for you. Come." She directed them toward the back of the room. A long archway led to a second room, the gambling area. "The little girl must stay here."

"I can't leave her."

The woman glared at Katia. "There is a place I can keep her until you're done."

CONJECTRIX

Katia looked down at Lottie, hesitating. "Will you be okay? I'll be right here if you need me."

Lottie shrugged. "I'll keep myself busy."

Katia watched her walk away with the stranger. Her gut told her something was wrong, but she ignored the feeling, blaming her paranoia of the place. Entering through the archway, she weaved in and out of the smoke rings and past all the drunken laughter to another archway with curtains. A pretty girl with bare shoulders and a tiny waist stood at the entrance.

"I'm looking for Land—"

"Yes, mistress." She slid open the curtain. "Your food is prepared."

Katia hesitantly entered, hearing a loud gale of boisterous laughter. The room was lamp-lit, with thick fabric covering the chairs and walls. As her eyes adjusted, she saw Landon sitting at a large, round table cluttered with little yellow discs. She walked over and saw a second, smaller table with a plate of food—chicken and vegetables. At the sight, she nearly lost her composure. Real food had never looked so good.

"Hope you like it," he murmured to her.

"How did you get back here?" Katia whispered.

"And you said my magic was useless." He smiled and went back to his game.

She watched the others play while she ate. The men were loud and drunk, some heavily bearded and some with confusing accents.

"Everyone, this is Ice," Landon introduced her.

A loud welcome followed.

"You much for cards, miss?" one asked her.

"Sorry, I don't play."

"Too bad," he returned with a crooked smile. "We're always looking for fresh meat to peel off the bone."

"She's my good luck charm," Landon spoke up.

"Like he needs one." The others laughed.

"She looks pretty lucky," another one said. This voice sounded different from the others—low and calm, like the sea tide.

Katia turned. He looked like the others—a bushy beard, the almond eyes—but there was something else. Something familiar. Katia caught herself staring and shook the feeling away. She had to be mistaken. It couldn't be.

"Then again . . ." The man flung his cards to the table, holding her with his gaze. "She never did bring me luck."

Without another thought, Katia leapt across the table, her hands scrambling for his throat.

Landon forced his way between them in an instant, trying to pull her off as the man gasped for air. "What is wrong with you?"

"Landon Rhees," Katia heaved in anger, "let me introduce you to my father."

CHAPTER SIXTEEN
Briggs

The tavern owner suggested they move to somewhere more private so as not to disturb other gamblers. After a few minutes and a cool glass of water, Katia relaxed enough to be in the same room as her father.

Katia just sat in a chair in the corner and stared, disbelieving, at the man who had helped create her, molded her into the person she was, and abandoned her like the coward he became. Did he not love her at all?

Landon entered the room after counting his winnings. He went straight to her father, who had won the most, and offered his hand. "Splendid game tonight. It feels good to play with someone as smart as me."

Her father shook it, smiling. "Same to you. I'm sure you agree, it's not how the game is going, it's how well you play with the mind of your opponent."

"Being misread is the fun of the game."

Her father placed his elbows on the table. "If you act rich and think rich, you play with the rich—and the rich are willing to throw money to anyone. Deep down, they want to lose. They want people to see all the money they have to play. Am I right?"

Landon looked impressed. "Do you use the Elmia Charm or favor the Monderan Magic?"

"My dear boy, I use no magic. Just years of practice."

"How many years?" Katia spoke up from the corner. Her arms were folded so tight that tiny ice crystals formed around them. "How many years did it take you to forget about your life?"

"That isn't fair, Tia."

"Don't call me that! You lost the privilege to call me that."

Landon spoke up, smoothing over the hostility in the room. "My real name's Landon, by the way. Landon Rhees."

"Briggs Ravenmoor," her father returned. "My wonderful oats sowed that creature in the corner."

Katia glared. "Landon, don't you dare—"

He smiled innocently. "I'm only curious about your wonderful oats. And how your father got here."

"I could ask the same question." Briggs' hand scratched his bushy beard. "If I remember right, I sold Tia off and that was the end of it."

Katia jumped up to strangle him again, but Landon was too quick and sat her back down. "We would love to hear your story, sir."

Briggs sighed. "It's not as interesting as you might think."

"I don't believe that—an adventurer like yourself, related to the lovely Katia here."

"Landon, shut up."

Briggs smiled half-heartedly. "Irina was the love of my life—that's my story. When I lost her, my story ended. Haven't been sober in about nine years. Drink numbs pain."

Conjectrix

"So does ignorance," Katia spat. "How dare you use my mother's death as an excuse to abandon me?"

"You look so damn much alike, it's easier not looking at you." Briggs puffed gently on a small brown cigar before continuing, "The sea washes away my misery, and I would return to it if I could, but sea legs and drunken fits make a wobbly captain."

Katia scoffed. "Serves you right."

Briggs took another long drag on his cigar and puffed out a thick cloud of smoke. "Well, I can see that my little winter bird hasn't changed much. Tell me, Landon, how is it that you have not yet been crystallized?"

Landon laughed. "Narrow misses." Katia slugged his arm. "You see?" He leaned forward in his chair. "Now, let me ask you a question. Where are we, exactly?"

"Tapoof. City of gamblers and traitors."

"Are we close to the Springs of Sephar?"

Briggs raised an eyebrow. "And why would you want to travel there?"

"Don't ask him any more questions," Katia ordered. "He won't help us. He only helps himself."

Briggs ignored her. "The best way would be by sea if you are trying to get away from the king's army."

Katia swallowed, clamping her mouth shut.

Briggs noted her gaunt expression. "Ah, yes. The army is here. The first place they came was to me."

Standing, Katia marched to her father. "You haven't cared about me in years, and it's obvious that nothing has changed. Turning your own daughter over to the army—"

"Kat—" Landon started, but she silenced him.

160

"No, Landon. I'm done with him. Come on." She tried to pull Landon out of the room, but he wouldn't budge. After a moment of tugging, she let go. "Fine! You two deserve each other."

She stormed through the curtain, only to stop right outside to listen.

Briggs laughed. "Quite a spitfire, that one. I can see some things never change. She gets wound up so tightly that when she snaps, it hurts. That's a warning, my boy. Watch out."

"Don't worry. I've been her punching bag for a while now. I better go check on her, but one question first."

"Shoot."

"Did you set us up?"

"Of course not," Briggs returned. "How would I know where Katia was? I haven't seen her in years. I figured she was dead for all I knew."

Katia had heard enough and set off to find Lottie. She kept rubbing her hands, trying to warm them, but the ice flaking off her palms looked suspicious.

Finally, she found the girl in the kitchen, alone. "Lottie, we have to go."

"Okay." Lottie seemed nervous as she moved a few items back into her little pouch. She grabbed Katia's hand as they exited. "Your hand is cold."

She released her, not wanting to hurt her. "Sorry."

"Are you in trouble? Did I get you in trouble?"

"No." Katia frowned down at her. "Why would you think that?"

Lottie shrugged and continued walking next to her.

Once back in their room, Lottie found a seat on the floor and opened her bag, revealing her treasures.

Katia collapsed on her bed, lost in thought. Her chest ached as old memories came to the surface. The same opium that had given her magic had driven her mother Irina insane, and she'd taken her baby brother Vanya's life before taking her own. After the tragedy, Briggs had crumbled, left with a poisoned misfit that reminded him too much of his old life.

The sting of seeing her father again had reminded her of all the things from her past, the good along with the bad. She remembered being in her father's arms as the boat rocked in the tide; the funny songs he sang to her underneath the blanket of stars; him helping her grab a slippery fish so it wouldn't escape the net. When Vanya was born, he was so excited to have a son. He'd loved his children more than he loved fishing.

So why did he leave?

Overcome by the memories, Katia wanted to cry, but the tears formed into small crystals on her eyelashes and she just picked them off.

After a moment, she glanced over at Lottie and her small pile of treasures. A few coins, a button, the purple marble, and . . . "Did you get a new trinket?"

Lottie quickly grabbed the items with her hands.

"Lottie, what is that?" Katia sat up. "Is that what I think it is?" She grabbed Lottie's hands and pulled the ring out of the pile.

"Kat, we've got to get out of here." Landon entered with her father behind him. "The soldiers are here. We need to go with your father."

"Come with me, Tia," Briggs added. "I have something to show you."

Katia glanced at him. "No. He's a traitor. He'll just try to sell us or make money off of us."

Briggs sighed with frustration. "Did you ever consider that I'm trying to protect you?"

Katia huffed. "Some protection. Sending me away so you could forget you had a daughter."

"I never forgot."

"Kat, stop this," Landon interrupted. "The soldiers are looking for you."

"Well, they aren't the only ones." Katia held out the ring. "Our debt was never paid."

Landon whistled low under his breath. "That adds to the dung heap, doesn't it?"

"Landon . . ." Briggs made eye contact and nodded. Without a word, he disappeared down the alley and out of sight.

"And where is he going?" Katia stammered. "Leaving again?"

"Would you stop that? He is not trying to trap us."

"What? Do you think you know that after meeting him for fifteen minutes?"

"I trust him, and you should too."

"I can't do that, Landon." Katia tossed the ring back to Lottie, who snatched it from the air. "He got rid of me. He doesn't want me here. He never did."

Landon grabbed Katia's hand, silencing her. She hadn't expected how warm his touch would be or how vulnerable it would make her feel. "What are you doing?"

"Calming you down." He held her gaze. "Listen. He wants to explain something to you. I don't know what it is, but he said he had to show us."

"What if it's a trap?"

"I'll give you Blizzard."

Katia laughed despite herself. "But he isn't yours—"

"I know," he cut her off. "But I love him more, and you know it, so that's what I can offer you."

Katia looked into his deep brown eyes and saw that he meant it, every word. "Okay," she conceded. "But if it's a trap and I'm right, you can never tease me again."

Landon smirked but agreed to the terms.

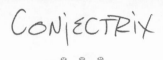

CONJECTRIX

❊ ❊ ❊

They gathered what belongings they could, covered themselves with cloaks, and fled into the dead of night. Landon fetched the horses from the stables but quickly discovered the clomping of their hooves on the cobblestone would give them away. Instead, he led the two horses away through a dirt path out of the city while the girls waited in a dark corner.

Time held very still as they waited for Landon to return. The night sounds of the city died down, save the wind whistling through the sandy rock.

Someone approached. *Landon*, Katia thought—before she saw a silhouette of a large man blocking the archway before them.

"She's around here," he said to someone behind him. "Search the Fighting Knight. She's wily, that one. I don't trust her. Best find her first."

"Yes, my lord," the other man returned and traveled down the corridor.

Lottie squirmed under her hood, trying to take a peek at the men, but Katia held her tight in place.

The shadow hovered for a moment longer, then departed.

Katia's nerves were rattled. She didn't notice she was holding her breath until Lottie tried to speak and she quickly covered her mouth.

Another shadow approached, drawing even closer. Katia felt her heart thumping in her chest. The shadow stopped right before them.

"Come on."

Katia almost screamed but knew better. When she saw Landon's face under his cloak, she wanted to slug him but instead took his hand. He led them through the winding stone to the outer wall.

Once there, he stopped. "I asked Blizzard to meet us by the last of the southern docks."

"You talked to the horse?"

Landon grinned. "He understands me, promise. Briggs is going to meet us around here."

"I still don't like this idea. There were soldiers. I think they were looking for us." She shook her head. "We're wasting time. Do you really think my father is going to meet us here?"

"I do," Briggs spoke up from behind them.

Katia turned to see him standing in the distance. "Come, we have far to go." He walked right past them and continued southward.

They marched for what felt like ages, accompanied only by the rolling clouds and the few stars that occasionally popped into view. A few times, someone would trip over rocks or boulders, but Briggs knew his way and warned of any major crevasses or dangers along the way.

"Are you sure you know where to go?" Katia asked at one point.

"I could walk it blindfolded."

"Which is practically what we're doing," Landon observed.

"We're nearly there," was all Briggs said in response.

The smallest sliver of light from the eastern horizon began filling in the sky. Outlines of the stones around them began to creep up in strange formations.

Landon swallowed, his voice solemn. "It's a graveyard."

Lottie backed away, silent.

Katia immediately knew where he'd led them and her heart sank down to her stomach.

Briggs' pace slowed as he reached a small hill.

In the half-light of the early morning, she could make it out—a large stone marker with a dark engraving:

Irina Sephora Ravenmoor
Here she lies waiting for her love.

CONJECTRIX

Katia fell to her knees, overwhelmed. Tears fell heavily, opening a wound that never properly healed.

Briggs knelt beside her, wrapping an arm around her shoulder. This time Katia didn't recoil but let her father hold her. Quiet moments passed in silence.

Finally Katia found the ability to speak again. "Why did you bring me here?"

"I wanted you to see."

Katia looked again at the stone. It was just a regular marker, nothing special or shiny like some of the others, only what a fisherman could afford. Then she glanced next to it.

There was nothing there.

"Where is Vanya's?" she asked. "Where is my little brother buried?"

"He isn't," Briggs returned, voice thick with emotion. "Last I saw him he was alive."

"What?" Katia could barely speak. Her head swam in different directions. "How is that possible? He was dead. You told me he was dead."

Briggs' eyes were hollow as they looked upon her. "I couldn't tell you the truth. It hurt too much."

"Tell me now," she demanded.

Sitting near her mother's grave, he could not deny her. Briggs sighed and settled back. "Your mother was so beautiful. I loved her so much. Irina—" he stumbled, "she was targeted by the King of Parbraven. A man named Reinoh."

Landon leaned forward, listening intently. "We've heard of him."

"Irina was one of the maidens of the Butterfly Islands, known for their royal blood and their incomparable beauty. Many of the monarchy felt that they could pick any one of them for their own, to use as objects of lust, not love.

166

"I wasn't much interested in revolution. I escaped to the islands, where I met Irina. She liked me because I was free from the rules of the kingdom. I followed my own path.

"She was such a rare beauty with her fiery red hair and a temper to match. We ran away and married. I didn't know at the time, but she had refused Reinoh before he was king and married me instead. I didn't know how strong her pull was over him; I only knew what it was to me. She could have been a queen, but she loved me so much, she married me."

Briggs stumbled in his telling, the secret he'd held for so long bubbling out of his mouth.

"I became a fisherman. We traveled around, one big adventure. She had little Tia, and I couldn't want for anything else. Life was perfect, except that I was always afraid my Irina would get caught. I had to keep her safe, away from the public eye, away from him.

"We were safe on the sea, free. But she got really sick before Vanya was born. I knew she couldn't stay on the boat, so I sent her with you to live here in Tapoof. I was with her when the baby came, but he was so sick, so small. She tried what she could to help him and sought the counsel of a healer."

He stopped for a moment, possessed by the memories. "But the healer was no healer, but a witch in disguise, all a part of Reinoh's plan. Reinoh's spies had found her on land. This witch was given instructions to drug Irina in hopes that she would forget about us and return to Southwick. Instead it drove her mad. You and Vanya were also targeted. By exposing you to magic, he hoped you might turn against me or become so powerful you could be a weapon to help him."

"How do you know all this?" Landon asked.

Briggs' eyes welled up with tears now, free-flowing and unstoppable. "I was there the day Irina died. I'd heard that Reinoh had come to Tapoof and knew the only reason would be if he'd found her. He had come to collect her, to take his butterfly back to Southwick. His own wretched wife had died, leaving him alone with his son. But I know he didn't love Irina like I loved her. How could he? He never knew what her love was like.

"He was convinced the drug had worked, but then I arrived. Once she saw me, the spell broke." Briggs got very quiet remembering. "She ran to me. She shouldn't have come to me. She might still be alive, not mine but alive. As she ran to me, Reinoh stabbed her through the heart. Triumphant to see me at such a loss. He snatched the baby while I tried to stop the bleeding.

"She was so beautiful. She spoke your name and little Vanya's name. She loved you so much. I needed her to survive. She was my beating heart."

Katia's tears fell down her cheeks, forming crystals at her chin.

Briggs held her gaze. "I sent you away to hide you. You look so much like her. Reinoh will know you when he sees you. He will find you. He will kill you. I was only trying to protect you."

Katia embraced him. There was no more wound to get in her way now. She let her magic move out of her, fed by the emotion releasing it. Cool strings of frost swirled around and around them, strengthening them together. Slivers of morning light glistened off the elegant crystals.

"We have to get Vanya back," she said into her father's shoulder.

His grip on her tightened. "We have no proof he's still alive."

Katia moved back to look at her father. All his strength had left him in the telling of his tale, the hurt overwhelming his will. "I'm not going to leave him to die in the hands of the king."

"Vanya doesn't know us," Briggs tried to explain. "He doesn't know about his mother or her sacrifice. Who knows where he is now, how he's been raised, if he's still alive."

Katia looked at her father with astonishment. "How can you not try? After all the sacrifices Mother—"

"I *have* tried, but there's no point!" he shouted back to her. The sound broke the morning, silencing Katia and surprising her nearly to tears. Briggs brushed his hand through his beard. "If Reinoh sees me, he will kill him, I have no doubt. To spare Vanya's life I have to stay away from him."

Katia stood. "Well, I'm not leaving him there to die. I'm going to find him."

Landon, who had remained silent for the most part, spoke up. "Kat, we aren't going to Southwick."

Katia turned around to face him. "Yes, we are. I can't leave him."

"We have no choice right now."

Her anger flaring, Katia pushed him in the chest. "I don't care about finding Naomi's sister now. This is my family."

She'd expected him to argue back like usual, but Landon's voice sounded compassionate and soft. "I'm sorry that this happened to your family, but we need to focus, Kat. Remember Naomi. What would she want us to do?"

"How dare you try to guilt me, Rhees? Don't bring her into this!"

At that, he finally snapped. "How could you forget so easily? She's sacrificing her life for you."

His words stabbed like a knife. "She would support me if she were here."

"Do you hear the drumming?" Lottie interrupted them, a peculiar smile appearing on her face. "They're coming."

Landon and Katia stopped. Plodding could be heard against the hard ground, distant but approaching quickly.

"The soldiers," Briggs said grimly.

Landon grabbed Katia's arm and moved like lightning. She turned to grab Lottie but couldn't reach her. The girl just stood there without reacting, like a ghost watching the world around her.

"How far to the river?" Landon asked Briggs.

Briggs rose to his feet. "Not close enough." And with that, he grabbed little Lottie and ran for the shadows.

Their own footsteps drowned out the sound of the approaching horses. Briggs was a careful guide, but the terrain soon turned from desert hard-pack to soft sand, hindering their progress. He let down Lottie and led her by her wrist. She struggled against him, trying to free herself from the grip.

On the left of them, the small trees and shrubs began to disappear while the taller desert palms and large leafy plants became more abundant.

"We're not going to make it," Briggs said over his shoulder, still struggling with the little girl's lagging. "Go to the trees."

They changed direction and turned west. Landon and Katia fell into the shadows when they reached the tree line, trying to see any soldiers advancing.

"Climb," Landon ordered. He helped Katia with a boost from his hands.

"Where's Lottie? Where's my father?" she whispered. "I can't see them."

"No time," he returned, climbing after her.

The overgrown vines helped them advance up the trunk. A cluster of large palms held together on top made for a convenient hiding place.

"Over there." Landon pointed toward a rustling in the leaves. Lottie and Briggs emerged, moving through to a safe area.

In the silence, they could hear nothing but the sounds of an awakening jungle. The sunlight moved behind the clouds.

Far along the dunes, shapes began to appear. A line of horses came advancing through the trees.

Katia's mind whirred. "How did they find us?"

"Someone can't be trusted. My bets are on the little girl."

"Lottie?" Katia shook her head. "I don't believe it."

As the morning light became stronger and the horses drew nearer, it was clear they had followed the signs of their quick dash to the trees. The obvious footprints stood out in the sand.

Landon swore under his breath. "They've got Blizzard."

Katia, too, spotted the magnificent horse with his new rider—the large captain from the lake. "They tracked us all the way here?"

Landon hushed her as they watched.

The large captain took out a pouch from under his shield and pulled out a stone. The horsemen behind him created a V formation, stopping right before the trees. The captain signaled to his left and soldiers dismounted, approaching the trees.

"Hold your positions!"

From above, Landon and Katia could see the soldiers had formed a circle surrounding Lottie and Briggs.

Katia couldn't just watch. She needed to act. She started to call her magic but Landon stopped her, covering her mouth.

From below came a struggle and the sounds of clanging. At last, Lottie and Briggs were pulled from the trees.

The captain examined them. "Well, this is not who I expected. A little girl with a drunken old pirate. But where are the others?"

"We don't know," Briggs said, earning him a blow to the stomach from one of the soldiers.

Conjectrix

"That's enough, Ravenmoor. It's clear that this little creature is not your daughter, but she'll do for now."

More struggling followed as both were bound and placed with riders. Briggs was knocked out cold and slung over the side. Little Lottie merely looked at the soldiers with curiosity and went without a fight. With a loud yell from the army, the horses plodded on toward the south, leaving a furious Katia and Landon covered in snow.

He shook it off, removing his hand from Katia's mouth to find bite marks. "Well, that was uncalled for."

"You big jerk!" Katia tried to slug him but about lost her balance on the branch. "They're gone! Why did you let them get away?"

"What choice did we have? Besides, one of them can't be trusted."

Katia understood who he meant and fumed. "How can you say that after he poured his heart out?"

"Oh, and now you're best friends? The story was touching, I'll admit, but it shouldn't change the fact that he sold you out."

Katia's mouth gaped. "Sold me out?"

"How else would they have found us?" Landon shook his head. "I could tell he didn't like telling the story, but it was rather lengthy and conveniently kept us in one spot."

There was truth to it, Katia couldn't deny it. She shook her head to clear her brain. "You are the one who told me to hear him out."

"Because he's your father. But fathers aren't perfect; they're people, not saints." Landon spat this out as if he knew from experience. "If it's not him then it's the little girl. Either way your heart is broken."

Katia sat and stewed for a long moment, not wanting to believe either was true. "So what are we going to do?"

"We're going to the Springs of Sephar like Spotswood asked us to."

"And leave them? I can't do that to Lottie."

"Lottie has caused more trouble than she's worth. We can't have her with us when we are trying to find the Springs."

"Well, I'm going to find them." And with that, Katia began climbing down the palm.

"Katia!" Landon tried to grab her arm, but she had already made it to the bottom. He moved as fast as he could to follow after. "Kat!"

By the time he caught up to her, she'd reached the spot where the soldiers had taken Briggs and Lottie. "Can't you see this is a trap? They'll want us to rescue them."

"I don't care." Katia studied the footprints on the ground.

"Will you stop thinking with your emotions and start thinking with your head?"

Katia stood back up, hands on her hips. "And what if it was Micah?"

"Well, it's not—and anyway, Micah can handle himself." Landon looked at her intensely. "We're getting sidetracked from what we're supposed to do. Micah and Ferra probably have the other sisters wrangled up and are sitting around, wondering what's happened to us."

Katia looked away, feeling a twinge of guilt.

"Naomi is depending on us and here we are trying to help your father, who—I'm sorry, but isn't anything compared to saving the world. And who clearly doesn't want anything to do with you."

The words seemed to have slipped out of his mouth without thinking.

Katia stared back at him, her almond eyes narrowing into little slits. Without another thought, she grabbed Landon's arm. Her magic wrapped around him quickly, constricting and pulsing.

Landon yelled at the pain. "Kat! What are . . .?" The magic moved to his chest, sucking out his breath.

CONJECTRIX

Don't really hurt him, Katia instructed her magic. *Just enough that he gets the point.*

Landon tried to move but stiffened up under her icy fingers.

"I'm so sorry Landon, but I have to try to save them. If I don't, I'm abandoning him just like he did me. Please try to understand."

Landon's face was frozen in shock, just like the rest of his body. Katia lowered him gently to the ground, staring for a moment at what she'd done before leaving him to thaw.

CHAPTER SEVENTEEN
JOURNEY TO THE SURFACE

Silexa lay under the tree next to the grave of her sister, looking at the fairy lights. She went there often to find peace. UnderElm was a sweet, harmonious departure from the harsh reality of her life. Ymber was dead. Bryant had gone to find her sister Vespa hiding in the southern marshlands, somewhere called the Musungu.

And with him was Zander, or at least she hoped. His disappearance left her angry and scared. Of course she was nervous for Bryant as well, but he was a seasoned fighter and a grown man; Zander was a boy and knew nothing of fighting. His valiant heart often got him into trouble. That truth was hard for her to accept—the truth that Zander might not return.

Up above her resting place, fairy lights distracted her. Little sprites flitted about in the dark, making busywork for themselves. She watched them, her thoughts drifting to the people of UnderElm.

The little community felt crippled without the prince to lead them, but it remained strong, for their situation had always come with the understanding that they lived in secret and had to stay sharp and witty.

Conjectrix

But when it came to leadership, the people looked to Silexa. She was an outsider, a princess, and in love with the prince of Southwick. Since Bryant left, she'd been consulting with the guards on their security measures and the overall well-being of the town. Everything looked sound, but Silexa knew it wouldn't be long before that changed.

She sat up as something startling sparked her memory—the Louving, the shapeshifter. Audra. Horror shot through her body like lightning. Why had she not thought of her before? She had been so preoccupied by Bryant's and Zander's safety that the thought had completely slipped her mind.

She immediately ran to Mother. Finding her near the kitchen table, she rushed to her, out of breath. "Mother . . . Mother, the Louving girl."

Mother seemed startled by the abrupt entrance. "Silexa dear, are you all right? Have you heard news?"

"No." Silexa swallowed. "I had the most terrible premonition. The Louving knows where we are."

"A Louving? My dear, I do not know what you mean."

"A changeling. A shape shifter. They can change their appearance to look like any one of us."

Mother looked at her intensely. "Are you sure?"

"Yes, we were looking out for her when we first arrived, but with everything else that was happening, I forgot the danger until now."

"Do you think she could be here now?"

"I don't know. It's possible." Silexa brooded, looking Mother hard in the eyes. "What do we do?"

Mother seated herself at the small table. "Well, Silexa, what do you feel we should do?"

"I think we need to leave."

"I agree."

"Is there a place that's safe?"

"Yes," Mother reassured. "There's a tunnel that was built in case of an exodus from here. It leads north to the Sister Elm."

"Sister Elm?"

"A special tree above ground. Our Elm shares the same roots. We will be safe there."

"But how will we get everyone out?"

Mother took her hand and stroked her cheek. "I will organize it, dear one. What I think you will need to do is create time."

"What do you mean?"

"Return to the surface and find out about this Louving and what is happening with the kingdom. We will need this information when we reach the Sister Elm."

❊ ❊ ❊

Plans were made immediately. Mother organized the evacuation. All made the sign of the UnderElm using the four fingers across the breast and agreed the symbol must be used to identify all belonging to their company.

Mother fitted Silexa with a long smock made out of lamb hide and sack cloth. She cinched a small knife on her thigh just in case and used her remaining shadesilk as a headscarf to hide the Everstar mark on her neck. A guide took her to an exit hidden in a far tunnel.

"This will lead you to a barn near the east wall," the dwarf named Sham told her. "Remember your path. The best place to find information is the taverns in the east. That is where the guards reside."

He moved the large stone by pressing his palm against it. The passage turned visible as if it had always been there. Silexa thanked him and moved on.

CONJECTRIX

Down she went through the dark tunnel with only a very small light in the palm of her hand. She felt around the walls that wound around like a burrowed rabbit hole. It became difficult to move in places since she was taller than the average dwarf.

The magic in her stone helped mold the tunnel through the difficult areas. As it narrowed, the path began to fill with straw. Someone had blocked the entrance. Pushing her way through, Silexa soon saw the lights of the city and felt the crisp night air.

The city of gold glimmered around her. Dark clouds hung overhead, reflecting the lamp lights from the city.

Her footsteps halted as she heard voices drifting from a nearby farmhouse. She turned to see a farmer and his wife talking near the hitching post. Hiding behind the haystack, she eavesdropped on their conversation.

"Dirty old king, that's what I say," the wife spat in disgust. "Serves 'im right."

"No need to say such things, 'Esta. None of our business, no how," the farmer returned.

"But what they gonna do now?"

"With the prince missin' and the king dead, who knows?"

The King: dead. Silexa froze, the words ringing around in her head.

The couple disappeared from sight before Silexa dared move again. Her mind clouded, thoughts racing about. She knew now Mother had been right to send her to the surface. They needed this information. Carefully, she crept to the street.

The night felt alive with news of the king's death, nearing the point of anarchy. She grabbed snatches of conversation here and there as she tried her best to mingle in the street with other gatherers.

Silexa slipped into a busy tavern. The noise of the crowd sounded in her ears like an angry hum, each voice indistinguishable from the next. Pressing her way to the bar, she ordered honey wine and took a sip. It burned down her throat.

The barkeep smiled. "Not used to it, are ya?"

She shook her head, embarrassed.

"Are you new here?" he asked. She didn't respond to him, but he went on, "Mind you, I keep to me-self. No need to tell me. Lot of diff'rent people come out when there's news like this."

Silexa pursed her lips together. "Can you tell me what happened?"

"Not much to tell ya. Reinoh's dead."

"But how did he die?"

"Suicide, people say." The barkeep glanced around. "Strange things happening. Don't like it none. There's an evil here. The Demon man." He touched his finger to his nose and nodded.

Silexa knew to whom he referred. Sharrod had taken over the city.

"Why would a king kill 'imself? He got everything, right? The puzzlin' thing—where's his son at? All of Southwick thinks he killed 'im and hid 'im in the maze of ruins under the castle, but I don't think that neither."

He went back to cleaning his glass. "Place ain't safe no more. I say leave before the shadows come." His thin smile dipped down under his crooked nose, his eyes surveying the crowd before resting back on hers. He motioned to the drink with his chin. "On the house," he said before helping someone else at the other end of the bar.

Silexa tried another swig of the honey wine. The bitter taste sent sharp sensations around her mouth and down her throat. Unable to drink anymore, she left the counter, heading for the door. She'd heard what she needed to hear. If Sharrod ran the city, she needed to return to Mother and get as far away from Southwick as possible.

She bumped her way to the exit. Near the door, a tall, blond man blocked the exit. His fair head stood out in the sea of dark hair.

"Please excuse me," Silexa said, trying to push through.

"Forgive me," the man returned. "I didn't mean to get in your way—the bloody crowds, you know."

He was plainly trying to joke with her, but she didn't care for it. "Please, I must get home." He moved out of the way and Silexa quickly exited.

"Wait!" he called out to her. "It's rather late for someone as pretty as you to be out and about on a dangerous night like tonight. Let me walk you home."

Silexa cringed. "No, thank you. I think I can manage."

The young man kept pace with her.

"Please, just go."

"But I've never seen you around this district before. I'm rather new here, and I could use a friend."

"I'm not the friend for you." She tried to speed up.

"No, wait." He grabbed her arm. "Please don't go running off. I saw you at the bar and thought you would be around longer. You hardly drank anything. I thought I would have more time."

Silexa tried to pull her arm away. "I really am sorry, but I must go. As you said, it's late and I have family that needs me. Please let go."

"Will I get to see you again? I didn't even get to talk to you. Will you at least tell me your name?"

As Silexa continued to struggle with his grip, she studied his face. He shouldn't be familiar to her, but somehow he was. "Giselle," she lied. "My name's Giselle."

He smiled crookedly. "I knew a Giselle once. Pretty name. I'm Vlad."

The name meant nothing to her. "I'm glad we know each other." She finally pulled out of his grip and began walking again. He kept up.

"I've only been in Southwick a few months, you know. Moved here from the Crest to the west."

Why was he telling her all this? Then something he'd said caught her attention. "You said you're from the Crest? That's far away. Why are you here?"

"I came for the feast, of course. What a mess that was."

Silexa hoped that her fear didn't show on her face. "The feast? That was some time ago."

"Yes. I'm good friends with the prince—well, I mean, I was. Haven't seen him though. I hoped if I stayed I would find him around."

"Do you think the prince is still alive?"

"Well, yes, of course."

"Why?" Silexa asked, furrowing her brow. "Most think he's dead. If the king was murdered, the prince must be dead."

"Well, I can see your point, but Bryant was a good friend of mine. I would hate to think he was dead."

"How good?"

"We went to school together . . ." He went on rambling about some school far away that made no sense to her. Silexa knew Bryant better than anyone else and had heard nothing of this Vlad.

They were walking down an alleyway that soon would fork. If she stayed to the right, she could loop around and get to the farm, but the last thing she wanted was this man following her. But she didn't know what lay at the left and would surely get lost.

It was time to make a decision. She could feel the hidden knife near her thigh and went over in her mind how she could reach it quickly. Without a second thought, she turned left.

CONJECTRIX

"Tell me," Silexa spoke up, "have you met anyone else here?"

"While I was in the palace I met a lot of influential people. Commander Lockwood, and Curtis, Bryant's Primitus."

"Why are you not in the palace now? The east side is full of quiet farmers—not very exciting, I would think."

"True, not much has happened," he agreed. "It was a suggestion from someone in the palace that I should spend time on this side."

"Which someone?"

"A boy named Ander, who was friends with—"

Silexa stopped and turned to him. She knew of who he spoke. Her eyes scanned over his face, searching for answers. Everything about the man prompted questions.

At first Vlad looked curious, but then his eyes intensified and a quirky smile stretched across his face. Silexa started to run, but Vlad caught her arm before she could go. She struggled as he pinned her against a wall.

"How did you find me?"

"I have my ways," Vlad smiled. "The Oracle said I should stay on the east side. It looks like it paid off."

Silexa struggled against him. "What do you want?"

"Revenge, for one thing." His eyes flashed. "That blow to the head was uncalled for. I'll also need that stone around your neck. Sharrod will be so pleased with me."

"There is no way you're getting that," she spat back.

"Over your dead body." He flashed an insane grin. "That's the idea, you know. There would be nothing better than collecting your blood. Having poor Bryant think his lovely sweetheart is nice and safe and then murdering him while using her face."

"Bryant is dead," Silexa insisted, but he cut her off short.

"No, I don't think so. The power of ascension has not been released. But that will all be taken care of soon."

"What do you mean?"

"Curtis tracked him to the Musungu." He loosened his grip to find a better hold. "And as for you? You'll need to come with me . . ."

Silexa took her chance. With a great shove, she broke away and pulled out her knife, slashing his hand.

Vlad yelled and went for her throat.

Silexa grabbed the stone that hung around her neck, feeling for the magic and asking for its help. The walls behind her melted, allowing her to disappear through. Vlad lost his grip as the stone wall began to close up around her.

She was in a dark room, lit only by the light of her stone. She found a doorknob, opened it, and entered an empty living space. She moved as quickly as possible through. It was just a matter of time before Vlad would find her.

Another door led outside. Once in the alleyway, she ran, dodging this way and that, deeper and deeper into the city until she wasn't sure what direction she faced.

She stopped before a large stone building, boarded up and vacant. Silexa grabbed her stone again and melted through the wall. Tiny cracks in the foundation allowed her to watch for anyone coming. It was hard to see in the darkness of the night, the dim lamplights casting shadows around the walls.

For a long while, she stayed there, watching, waiting, and thinking. It was clear now that Vlad was a Louving, the same Louving she'd feared. Now she knew two disguises of hers: Vlad and the little girl Giselle, who'd led them to the entrance of UnderElm.

Who knew how many others she would use in order to get to her?

CHAPTER EIGHTEEN
REGRET

*S*tirring in and out of dreams, drifting away from Reynolds and Arie, away from the trolls in the mountains and out in the world. Flying over hills and people, trees, rivers, and endlessly moving, like floating in continual waves of the sea.

Faces she remembered, mixed with others . . .

Silexa, her lost sister . . . alone, crying, lost . . .

Zander . . . in haze, wandering in mist . . .

Taren, his face alight with fire . . .

. . . But Reynolds returned in her dreams and asked her to wake . . .

. . . and she did.

The waking world made very little sense. Naomi felt herself being carried and cradled in different arms. Reynolds watched her very closely. He didn't speak; there seemed to be nothing to say. Naomi would drift back to sleep and wake again to see him there watching, just the same.

. . . Drifting again . . .

Searching . . .

A frozen mountain . . . blue eyes shining in ice . . .

. . . desert sand and heat mirages of horses and a small girl following her . . .

. . . to a fiery mountain down deep in the earth . . . the living eyes, bright and yellow, know the soul. He lifts his giant mouth and erupts in angry flame . . .

. . . and Reynolds returns. "Wake, Naomi."

. . . and she did.

Naomi finally woke out of her dreamy state. Her lids felt heavily in the darkness of the night. A shadowy figure held her tiny hand. Her head swiveled, slow and heavy, as she tried to take in her surroundings. The warm fire near her feet made her flinch as she remembered the heat and flame in her nightmares.

"Calm down, calm down." Reynolds sat next to her, tending the fire. He released his grasp once he noticed her movement.

Naomi looked around. All seemed quiet. The dark fire smoldered low with embers. As she sat up weakly, the ringing in her ears lessened, and she gained increasing awareness of where she was.

For the first time since drifting off, she saw her skin, if only by firelight. It had always been white, but when she'd walked into the fire, it seemed to have damaged it. That was a surprise. It might have only been the low light from the fire, but her flesh now had a strange iridescence, shimmering like a pearly coat.

"What is that?"

"Scarring, I imagine," Reynolds replied. "It's getting better. It was much worse."

Naomi touched her arm and felt the tender sting. Without thought, she pressed her hand to her chest and the Vivatera. While it had once rested so peacefully before, now it pushed back with a violent force, seizing her breath.

Conjectrix

"Whoa." Reynolds grabbed her hand and made calming motions. "Come on, now. Come back to me . . ." He continued calming her, his voice soothing, until finally she relaxed.

The stillness of the night surrounded them, isolating Naomi's confusion. She looked up at Reynolds with concern. The magic had attacked her. What was the Vivatera doing to her?

After a few still moments, Reynolds returned his attention to the fire. "Are you feeling better now?"

Naomi didn't know how to respond.

"The seizures started soon after the fire and the only way to stop them was to—" He cleared his throat. "I needed to make sure you were okay, so I combined our magic. And I know I was invading, but I did it for your safety. I promise I didn't go anywhere in your thoughts that you wouldn't have liked me to. I just did what I could to— " He stopped again, this time falling quiet.

Naomi remembered her dreams. She hadn't imagined him; he was real, always watching her. He had entered her thoughts gently but found a way to control her dreams nonetheless. Nothing felt safe anymore. She knew he wasn't oblivious to her feelings, but having him into her thoughts felt like a betrayal.

She looked away. The stars above shone bright, a warm cocoon of scrub trees surrounding them. The slick rock from the pass had disappeared, replaced with harsh sand and crumbling rock. Past the fire, she saw shapes—two figures: Gurr standing guard, and Arie asleep against a rock. They were still with her.

"Where are we?" Naomi muttered.

"Near the foothills of the Ignis Mountains. Lucky for us, no trolls followed us here, as far as we can figure—except for your troll friend, who I must admit has been very loyal to you. At least, we think so. We can't figure what he's saying, but Arie and I figure it's in regards to you. He has slept very little and insists on watching over you each night."

Naomi smiled at the thought.

"The clouds are disappearing, as you can see." Reynolds pointed to the stars. "And the sun nearly kills us. Nothing lives out here, and there's hardly any food or water. The ground is hard and tiring to move through. A salty sand covers the surface, but try to move over it and it forms around your feet like clay. It's miserable.

"I doubt your sister is here at all. How could she live out here? Our goal today was just to make it to this little patch of trees. I thought we might find a rabbit or rodent to eat. We've been resting ever since. Just waiting . . . " He trailed off again.

Naomi sat still and listened to her heart. It occurred to her that this was the most information he had ever given her in one sitting. "Thank you for telling me."

She looked at her skin again. "What's happening to me?"

"I don't think walking into fire was such a good thing. By the look of it, your magic tried to protect you, but failed."

Naomi frowned. "I thought I would be fine. I thought the fire would help me."

"Never push your magic to its limit," Reynolds cautioned her. "You're not invincible, Naomi, as much as you think you are."

The way he spoke her name gave her a pang of regret. She hadn't thought of what she might be putting him through.

"If you die and I can't save you, then you'll be trapped like all the other ghosts here," Reynolds went on, his voice low. "You can and will die if you are not careful."

The words triggered something in her memory. "Where is Nobbs?"

"Dead. It's strange, but he saved you."

It stung to hear the words out loud. Naomi grabbed her chest again, afraid she might fall under another spell, but it was only heartache from her loss. But then, he wasn't really dead, was he? "Do you think he returned to where he came from?"

"What do you mean?"

Naomi stared at the fire. "When you suspected I was dreaming in the Netherfields, you were right. I was being dragged by wanting souls and he pulled me back to you."

Reynolds looked astonished by this news. "Why didn't you tell me?"

"There was no reason to." Naomi tried to keep calm. "Nobbs could watch me in that realm much like you did now."

"How?"

"He was a man's soul traveling in the body of a creature. He told me how he managed to persuade the grumbears to help him and others like him. They were in possession of the bodies but not the souls. Do you think he returned?"

Reynolds frowned, ignoring the question. "Did you allow him into your dream?"

"Like you?" Naomi retorted. "Were you an invited guest?"

"That is different. I'm trying to protect you."

"That's exactly what he did. He saved me."

Reynolds threw something in the fire which scattered ashes around. "Don't you understand you're making it too easy for them to find you?"

Naomi's eyes widened in surprise, her voice dropping to an angry whisper. "I don't know how to control it. You speak like it's my fault."

Reynolds ran a hand through his hair, frustrated. "I thought we could control it with the Conjectrix. I thought that was why Spotswood gave it to you, but it seems I was completely wrong about it. It's probably more dangerous having it. It tells us too much and you're too vulnerable to use it."

"But what does it matter?" Naomi snapped back. "It didn't save me from the fire; Nobbs did. He saved me when you couldn't."

"What are you talking about?" She had never seen Reynolds so angry. "I'm with you—here! Right here! And I shouldn't need to make that kind of decision. You shouldn't have walked into the fire."

"You were there, but you couldn't protect me," Naomi insisted. She felt the heat rise in her cheeks. "The souls grabbed me. They were ready to drag me into that river. Nobbs found me when you couldn't. He could see that world because he belongs there."

"Only because you keep things from me. You need to tell me things."

"Why? So you can tell me to stop doing things when I don't know how? Why even bother protecting me? It's hopeless. You've already lost."

Reynolds stood up quickly, a war of emotions on his face. Naomi blinked in surprise. He was hurt. She hadn't expected that at all. Reynolds was a rock—his feelings completely unaffected, his silence profound.

His eyes narrowed, the feeling there more revealing than anything he'd ever spoken aloud. The expression translated down into her soul, one simple question—Why? He kicked the dirt on the ground, putting out the remaining fire, then disappeared through the scrub trees.

Naomi placed her hand on her chest, once more preventing a faint. The argument had been necessary, she knew. Despite the pain she'd caused him, it felt good getting a reaction from him. But his anger haunted her imagination and she lay quietly in the dark.

She thought Reynolds would return, but he didn't. After a few moments, she reached around her cloak and found the Conjectrix, hoping

189

it might bring comfort. Reynolds had warned it might be dangerous, but she didn't care. It was a connection to those she loved. Warmth came immediately when she rubbed it with her fingers. Different images mixed together, like a collection of someone else's memories. It reacted with such excitement, like it was waiting for her attention; it needed to show her something.

There was a girl in the image. It was the same girl Naomi had watched while in the cave. This girl was traveling with Katia, she knew, but as she focused in, it became clear the girl was alone. A small plate of food sat in front of her, though she wasn't eating. She looked nervous, maybe scared.

A shadow moved over the girl's face. She was not alone after all, but talking with someone. Another image formed near her. Naomi caught a glimpse of something lean and blond, but it was hard to focus on something so small.

The image flashed out and Naomi dropped the ball. It rolled down her cloak, resting at her feet. Her focus disappeared as Reynolds' words ran around in her head. The Conjectrix was not bad; it was a tool and it could help her. Even thinking it increased her compassion for those she saw. Naomi didn't know this little girl, but she would take care of her if she could.

All at once overcome with a hollow, overwhelming feeling of responsibility, she folded up her knees and sobbed.

Help!

Weakness overtook her like a rushing wind. Feeling an incredible dizziness, she dropped to the ground, gripping it as if she were about to be swallowed by the sky.

No! Leave me alone!

Please don't.

Voices filled her head, echoing with confusion. A warm hand fell on her shoulder. *Reynolds.* A million apologies filled her heart. She looked up—only to see Arie's face staring back. She grabbed his hands, warm and comfortable and unfamiliar, and felt like a little girl under her big brother's protection. The darkness took her.

SCREAMING!!

Plea for help . . .

> *It rings through time . . .*
>
> > *Through space . . .*
> >
> > > *Through distance . . .*
>
> *Awake!*
>
> *. . . search . . .*

The magic stirs to act!

Crying in the corner.

Her eyes shining dark with tears.

She knows the secrets—she felt the touch.

> > > *A dark cupboard, the evil waits . . .*
> >
> > *The disguise fools the others—the blood sweet with liquor.*

The girl is crying, holding a stone . . . a purple marble . . . close to her.

She is scared at what she has told . . . of what she knows . . .

The scream is silenced

The stone still tight in her little hand.

> > > **FLASH!**

The evil is gone as the blood spills freely.

Time slips . . . away . . .

> > *Save her!*

Grip still tight . . .

> *I can find her . . .*

The gurgling voices—the crushing . . .

Save her!

Heartbeat slipping . . .

Save her!

Fibers weave from the stone—express the magic. Make it whole.

Come to me. Bring me to her.

Connected!

Brilliant!

Wrapping lovingly around the little child.

Save her!

Who can help?

. . . Help me . . .

. . . Take me . . .

FLASH!

Cold . . .

Snow . . .

Jeanus.

. . . losing connection . . .

. . . losing concentration . . .

. . . help her . . . please . . .

FLASH!

The breach begins . . .

The SOULS enter . . .

Hands grab and ensnare . . .

The glowing eyes . . .

. . . he has found me . . .

Struggle to be free!

Hands . . . more hands . . .

Grabbing

Pulling down
S T R E T C H into P A I N . . .
B R E A K F R E E
CRACK!

❀ ❀ ❀

"It's not my fault," Arie yelled back at Reynolds. "I had nothing to do with it. If you want to blame anyone, blame yourself for leaving."

Reynolds shoved his brother. "I just went for a walk to find some food. She was very weak. I was thinking of her."

Arie pushed him back. "You weren't thinking of her at all. You were thinking of yourself and your wild ego."

Reynolds had heard enough and tackled Arie around the neck. Arie reacted with a swift punch to his stomach. They toppled to the ground, wrestling. After a brief struggle, Reynolds flipped Arie on his back, pinning him down.

"She just vanished," Arie protested. "I turned my back and she was gone. I promise, I did nothing to her."

Gurr watched the grown men roll around like animals, a look of amusement in his eyes. He soon lost interest, though, and started toward the mountain without another thought of the fight.

Arie took advantage of the distraction and grabbed Reynolds' arm, flipping him, knocking the wind out of him. Reynolds lay still, finding his breath. "Fine," he exhaled, "you win."

Arie stood and wiped the blood from his nose. "I win only because you've lost so much more." He pointed a finger directly at his brother's face. "Tell me how you let a girl like that get away."

Reynolds looked up to the heavens. "I don't know. I never know. I don't know what to do."

CONJECTRIX

"Go find her! Follow that big monster and go rescue her."

Reynolds moved his hands to his face, utterly giving up his fight.

"That girl is beautiful and strong and charming," Arie continued. "How could you push her away like that?"

Reynolds sat up, resting his arms on his knees. "I'm trying to keep her safe."

"Fat lot of good that did you. Staying away is a better way of protecting her? What a stupid thing to say."

"Hey, don't talk about things you don't understand. It's dangerous being around her."

Arie rubbed his sore arm. "It's not dangerous. She's tiny."

"Not like that." Reynolds tried to stand. "It's not real. None of it is real. It's an illusion, the whole thing."

"Illusion?" Arie offered a hand to his brother, who took it. "There's no illusion. She's flesh and blood, and you are a jackass."

Reynolds lowered his head, ashamed. "I'm pulled toward her. I gravitate to where she is. And it's getting stronger."

"It sounds like you love the girl."

Reynolds turned and shoved him again. "Don't you get it? Love isn't possible."

Arie shoved him back once more. "I will admit, Naomi has a charm around her, the kind that makes you feel nearly invincible. But what I'm talking about is how *she* feels. That is no illusion. And if you would stop thinking about yourself, you would see it."

Reynolds stared down his brother, feeling the fight die within him. "You don't understand. It's impossible. I can't. Not now."

He turned again and walked toward Gurr, who had ventured far ahead, near the end of the scrub, closing in on the boulders near the foothills.

Arie ran up behind him. "Stop being such an idiot—"

"She doesn't love me," Reynolds spat out. "I ruined her life!"

"You saved her! She doesn't want a *life* without you."

"How would you know?"

Arie gripped his shoulder and forced him to hold still. "I know enough about regret. I know what it feels like to be so close-minded and stupid. You have a chance. Don't lose it."

His emotions threatening to overwhelm him, Reynolds struggled to keep calm. "I don't think I can save her. The magic will kill her. I thought there was a way, but I don't know anymore. Taren was right."

A screech in the air interrupted any other thought. Reynolds reacted, grabbing his sword. Arie raised his hand to block out the sun.

A shadow moved across the desert valley. A long body, red like fire, sunlight glinting off its scales, casting blind flashes of light in different directions.

"Arie, down." Reynolds tugged on his brother's shoulder. "It will spot us."

"A fire eater." Arie let out a sigh of wonder, squinting at the dragon. "I knew you could not hide forever."

Reynolds ran for the shelter of a large boulder, but Arie didn't move. Instead he walked farther out into the open.

"What are you doing?" Reynolds shouted.

Arie lifted his arms out and arched his back. "Tasting regret one last time."

The large beast swept around in the sky, targeting Arie. Its shadow moved closer and closer, barreling down at a frightening speed.

"Arie!" Reynolds screamed, but still he did not move. "Arie! Run!"

CONJECTRIX

There was no other choice. Reynolds ran for his brother, but the thick, crusted sand slowed his every effort, sinking him in deeper and deeper.

Large claws snatched Arie from the ground like a small rag doll. Reynolds barely managed to grab around his legs before his feet left the ground.

Chapter Nineteen
SHEDRA'S SON

The freezing in Landon's chest spread instantly, numbing his limbs in place. Katia had disappeared from sight and the cold burn spread so furiously through his body, he could not make it stop. Shooting pain spread everywhere.

His magic. Landon needed to reach his magic. His brain could scarcely think beyond the pain, save for his anger. Resentment filled his heart as he slowly felt himself freeze to death.

With every ounce of energy he had, Landon called out for his magic. He closed his eyes, trying everything he could to seek help. He thought of his mission, of his failure, of Katia, her father, and the Traveler girl. It was all a mistake. He was all alone, without hope and without life. If he ever saw Katia again, he might strangle her.

But before he could envision the meeting, Landon blacked out.

❀ ❀ ❀

A gentle light passed before his closed eyes—a fire, perhaps. He felt warmth, like blankets covering him up to his chin. From far away, he heard a tiny mumbling surrounding his ears. His muscles twitched, unfrozen and happy to move.

CONJECTRIX

He slid open his eyes to find a dark room lit only with a small candle.

"Oh, my goodnight, he's awake. Wen, he's awake," an old woman's voice cried out. Someone scurried to his side. Without warning, two faces popped over his covers on each side: an old woman and an even older man.

"Hello, deary," the woman said. "Been out a long while now, haven't ya? Feeling a bit better, are ya?"

Landon just stared.

"But you're recoverin' now," the old man added. "Bit of rest and some tea may make you right as rain. Warm you right up."

He handed over a cup with a warm drink in it. Landon sipped a little. It tasted of licorice and cherry drops—not his favorite, but it would do. "Thank you."

"Oh, my stars, Wen, he speaks," the woman clamored with excitement. "Lord be praised. We were worried for a moment there. Thought you were a hopeless cause, but Wen here thought you all right, he did, and I thank him for it. He has the patience of an angel."

Still disoriented, Landon tried to sit up. The stiffness from the freezing had taken a toll on his muscles.

The old man pushed him back gently. "Steady, now. You've had a rough stay. Let us just take care of you and we'll get you up and back on your feet soon. I'm Wenlock Brighton, by the way, and this is my lovely wife, Henali Mae."

"Just call me Mae, dear."

"Thanks, really." Landon grabbed his skull. "My head is pounding."

"Well, I would think so after what you have been through." Mae considered. "I don't know quite how long you been out. We've only had you—what, three days or so?"

"Yep," Wenlock agreed, "three days yesterday."

198

"What?" Landon tried to sit up again, but his head began to swim. "I have to go."

"Not so fast." Wenlock put the tea back to his lips and made him drink. "You're stuck with us for a while, so you might as well hear the story."

Landon coughed out the tea. "Story?"

"Of how you got here, my dear." Mae placed a warm cloth on his head. The soothing touch of the heat felt better than any tea, and his throbbing temple eased a bit. "As I said, we don't know how long you'd been there. I think the vultures figured you dead—that's how you got the peck holes by your ear."

Landon lifted his hand up to feel the tiny scabs on the side of his head.

Wenlock continued, "Someone found you—"

"Oh, yes, a dear friend."

"Yes, and knew we might be of some service to you, and brought you here."

"And who is this dear friend?" Landon asked.

"A drifter like you," Mae answered. "We call her LeAndra; it fits her well."

"And where is here?"

Wenlock shushed him. "We cannot tell you. It's a secret. When you are all well, we will show you the way out."

Landon struggled with the whole idea. "Listen, I'm sorry for being a burden, but I really can't stay here. You see, I've lost my companions. Some were taken by the soldiers from Southwick—"

"Did you see any soldiers?" Mae interrupted, turning to Wenlock.

"Don't reckon. Haven't seen soldiers here for quite some time, maybe since the last war."

"No, listen," Landon tried again. "There was a girl—"

"Yes, and she brought you here."

"No, not that girl, someone else, someone with red hair."

"What hair color is LeAndra's, Wen?"

"Light brownish, maybe. It's hard to think of her without the hood."

"Oh, but her eyes are as cool as ice. The lightest blue I have ever seen."

"No," Landon interrupted them both. "I have to find my friend with the red hair—a girl, yes, but not LeAndra. She went in the direction of the jungle."

"The jungle, my dear?" Mae frowned. "You mean by Tapoof?"

"Yes," he said with relief as he finally recognized something.

Wenlock looked grave. "Sorry to tell you this, but we are quite a ways from Tapoof. No getting there now. What—three days journey on foot, would you say?"

"Sounds about right."

"This can't be happening," Landon said to himself.

"What do you need this girl for?"

Landon shook his head to clear his thoughts. "She and I didn't part well. I need to make sure she's okay."

"Ah." Mae smiled, which created a deep dimple in her right cheek. "It's like that, is it?"

"No, no." Landon almost laughed. "I'm not in love with her. Really, that's not why. We have something we need to find."

"Oh, a quest." Wenlock rubbed his hands with delicious enthusiasm. "Nothing better than a good quest. What is it, my boy? I'm up for the task." He moved his arms with a flourish, like a brave knight.

Landon watched the spectacle with a raised eyebrow. "No, I really can't say. It is a charge for me and her alone. We made a promise— that's why she froze me, because I asked her—"

"She froze you?" Mae's voice flooded with motherly concern. "Well, that doesn't sound like a good friend. Best be done with her."

"I can't, please . . ." Landon's exhaustion returned. "Please, help me find her."

Wenlock patted him on the knee. "We will try our best. Can't promise anything, though. News doesn't travel this way very fast. Maybe when LeAndra comes to visit, she will know."

"Excellent idea, Wen."

Both of them looked on Landon without saying a word. The silence felt unnatural. "I think I'll get more rest, then," Landon said finally, resting his head back against the pillow.

"An excellent idea, truly excellent." Wenlock stood to go. "Rest, my boy, and we will talk when you are feeling better." He paused at the doorway. "And what may we call you?"

"You may call me Landon Rhees."

Mae and Wenlock looked at each other.

"Rhees?" Wenlock questioned. "You say Rhees?" He came closer and peered at Landon's face. "As in Hammond and Sheldra Rhees?"

Landon's eyes widened. He hadn't heard his parents' names in so long that he had almost forgotten them. "Yes."

"Oh, Wen . . ." Mae smiled back down at him and grasped his hand. "What is it?"

Wenlock clapped his hands and began to dance a funny dance around in circles. "Landon Rhees, what a pleasure!"

"What is?"

"What do you know? We're family."

"Huh?"

"Sheldra was my favorite niece." Wenlock's little jig continued up to the foot of the bed. "I remember her marrying Hammond—fine fellow, from Cedar, not far from here. Didn't know much of their family, but no matter. I lost contact with them when Hammond found himself in the Great War. Both dead. I didn't know they had a son, though. Foolish of me to not think of it."

Landon couldn't believe it. "Are you tricking me? You're seriously my great-uncle?"

Mae grinned so brightly that it practically lit the room. She squeezed his hand even tighter. "Wen, I think you have excited him too much. Now he will never go to sleep."

"Him? What about me?" Wenlock continued with his dance, but saw the look on his wife's face and slowed until he stopped. "All right, woman, if you insist." He moved closer to Landon and looked down at him. Small tears of joy filled a wrinkle near the corner of his eye. "We'll talk more tomorrow."

Wenlock snapped his fingers and Landon felt the burden of thought being lifted from him. With heavy lids, he fell back to sleep.

❄ ❄ ❄

When Landon woke again, the light of day had filled the room. The small chamber had pocket windows made of colored glass, spilling rainbows across the curved ceilings.

Next to his bed sat a tray with fresh, hot breakfast. Landon began shoveling it down like a starved dog. It tasted better than anything he remembered; the flavors were so full and the berries sweeter than honey.

Mae came in halfway through his biscuit. "So glad to see you eating." She reached over and hugged him—not an unwelcome gesture, just awkward. He would have to get used to the attention, he thought.

"I have some clean things for you here, if you don't mind the patches and old man smell. Wen hasn't fit in these for years, but I think they

202

might do for you." She leaned in close. "You see, he's shrinking, but don't say anything to him. He thinks he will someday be back to this height. I say it's impossible." She smiled and left again.

Landon's muscles tightened as he strained to get dressed. A strong ache ran through his body, but he fought through the pain; he was just warming up the muscles he hadn't used in a while. The clothes did smell of old closet and looked a little tattered and well-used, but they fit him just fine.

He stepped out of the room and found a small set of stairs that led to an open room full of windows. It caught him off guard to see so much of the outside world—not only leaves and trees, but distant land, water, and sky.

"Whoa."

"You like it, do you?" Wenlock asked him from around the corner. He looked up from a telescope and quickly scribbled on parchment before returning to the eyepiece. "This is the observatory. You're welcome to look at anything you like in here."

Landon took a good look at the room. It was circular with stairs leading down to the other rooms in the home. A mess of books and instruments cluttered every flat surface, along with papers and drawings, potions and apothecary. "What do you do up here?"

"Anything I please." Wenlock adjusted a knob by the eyepiece. "Come and see."

Landon walked over to where his uncle stood. The window was covered in large green leaves from the surrounding trees. "What am I supposed to be seeing?"

"Just look."

Landon leaned in and looked through the eyepiece. Instead of the nearby leaves, he saw the desert—the Salt Dune which he remembered crossing. "Amazing. Should I ask how you do this?"

Conjectrix

Wenlock just laughed. "Good to see you up and dressed. Those are my favorite trousers—don't ruin them." He smacked Landon on the shoulder and sat down next to his papers.

"What are you writing?"

"Patterns," Wenlock returned, without looking up from the paper. "The world moves in patterns, my boy. Similarities reappear in cycles. Numbers are a constant."

Landon didn't quite follow but was curious. "So, you're looking for patterns?"

"Yes, but more than that. You talked last night about the girl with the red hair. I thought I might try to track her."

Landon looked in the glass again but didn't see anything different. "Is this where I was found?"

"Oh, I don't think so, but I'm looking for patterns that might lead me from that point to somewhere where she might go, or be drawn to, understand?"

Landon shook his head. "Your skills are far beyond mine, Wenlock. What else can you see up here? All of Parbraven?"

"Nah." Wenlock laughed. "I don't have strong enough instruments for that, but I can see anywhere around here. There are some blind spots—like shields that I can't see past, but all you really need is the numbers to find it."

"Can you see Southwick?"

Wenlock's face lit up. "Ah." He scampered like a rabbit over to the other side of the observatory to a larger instrument, then began rummaging through papers and muttering to himself. "Ah-hah!" he shouted, moving the eyepiece to the numbers on the paper. "Just a few adjustments. There. Come see."

Landon followed his uncle to the other side and looked. He could see it. It was far away, but he could still see it—the turrets, the surrounding walls, the crashing ocean, and the sloping mountain of ruins.

Wenlock jittered with excitement. "Interesting place right now. The patterns are jumbled. Something is scrambling them all up, so I cannot get closer. That tells me that something terrible is happening inside."

"How can you tell?"

"Patterns are natural. Numbers are constant. If I can read neither, then it is unnatural and fluctuating."

Landon's eyebrow went up. "I guess that makes sense."

"No, it doesn't." Wenlock took over the eyepiece. "It doesn't make sense, that's what's so frustrating. All I see are patterns. If there are no patterns, you are invisible to me and possibly to others, too. So, I try to see what I can from here. Still plenty of activity."

Landon looked over some of the papers. None of it made sense to him. "I know something about what is happening."

Wenlock looked up. "Best not tell me what you promised you wouldn't. I'm safer not knowing what kind of trouble you're in."

"Fair enough."

Mae came up from a lower level. "Well, my heart be praised. You look like a young Wenlock, you do. Did he say that much to you?"

"No, just that I couldn't ruin his favorite trousers."

Wenlock glared but went back to his numbers.

"Funny that I never saw the resemblance until now, but you do have some features of your mother's—the smiling eyes and such. But she was so fair. Your father had the dark eyes and brown skin. Looks like you're a great combination."

Landon smiled at her sweetness. "I don't remember them much, honestly. I remember them leaving and then being told that they were killed and being forced to live with a family that hated me. I ran away soon after that and joined the Travelers."

"Oh." Mae's expression fell. "Well, your parents were good people, snatched much too young. Your grandfather is still alive, though. Where is Sal now?"

"Last I heard, he was peddling in Henthrop." Wenlock glanced back at the pair. "Best not talk about him; he's a bit bonkers."

"I don't know much about your father's side of the family, but I bet they were all honorable people like your father, and devoted themselves to Southwick and that silly war and got killed and such."

Landon smiled ruefully. "I don't have much interest in my family."

"Yes, but we are family now," Mae returned gently. "I promise, I won't be acting like your mother or anything, but I still value the find all the same."

Landon understood. "When do you think I'll be well enough to leave?"

"Wen has some terrific healing elixir that works pretty fast. We get wounded people now and again and they're out of here within a few days."

"But it would be better if you knew where you were going, don't you think?" Wenlock spoke up.

"Yeah, if that's possible."

"More than possible." Wenlock searched for some blank parchment. "Do you have something that belonged to this girl?"

"No, I don't think so."

"Do you remember what she looks like?"

"Of course."

"Mae?" he asked, but Mae had already grabbed some drawing pencils. "Okay, you need to describe her to Mae and she will draw the pattern for me. I'll put in the calculation, and there you have it!"

"Wen makes it sound so simple, doesn't he?" Mae smiled and shook her head. "I need you to really think, really remember the little details. It's the patterns that make her unique that will help us find her."

Landon sat and closed his eyes. He tried to really think about Katia, but some of the memories blurred together. Then he remembered her face, full of panic and despair; the way her hair fell in her face after being covered in mud; the embarrassment after he had washed in front of her.

"This is good," Mae told him.

Landon opened his eyes. "But I haven't said anything."

"No need to, my dear. I can see images related to your feelings. Is this looking close so far?" She turned the parchment over and the outline of Katia's face looked back at him.

"Yes, that's amazing. Her eyes are slanted, though."

"Oh, she's from the Dunes." Mae went on sketching.

Landon closed his eyes again, thinking further. The day she made the Ice Queen, back even further, to the day they first met on the way to the Willows. She was so scared and sad; her hair was longer then, but her little upturned nose was still the same as it had always been. He remembered comforting her as she cried—tears for her father and the death of her mother.

Guilt overwhelmed him. He felt selfish for saying they should continue on and not find her father or Lottie, or even her brother.

"That's quite a bit of sadness," Mae said gently. "Doesn't she ever smile?"

Landon looked at the sketch. The eyes were perfect, filled with searching and longing—and emptiness. "If she smiles, it's not when I'm around."

Mae finished her sketch. "Here you go, Wen. He thinks I did well."

CONJECTRIX

"You always do well, my love." Wenlock took the parchment and winked at his nephew. "She's very pretty, Landon. Okay, let's see . . . I'm just evaluating her patterns, the shapes and turns, curves, contours, and balances in her features."

His fingers went to the parchment and he began to write the numbers. On he scribbled, endless numbers and calculations scrolling over and over.

Landon watched his great-uncle, amazed at how quickly he worked.

"Hmm . . ." Wenlock moved to a different instrument a few paces away and began entering numbers and adjusting. "Damn magic. Pesky little thing."

"What is it?"

"She's got a grumbear with her."

"A what?"

"Stupid magical creatures," Wenlock grumbled into his eyepiece. "Never can see very well around them. Always ruining my fine numbers. Don't taste too good, either. Magical creatures never do, you know—just a tip."

Landon glanced back at Mae, who wore a look of enjoyment watching her husband work.

"Well, I think I might have found her."

Landon rushed to the instrument. "Tell me."

"There's good and bad news. She is not far from here, just near the falls."

"But?"

"Well, she's walking into a trap."

"What do you mean?" Landon looked in the eyepiece. He didn't see much of anything—lots of trees, a trickling stream, a boat, and the little dark head of a girl who was with a soldier. "I don't see Kat, Wenlock."

"I told you, your friend is hard to see with that stupid magic around her."

"But what am I looking at if not her?"

Wenlock checked the numbers again. "That is the calculation I got from her eyes."

"Her eyes?" Landon looked again. "Where is her father? I can't see him, either."

"If that is who she searches for, he will be there."

"But why do you say it's a trap?"

Wenlock pointed to a corner on her mouth. "There."

Landon stared at him. "It's a picture."

"Yes, but look at what the mouth is telling you. Someone is keeping secrets—someone she trusts. I think she knows something else is going on, but is too afraid to believe it."

Landon again surveyed the scene Wenlock had found. "And where is this, again?"

"At the Springs."

Landon shot up. "The Springs? The Springs at Sephar? That's where I am?"

"Well, very nearly."

Landon ran a hand through his hair. He couldn't believe he was so close. "Tell me, do you know a girl by the name of Fontine?"

"I don't know that I do. What about you, Mae? You know more people around here. Ring a bell?"

"Isn't Fontine a pretty name?" She hummed as she straightened a few things scattered across the tables.

"Listen, lad." Wenlock took Landon's shoulder. "We'll set out tomorrow. Let us send you out right, get you some new things, some instruments. I can't let you face these barbarians without proper preparation."

"Will she be all right?"

Wenlock threw up his hands. "What am I, a fortuneteller? The grumbear is lucky enough. They're creepy little things, but crafty and useful. We'll just have to hope she can stay out of trouble until we get there."

Landon perked up. "We?"

"Ha ha!" Wenlock began his little dance. "This is high adventure, my boy. What I was made for! Tomorrow."

Landon couldn't help but smile. "Tomorrow it is."

CHAPTER TWENTY
GRUMBEARS

Katia ran as far away from Landon as she could, away from the sandy desert of the Salt Dunes to the tall tropical palm trees of the jungle. Fueled by her temper, she set her mind on finding Lottie and her father. She couldn't think about the state she'd left Landon in, or what might happen to him, or the pain she had caused.

Stop it. No more thoughts of Landon. Focus.

The sandy footprints from the dunes disappeared as the hilly terrain turned to a muddy, humid jungle. The bracken of the forest floor covered any path made by horses or men.

Panic set in. There should be a river. Landon had mentioned a river back by her mother's grave. Katia continued on, listening for the sound of rushing water, though she heard it.

The deeper she ventured into the jungle, the higher and thicker everything became. The dense trees trapped the cawing and screeching of birds and the hum of insects, sending them bouncing around each other, disguising their location. Her only weapon was her magic.

The tall trees stretched up and up. At once, Katia was struck with an idea: if she climbed one, she might be able to see the river. She approached a likely specimen, trying to get a hold, when she felt something sticky. She lifted her hand and watched a long white strand trailing off her fingers. An intricate webbing tied the trees together. In the center of the web was not one, but an entire family of large, fist-sized spiders.

She screamed and tried as best she could to wipe the web off her hand. The sound sent the spiders scurrying and she took off running, brushing herself as she went. A dozen armed soldiers had become a normal occurrence, but a few hairy spiders scared her to death. Her thoughts turned to Landon and how he would have made fun of her for running. *No*, she instructed herself. *Don't think of him.*

The sprint took her deeper into the jungle than she'd hoped to travel. The path had disappeared entirely. Panic overtook her. She was no longer trying to get anywhere in particular, just somewhere familiar.

The deeper she traveled, the worse it became.

Fear finally collapsed her effort. Katia couldn't go on and conceded. She was lost. The jungle had won. She thought of crying but was too angry. How dare Landon disagree with her? She had to find her father and poor little Lottie. Crystals began to form on her palms, but she lost the will to use them.

Katia grabbed some large fronds, shook off the bugs and sand, and placed them over the top of a fallen palm, creating a little hut. After checking around her for more spiders, she sank into the shelter, curled into a ball, and cried. The strange comfort of this helped her fall asleep.

She woke to a curious screeching coming from above her. The jungle had darkened, but she could still see the outlines of things. Something the size of a cat had landed on the leaves of her shelter. Katia froze, silent with fear, as the creature moved around, sniffing the air.

It stopped. Katia held her breath. Suddenly, it swung down and looked under the shelter directly at her.

She squealed, backing away. The animal had very big eyes, orange and intense, the color of fire. It swiveled its head around like an owl, evaluating her. It blinked a few times, then flipped around and disappeared.

Katia peered through the leaves of the shelter to see a dozen pairs of glowing eyes looking back at her.

Every fiber of her being went cold. She wanted to jump up and scream and run, but she just lay there, frozen.

One screeched at her. She didn't know what to do. The creatures were furry and small, like tiny little monkeys with their long curly tails, though their faces were more like small bears. She started to think they looked adorable—until another one screeched at her, rattling her nerves. These tiny things were going to tear her apart.

"I'm sorry I froze you, Landon," she whispered to herself. "I could really use you now." She envisioned her death, chewed to pieces by fluffy jungle monkeys.

Many more began to screech. The mass moved like one giant swarm.

Katia covered herself, expecting their claws to rip into her skin . . . but nothing happened. She looked back and found only one still on top of the shelter.

It gave a low growl.

Katia swallowed, her eyes searching for a weapon to smack it with.

It growled again. This time she heard something that sounded like a word.

"Furrund."

She stared. "Furred? What does *that* mean?"

It did it again. "Furrrund."

"Wait. Are you saying 'friend'?"

A multitude of screeches echoed in the trees behind it.

CONJECTRIX

Katia looked at the animal more closely. "You talk? You're a friend?"

The animal blinked. "Rrroowden."

"Is that your name?" Katia guessed.

It blinked yes again.

"What are you?"

"Grrumberrrs." It repeated it a few times.

"A Grumbear?"

Yes.

"This is amazing! I can understand you."

The screeching from the others made her nervous again.

Roowden silenced them. "Urrvurrsturrrrr." His little face was very intense as he spoke.

Katia frowned. "I don't understand. Of oyster, over stir . . ."

Roowden swung to the ground and picked her pocket.

"Hey." She batted at the animal until she saw the piece of cloth it dug from her cloak— It was the delicately embroidered Everstar—the gift from Spotswood.

Katia stopped, understanding. "Everstar."

Roowden blinked again.

Katia sank to the jungle floor. "How do you know about the Everstar? Is Naomi here?"

"Fffarrr," he growled. "Nnnott."

"Tell me, please. How you know of the Everstar?"

He placed his paws to the ground. "Rwoooownd. Weee see hurrrrrr."

"I'm not understanding," Katia said hopelessly.

Roowden moved closer to Katia, sniffing her. "Mmmmm . . ." He smelled her wrists. "Mmmujick eesss sttronnnng. I's smmmmmellls itt."

"You smell my magic?"

214

He blinked yes. "Grrumberrs smmell thu urrrth. Smmell mmujick. Furrund of mmujick, uv Ssspodswod."

Katia wiped her eyes, still tender from earlier. "I'm trying to understand, really, but I'm so lost."

Roowden took his paw, stroked her hand, and bowed. He screeched something to the other grumbears, who responded with sounds of delight. Slowly, the animals began to swing away through the jungle. Roowden jumped, bounded off a trunk, and landed on Katia's shoulder.

Her first reaction was to squeal, but his soft tail curled around her neck, comforting her.

"Gooo. Follllloww." His paw stretched out toward the path of glowing eyes.

Katia could think of nothing else but to follow them. The thick ferns lessened as she crossed a small ridge. Before her eyes lay a brilliant ring of trees. Little holes in the trunks emitted soft blue lights, and large nest-like homes had been built between the branches. The orange eyes now encircled her—the blue lights like small stars twinkling among tiny suns—a little wonderland filled with enchantment.

In the middle of the ring were a series of large mounds. Roowden jumped down from her shoulder and ran to the nearest one. A few little eyes popped out of the opening, then vanished.

Roowden appeared again a moment later with a pouch. The eyes reappeared behind him, belonging to the gentle, soft face of a grumbear—his mate perhaps, watching what he was doing.

The pouch was black, man-made, and large in his paws, though no bigger than Katia's thumb.

Roowden placed it in her hands. "Opppunn."

Katia flipped over the pouch and a small purple marble rolled into her hand. She stared, astonished. "Where did you get this?" Her fears went immediately to Lottie, wondering what had happened to her little friend.

"Furrund. Ssspodswod."

"Spotswood gave this to you?" She looked closely at the marble. "What do I do with it?"

Roowden took his paws and rubbed the ground in a circle. "Rwoooownd. Weee see hurrrrrr."

Many of the orange eyes moved down the trees to get a closer view of the spectacle, filling the ring with a strange ambiance.

Katia could only think of repeating what Roowden had done. She placed the marble in her palm, put it on the ground, and rolled it in a circle.

Dust began to swirl in tiny spirals, much like Micah's magic. As she continued to roll it around, the ground began to glow.

Screeches of delight filled the ring as the magic moved faster, glowing orange, then moving to bright white. Katia's own magic reacted, too, mixing crystals of icy brilliance, frosting a ring of magic.

And then she saw her.

Naomi's face stared out, a delicate image in the ice. She looked sad, hurt, tired. Where was Reynolds? It looked like she needed help, but she was so far away. Katia reached out and touched the image.

Reacting to the touch, Naomi smiled within her pain. She looked around but couldn't see Katia. She touched her mark and rubbed it.

The image vanished.

Katia smiled. The white ring faded away, but the memory held strong. The sight of Naomi filled her again with hope and reminded her of her mission to find the sister lost in the water.

"Can the marble show me other people?"

Roowden blinked yes. "Kaarrrrfulll. Mmmujick husss mmmaarckss."

Katia understood. Others could see the magic, which meant she might be putting her friends in danger by searching for them.

"Roowden, are you the only one of the grumbears that can talk?"

Roowden scurried away in the trees. Katia watched him go. To her complete surprise, she saw not only the glowing eyes of the grumbears, but human faces in the mystic halflight. Visible ghosts stood around the ring, watching her, watching Naomi. Faces of men and women left as Stains.

One came forward—a young man with a sweet countenance—and smiled. He didn't say anything at first, just stared at the place where Naomi's image had appeared.

"I know her." His voice carried through the air like a whisper, though his mouth hadn't seemed to move at all.

"Who are you?" Katia asked. "Should I know you?"

"I am Dobbins Foger," his voice echoed in her mind. *"I am here at the place of my origin. My grumbear sacrificed his body to help me save her. Your Naomi."* He looked onward past Katia, seeing something beyond what human eyes could see. *"We are tired and ready to sleep. She can save us."*

"Save you? From what?"

Others joined him now, standing close together. *"Our souls need rescue. She can save us. Please, help us."*

"Of course I will," Katia replied without thinking.

The shades disappeared, leaving only the orange eyes behind.

Roowden moved back to his mound and brought out the soft-faced grumbear. "Floowdurr."

Floowdur batted her eyes, embarrassed. "Yesss, misss." Her speech was higher in tone and easier for Katia to hear.

Roowden pushed her forward. "Floowdurr wulll sssshooo yoooo."

"Show me?"

Floowdur wanted to hide, but Roowden stood firm behind her. Her tail moved up to cover her eyes. "I lead yoo to hoo yoo seek."

Katia fell instantly in love with the bashful little creature. "When can we go?"

Roowden moved his paw in an arch. "Lllyyyttt."

Katia felt overcome with relief. "Thank you so much." She turned to the others looking on and bowed awkwardly—the only thing she could think of to do.

The grumbears screeched with delight.

Floowdur came to her hands and gently nibbled a kiss.

It was the sweetest thing Katia had ever experienced. These tiny creatures changed her heart and restored her hope.

CHAPTER TWENTY-ONE
Musungu Haunts

Zander didn't dare move or breathe. Fear paralyzed him, rooting him in place. The hands wrapping around his throat were not human hands. The flesh felt thin around the knuckles, the bones like sharp sticks poking into his flesh.

And as sudden as it happened, the hand vanished with a gust of wind, sending leaves swirling around him. His heart pumped heavily. *"Move,"* a voice in his brain instructed, and he jumped to obey.

He retreated into the mist until his back rested against a tree. His eyes fell upon the hand that had held him moments before—not a hand at all, but the dead mossy branch of a tree. He felt around his neck again. He could have sworn the hands were real, but there was no proof of it. The sight of the eerie branch softened his fears, if only a little.

Mist swirled around, rising and falling with each of his breaths. It crept, fingerlike, along the ground, grabbing and snatching. Images appeared in brief swirling puffs, then faded away again—faces of children, mothers, and fathers coming and going around him. Zander blinked to clear his eyes, but the images wouldn't go away. They glanced at Zander and marched past without caring.

Conjectrix

The Musungu had lived up to its reputation; Zander was in every way spooked.

Footsteps passed where he had just stood, the fog concealing him from sight. The ethereal faces around him looked as intrigued as he. Someone else had come to the Musungu.

"Follow them." Zander didn't like the idea, but the voice came again. *"Quick."*

Zander crept out of the safety of the tree and followed at a distance. Muddy boot prints marked the path. He heard little snippets of argument and what sounded like a struggle. The footsteps trailed off to the right, but Zander stopped where he was.

"Follow to the lake."

The faces in the mist looked like they were smiling, urging and encouraging him on. He did as they asked, approaching the lake before him.

It was unlike anything Zander imagined, still and clear. A purple hue hung around the water's edge, with white powder ringing everything it touched. Around the edge, large trees grew tall, with long branches covered in webbed moss, closing in the water and keeping it in isolation.

Zander's airway tightened. A pungent stench of decay left a burning in his throat. He brought up his tunic to cover his nose.

In the middle of the small lake sat a lonely island, full of clusters of thorny bushes and crooked trees covered in thick moss. The purple aura spread throughout the briars and branches.

"Come to me." The voice surrounded Zander now. He felt it inside him, pulsing through his veins. Whispers moved around him like tiny puffs of wind, filling the air with a busy hum.

Zander looked again at the water. He didn't dare tread in the beautiful crystal harmony.

"Come, Defender of Everstar. Come across the water."

Everstar. He felt the lovely word around him like sweet kisses in a breeze. Taking courage, he tried to test the coolness, but his foot did not penetrate the crisp water. The whole of his foot landed on top, like walking on glass. He pressed his weight down. It held him as he moved his other foot, stepping forward. The faces watched on as he walked carefully to the island.

Once Zander stepped both feet onto the boulder-lined shore, the faces disappeared into a mist. He was alone. The hum of noise disappeared, and all he heard was his own breathing. The quiet voice that had guided him across the lake vanished. Glancing around, he spotted a large pointed hat approaching the place where he had left the water's edge.

Curtis, the man who had killed Zeth without a thought, stood tall over three dwarves. The sight started Zander's heart thumping. He crouched behind the boulder, out of sight. Thorny briars scratched and poked through his skin as he crawled into a small hollow, trying desperately to listen, but it was difficult to hear, as if the fog muffled the sound around him.

Zander tried to move forward, but his skin caught on the thorns. He bit his tongue to prevent any sound from escaping. The swirls of mist cleared his line of vision. He could see directly down to the shore. Zander recognized one of the captured as Brandell, the fairy whisperer. But where was Bryant?

Curtis had Brandell by the wrists.

Little snippets of the argument drifted across the water. ". . . tell me where to find her."

"You won't find her. The magic here will conceal her. This place is a trick. Everything hears. Everything listens."

Conjectrix

Curtis shoved Brandell to the ground. "Tell me this, little man: what happens to you if you stay in the Musungu?"

Brandell tried to scamper to his feet. "Your soul will be consumed by magic and—"

Curtis smiled, finishing his sentence. "You'll be eaten away from the inside out."

A wind gathered at the shore. Zander heard in it the quiet whispers of the creeping fog. A few faces returned, standing near him. The people were not frightening to him; they were merely curious to see what was about to happen.

Curtis grabbed one of the other dwarves, bound by a rope. Zander recognized him as Jarem, one of the smaller dwarves. He looked helplessly at Brandell as Curtis took his hands and held him over the water.

Splash. Zander jerked at the sound, astonished.

Suddenly the little dwarf started to scream—excruciating, painful shrieks. The water bubbled around the dwarf as he flailed about, sizzling his flesh. Blisters grew on his skin, bursting into oozing sores. Zander watched on, too horrified to look away.

A moaning came through the wind that whipped into a small tornado. It migrated to where the small dwarf shrieked in his agony, and lifted him out of the water. The dwarf was no longer visible; all that rained down from the cyclone were bits of crushed bones.

Zander gasped in horror.

Curtis's attention turned.

"Get out of sight."

Zander tried to back away but got snagged again by the briars, the painful thorns cutting into his shoulders and arms. As he wiggled free from the snag, a slimy, muddy hand covered his mouth, and another arm grabbed him tight around the middle.

"No sounds." For a second, Zander thought he had heard the voice again in his head, but he felt the strong body pull him back out of sight.

Zander's mind whirred. He thought of the faces in the mist—maybe they were real? Maybe they wanted to hurt him or take him away? The hand felt real, warm and wet. He could smell the foul stench of the swamp on the boney fingers. He choked on his breath as he was forced to breathe through his nose.

The mysterious person pulled him behind the briars, out of sight of the commotion on the lakeshore. Zander felt his head being pushed down as his body was pulled through a small opening in a rocky cluster into a dark enclosure. The hand continued to cover his mouth as he was guided near a thatched wall.

"I'm going to let go." The hand slipped off Zander's mouth. Lamplight brightened the dark space, revealing the person who had pulled him away from the briars.

A young woman sat covered in dried, caked mud. It was difficult to discern the details of her face, but Zander immediately knew her. Her eyes glistened dark blue under the warm flame of the lamp—just like Silexa's had in the cave underneath Southwick.

"Y-you are . . ." Zander started, but didn't need to finish. She nodded.

"Vespa. And you are Zander."

Zander sat back in amazement. "How . . . ?"

Vespa made a little flourish with her hand and pursed her lips, letting out a slight buzzing sound. The front pocket of Zander's vest moved as the Highthorn flower rose up and twirled until Little Lovely emerged once more.

Zander looked in awe at the spectacle, unable to find any words.

Vespa read his expression. "I knew you were coming." She motioned to Little Lovely. "Each of us got to choose who our protector would be.

CONJECTRIX

I chose something a little more elegant, more secretive than the loyalty of an animal—a fairy from a peachnut tree. A few of my sisters laughed at my decision, but now I know the language of their kind.

"Fairies don't live very long," she continued with a sad smile, admiring Little Lovely. "Mine didn't, but her friends continue to serve me well."

She buzzed a little something with her lips. Little Lovely flew over to her shoulder and buzzed something back. "Their wings send different vibrations, like how bees communicate. It's hard to hear unless you are listening for it." She buzzed again and the fairy danced.

Zander liked Vespa very much.

"Little Lovely says you don't communicate very well. I confess, in this we are similar. I haven't had much practice at it lately." Her lip curled upward, reminding him of Naomi's smile. "The Haunts here aren't much for talking, you know. You sure have a special little lady here, though."

Little Lovely twirled again for their benefit.

"Little Lovely says you told her a secret that is very special. Can you tell me?"

Zander didn't know how to answer.

Vespa looked down. "It doesn't matter if you tell me. I know why you're here. You must know about me or you wouldn't have come."

Zander frowned, confused, watching as she grabbed the chain around her neck and pulled it up. There, just like Silexa's, was a beautiful deep purple stone embedded in a medallion of gold. "Nox. Dark earth, nocturne, life in the soil—that's what I protect. Many think nothing can live in the Musungu, but it is brimming with life. This place is stained with magic, and I thought it would conceal me."

She trailed off, her face clouded with thought as she placed the medallion back under her clothes. "Why are you looking for me?"

Zander sat up. "S-Sil-exa."

She sagged forward, her knees sinking deeper into the mud. "You've seen her, haven't you? My sister?"

Zander smiled and nodded.

"Please, tell me what has happened."

Zander tried but stumbled again on his words. "Th-the prince knows," was what finally came out.

"That was why she disappeared? She's in love with a prince?" She laughed. "I'm not surprised. Silexa has always wanted more than what she could have. Is she gathering us? Have you met any of the others?"

That was a question Zander was not prepared for. His face fell. He didn't dare tell her of the tragedy that befallen her lovely sister, Ymber.

Little Lovely swooped close to Vespa's ear and told her of the news of her sister's death.

She grabbed her chest, tears streaking clear trails down her muddy face. "This is a confirmation of my fears. I came here to hide from the truth, but there is no running from the pain we all must bear every day."

Little Lovely buzzed again animatedly, as if trying her hardest to communicate something important.

"Right, yes, I know." Vespa nodded, wiping her eyes. "Let me just grab a few things." She moved around the small hut, pulling out trinkets, scarves, money, and placing them all in a rucksack.

She glanced back at Zander. "Little Lovely tells me that you are going to lead me to a place called UnderElm. Tell me this: do you know those men out there across the lake?"

Zander nodded. He felt more comfortable talking now and tried to open up. "The d-dwarves are my f-friends."

"And the tall man is not, correct?"

Zander nodded, swallowing back his fear.

Vespa came closer to him. "Give me your hand, Zander." She lifted his palm and placed it in hers. "Thank you for coming to rescue me. Someday, I know you will tell me your secret and I will cherish it like the fairies do."

Her face turned serious. "The Musungu can be a very dangerous place. The Haunts that live here will not hurt you, unless they feel threatened. The magic that stained them is not natural. It is the most poisonous kind I have ever seen. When they feel anger," her eyes intensified, "—and you must remember this—they enter your body and the stain is so powerful, you melt away and never return. Do you understand?"

Zander nodded. He understood all too well.

"Do not disturb the water. I can protect you across, but any ripple or even a tiny pebble will start the cyclone. And do not harm the trees. They are living and will fight if necessary."

She started to lead him outside when she quickly turned around again. "One more thing. If something happens to me, take my stone. Take it before the stains get me and run as fast as you can."

Zander understood the importance of what she'd asked of him. He had borne Silexa's precious stone once and now he had been asked to do such a favor again.

CHAPTER TWENTY-TWO
SNATCHED

A gentle trickle of sweat beaded down the back of Naomi's neck onto her fine, thin scarf. The smell of sulfur mixed with dust filled her senses, accompanied by a constant ringing in her ears. The jagged rock face scratched against her back. Ash dust brushed her hands and face, sticking to the sweat on her body. A dark sky hung overhead, brimming with thousands of stars twinkling in the clear night. The sight confounded her. How had she gotten to Mount Ignis? A moment ago, she'd been dreaming of a young girl in trouble. She'd helped her, and the vortex brought her here. In her palm, the Conjectrix pulsed, hot to the touch.

She admired the glow of the faces in it.

Jeanus smiled up at her, as if looking through a window. She had only met the woman once in an apple cellar which seemed a lifetime ago, and she had been carrying the Conjectrix with her. Naomi remembered her eyes were blind to the outside world, but through the magic of the Conjectrix, Jeanus could see the danger and intervene.

Naomi understood it now better than anyone, next to Spotswood. The Conjectrix wasn't meant to help her connect with her friends or to keep her from dreaming. It was a powerful conduit that communicated through space and time—a thinking object that sent information to those in need of help. And Naomi was its vessel.

The image of Jeanus disappeared and someone new came into focus. Her fist grew tight around the orb, holding it still as she stared hard into its depths.

Taren. The magic in her veins became frantic. He had found her, as if he had been waiting for her to use magic. Heroism would reveal her. He *knew*.

Energy pumped so fast through Naomi's body that her only thought was to flee. Anxiety flooded in, an overwhelming rush of emotion, knocking her back to the rock. She closed her eyes and asked for help.

She found her magic swirling in a terrified frenzy. It had wakened to something horrible. Her magic was always so calm and reasonable; now it danced in erratic patterns from here to there, too fast for Naomi to follow.

Finally it moved up her arm and held on like a frightened child.

"He is here," it said in her mind. *"He waits."*

"What do I do?"

"Seek shelter. Protect us."

Naomi opened her eyes and evaluated her surroundings. There were openings all along the ledge left from old lava flows. One of them had to lead inside.

Carefully, she crawled up the rough rock, using the pocket holes for footholds and finger hooks. A close-knit web of caves weaved in and out above her. Halfway up, she heard a high-pitch screech and saw the dark shadow of a dragon circling around the mountain.

Naomi crouched reflexively, her shadesilk cloak covering every inch of her. She glanced up, seeing the rough scales and tough leather that covered the body of the creature. Large, sharp claws grabbed the rock with intense force, scraping and climbing as its wings bent around its shoulders. Its teeth and eyes were sharp, glowing yellow from the heat in its belly.

She had heard of the existence of dragons, like many other tales told to frighten children, but it had been hard to believe until now.

As the creature entered a hollow near the mountain peak, it dislodged some loose rock, sending it tumbling down toward Naomi. She huddled in a hollow, safe but with only inches to spare. She quickened her pace. It was too dangerous being in the sight of such a beast, so she scrambled for a large opening on the side of the mountain.

Feeling her way around, she slid in and out of the tunnels and crevices. The jagged lava rock poked through her clothes and scraped her skin as she moved within the narrow formations, unnatural for human passage.

A larger tunnel lay before her, filled with reflective light. As she carefully inched toward it, she stopped, pulling her cloak tightly around her body. Voices were coming from inside.

Still concealed beneath the shadesilk, she continued forward. She soon found herself in the shadows of a large cavern above a river of lava, its orange-red glow near blinding her. Even from her distance, she could see the steam and smoke hissing out, its bubbling pops singeing everything in its path. The air was filled with sulfur and burning.

As the lava river flowed around the jagged rock, images began to appear. It wasn't a trick of the heat; Naomi could see their faces rising up through the molten rock and then disappear again. With a start, she came to a stunning realization—she was beholding the horrible beauty of the River of Souls.

Two figures stood silhouetted by the firelight. Naomi quickly moved out of sight and continued down the path. She found what looked like a tunnel, but it stopped abruptly in a dead end. She tried several different openings, but each time came back to the same place. Spotting a slope close to the edge of the opening, she decided to risk it.

Naomi kept covered as best she could and held tight to the jagged mounds of rock before her. She must have grabbed one too hard, for it stabbed into her palm. Flinching, she lost her grip, sliding a few inches. A few loose rocks skidded away from her and plummeted over the edge.

For the first time, Naomi thanked Reynolds for the boots and thought it lucky she had not taken them off like she'd wanted to.

The tunnel narrowed and tightened as it wound higher. Nimble and small, she maneuvered through the tight spaces, guided by a faraway firelight. On and on she traveled.

She stopped. She had come to an archway. A scraping noise sounded above her. Looking up, Naomi saw a long, sharp claw stretching out overhead. Heart in her throat, she turned and spotted a large yellow eye, smoldering like fire, staring at her through a web of rock. It sniffed the air and snorted a low grunt.

Naomi froze, staring at the fire eater.

Its large claw moved again, scraping to get her. She screamed, the sound echoing around and around, alerting others to her presence.

Something crunched behind her, and then the wall of the tunnel collapsed as a long claw smashed through.

Naomi ran, not knowing where she was heading, not daring to look behind her. At the archway, a flat plateau of rock stretched out before her, ablaze with heat; steady waves of steam drifted upward. On the other side lay an entrance to a tunnel.

Glancing back, Naomi saw the fire eater approaching, screeching a horrible cry as it lunged for her. She dodged to the right, narrowly missing its claw.

With no other choice, she leaped for the other tunnel.

Her feet found hold on the rock, safe at last—then she skidded as fast as she could. Two blinking yellow eyes met hers from inside the opening, slowly moving toward her—smaller and deep purple in color, a child perhaps of the thunderous red clawing beast behind her.

Feeling pinned, Naomi turned, searching for some escape. More glowing eyes stared at her from within the various pockets.

She had landed in the middle of a den of dragons.

The red fire eater huffed. It turned its head, steam rising from its breath.

Naomi panicked. The heat extinguished the breathable air. Her feet slipped across the rock surface as she searched for a way out.

It was then that she saw him, standing near the edge of the plateau on a ledge that led out into darkness.

Taren.

He stretched out his arm. "Come! Take my hand!"

Naomi didn't know what to do. There was so little time and her head couldn't think fast enough to process what was happening.

The fire eater swiped its big claw. Naomi reacted on instinct, grabbing the hand of the person whom she feared more than anyone, the person who had very nearly succeeded in killing her.

The shadows swallowed Naomi as Taren dragged her away from the fire. The air changed from thick heat to fresh and cool. The tunnel led them to a path that wound around the mountain, lit by the starry sky.

Taren held her hand tighter than was natural. His magic hovered close at her fingertips. She could feel his anger, as dangerous as always, but there had been no other option. Magic pumped in her veins, her heart racing. She tried to think of a way to escape, but the screaming in her head that resonated throughout her entire body prevented any rational thought—screams of terror.

The path wound back again into a small hollow in the mountain. Large lava rock shaped formations like windows, opening up to the sky, the moon and the stars framed like a tapestry. Taren stopped, let go of her hand, and walked to the edge.

Naomi stood in silence, not knowing what to say. Taren, too, was quiet, unspeaking. At last, she found her courage. "Why are you here?"

Taren fiddled with a rock, slow to respond. "Where is Reynolds? I thought he would never leave your side."

"I don't know."

"He left you alone?" Taren glanced in her direction, but quickly turned away again, not making eye contact. "He's braver than I gave him credit for."

It grew quiet and uncomfortable once more. Naomi couldn't hold her question any longer; she had to know. "Why did you save me?"

"The fire eaters are very protective of their young," Taren answered. "And burning in the belly of a fire eater is a terrible way to die."

She wouldn't let him side-step that easily. "What *are* you doing here?"

Taren turned again, his smirk half-visible in the starlight. "The same thing you're doing, I imagine." He shook his head. "But your sister isn't here. It was a beautiful lie. You were led into a trap."

Anger propelling her courage, Naomi ventured closer to him. "You're the liar. This is not a trap—"

He finally turned and faced her, his eyes black in the moonlight, emotionless. "My father is here. You remember my father, don't you?"

Naomi shivered. Lockwood, Commander of the Southwick armies, who had killed her beloved guardian Malindra.

"He's here to take you. He wants you. I was sent to take—" Taren trailed off, stuck on his words. He sounded almost . . . nervous.

"Why me?"

"It had nothing to do with you." He sounded disgusted. "And it didn't have anything to do with Reynolds, either. It had to do with what you had around your neck."

Naomi didn't understand. She felt around her throat; the scarf was there still, as it always had been, but then a thumping in her chest awoke the memory of when she'd last saw Taren. "What are you not telling me?"

"Just because I can't read your magic doesn't mean I don't know how magic works. I probably know it better than any living person." His voice grew angry with the telling. "I can't escape it. It's always in here, telling me things. I can't get rid of it."

A small laugh erupted from his throat like a cough. "Do you know how you're going to get rid of it?"

Naomi stared blankly. "Reynolds said—"

"Reynolds." Taren scoffed. "Reynolds doesn't tell you anything. He thinks he understands the magic, but he doesn't. He thinks it will act differently, like there's another way, but there isn't. The magic has told me so."

Naomi tensed. She didn't like the tone of this conversation. "What did it tell you?"

"That you have to die."

A hot blush of anger flashed in her cheeks. "I did die! Is your memory really that short? You did it. You killed me!"

He sat on a ledge, looking defeated. "No, I didn't. Not really. Reynolds is the one who will kill you."

Naomi pulled over her vest to show the melted Vivatera sunken in her chest. "This saved me. It chose to save me."

Conjectrix

Taren's hand came up to his mouth. "It worked. I knew it would. I know it had." He found Naomi's eyes. "It told me it would work. I just obeyed."

Naomi stared, not knowing what to say. Anger still spread all over her, the magic inside nearly bursting to get out and attack. What he said couldn't be true. She still remembered the piercing, searing pain, the gurgles in her throat when she couldn't breathe, her strength leaving her body. And now he claimed he hadn't meant to harm her, that he'd known all along the magic would save her.

"I don't believe anything you say." The words tumbled out of her mouth.

Taren's expression changed, the coldness of his exterior melting before her eyes. "How could you believe I would want to kill you?"

"Because I wear the proof."

"The proof that it worked." He stood and came closer, the tension between them so thick Naomi almost forgot to breathe. "When you were young, Reynolds left you a trinket." His hand swept gently over the scar on her neck. The touch made Naomi uncomfortable and nervous. "The Vivatera was his then. But I knew what he didn't, so I made the decision for him."

Naomi couldn't speak. She swallowed her nerves back down her throat.

"Reynolds can't save you from the mess he created. There is no alternative. It must be a sacrifice. The magic needs to be whole and you're magic came from it. It wouldn't be whole without the Vivatera. It was purposefully done."

Finally finding her courage once more, Naomi slapped him hard in the face.

Taren brought his hand to his mouth and touched the spot. He gave a little laugh. "The Vivatera had a choice. And it still has a choice."

Naomi heard the words, but a severe pain overpowered her—a hot, spasm that overtook all her sensations, her movement. Her body collapsed into a fit of shakes. She felt strong arms around her, holding her still, before she blacked out.

CHAPTER TWENTY-THREE

SERA

Grab on!" Arie shouted, extending his hand out to his brother.

Reynolds struggled for a grip as gigantic wings flapping above sent a steady stream of wind whipping around him. He hooked his hand around Arie's wrist in a firm hold and swung his body up next to his brother.

The feeling was both terrifying and exhilarating as they traveled across the wide desert in the talons of a dragon. The mountain drew closer and closer. Suddenly, the dragon dove through a large opening near the mouth of the volcano, sweeping them into darkness.

The creature wound through the vast caverns until a large opening came into view and it slowed and descended. Just before it landed, Reynolds felt Arie grip his shoulders and shove him down to the rock below.

Rocks skittered across the surface as the fire eater hooked its sharp talons into the cavern floor, and Reynolds covered his head from the jagged rainfall. The beast let out a large cry before folding in its wings.

Arie lay sprawled out where he'd fallen near the tail of the dragon, a small trickle of blood on his temple. Without hesitation Reynolds pushed through the dirt and scrambled over. At his approach, Arie's eyes open with an amused smiled on his face.

"Why the devil did you push me—?"

Arie's palm shot out, covering his brother's mouth as he shushed him. His other hand pointed to the dragon. Its large, bulbous eyes stared down at the pair. They were the color of fire, full of intelligence and depth, observing them with calm curiosity.

Reynolds held still as the dragon analyzed him.

Movement near the top of the cavern caught his attention and he turned his head. A creature blurred toward them, looking as though small flames traveled down from its head to its feet. It leapt over the large claws of the fire eater and landed with equal grace.

Reynolds stared. His eyes had deceived him; it was not a flame, but a girl. Her red hair flowed long down to her waist. She dressed in tattered, burned clothes, her cloak deep red with a shimmer of scales just like the dragon. Her beauty was unearthly, her piercing eyes violet under the flickering light.

She came closer, her mouth hard as stone with a gaze full of determination—and glared directly at Arie.

She didn't make a noise but stopped right at his feet. Silence filled her penetrating, stern look that soon became uncomfortable.

Arie slowly stood up and dusted himself off. He returned her gaze.

Out of nowhere, the girl slapped him across the face. The sound resonated around the walls. His skin burned an angry red, but the amused smile never vanished from his face.

Reynolds' hands went to the hilt of his sword in reflex.

But then the girl leapt forward and kissed Arie straight on the mouth. She pulled back again and went to slap him, but he caught her hand before she could.

237

CONJECTRIX

"That was a stupid stunt, Rass," she said, struggling to get her arm free. "Ignis is a dangerous place right now."

"And when has it ever been safe?" Arie let her go and she adjusted herself again.

But she couldn't seem to help herself and moved in for another kiss.

"Why *are* you here?" she asked pulling back once more. "You can't be here. I always dreamed you'd come, but you never did, and now you're here when you can't be."

"I wanted you to meet my brother, Reynolds."

"And *now* I meet the family?" The girl turned and studied Reynolds. "I didn't know you had family."

Arie smirked. "It's been a while since we considered each other family."

Reynolds, who still had his hand on his sword, smiled dimly.

The girl shook her head at Arie. "You're an idiot. You can't be here, as I said. It's too dangerous. Men are here from Southwick. I think they're looking for me, or something."

"Yes, you would be right."

Reynolds finally connected it. "You're Sera."

"Good eyes." She turned back to face him. "Tell me, what has Rasmussen told you about me?"

"Nothing."

Sera slugged Arie's arm. "You didn't even tell your brother about me?"

"You told me not to," Arie defended himself, rubbing his skin. "I didn't say a word to anyone."

Sera smirked, satisfied.

Watching Arie's face as he looked on the girl, Reynolds doubted he would hold a grudge. "Do you have any food? We're starving."

Sera looked at both of the men and nodded. "Come on." She moved toward a hole under where the tail of the dragon lay. "Don't mind Webster. He's a bit grumpy today."

She led them to a large cave. Once inside, she rubbed her palms together and a sparkle of light lit up a torch on the wall, revealing a bed of straw and a few wooden boxes. She pulled out jerky and a few dried apples from one of the crates.

"Not much keeps out here, but I have enough to share." She brought the food back, sat on the floor before them, and crossed her legs. When they had a good few bites, she interrupted, "So, who wants to do the explaining?"

Reynolds swallowed down his mouthful of apple. "I think I should. The men are here because of a girl—a girl named Naomi."

"And why would this girl come here?"

"She's looking for you." Sera's stare smoldered, waiting for an answer. Reynolds took a deep breath. "Her real name is Redemia, daughter of Prolius."

Sera laughed. "A daughter of Prolius? And she bought into that lie? How ridiculous. There isn't a Redemia."

"No, you don't understand," Reynolds interrupted. "She does exist—"

"Boy, I am the oldest of the Prolius children. I was twelve when we left Southwick. I understand more than anyone else what it was like to live there, under siege and terrified, helping my sisters survive."

"But your mother was pregnant."

Sera stopped, seeming upset by the sudden resurfacing of such unpleasant memories. "Yes, she was. She lost the baby—"

"No, she didn't."

"What a bold-face liar." Sera jumped to her feet and began pacing. "I don't believe you. What would you know about it?"

"I was there with her."

Sera spun around and launched a cheese knife at Reynolds, which stuck in the ground between his legs. "Stop. Just stop it. You're speaking nonsense."

Reynolds stood cautiously, keeping his voice calm and even. "It isn't nonsense. It's absolute truth. She lives and she's here and she's cursed, just like the rest of you. If I were you, I wouldn't believe it either, but I was there. I was in Southwick. I saw the little girl myself. I watched your mother hand her over to Malindra as a baby, and I've been protecting her ever since, until last night when she suddenly disappeared. So, please, help us—"

Sera moved her finger to his mouth, silencing him. "You're serious?" She looked at Arie, then back at him. "She survived?"

"I promise you, she is real."

"I can't believe it!" She jumped up and down in a small giddy fashion—no longer the fierce warrior of the dragon caves, but a little girl in a palace waiting for news of a sibling, soon to arrive.

"I remember placing my hand on my mother's stomach to feel the tiny kick. Oh, my poor father. He never knew her. Some of the others were too little to understand. But that kick brought me a new hope that we would be okay. Then we were sent away, and when my mother met us, she told us the baby died . . ." She trailed off, lost for a moment in her own thoughts. "Is she really alive?"

"Yes, yes," Arie interrupted, seeming to have grown tired of the subject. "Now, can we find her so she can tell you all about her happy childhood?"

"But what about you?" Reynolds turned to Arie. "How do you know *her*?" He pointed to Sera.

"From Southwick."

Sera smiled and nodded. "That's where we first met, but it wasn't until years later that I saw him—a young, drunk, jerk of a soldier from Southwick who I hated." She winked at Arie. "Still kinda do. But that is much more boring than your secret girl risking her life to find me."

"My girl?"

She cocked her head to the side. "Oh, sorry, did I say something wrong?" she asked, all innocence. "Where do you think she might have gone?"

"The river. I think they have lured her there."

Sera's head shot up. "The river? She's in worse shape than I thought. Why would the souls want her?"

"There might be a lot of reasons, actually, but one might have to do with a blood promise made with a troll."

Sera mulled the words over. "This girl is getting more interesting every second."

Reynolds shook his head. *You have no idea.* "Last night, she said she saw you in a sort of vision. Near a cave with three dots, I think."

Sera's eyes went wide. "Three dots? That's the Marking Stones. It's where *she* lives."

"*She?* Who's *she?*"

"She'll take her. I'm sure of it. That's why they're here." Sera rushed to an antique box and fumbled around in it for something.

Reynolds followed. "Where are they leading her?"

"To Hell, my brother." Arie slapped him on the shoulder grimly. "As I told you."

Sera abruptly rushed out of her small home and the two men followed. She ran up the slope near where the fire eater rested its head, whistling an echoing, high sound. The dragon blinked its eyes and looked at her as if it understood, speaking back to her in a way it was impossible to follow. After a moment, Sera ran back down.

"The tunnel is too narrow for him to take us, but if we need him, he will hear my whistle. Frieda will come, too, even if she has to leave the little ones."

Reynolds stared. "There's more?"

"Oh, yes," she confirmed. "Lots more." Without another word, she left, the men scrambling to follow.

Reynolds' head swam with more questions. "You live with them? How?"

"I charmed them. I figured a smart boy like you would know how that all works."

Reynolds brimmed with admiration. "I continually underestimate how powerful you sisters are."

Sera stopped, turned facing him, her look no longer one of amusement. "I would change it in a heartbeat. This curse is not one to be taken lightly. That's why I felt I needed to come and hide here, away from my sisters, and protect the river. Fire is the warrior of death. You know of the river, but you have yet to see the chasms, the flames . . .

"This really is the most horrible place in this world. It's haunted and evil. Demons from the dead raise up through the earth. And I can't fight that. There's nothing on this earth that can touch it. The fire eaters are the only thing that can help me cope with it. Help me through it. Remind me how to love."

Her head sunk down. Arie tried to take her hand but she pulled away and marched on again, alone.

Glaring at his brother, Arie followed.

Reynolds trailed after, the conversation lingering in his mind as he walked.

Small rumblings shook the walls around them. It took a few seconds to calm before Sera thought it safe to walk on.

"What was that?" Arie asked.

"I don't know."

Reynolds didn't like it at all. "You said men from Southwick were here?"

"Just a handful, really. A bunch of bumbling guards. But there are two I have felt. The leader is a big man, I think. I don't like the look of him. Nasty mustache. But the other is smart. His son, I think. He is a fire whirler also—I can feel it. He is the one I worry about. He looks beyond his years."

"You can feel it?"

"It's the same language."

Reynolds stopped. *Fire whirler.* An image flashed in his mind, a wall of fire deep in the Echoes. How could he have been so stupid? His heart pumped faster, his walk becoming a run down the tunnel ahead of the others. There was no mistake this time. Taren would not win. Reynolds had to get to Naomi. He had to find her before Taren could do anything.

With every step, he became more anxious to find her. He felt the heat of the mountain, the sound of the churning lava and the dragons' roars, but the loudest noise was his own heart pounding in his chest, drumming in his ears.

How could he have been so stupid as to leave her side, to take his eyes off her for one moment? She had provoked him, true. But when had he lost the upper hand with their friendship? He was the one holding the secrets. He'd had everything in control, once.

But their recent experiences had changed both of them, so much so that there were hardly any secrets left to separate them. The truth had brought them closer together and driven them further apart all at once.

Now, because of his stupidity, he was going to lose her.

Another rumble shook the chamber, not as intense as the first. His heart lurched. Naomi had to be close. Unable to help himself, he rushed into the darkness.

"Wait!" Sera called after him.

"He's going to kill her." Reynolds reached a fork and slowed, looking at both ways. Sera and Arie caught up to him.

"Stop," Sera demanded. "Tell me what's happening."

"I've got to find Naomi." Reynolds was talking to himself more than anyone. "He's going to kill her. I know it. I know it."

CHAPTER TWENTY-FOUR
Memories of Soft Silk

Silexa huddled in the cold, empty house, bare of all essentials, and filled with an accumulation of years of dust, suffocating in its continuing stillness. Occasionally, a rat tunneled in and out, and though Silexa didn't like him much, it was nice knowing that something else lived in this space. Eventually, though, the creature found nothing of interest and left her alone again.

Daytime moved to night and soon to day again. She marked her own breathing to pass the time. In and out. In and out. She felt herself spiraling into madness, slipping to despair—hungry, anxious, and restless.

As more days passed, time slowed even more, and she started to become paranoid. Her thoughts drifted often to the village of UnderElm. Mother would wonder where she was. It was not fair to leave her to lead the evacuation without Silexa's help, but what could be done? If she hadn't made this detour, the Louving would have found UnderElm and their protection would be lost.

She thought of Bryant, of Mother, of Zander—all out doing something heroic, while she hid in silence and did nothing. Sleep proved elusive, her dreams filled with horrifying images of burning, screaming, and pain.

But, above all, hunger overwhelmed every thought. In desperation, she searched the house again for food, raiding the empty place for anything to eat. She got lucky and found a few jars of questionable content left in the back of a high cupboard. Hunger overcame her common sense and she ate a few of what could have been fermenting pickles. At first she felt satisfied by the food, but later her stomach ached and burned. She curled up in a corner, holding her stomach, crying through the pain, until finally, exhausted, she fell asleep.

Crack! Silexa woke at the sound of something being smashed. In the complete darkness, she couldn't tell if her eyes were actually open. No light of any kind came in, nothing from the city lamps. At night, Southwick looked like a city of shimmering gold, but that had changed. Extinguishing the lights was deliberate. Something was happening outside.

Boom! More sounds, more screams. Something had fallen. She heard the breaking and splintering of wood close by.

She moved closer to the wall, listening. There was screaming, crying, and shouting, not unlike her dream. She couldn't tell where it originated, just that it was close, possibly down the street. There wasn't much she could tell from the noise.

As she listened to the activity outside, she became aware of the light slowly filling the room. At first, Silexa thought her eyes were just adjusting to the darkness, but the light didn't go away. She turned and her heart nearly stopped.

A bluish light illuminated the small, dark corner where she had slept. Her eyes must be playing tricks. Silexa squinted, trying to find the sharpness and angles of the person holding it, however faint they might be.

The aura hovered near her face. *"Silexa, I have found you."*

Silexa trembled. She knew the face staring back at her through the aura. It was not one the Louving could imposter. "Ymber?"

Ymber's lovely face smiled, her long hair reflecting like liquid silver. *"Come, we don't have much time."*

Silexa was still in shock. "Ymber? I don't understand—"

"I will explain what I can as we go."

"Where are we going?"

"Away from here. Southwick is not safe. They know you are hiding here. The Oracle can see you, no matter where you run. They are destroying this district to find you."

Silexa rose to her feet and followed without asking any further questions.

Ymber guided her through the house to a door near the back. *"I will meet you when you reach the tunnel, on the other side of the wall. There is a tower that watches over the wall. It has a single lamp light. Follow it. The tunnel entrance is just beyond the tower. When you cross the wall, you must be careful—it leads only to the sea. Do you understand?"*

Silexa nodded and stretched to hold her, but there was nothing. Ymber had vanished. Taking in a deep breath, she opened the door.

Outside smelled of burning wood and ash. Thick billows of soot floated through the air, though she couldn't see any fire. She traveled cautiously through the narrow street. An eerie quiet followed as she walked.

Sounds around her grew louder and louder. She heard a long scream, accompanied by footsteps. Silexa slid to a side wall and watched others move past her. It was a family: a crying mother, an injured son being carried by a father, and other children varying in age. They did not speak nor look up as they past, but briskly walked on into the darkness. After a few hesitant seconds, Silexa slipped behind them, following.

They scuffed and shuffled one way, then the other, keeping as silent as they could. Finally the father spoke in a whisper. "This is not the way. We are lost."

Silexa stayed back but listened to the small argument that followed. The family was looking for a way out of the city. They started moving again, this time right. Silexa continued to shadow them. They had a little girl no older than three trailing in the back. In her hand, she held a cloth doll with small black button eyes. The girl was being tugged along by an older brother. As she struggled to keep up, the doll came loose and dropped to the street.

"No!" the girl wailed, but her brother covered her mouth.

Silexa stopped and picked up the doll. She moved forward, trying to hand it over to the father, who stopped his family, stepping in front of them as if to guard them from her.

He looked her over before speaking. "The soldiers are smashing our village looking for someone. You're who they're looking for, aren't you?"

Silexa wasn't sure of the implications but knew it was true. "I think so."

"I've lived my whole life in this city—penniless, but happy with my family. Who are you to destroy that?"

"Please." The wife came over and grabbed the injured boy from his arms.

Silexa looked the father square in his eyes, not holding back any of her emotions. "I am to marry Prince Bryant."

The mother with her small, sad face smiled with her eyes. The father did not.

"The prince is dead, and we are in chaos without a king. Southwick is now controlled by someone named Sharrod who has sent out men to find—to find . . ." He stopped.

Silexa saw his despair. "I assure you, the prince is not dead." She tried to sound confident. "I know how to fix the city. I will lead you to safety."

The father looked too angry to speak.

The little girl who'd dropped the doll came up to her father. "May I take my dolly?"

Her father grabbed her hand hard but nodded. Silexa handed it back, smiling.

The father seemed to have been softened by his daughter. "You can get us out?"

Silexa nodded.

"Show us."

"There's a tower, a watch tower. Help me find it?"

The wife again tugged on his sleeve. "The tower is back to the south."

"We can't go back there—"

"I can protect you."

Stern-faced, the father picked up his daughter and moved briskly back through the streets they had just traveled, the rest following after.

There was another boom and shouts to the left. The father found a crossing and turned right, then another left. The soot cleared a little, but nothing could be discerned through it.

A faint light grew before them, but approaching footsteps drowned out any relief they might have felt. Soldiers. The father pushed everyone into an alcove.

"I can see the market square," he said. "This is where the soldiers came in. I don't think we can pass without notice." He glanced back at Silexa, seeing her confusion. "They sealed the district. No one is allowed to leave until they find you, if you are who you say you are. And the moment they see you, they'll be after us all."

"Don't worry. I can protect you." Silexa grabbed onto her stone and felt the wall for security, communicating with the rock, feeling its willingness to help. "We need to get closer to the tower."

The father didn't like it, but the mother's sweet hold on her husband had power to sway him. "Be brave," he spoke to his children. With that, they moved down the street toward the tower.

Soldiers were talking to each other, searching about, while others guarded the entries. The tower was only streets away. No one was looking their way.

Silexa picked up a fist-sized rock and held it cupped in her hands. It heated at her touch, turning a blistering red. With deft aim, she threw it toward the opposite corner. It hit a crate and burst into flames.

All the soldiers were taken off-guard.

The father ushered the others ahead of him. The youngest of the family had just slipped around the corner when the soldiers took notice.

"Hey!"

The father acted quickly knocking the soldier hard in the face with his elbow.

"Quick!" the father yelled to Silexa, who aimed another rock. She turned and ran down the street toward them. The soldiers were not far off and moved quickly.

Silexa grabbed hold of her medallion and entered the tunnel. As she ran, the fingernails of her other hand grazed the stone walls. The gentle magic woke the rock, and the wall soon began to break and splinter into shards like shale crashing down behind her.

She managed a quick glance over her shoulder to see a few of the soldiers closest to her treading on the debris and sliding down to their knees. As the rock loosened, it came down with so much force that it began to cascade, pouring from the ceiling above.

The father turned, witnessing the sudden rush of rock. He grabbed Silexa's arm, pulling her forward, then froze. Behind them, the thin layers shot out like blades, cutting into the advancing soldiers. Soon the entire force of the rock wall moved down in an avalanche and completely covered the entrance.

Silexa stood, staring, still holding on to her stone.

"Come on," the father urged.

Together they ran through the maze until they reached the tower. An iron gate blocked the passage. The rest of the family huddled in a corner, waiting for them to appear, their frightened expressions melting away when they saw their father.

Shouting resumed, filling the streets again with the sound of pursuit.

"Hurry," Silexa whispered. "I can get you through."

They rushed to the gate, where Silexa placed her stone against the bars of iron. The slats began to move and melt away from each other, creating a hole big enough to climb through.

The father pushed his children through, one by one, to the other side. He helped his wife, who paused to kiss him, before he entered himself. On the other side he extended his hand to Silexa, who did not take it. "Come!"

"No." She released the stone and returned the metal back to normal. "I have a different path to take."

The father grabbed her hand before she could depart. "Please, it is not safe."

"Take your family and travel out of Southwick. Go where you will be safe."

251

Conjectrix

"Salvador," he spoke. "My name is Salvador."

"Silexa."

"I understand why they are after you now." He smiled, nodding his head. "We would be honored to have you as our queen." And with that, he disappeared with his gentle family.

The sounds of the rushing soldiers drew closer. Silexa stood near the gate by the south wall and pressed it with her stone. The rock melted, opening out to the sea beyond. She slipped through and touched the wall, sealing it shut.

The cliffs beyond dropped to the sea below at a sharp angle. Ymber had indicated it would be steep, but Silexa had not imagined *this*. She continued downward, holding onto grass and rocks to steady herself. The winds lifted the smoky haze away from the dirty streets of Southwick.

Silexa found a lip in the rock and peered into it. From there she could see a deep cave, hidden with craggy vines and moss. She pushed her way through and took a breath. After days of feeling terrified, she finally felt safe again.

"I knew you could do it." Ymber's aura lit the darkness.

Silexa sighed and gave a weary smile. "You saved me. Thank you."

Ymber's eyes were distant. *"Come. I don't have much time."*

They started walking down the tunnel. "I couldn't be more pleased to see you," Silexa felt prompted to say after a moment, "but it is very unexpected."

"I do not remember everything. I do not remember how I died. I know I am no longer alive, but I do not understand why I am not dead." She turned to her sister. *"I love seeing you, but I hate being here."*

"How did you know where to find me?"

Ymber smiled and kept moving. *"I hope to show you."*

"Show me what?"

"I think you will remember. That is as far as my memory will go."

Silexa slowed down. "Where are you taking me?"

Ymber continued on down the tunnel. *"There is a pull surrounding me, like a bowstring that bounces me there. If I think of traveling away, I'm pulled back. I am not of the sun but of the earth, and I cannot escape."*

"How did you know I was in trouble?"

"I found the dwarves. They left their underground home. They passed by not far from my boundary. I heard them talking. Someone mentioned you, a woman."

"Mother."

Ymber closed her eyes. *"Yes, Mother. I remember a little now. It feels like a dream. She worried. You went to the surface and you did not return. I thought I would help. I am limited in where I can go, but I wanted to help you. I'm so glad I did."*

Silexa listened to the story, amazed. "How did you find me?"

"The magic gives you away. I can see it clearer as a Stain. I am made of it. I was led to it." Ymber turned to her sister. *"I do not understand the outside world anymore. I am not welcome there. I know I will not die in it, but I will cease to be me. I will not have the liberties of my memories. I would stain others and disconnect and destroy . . ."* She seemed unable to piece her thoughts together and so fell silent.

Silexa's heart grieved for her sister. The stain of Ymber would never replace the good person she'd known and loved. The sad reality became clear to her; when Silexa died, her fate would be the same. The magic would remain while her body would pass away.

CONJECTRIX

They continued down the secret tunnel which led them back into the catacombs running under the city. When columns appeared, Silexa stopped. A large space opened up beyond but was eclipsed in darkness.

"Use the box."

A small marble box sat on a bench before them. Silexa lifted the lid to reveal white dust with tiny gold flecks. Sunsparks. She snapped her fingers and a beautiful ball of fire appeared in her hand.

"There are torches near the wall."

Silexa grabbed one and filled it with fire. The place became instantly brighter, illuminating the marble room with veins of ornate designs twisting around the floor in wonderful patterns. "Is this where we're going?"

"No. But it is close. Do you recognize it?"

She walked away, leaving Silexa alone in a world formed of old memories. She knew where they were, and Ymber was right; she didn't want to go. She stood, rooted where she was.

Ymber turned around. *"You need to come."*

"I can't," she whispered. "I can't go in."

"You must. There is something you must see. There is something that must be explained."

Silexa could not move. She felt frozen, petrified to return to her own childhood nightmare.

"I will be with you." Ymber moved back to her sister's side. *"Come."*

Silexa slowly stepped forward, like walking in a dream. They traveled down hallways of amazing detail, still as beautiful as when it had all been new. A memory of running through the marble pillars in a soft, silk dress came to her mind, perfectly preserved and hidden even after all this time.

"Are we in the palace?"

"Southwick is built up of ruins upon ruins, higher and higher. We are not as underground as it would appear. They sealed this part away. All the windows are blocked by other walls." She turned and pointed to a crack in the foundation of the structure above. *"I hear rumbling every once in a while. I do not know what is near, but I don't believe anyone would enter here."*

Silexa thought of the room Bryant had placed her in the palace, hidden far from everything. It hadn't look anything like this. She'd always believed this place had been destroyed.

"This way." The hallway narrowed into an odd shape, like they were at the back of a staircase, but still they moved forward.

Silexa stepped into a dark room. A strong wind whistled through and blew out the torch.

"Ymber," she whispered, her voice echoing around the room, but there was no answer. She took a few tentative steps down a circular staircase.

All at once, a, blue veins of light appeared in patterns across the floor, each moving in a different direction, each with its own purpose. The lines formed into the shape of mountains—her mountains, shooting up to the sky. Suddenly, the whole room was alight with strands of energy. Where the final point ended, there was a broken platform.

She had stood there as a little girl—right there on that platform. That was where the lightning had struck her, burning with a curse.

Silexa looked around again, envisioning her sisters standing with her. She remembered the excitement of a loving father presenting his daughters with such wonderful things. It was so beautiful—the fantastic medallion their father had fashioned out of the stones he'd found.

The vision melted away when she saw Ymber again standing on a platform to her left, just as she had eighteen years before.

"The stones must return here."

"But it's too dangerous. The magic is too strong when we are together."

"This is where the magic took us, changed us. Do you remember?"

"Of course." Silexa wiped the tears off her face.

Ymber moved to the center of the star. *"I am imprisoned here, sealed here. When you leave, I will be alone and immortal again. I shall go mad without you."*

"No." Silexa moved to her. "No. Come with me."

"I cannot," Ymber returned, sad but tearless. *"You know I am gone. I long to move onward."* She looked into Silexa's eyes. *"Rescue me."*

The plea was too much and Silexa broke down. It was like having her sister die again, only this time she was the cause.

"The stones can reunite here in this room. If all the stones come here, we can be free from the curse."

"But what will happen to us?" Silexa asked again. "Will I die?"

"Death will bring you here. Something must be done. Please help me. Promise me."

Through her weeping, she could see the torture in her sister's face. "Yes," she whispered. "I will."

CHAPTER TWENTY-FIVE

EXODUS

Ferra and Micah continued on their journey, with Browneyes accompanying them. The landscape changed gradually from the thick forest to rolling foothills and sparsely clustered trees. Small ravines connected the groves with sweeping, scalloping valleys.

Micah decided to climb the last tall tree in the forest, right before the woodland disappeared into endless hills, to take a look around. "I see it!" he yelled from the highest branch. "I see tall, white stone far in the distance."

Ferra sighed in relief. It had been a long journey traveling in the forest; she had nearly given up the idea of finding anything else. She turned to see Browneyes sprawled out on a limb high in the tree. "Sorry for doubting you."

Browneyes smirked in satisfaction. "I said I would help you."

Ferra grimaced. "Yes, I know." The remark was a painful reminder that she still mistrusted the Louving, even after saving Micah's life and guiding them on the right path. But over the past days since their midnight talk, a reliable relationship had formed between them, and she couldn't deny that the Louving had helped guide them here.

But now's the time, Ferra thought. It was time to separate from Browneyes.

"How long do you think it would take us to get to Southwick from here?"

Up in the tree, Browneyes shrugged. "We could be in the castle by tomorrow night."

"So, what now?" Ferra asked rather bluntly.

"I really like this tree, you know? There is something so calming about sitting high about everyone else. Don't you think, Micah?"

A muffled response came from above, but Ferra couldn't hear it. She felt herself losing patience. "Listen, you did what you said you would do. You brought us to Southwick. I think we can manage from here."

"I need you to help me find Reynolds. That was the deal."

"But I don't even know if he's there—"

"But he will be," Browneyes interrupted. "I can't believe how selfish you're being, Ferra of the Forrest. A daughter of the mighty Prolius should be considerate to those in need."

Ferra shook her head. "I'm not the selfish one. I never sought your company. I never asked for your help. I'm an excellent tracker and could've found my own way."

"Oh." Browneyes' eyebrow lifted. "Did I touch a soft spot?"

"We're done—Micah and I. We are going on without you."

"But we were such a nice company."

Ferra paced along the ground like a bear. "I can't trust you. I know you're here because of some selfish reason."

Browneyes' face grew sad. "So, we're not friends after all. That makes me so disappointed, Ferra."

"You couldn't get Reynolds to love you even if you tried. He's in love with Naomi."

Browneyes laughed. "No, I don't think so." She swung her leg over the branch and sat up. "How well do you know him, huh? I know all of his secrets. He could never love that girl; there's too much guilt."

Ferra thought over her words. She didn't know Reynolds as well as Browneyes might, but he didn't act like the bad guy she portrayed him as. "So, what's your plan? Now that we are uncovering secrets, how are you going to get Reynolds to love you?"

Something rustled in the trees behind her, perhaps footsteps. Ferra pulled out her knife and crouched behind a bush. She looked back to see that Browneyes had perked up, interested in the sudden approach of people. Higher, she saw Micah motioning with his arms.

Ferra crept forward through the bushes to the edge of a long drop. Through the hills lay some scattered rocks, caves, and shrubbery. Out from the closest cave came a dwarf, walking briskly with purpose, like a scout. He carried his axe out in front of him, looking very much as if he mistrusted the outside world, and hurried along to another hillock and disappeared. *What a strange sight.* "What is a dwarf doing out here?"

A minute later, the same dwarf ran across the grass back to the cave he had come from.

Ferra leaned over through the bushes and branches to see the other side of the hill.

"What do you think?" a voice behind Ferra startled her. It was Browneyes, followed by Micah.

"There's another cave below us." Ferra looked down at the hole in the ground. "It leads right underneath this tree here."

"Let's check it out, shall we?"

"But what if the dwarves come back?"

"What fun that will be." Browneyes was already moving down the slope. "You're an adventurous, spirited girl, and this is far better than arguing."

Conjectrix

Micah smiled as he passed, patting Ferra on the back. "Oh, happy joy! This is good news."

"Why do you say that?"

"The ground talks. Dwarves are friends of the ground. They can tell us news of Southwick. Do you not see this?"

Ferra hadn't thought about it. Her consuming thoughts of Browneyes had clouded her logic. She followed them down into the cave.

The opening was very tight. Browneyes and Ferra had to crawl, but Micah fit well enough. The tunnel wrapped around large roots from the tree above, then dropped suddenly, sloping downward.

Ferra tumbled down, landing on both Micah and Browneyes.

Browneyes shoved her. "Get off."

Micah adjusted and sat up. "Do you see it?"

"What?" Ferra asked, dusting herself off.

"The lights!"

The girls looked out across the vast space. Sure enough, little lights appeared, floating around in no particular pattern. They varied in size and color and brought a strange brightness to the large room they now found themselves in.

Browneyes stared in wonder. "They're fairies. Do you know how long I've wanted to see one of these?"

"I never thought you were the fairy sort."

"Just because I kill people and drink their blood doesn't mean I'm not a female, with girlish inclinations," Browneyes returned sarcastically. "Fairies are magic, like me. We come from the same root, like family in a way. I've never had family."

Ferra found this statement rather strange coming from the Louving, but kept her mouth shut.

Dirt fell from the slope. Someone was coming. The three of them quickly hid behind a root.

"Who's down here?" a voice shouted in the dark. It was a woman's voice, harsh.

No one said anything.

With a snap, the fairy lights illuminated brightly, revealing the entirety of the roots and undergrowth. It was an amazing maze, weaving in and out around colored leaves and nocturne flowers. The light was so bright that Ferra, Micah, and Browneyes squinted to see.

"Who are you?" the woman asked.

Ferra stepped out from her hiding place. "My name is Ferra—"

"Good Heavens," the woman interrupted. "What on earth are you doing here? A daughter of Prolius so close. Silexa was right."

"Silexa?" Ferra answered, astonished. "Do you know her?"

As their eyes adjusted to the light, a small staircase chiseled in the dirt became visible. A kind-looking dwarf woman came down to meet them. "Silexa is my friend. My name is Mother. We are in exodus from Southwick."

"Where is she?"

Mother moved down and stood before them. "Who are your friends?" she asked before continuing.

"Micah Shadower," she introduced. "And this is Browneyes, our . . . guide. We're traveling to Southwick."

Mother nodded in understanding. "As you should, but I ask you not to travel yet."

Near the opening, a few more dwarves appeared, checking out the cavern.

"Let us talk later," Mother stated, then lowered her voice to a whisper. "Please, can I ask for your help?"

"Of course," Ferra returned.

Micah bowed. "I am at your service."

All eyes turned to Browneyes, who looked occupied in thought. "Oh, yeah, sure. Love to."

"Thank you," Mother said, then began organizing the dwarves who'd just entered the cavern.

The number of dwarves surprised Ferra, like ants marching in an ant hill. Each family set up a little dwelling around in the roots. There were few provisions left, so she volunteered to find them food, taking Browneyes with her, while Micah helped set up the tents.

Ferra gathered berries and roots the dwarves could use for stew, along with charming a few rabbits for food.

"Doesn't that feel like cheating?" Browneyes commented, watching the rabbits run into the sack under their own free will.

"They know what they're doing. I don't keep it a secret from them."

Browneyes poked at the ground with a stick, not helping at all. "But what's the fun in that?"

Ferra stood, cinching up the sack. "You don't have to stay. I don't think Mother would mind if you left. There's nothing to benefit from here."

"Oh, I think you're wrong. This is actually a perfect opportunity."

"How's that?"

Browneyes picked a flower and blew on its petals. "The dwarves know a secret way into Southwick. What could be more perfect than that? We could be in the palace and no one would know."

Ferra had also thought about this. It was a good idea. "But why stay? You could leave now if you wanted."

"Stop trying to get rid of me." Browneyes walked forward, pointing the stick right at Ferra's heart. "You can keep a better eye on me if I stay, you know."

Ferra didn't much like the stick pointed at her, but as much as she disliked Browneyes with her, she had to admit, her point was valid. The Louving girl was too dangerous to let loose.

As they returned to the cavern, she glanced over once to see Browneyes smirking, all the while stroking the vials of blood— other people's blood—she wore around her neck.

CONJECTRIX

CHAPTER TWENTY-SIX
DEATH IN THE MUSUNGU

There were only five left from the original twelve: Thornock at the front, with Gunthar right behind; Therham and Gersham, the twins; and Bryant, bringing up the rear. Each was bruised and worn out from the trap they had walked into. The assassins had hit the company from behind and captured many. Regardless of the precautions Bryant had taken, no one emerged unscathed.

He winced, reflecting on the incident. His arm was now bandaged from where an arrow had pierced his flesh, but he felt very little pain. He felt fueled by Curtis' betrayal. In all the mayhem, Curtis had used his assassins as distractions to escape. He would not get another chance to do the same. Not ever again.

Mist spilled over everything it touched, and as the terrain began to slope downward Bryant tried to proceed with caution, listening for any sound that might reveal Curtis and his assassins.

An arrow whizzed through the air and pierced Thornock's shoulder.

"Thornock!" yelled Gunthar. Another arrow flew.

"Behind the trees!" Bryant ordered. The party moved quickly behind cover. Thornock struggled and fell to the ground.

"We can't see where they're coming from," Gersham whispered.

Bryant refused to give into the terror. "I think they're as blind as us. Gunthar, shield yourself and try to get to Thornock."

Gunthar, the mightiest of the dwarves, carried a large wooden shield. He braced himself and ran to where Thornock had toppled, and reached under the fallen man's arm, taking hold of his waist. An arrow hit the shield hard from the southern side but didn't penetrate it. With great effort, they made it back behind the trees.

Bryant examined Thornock's wound. It was deep, but he would live. He pressed the front of the dwarf's chest, feeling around. With one quick lurch, he pulled the tip out of his shoulder.

"Gunthar?" he asked, but the stout dwarf was already ripping a long piece of cloth from his tunic to fasten a bandage.

Bryant lowered his voice to a whisper. "We cannot stay here. I need you to you lead the others down into the swamp. I'll try to track down the assassin. The arrows are coming from the right. I think they're close enough to see us."

Without a word, Gunthar gathered the twins, lifted his shield, and moved downward. The arrows again began to fly. Bryant's keen eye tried to follow the trajectory to locate the source.

"Linger here, my friend," Bryant instructed Thornock. "Catch up with us after I draw away the fire."

Thornock's breathing was heavy. "Yes, my lord."

Bryant positioned his ear to the trees. With caution, he crept around a cluster, toward the direction of the arrows.

The mist parted in swirls as he ran. He caught a glimpse of the black and red suit of one of Curtis' assassins. The fog kept him from the archer's sight until he locked eyes with Bryant. An arrow flew through the air, hitting the tree next to him.

CONJECTRIX

Bryant swiped at the tangled moss and trees with his sword, trying to reach the man as fast as he could. Another arrow came at him, nicking his wrist as he swung his sword to block it. He inched closer as the henchman reached for another arrow. With a blow to the head from the hilt of his sword, Bryant knocked him out.

Kneeling on the man's back, he tied his hands together, using the bands around the assassin's own wrists. After securing them, he scanned the area him for any other sign of attack.

A heaving wind blew by, sucking the mist in and out as if the swamp drew breath. All went silent. An eerie stillness penetrated the air, like something had died.

Bryant looked around, holding fast to his sword, unable to shake the feeling that he was being watched. Someone was hiding, waiting for him to make a mistake. He wouldn't give Curtis the satisfaction. He looked hard for the black and red uniform, but the fog only increased.

The air began to swirl, startling Bryant. He jumped back, preparing to strike. The face of a man appeared, his eyes piercing into Bryant's soul, then vanished.

Another trick of the mist. Bryant didn't know what to make of it. He moved toward where the face had appeared, jabbing with his sword, but there was nothing. He swiped again and the mist exploded around him, swirling so frantically his eyes couldn't follow.

"Run!" he heard from beyond his sight. Gunthar.

Bryant turned to follow the voice, but a mist-like barrier formed around him. He hacked at it with his sword, but it only solidified, thick and impenetrable.

Shouting filled his ears. Bryant pressed against the barricade of fog, forcing his shoulder through. Thick pressure squeezed against his chest, the mist blocking every chance he had.

The face returned. It appeared first in the wall, then slowly drifted away, watching him. The sunken eyes looked hollow and skeletal; strings of hair fell down to disembodied shoulders.

Bryant stood, prepared for anything the Musungu had created.

"Go back," it said in a whisper that rang in his ears.

"Who are you? What do you want of me?"

"You are intruders in our home."

Bryant thought fast on his feet. "We're searching for a girl. She is all we need."

"Go back."

"Not without her." Bryant was firm in his defiance. "Tell me who you are."

A strange smile moved across the specter's face. *"Shivra, Older of Nightshade. We are the cursed and the poisoned. Leave now and you will not be harmed."*

"What will harm us?"

"The curse. The poison. The Musungu is well-prepared for predators like you, searching for magic that is not yours."

Bryant thought quickly. "The curse is not of your making. I know how to lift it."

"What you speak is impossible. The Musungu is forever."

"No, it is possible. The girl is the key. If you're protecting her, give her to me. She is part of the puzzle."

Shivra's ghostly head stared down Bryant, neither anger nor humor in his expression. His glare felt like ice moving down Bryant's spine, but this was not the time to fall prey to cowardice.

". . . and I give you my word," Bryant added in a rush. His shoulders hunched. "If what I say is not true, you may keep my soul."

CONJECTRIX

The face smiled grimly. *"Your word is as good as death."* And with that, a shot of mist pierced Bryant in the hand.

Bryant winced, feeling the burn spread throughout his hand. He dropped his sword to shake it out.

"You are poisoned," Shivra said with great satisfaction. *"That is your promise. The poison will kill you and you will return here to live out eternity as a lost soul. You are bound to the curse. Now, it is up to you."*

The burning continued through Bryant's arm and into his chest. He let out a gasp as it penetrated his heart and began pumping through his veins. It accelerated like a rush of hot liquid filling every inch of his body. He felt like he was melting, but his limbs wouldn't move. Sweat dripped down his brow and burned every pore. He saw white and then—

... nothing.

❈   ❈   ❈

Vespa led Zander around the briars to a peninsula out of sight from the shouting. The faces were starting to take a clear interest in the strangers who had entered their domain.

"Hold on to me," she said as they neared the water. She held out her hand and moved onto the surface. Again, it did not splash. Zander looked closely and saw her grasping the medallion tightly, speaking so low he could barely hear her.

"Zander, do not look at them," Vespa whispered once they had finished crossing, referring to the faces in the mist.

He moved his eyes to her hand instead.

"The more you look at them, the uglier they appear. That's when they get angry. Make it seem like you take no interest in them. They should leave us alone."

Zander obeyed and stood up straight, striding with confidence with Vespa at his side. The mist swirled around them, the eerie feeling of being watched following him as they worked through the muddy patches and clusters of briar. Soon the feeling began to disappear—only to be filled with new sounds of horror.

"Are you ready to help me now?" Curtis was saying with a sneer in his voice. "Or would you like the same fate?"

"Please. Stop. I've tried." It was Brandell.

Zander stopped in place. What was happening?

"Try harder. I could add another scar to his face. It might improve it. But what is the use? I think the water might help his complexion."

"No! Don't!" Brandell yelled. "The fairies won't answer. I can do nothing else."

Curtis laughed. "Well, then I guess I have no need for either of you."

"No!" The shout was not Brandell's or Hix's or even Curtis's—it was Zander's.

Vespa quickly moved out of sight, dragging Zander with her, but anger rushed through him. He hadn't felt that way in a long time and needed to act before the energy inside consumed him. He fought Vespa's grasping hands.

"Trust me," she whispered.

All went quiet at the water's edge. Zander craned to see what was happening.

Vespa crouched down and pulled out her medallion. She began rubbing it as her lips made a sad buzzing sound. The buzz turned into a hum, the hum into music.

All around them, things were changing. Something took over the music and carried it through the mist. It was unlike anything Zander had ever heard, a melancholy sound he could feel in his heart. It made him sad and wistful. He didn't like it, but he couldn't pull himself away either.

The whole swamp knew the music and joined in—swaying with the wind that blew with the harmonies, like breathing in life. The air no longer smelled of thick, stagnant muck, but of jasmine on a hot day, a strange and wonderful phenomenon.

Zander felt the music inside him, like he was a part of it. It filled his breath and pushed him up. He could no longer stay put and walked forward, entranced by the feeling inside him. From behind a large stump, he could see everything.

Curtis stood with two of his assassins who each held a dwarf captive—Brandell and Hix. The mist swirled around them.

"What is this trick?" Curtis swiped at one of the faces. "Who are you?"

The faces gave no reply.

The wind picked up again with heavy breaths, heaving and blowing. Hot wind, not the same as the sweet jasmine breeze, pushed and pulled with each breath. It took Zander by surprise and knocked him to the ground.

Curtis spotted him immediately.

Zander tried to get up but slipped around in the mud.

Curtis pulled out his sword. He shouted, but the music and wind muffled his voice.

A small inlet of water lay between them. Zander quickly grabbed hold of the vines of the tree and crawled to his knees, anchoring himself as the wind pushed him with a strong downward force. He had a plan, though foolhardy; he acted from the heart, without thought.

Still grasping the vines, he tried to walk across the exposed trunk to stand between the land and the water. The wind grew even stronger with the consuming breath of magic, nearly pushing Zander down into the water.

Curtis had nearly reached him now. Zander felt trapped, like a sacrificial lamb.

"Well, the runt survived after all," Curtis sneered as he reached the inlet. Disdain emanated from his intense glare. His sword nearly reached Zander's throat. One good swipe could cut him clean open.

The wind increased once more, making everything move with its sway. Zander wrapped his hands around the vines, but the moss from the broken tree made everything slippery and he began to lose his footing. He saw the frustration in Curtis's face as he aimed the sword.

"You impudent boy!" Curtis yelled over the wind. "So valiant in your bravery, but you don't understand that you've already lost. Your precious Silexa is dead. UnderElm is taken—and you are the cause of it all."

It must be a trick, Zander told himself, but the words terrified him.

Another gust came, the strongest yet. This time, it succeeded in knocking him off the trunk. Zander's legs dangled freely in the air as he gripped tightly to the vines. Curtis also lost his balance but managed to slash a deep cut in Zander's leg.

Zander's scream of pain was drowned again in the music of the howling wind. It called his name, inhaling the warm breath of the living swamp and exhaling those it wished to help. It said it again, much closer. Zander turned and saw Vespa holding out her hand. She crept near the base of the tree, moving closer to help him.

But Curtis had seen her, too. Their eyes met, and his rage bubbled to the surface, the greed in him writhing as he spotted her medallion. He took one step closer, into the water.

That was all the faces needed—one act of defiance to incite their rage. The music changed into their screams, their faces melting into

271

hollow shades. The ghosts flew around in a frenzy of excitement, following the patterns in the wind.

Curtis hurriedly backed out of the water, but not before the rushing cyclone returned. He frantically patted himself dry, but the water burned and sizzled underneath his skin.

"We have to move." Vespa's yell was barely audible above the howling. The cyclone moved swiftly with terrible force, pulling them both closer to the water as the ghosts continued to swirl around.

Zander grabbed her arm and tried to inch back to land, but the wind was too strong. His grip slipped as the vines began breaking with the force.

"Hold on!" he heard Vespa yell, but with every breath of wind, he slipped more.

Curtis's leg was covered with enormous blisters. He yelled in pain as he tried to drag himself from the cyclone, digging his sword deep into the mud and holding on for dear life. The cyclone wrapped around his legs, sucking them dry. Curtis screamed at the intensity of the pain and lost his grip, falling into the cyclone and disappearing into dust.

Zander, still struggling to hold on, looked on in horror. He watched the top of Curtis's hat disintegrate in the air. At last, satisfied with its kill, the cyclone began to die down and move away from the shore.

But the wind was still strong and Zander's arms were about to give out. His body waved like a flag over the water.

Vespa held Zander as tight as she could, but she, too, was slipping in the mud and moss. From behind, hands grabbed her around her waist and pulled her away. Zander looked up to see four dwarves helping her. Two moved forward and grabbed Zander just as her grip failed. At last, they were pulled out from the tree and away from the water.

At first, Zander didn't understand what had happened, but looking around, he recognized the dwarves immediately: Thornock was hurt but determined; Gersham, Therham, and Gunthar all looked well enough.

Vespa looked at Zander's leg. "Oh, the cut looks deep. Here." She pulled a silk scrap from her pouch and fastened it tight around his calf. "Better?"

Zander nodded.

"Where are Brandell and Hix?" Thornock yelled. Zander pointed in the direction and two of them left to find the others.

"W-where's Bry-ant?"

Gunthar looked around and shook his head. "We left him to deal with the archer. We got lost in the mist until the howling started. I thought he would be here."

The wind was changing while they spoke. Vespa had risen to her knees and was singing again. The breaths of the wind changed back to hums.

"What is she—" Gunthar started, but Zander stopped him.

Lights began to appear all around them—on the briars or Jushery shrubs, as well as the flower in Zander's vest pocket. The lights floated closer to Vespa, then disappeared as she buzzed her lips.

"What was that all about?" Thornock grumbled.

"Fairyspeak," came a voice from behind them. It was Brandell and Hix, standing with Therham and Gersham.

Brandell looked on in amazement at the lights. "She has asked them to find Bryant."

"Where are the assassins?" Gunthar asked.

"Gone," Gersham returned. "Took off after the cyclone came."

Zander embraced Brandell, then reached into his vest pocket and brought out the glowing flower that hid his beloved fairy. "S-she has m-missed you."

In tears, Brandell buzzed his lips, bringing out the fairy. She danced around, excited, and kissed him on the nose.

A bed of lights returned down the path, carrying the fallen Bryant. They laid him down on the trail. Vespa moved to him quickly, evaluating him. "He's been poisoned."

"By what?"

She looked at his hands. His veins were purple. "By the Nightshades—the stains of magic that find us so interesting."

Zander looked at Bryant, overwhelmed with guilt for endangering the mission that had led to this result. "Is he . . . ?"

Vespa shook her head. "I don't know. There is nothing I can do."

Little Lovely twirled close to Vespa's ear, whispering something to her.

Vespa frowned, turning to Zander. "She says she can fix it, if you'll let her. She wants to."

"Of course. Anything t-to save him."

"No." Brandell came forward. "I won't let her."

Vespa lowered her eyes to the fairy. "It's what she wants to do. She's excited to help."

Zander's excitement turned to sadness when he realized what she was going to do.

Little Lovely kissed Zander's nose, then fluttered over to his ear. "I have a secret. Do you want to know what it is?"

A tear dripped out of the corner of his eye and rolled down his cheek. He nodded.

She fluttered over a few of the Highthorn flowers, then moved to his palm, dropping in a little seed. "A gift for you. Highthorns will always protect you. Carry this with you on your journey and plant it by something you love." She fluttered away but came back to his other ear.

"Saving your prince will save you. My secret—I will live within him. You will see. My last gift to you."

She flew away again to Brandell. He would not accept this as easily as Zander, but after a moment of tears, he agreed to let her go.

Little Lovely danced around the others before resting back on Vespa's hand. Rubbing her stone, Vespa sang a sweet, melancholy tune.

The little fairy spun around until it looked as though she'd fallen asleep. Vespa's song changed, moving the fairy very fast and changing her back into a flower spinning in the air, a beautiful purple liquid inside.

Vespa fell silent. The heavy breaths of the Musungu also grew quiet in solemn remembrance of the sacrifice Little Lovely had just offered. Though the song ended, the hum remained, filling the souls around the new little flower. Vespa lifted it out of the air and raised it to Bryant's lips. The nectar ran down his throat, filling his body and soul.

A minute passed with no reaction, but soon his skin began to return to his olive complexion. His eyes flickered open and he looked around at everyone staring at him.

Bryant sat up. "Did I miss something? And what in bloody blazes are these things?" He motioned to the fairy lights around him, which quickly disappeared.

He struggled to his feet and spotted Zander, a great big grin stretching across his face. He grabbed him around the shoulders. "I knew you would do it. You did it!"

He caught sight of Vespa next and picked her up, too, in his mighty grasp. "Zander is amazing! I knew he would find you."

Zander smiled. "Meet Vespa."

Bryant swung her back and placed her on her feet. "Very nice to meet you." He bowed. "I am very much in love with your sister."

CONJECTRIX

Vespa seemed less than impressed with all of this, frowning at Zander. "Is he always like this?"

"No."

Bryant checked his neck and his hand. "I feel different. Happier, and strangely warm inside."

No one wanted to bring up what they had just witnessed. In time, the truth would come out.

The mist again began to thicken around them.

"We need to leave here," Vespa ordered. "Before the Nightshade get curious."

Bryant returned to his tough persona. "Of course, yes. Do you know of a Shivra?"

Vespa's face paled. "Shivra did this to you?"

Bryant furrowed his brow, as if it were difficult to remember. "I . . . I had to fix it or . . . or I would return here and I would remain here forever."

"So, what has Little Lovely done, if not fixed this?" A teary-eyed Brandell asked. "Was her sacrifice all for nothing?"

Vespa shook her head. "Good will come from her sacrifice, but we will have to wait and see what will happen. Shivra always makes good on his promises."

"Sorry," Bryant said. "Will someone explain how I've upset everyone?"

Zander wiped away his tears. "On the way."

"Yes, all right," Bryant agreed, rather confused. "Lead on, then."

CHAPTER TWENTY-SEVEN
THE SPRINGS

Landon set out with Wenlock to acquire provisions, as well as to learn how the instruments worked. Landon looked through endless calculations that, if entered correctly, would show him people or destinations. It was incredibly fascinating, and completely complicated. The exercise helped him gain respect for his energetic, if not a little eccentric, uncle.

Mae provided meals and light, pleasant conversation. It was obvious that she was not keen on the idea of Wenlock leaving with Landon, but she never sought to change his mind; she only wanted to support and love him.

When morning came, Landon felt anxious. He needed to get to Katia if he could and rescue her from whatever danger Wenlock predicted. This nonsense had diverted their mission and he felt pressure to get back. Landon liked Briggs Ravenmoor—really liked him—and wanted to trust him for Katia's sake, but it was clear now that there was more going on than he was saying.

There was also something about Lottie that bothered him and he couldn't put his finger on what it was. Lottie knew secrets—specifically,

CONJECTRIX

the charge he and Katia had about finding Naomi's sister of the water. Landon had a suspicion she would tell anyone anything if it played to her favor.

Up in the Observatory, Wenlock was ready. He had dressed for an adventure with a large brimmed hat, tall tan boots with creative buckles and pockets, and a sash fashioned with all manner of knives, potions, and such.

Landon had what he'd come with; his pack full of new food, his sword, his magic, and his wits. "Got enough there, Wenlock?"

"You may mock until I save your life with my exploding bag of tricks."

"Well-noted."

Both of them gave a swift kiss to Mae as they left. Wenlock led him down a staircase that looked much like the others, but when he opened the door, leaves assaulted them. Green branches filled the view. Landon looked down, which he shouldn't have done. "You live in a tree house?"

"Of course." Wenlock began moving a contraption that would lower them down. "How else could I get this view?" He smiled as he walked onto a platform in the middle of a cluster of branches. "You coming?"

Landon hesitated a moment, then stepped onto the platform. Wenlock slowly began pulling on a rope, which jolted at each movement. Everything slowly eased downward. There were no sides on the platform to hold them in, which was rather disorienting—like descending through the sky. Landon moved over to one of the ropes and held on as best he could, clinging for his life.

Down and down they went from the daunting height.

"How in the world did you make your home up here?"

"Oh, I've lived here a long time." That was Wenlock's only response.

The massive trunks of the jungle were a thing of beauty, unnatural and full; any sounds were absorbed in the thick wood.

The platform landed on a soft mound and Wenlock and Landon leapt off. Slowly the platform began to wind back up the tree.

"Is that the only way up to your home?" Landon asked, watching as the platform disappeared.

"Of course not. It's just the fastest." Wenlock situated his pack and looked through a tiny lens. "Well, my boy, let's see what adventure waits us!" And he strode out into the jungle.

Landon followed his uncle through the trapping, claustrophobic trees, watching his erratic movements with a careful eye. A few times, Wenlock ducked behind trees, hiding from something. Landon didn't know what to make of it and stood there in the open, unsure if he, too, should hide. This happened multiple times and Landon soon followed.

After a brief time crouching behind a bush, Landon cleared his throat. "So, what exactly is out there?"

Wenlock shushed him but turned. "Stupid little creatures tell the trees everything."

"Where are we headed?"

"We need to head to the waterfall and find LeAndra."

"LeAndra? Who is—?"

Wenlock shushed him again. "You never know who's listening."

Landon kept silent, without a clue of where they were going or what they were doing.

Their surroundings changed from the thick jungle trees to a lean, willowy forest. The ground softened against their weight. Wenlock jumped around the grassy soft patches like a toad, avoiding leaving his footprints. Landon tried to do the same but failed, expelling so much effort, he felt like a buffoon.

It was afternoon when a trickle of water finally filled their ears.

CONJECTRIX

Rocks became boulders and grass became stone. A small stream lined a path down the rocks.

Wenlock rubbed his hands with joy. "We're close."

"Where?" Landon still couldn't see a river or waterfall.

But Wenlock didn't answer. He motioned for Landon to follow him around a rocky slope, nimble as a rabbit. The trees slanted sideways, pushing out from the hilly ground. Landon struggled to follow, trying to find a hold in the bendable trees. He twisted around and found a black rock jutting out of the mountain, slick and smooth.

Wenlock stood with his hands outstretched, feeling around the grooves. He pressed on the stone and placed his ear to it, and listening. "Nope," he muttered to himself.

He shuffled down the wall, listening and feeling around. He stopped again and smiled. "Ha ha!" He gave a happy dance, grabbing a purple pouch tied to his sash and opening it. Reaching in his hand, he pulled out a handful of black dust with silver flecks in it.

With a flick, he tossed some of the dust in the air. It looked like smoke rising until Wenlock gently blew on the cloud. The particles drifted around the rock, the silver flecks sticking to the mountainside. It was an amazing illusion, the shimmering outlines in the cracks visible like an opening in the wall—a wall that wasn't really there.

"Ready?" Wenlock asked excitedly.

Landon looked at the illusion. Magic wasn't new to him, of course, but it was always amazing. "I guess so." He wasn't sure what he should be ready for, so he just shrugged.

Wenlock walked right in and disappeared.

Landon reached out to feel the wall that shouldn't be there and stumbled head-first into the cave.

"You coming?" Wenlock hollered back impatiently.

Landon picked himself up. "Yes."

Wenlock snapped his fingers and a small blue flame appeared.

"Are those Sunsparks?"

"Close—moon sparks. Not so bright, you know." Wenlock moved forward and held out the light.

Landon followed him down the tight cave the best that he could. The moonsparks dimly lit the space in front of Wenlock. Landon couldn't see the protruding rocks above and smacked his head a few times. He progressed at a crouch with his hands outstretched just in case. His uncle got ahead of him with the light and the dark shadows stretched out. Moisture in the air covered his fingers as he felt his way on.

Up ahead, he saw his uncle stopped at the opening of an archway, looking beyond it, into a vast space.

Landon moved to stand by his uncle when he felt a small whiz of air next to him. He grabbed at his ear and felt wetness. He grabbed Wenlock and forced him down. "Someone is attacking," he whispered.

"What nonsense." Wenlock tried to straighten up, but then another whiz came at them and they both ducked. "Oh."

Landon took cover behind a tall shield of rocks. The light faintly reflected off the walls. Straining, he could see the reflection of a pool of water with tiny streams flowing in and out.

"LeAndra!" Wenlock's voice echoed around the cavern. "It is I, Wenlock Brighton, at your service." He tried to get up. "Please, we are here seeking your assistance." Another assault flew at him and splashed next to his feet.

"Leave, Wen," a soft female voice echoed. "We have been betrayed."

Another blast hit next to Landon and he steadied himself.

"No, my lady." Wenlock tried to walk forward. "It was not us." This time he was hit square in the face.

CONJECTRIX

Landon ran forward to his uncle, stopping in surprise. Instead of a bloody, horrible mess, Wenlock was soaked with water from head to toe. He rubbed the moisture from his eyes.

"Will you please stop throwing water at us?" Landon shouted.

Silence fell—everything but the gentle trickling of the water.

Out stepped a girl in a dark hood, dripping with water. "Wenlock, you need to be careful. I'm warning you now to go away, back to Mae. I've been betrayed."

Landon studied the girl. "Are you the one who rescued me?"

The girl raised her arm again defensively. "A lot of good it did. I should have left you to die."

Landon moved toward her. "I'd like to thank you—"

More water jetted toward him.

"I have been betrayed." Her voice shook with anger. "And you know I have."

Wenlock stepped forward. "He doesn't know anything. He's been with me and Mae, like you asked."

"But his friends are here."

Landon squinted in the light of the moon sparks, searching for any resemblance. "Fontine?"

The girl froze. "I don't know what you are talking about."

"You're her. Aren't you? Your name is Fontine."

She stood, defiant. "That is a dangerous name and I pray you not to use it."

Landon fell to his knees, crumbling with relief. "I came here to find you."

The girl's defenses went back up as she retreated into the water. "See, Wen? See? He has betrayed us. He has used us!"

"What?" Landon rose up once more. "No I haven't."

"Don't trust him," she warned Wenlock. "He has magic. He will use it against you."

"I have not seen any magic."

"I have seen it," LeAndra insisted. "He called out to me. That was how I found him. He is a trickster."

Landon had heard enough of all these accusations. "Let me explain," he tried, but she hit him with a blast of water, stinging with icy cold.

He had had enough. Landon ran toward her. She had no time to react and within seconds Landon had grabbed around her waist, preventing any further attack.

Wriggling, LeAndra broke free of his hold, smashing him with a wall of water. Landon pushed her down, and both went splashing into the pool.

"Stop!" Landon shouted between thrashes. He tried to pin her arms, but she was fast and slipped out of the grip in time to punch him in the jaw. "I'm friends with Ferra! Your sister! I've come to find you!"

The words caused the girl to freeze mid-punch, her fist suspended in the air. "What did you say?"

"You know what I said." Landon bit back his anger, rubbing his jaw. It stung a little, but she had been too frantic to put much power behind it.

"What do you know about Ferra?"

"I know that she has a mean right hook." Landon remembered the blow he'd received after he tortured one of the mole creatures in the Durundin. "Like you. Did you teach her that?"

LeAndra half-smiled but still seemed suspicious. "Nobody calls me Fontine. The name gives me away. Why are you here?"

Landon's shoulders fell with a sigh of relief. He gave her a spontaneous hug, while she stood rigid and alarmed. "I have a lot to explain, but I don't have time right now."

He pulled back. "And what did you mean I betrayed you? You don't even know me."

She studied him with her dark eyes. "You know me as Fontine."

"Yes, I figured it out." Landon struggled to put the puzzle together. "But I didn't when we wandered in here."

"How did you know where to find me?"

"I didn't."

Wenlock stepped forward through the shadows. "That would be my fault. I sought out your help, my girl, because I knew you had the means to stop this."

LeAndra frowned. "I don't understand."

Landon turned to his uncle. He didn't understand either. "You knew she was a daughter of Prolius and didn't tell me?"

Wenlock just shrugged. "Mae has seen her—the one meant to kill you, LeAndra. The patterns confirmed it. We searched the numbers yesterday, and she is here."

Landon was even more confused than he had been before. "The numbers?"

LeAndra looked accusingly at Landon. "Did you bring her here?"

"Wait? Who is *her*?"

Wenlock shook his head. "She came with the Wanderer."

Landon's mind whirled. "Are you telling me Katia is going to kill her?"

"Not the red-head," Wenlock assured him. "But you saw the picture Mae drew. Somebody was keeping the secrets. It was there in the cover of her mouth. You saw it."

Landon nodded, still unclear of *what* he should remember about the picture.

"When we looked up the location for the girl in the picture, she wasn't there, but there was someone else, remember? Who was that someone?"

"I don't know!" Landon exclaimed in frustration. "I don't know what you're talking about."

LeAndra turned stone-like. "Mae saw her? She saw it happen, didn't she?"

Landon ran a hand through his hair, trying to clear his thoughts. "Okay, let me get this straight. Someone—some mystery girl—knows about LeAndra—knows she's . . . who she is. Knows she's here when nobody should know. So, someone who did know said something. Am I following?"

Wenlock ignored Landon's attempt at understanding and continued. "But you must know the patterns didn't match. Mae sketched what she saw and it wasn't the same as what I saw. The calculations and the vision always match, but this was different. She was older, much older than a little girl should be, with blond hair, if I remember."

"Are you talking about Lottie?" Landon asked. "I saw her in the eyeglass. She's just a little girl. But her hair is black."

Wenlock rummaged through the pockets on his boots and pulled out a piece of folded parchment. He gave it to Landon, who opened it carefully. LeAndra grabbed the corner to see.

This was a mistake. It had to be. The picture on the paper didn't look anything like Lottie, but he knew the face. He had seen it before. "I know her." Landon swore under his breath, flipping the page with his figure. "She's a Louving."

❊   ❊   ❊

Katia splashed her face with cold water from the river after scooping a large portion with her hand to drink. The water felt so good after so long in the humidity of the jungle. The days all blurred together now, with nothing in her sights but the trunks of the trees. But the river was what she wanted to see; the river was where she needed to go.

CONJECTRIX

To actually feel the river's water against her skin—it was the best feeling in the world. She wanted to jump in it and swim, but her furry companion, Floowdur, urged her forward.

"How much farther, do you think?"

"Spreengss isss close, my misses."

Katia stood again and began marching up the bank, following the bend in the river. In the distance, she spotted the Springs of Sephar. They were just as spectacular as Landon had said. Along the large mountain cliffs, the two rivers cascaded separately down until they pooled together and roiled out in one giant, rolling waterfall. The sight was breathtaking and caused Katia's mouth to drop.

"Missess!" Floowdur squeaked. She pointed to a big black ship near the bottom of the falls. The grumbear jumped back up around her neck. "Go bakk to da shadow, missss."

Katia hid in the security of the forest. She maneuvered through the trees, up around the banks where the ship had docked, staying out of sight.

"What do I do now?" she whispered to Floowdur.

The little creature gave no answer.

Katia squinted, trying to see any movement, but soon gave up. "I have to get closer. You don't have to come."

Floowdur scurried onto her back before Katia could tell her not to go.

"But if there's danger, I can't allow you to get hurt. You run away, back to Rroowden, okay?"

"Yesss . . ." She wrapped her tail around Katia like a scarf.

She inched forward, staying close to the trees and out of sight. The slick rock of the mountain became visible from the shore as it sloped upward. Because of the incline, climbing became difficult—trickier and slower—but she needed to stay hidden. A few rocks slid out from under her feet, but the thundering falls muffled the sound.

She edged around the slick mountain, close enough that the front of the ship grew visible. But then, a sound echoed around the slick black walls, nearly making her fall. It was a scream—a girl's scream—Lottie's scream.

The sound startled her and her footing slipped. A rock tumbled down to the water's edge and made a large splash. Katia scrambled back up the slope, hiding. Her hands ached as she held to the rock, her heartbeat tripling.

She closed her eyes, trying to talk to her magic, just in case she needed it. The delicate white light danced behind her eyelids, ready to play. It flashed around in its excitement—a warning.

Katia flicked her eyes open and peeked around the corner. Someone's head move below her in the forest. It was only one, but she knew he wouldn't be alone.

"Stop!" a shout came from the background, somewhere she couldn't see. "Too far. The boulder fell here."

Katia tried her best to become invisible.

A head looked up to where Katia hid. "Well, hello there."

Katia reacted without thought. The rocks cascaded down, carrying her along with them. She reached out her hands and grabbed the man's face. The soldier screamed as the icy touch instantly froze his expression. As she stood, trying to ground herself again, she saw the other soldier running through the trees, swinging his sword toward her.

She dodged behind a tree as the blade cleaved into the wood, narrowly missing her head. The soldier followed with another swing, but she ducked again just in time.

Floowdur jumped from her neck and dived at the soldier's face, scratching and biting. He squealed and tried to rip the animal from his body. The distraction gave Katia a chance to run.

Her instincts told her to go near the shore. She was in the open and it wouldn't take long for someone to spot her. More soldiers were making their way toward her from the ship, some cutting directly through the water.

There was no escaping it; she had to fight. As soon as she reached the water's edge, she placed her hands to the surface. Ice crystals spread rapidly through the water. The soldiers struggled to move their limbs as the magic trapped them. Others slipped on the icy surface

Katia seized the moment and, with a running start, slid across the ice, closer to the ship. Her new plan: find her father, save Lottie, and steal the ship, making her escape on water.

She slid past a frozen soldier and neared the bank. Three large men stood with their swords ready. Speeding ahead, she braced herself for impact as she crashed into the middle guard, knocking down the others. Katia leapt forward and grabbed the rope tying down the anchor. She began climbing, but her grip grew cold and she slipped. She tried again but failed. The rope wouldn't work; she had to get to the plank leading up from the water.

Below her, the fallen men struggled to their feet. Katia dropped and kicked, making one stumble back again. Another grabbed her around the leg. She reached for his neck. He drew back and she wiggled free of his loosened grip and fled.

"Get her!"

Katia ran up the gangplank and hopped aboard.

Stars of ice shot out from her hands, hitting two henchmen who had advanced on her. One staggered and she kicked him overboard. The other grabbed his face and sank to the deck.

The rope to the anchor was only a few feet away. She ran to it, grabbed her knife from her boot, and started cutting as fast as she could. Without the anchor she could get away. They would be free.

From the corner of her eye, she saw soldiers advancing. She tried blasting them with whatever her magic could. Her freezing touch wasn't working. Katia tried again to blast out her magic, but she felt assailants surrounding her.

A hand grabbed her arm and held tight. The pain made her drop the knife as she turned to see the large leader from the Southwick Army—the very one from whom she and Landon fled so many times before.

"Game's up, girlie." He spit as others laughed.

Katia flailed against him, but her strong will was nothing compared to his bulk, and she crumbled at his grip.

"Tia!"

Katia turned to catch a brief glimpse of Briggs in the corner, struggling, before being knocked in the head and collapsing to the deck in a daze.

"No!" Katia yelled and fought harder to get free. In her tangled position, she pushed against the bulkhead for leverage and managed to knock another soldier down. The leader slammed her head against the bulkhead. Katia lost focus, the ringing in her ears blocked out any other sound. Greenish outlines of people blurred into each other as she strained for sight. Blood streamed down her cheek. She felt another smack against her face and fell to the ground.

Soon arms surrounded her, holding her tight, pinning her hands behind her.

"Commodore, who is that?" Lottie's sweet voice broke through the ringing.

"Lottie," Katia gasped through the pain. "Are you hurt? Are you okay?"

She felt a gentle hand take hers. "Yes, I'm fine."

Katia squeezed it for comfort. Her vision was clearing; definition was returning. She could see Lottie standing before her, reaching forward to Katia's temple to wipe off some of the blood.

She heard laughter but didn't know why.

"We need her alive," the commodore said. "Don't be getting any ideas. She's for Reinoh, not for you."

Lottie just smiled sweetly. "He wouldn't know the difference."

"Her life is not your decision." The commodore pushed others forward, dragging Katia to where her father lay and dropping her in a heap.

Lottie only stared at Katia with indifference before looking back to the soldiers. *What happened to her?* Katia wondered. *What did they do to her?*

Through the confusion and pain, Katia felt the warmth of her father's fingers. She grabbed his hand and clung to him and cried.

CHAPTER TWENTY-EIGHT
THE WATER WHEEL

A piercing scream reached Landon's ears. He recognized it immediately and began running.

"Wait!" Wenlock shouted. "Wait for the old man."

Landon skittered to a stop. "She's here, Wenlock. It's Kat." He began trotting again.

"Think," Wenlock shouted after him. "You need a plan, you headstrong idiot!"

LeAndra, who had been right behind Wenlock, began running also.

As Landon moved along a ridge on the cliff-side, a dark ship became visible. He stopped. "We'll never get down there in time," he panted. "She doesn't know that Lottie's a Louving. She loves that little girl. That stupid girl!"

"Will her magic help?" Wenlock asked.

"Her magic? No. It's crazy."

LeAndra caught up to them. "Who's crazy? The girl or the Louving?"

"The girl, Kat. Her name is Katia. That was her scream. I've heard it enough to have it burned in my memory."

"What kind of magic does she have?"

"Ice," Landon answered off-handedly as he strained to see what was happening aboard the ship. "It was her handiwork when you found me nearly frozen to death."

LeAndra looked impressed. "She did that? Ice is really complicated. The patterns are hard to manage. Does she have good focus?"

Landon had never considered it. "She could improve, probably."

"Is she quick on her feet?"

"Yes, absolutely."

"We'll have to trust her instincts, then. Follow me."

❄ ❄ ❄

Katia's heart was broken. Lottie had betrayed her. She felt as if the wind had been knocked out of her, her mind spiraling with disbelief. Everything else fell away, all sound disappearing, as she was buried under a mountain of guilt and humiliation. She should have never left Landon behind.

Shaking. Someone was shaking her knee. She looked down and found her father trying to get her attention. A voice called out. Someone was talking to her.

"I don't care," she said to no one.

"But you will." Lottie's voice pierced her. "There's more you care about than just the little girl."

Katia looked up and stared into the face. It was all wrong. The brightness and glow in her eyes was replaced with a sharp glint of amusement. "Who are you?"

Lottie laughed. "Harrow sends his love."

Harrow. The mention of the Lord of the Underground sent heat through Katia's veins. His shriveled, withered face stood out behind her eyelids, the snowy lion rampaging on him before he vanished, before the bridge collapsed.

"You're a Louving," Katia's lips barely uttered the sound.

An evil laugh confirmed it. Mist rose from the water and surrounded little Lottie, and before Katia's eyes, she vanished. In her place was a tall, thin woman with sharp, angled features. Her ears pointed slightly, less severely than her chin, but couldn't be hidden by her long blonde hair, wound tightly in a braid.

There was nothing left that resembled Lottie at all. The menacing eyes remained.

"Why would you do such a horrific thing?"

The Louving smiled. "My name is Fronzi, like it's of any interest to you. I thought I might mention it, in case you ever need to explain how you got captured or how your father died."

She flipped her hair as if she didn't care much about the conversation. "As for the little girl, I'll tell you the truth, if it makes you feel better." She looked Katia square in the eye. "Children are the easiest to trap. They're so trusting and gullible and scared. She was so scared. She spilled the most amazing secrets—"

"And you still—?" Katia couldn't finish.

Fronzi's mouth turned down a little. "This is business, girlie. Your friend gave me an opportunity."

Katia's chest heaved with emotion. "Why her?"

"Oh, I think you know why." Fronzi reached around her neck and pulled the little bag of trinkets. "She had a secret as well, you know. You were too consumed in your own world to realize what this girl was about to do."

"What do you mean?"

Fronzi held up her hand. Lottie's beautiful ring slipped onto her slender fingers. "Do you know what this does?"

Katia blinked in surprise. "It reveals secrets."

CONJECTRIX

Fronzi laughed. "She showed me in the tavern how it worked. The moment I put the ring on and touched her little hand, I knew all about you and your boyfriend's plans. I also learned something else—something I was very pleased to know. I learned where the blond is."

Katia's attention flickered. "Who?"

"The blond you so desperately tried to protect in the Echoes—the one Harrow was looking for. I found her."

"How?"

Fronzi reached in the pouch and pulled out the small purple marble. "This. You must have been too stupid to know what this is or you would've never let the girl near it."

Katia stared at her, stunned. Fronzi was right.

"This travels far distances—through mountains and time. Your little darling could see others in the bead. I believe she thought she might get in trouble if she told you, so she kept it from you. I saw her talking to it before I approached her in the kitchen. I snatched it from her dying hands."

Tears reformed in Katia's eyes.

"Did it ever occur to you the little girl might have known what you are?" This time it was her father that spoke.

Fronzi's cold smile disappeared.

"Don't you think she was communicating it to the others?"

The Louving grabbed Katia's knife from the floor and came close to Briggs, holding it dangerously close to his throat. "Why would I care?"

"You think your crimes will go unpunished?"

She flicked the knife and a small drop of blood trickled down his neck. She caught it up on her pinky and licked it. "I don't need you alive, you know. Just the girl."

The knife twisted again in her hand as she moved it toward his heart.

But the rumble of the falls sounded closer than before and stayed her hand.

Fronzi turned her attention to the sound. "Is it supposed to do that?"

Katia couldn't believe what she was seeing. The falls had grown in size, nearly triple what she remembered. The amount of water coming into the river created wave after wave, rocking the large ship and knocking a few soldiers off their feet.

Katia seized the opportunity and froze the binding cords around her hands, breaking them with a swift jerk of her wrist. As the next wave hit, she scrambled to her feet and kicked Fronzi right in the chest. The Louving was startled but quick, and ran at her with the knife.

The next wave hit and knocked them down. The knife skidded across the deck. Fronzi grabbed Katia, sending them rolling with the rocking ship. Fronzi was a dirty fighter, tearing at her with her fingernails, scratching and biting, but Katia landed firm punches.

The knife slipped again as the boat rocked in the roiling waters, each girl scrambling to reach it.

The waves hit even harder, throwing a few of the soldiers overboard. Briggs wedged himself in a corner, bracing for each surge as the water crashed against the hull.

Katia lunged for the knife but got knocked off her feet and rolled. Fronzi almost had it until Katia kicked her in the mouth. The blood didn't seem to bother Fronzi, just made her more excited, more crazed.

Then suddenly, the sound of the crashing falls fell silent. The ship still rocked with the motion of the river, but it was steadying in the wind. Katia turned, distracted by the lack of noise.

The top of the falls still poured down, but the falling water never reached the river. Instead, it began winding back up in a continuous wheel, enlarging every second—and moving toward the ship. Seeing the ball of water, many of the soldiers jumped from the ship.

In Katia's distraction, Fronzi took grabbed the fallen knife. She slashed in a wide arc toward Katia's throat.

"Tia!" Katia turned to her father's voice. She had no time to react and reached her hand up to defend against the attack.

FLASH!

Fronzi stumbled backward, her own arm cut. A white, freezing wind whipped around her. The tiny shards of ice pierced her skin. Katia stood, hands outstretched as her magic bound the crazed Louving.

Again, her father's voice caught her attention. "Tia! The water!"

The wheel of water had moved directly over the ship. Torrents of water stormed down on them.

Katia released her magic and ran back to her father. Closing her eyes, she asked for protection. A layer of ice quickly encompassed the two just in time.

The massive wheel dropped on the ship, completely engulfing it.

Katia held tightly to Briggs as the raging water rolled over the ship, engulfing it with water. Bubbles rushed toward them as they watched within the frosted globe. There was nothing but cloudy blue water.

Cracks formed in the ice with each pounding. It began to melt from the onslaught. Katia tried to keep it sturdy, but the water still seeped in.

Then the ship began to steady and the continual blue of the water faded back to a bright gray.

A figure appeared, pounding on the ice until a deep crack formed. The ice shattered and the murky light of day came through.

"Kat!"

Katia felt herself lifted and held in a tight embrace. She was so frozen from the ice, the warmth of the body felt welcoming. Looking up, she saw Landon's angled jaw above her.

Elation swept through her. She threw her arms around his neck. "Glad to see you, too," he whispered in her ear.

She held him for what was probably too long but didn't care. "I thought I had killed you. How did you find us? Where's Fronzi?"

"The Louving? Probably downstream somewhere."

She let go and looked around her. There was no sign of the Louving or the other soldiers. Instead, she saw an old man and a young woman with warm blond hair and deep aqua eyes.

"I don't understand what happened." Katia squinted at the girl standing on the far side of the ship. "You found her, didn't you?"

"With the help from my uncle, here." He motioned to his side. "This is Wenlock."

Wenlock made an artful bow before returning his hat.

Landon brought her directly before the girl. "Katia, let me introduce LeAndra."

The girl stood as still as a calm sea and looked her square in the eyes, extending her hand. "Actually, it's Fontine."

Katia impulsively hugged her. "Thank you for saving my life."

"Hey! She had help!" Landon interjected.

Fontine moved back to get a better look at her. "It wasn't me. I could have easily killed you, but Landon assured me your magic was quick and you would know how to save yourself."

Unable to help herself, Katia retreated back in Landon's arms.

She heard a smile in his voice. "So, I'm guessing you don't hate me."

"Oh, no." Katia spoke into his chest, too embarrassed to meet his gaze. "I hated myself after I left. I've never felt worse in my life." Her tears began staining his shirt.

"Hush," Landon tried to calm her. "It was only the worst pain in my entire life and I nearly died. But saving your life makes up for it."

Through her tears, she saw the pain and sadness of the journey in his eyes, the ache of the separation and the betrayal of her leaving him to die.

"I'm so sorry—"

Landon leaned in and kissed her, silencing any further doubts. Whatever she needed to apologize for, it no longer mattered.

When he pulled away, Katia felt speechless.

"Not to ruin the party," Wenlock interrupted, "but I do see some floundering soldiers down there splashing about."

"Do you think this ship will still sail?" Landon asked.

"No problem." Briggs inspected the mast. "There might be a few repairs, but I have to hand it to the Monarchy for making one hell of a ship."

Landon grinned. "Good work. If we sail downstream for a while, we could drop off Wenlock—"

"I'm not going to leave now, my boy," Wenlock answered with dignity. "This is where the great adventure begins."

"I can't keep you with us. Mae would never approve."

Wenlock patted him on the back. "Good point my boy, good point. We'll need to be careful not to tell her." He winked before walking away to help Briggs.

Landon smiled and leaned into Katia. "Fontine doesn't know the story. I need you to tell her."

A thrill ran through her. Katia placed her hands on Fontine's and sighed. "I have a lovely story to tell you."

Fontine nodded. "I guess I have time to listen."

CHAPTER TWENTY-NINE
The Keeper

Naomi awoke from her wandering dreams, alone and confused. A small candle lit a corner of the hollow in the mountain. She lay her head against the jagged stone wall, still seeing Taren's face in her mind. He terrified her more than ever, the truth of his words crippling any will she had to flee. She knew Taren was right—her life would end here among those trapped in the River of Souls.

A bowl of cold broth sat near her. She'd dreamed of the broth, of warm honey filling her stomach and making the ache go away, but now she just stared, mesmerized by the flickering shadow of the candle on the liquid surface.

Her mind wandered to places it shouldn't, all as the Vivatera pulsed strong in her veins. It wanted out of her body. Something beyond Taren had scared it. Her magic throbbed painfully through her head and down her spine. There was no place to hide—not anymore.

No one came. No one checked on her. She sat alone in the silence with nothing but her thoughts to keep her company.

Slowly, a long shadow crossed the wall of the hollow where she was being held. Closer it approached, until it shrouded everything around it in shadow, casting a frightening image of a man. Little by little, the prominent face became more apparent and more frightening. This face was etched into her dreams, haunting her memories, with a murder she'd witnessed at such a tender age.

Naomi's anger rose, her magic pained at his presence. She tried to stand but didn't have the will.

"Well, well," Lockwood sneered as he stood before her. "Aren't you an elusive little bird? Malindra's darling pet."

Naomi couldn't say anything. Fear held her tongue.

"Time solves everything, don't you think? With time and reflection, every mystery can be solved." He laughed, a sound that made her spine tingle. "Do I make you nervous?"

Naomi didn't answer.

"Stand and follow me."

She found her courage to speak. "Where are you taking me?"

"You are a thorn in a perfect plan." Lockwood turned the firelight, revealing Taren standing behind him. "Thorns need to be plucked out."

Naomi's terror returned. She struggled to stand.

"Sharrod has someone he wants you to meet."

Taren took her elbow and marched her behind his father. Naomi went without fighting, feeling as if she walked in a fog, waiting for something to make sense.

She felt sweat drip down her back as the intense volcanic heat grew closer. She glanced at Taren. Her mind flashed back to the last images of him before he plunged the dagger in her chest.

She gasped, nearly losing her balance. Taren grabbed her arm again to steady her. She stared. He looked forward without blinking, betraying no emotion. Why was he here at all? He was an enigma, a puzzle she couldn't solve.

"Show me."

Naomi lifted her head. A voice entered her mind, like a ghost. Her eyes turned left and right, but no one said anything.

"Closer."

Naomi blinked and turned. Come closer to where? The march continued on. She turned to Taren, looking for answers, but he made no indication that he had heard anything at all.

The path dropped down into an awkward spiral. Light increased around them as they drew closer to something—somewhere.

"I wait, little one."

Naomi froze. She knew she hadn't hallucinated. It wasn't the heat or the pain that caused the voice. Someone had called her. Fear seized her. She knew that voice. The river held many dead, but she couldn't imagine it holding someone she loved so much.

She turned to Taren, whispering. "I know you heard it. I know it."

Taren's expression didn't change and he pushed her along.

Her magic no longer thumped but trembled inside her. Her knees were going to give out. She didn't want to go any further. She couldn't bear beholding Malindra's damnation.

The voice echoed, ringing through the walls.

"My Everstar."

No, Naomi thought. *No. Don't say that.* A hollow resonation of the voice haunted her inner ear. The name circled 'round and 'round, hissing. She grabbed her ears as the vibrations increased. *Stop, please stop.*

Taren grabbed her wrist. The ringing disappeared immediately.

Naomi looked at him, frightened. Everything on the surface was controlled, but his eyes told a different story. Naomi searched his gaze, but she could not read him. She never could.

CONJECTRIX

"Get ready," Taren whispered without looking at her. He slipped his hand from her wrist to her fingers, intertwining them with his own.

"Ready for what?"

Taren remained silent.

"Don't do this," Naomi whispered.

He turned and faced her now, intimidating her every thought.

"Please, Taren. Live a life you would be proud of living. Do the right thing."

Taren moved his hands to her collarbone and traced it. The touch made Naomi's magic flare up, the sensation catching both of them off-guard.

Taren pulled back his hand. Surprise and amusement covered his face. "I can see that some things are beyond forgiveness." His eyes felt as if they were prying deep into her thoughts.

He turned to walk through an open doorway ahead.

Naomi watched as his hand grazed the outside wall of the archway, touching three small, circular stones.

Three small stones . . . and it clicked.

The trolls surrounded her, all chanting. Naomi, ready to fulfill a promise, walked in the fire.

A woman stood there, glorious and terrifying. At first, Naomi thought it might be her sister, but it was not. This demon sought her out to destroy her, to invite her into the fire.

"I will keep you."

Naomi stared at the stones again. Taren had tried to communicate something to her. This *was* a trap. She needed to prepare.

Lockwood stood in front of her now. "Come on." He pulled her forward through the archway. A warm, glow of fire lit the tunnel walls. She turned and light fell over them, like entering the sun. Naomi saw the brilliance of the lava—the heat rising from the pots, spilling into the pools until it cascaded out and down the side of the walls. A ghostly curtain of steam rose up from a split in the floor, leading to the earth underneath.

Lockwood walked to the middle of the platform, surrounded by a few of his guards. Taren joined him at his side. The guards led Naomi to the center, still tied. They forced her to the ground before Lockwood.

Naomi cleared her mind. Her magic no longer hid away but rushed to the surface, flowing in powerful surges. She didn't struggle with her bands. The magic confirmed to her that they would not hold. She could burn through them when she wished. Even as the thought crossed her mind, the gentle prickle of heat surrounded her wrists.

"Taren told me of your incredible power, and yet we have you here bound, ready to die."

"Dying has nothing to do with it."

Lockwood sneered. "How can you kneel so confidently before me? Do you know why you are here?"

Naomi glared. "I know everything. I know more than you."

"More? I don't think so."

"I've seen you before." Naomi's confidence grew. "I watched you murder Malindra. You searched for me. What did you find?"

"You are a casualty of magic and need to be dealt with."

"What about Taren?" Naomi asked, poking at his weaknesses. "Was he a casualty? Didn't you send him away so he wouldn't damage your relationship with the king?"

"Don't speak of things you know nothing about," Lockwood spat back. "If the dagger couldn't kill you, she will—"

A small rumble from the ground interrupted his monologue, returning a greedy smile to his face.

CONJECTRIX

Naomi's head rang with voices once more. *"We wait. We are ready. We are one."*

A single scream rang out. Naomi tried to cover her ears with her tied hands, but it came from her own head.

Lockwood's lips moved, but she heard nothing of what he said. All she heard was the scream. *Make it stop. Make it stop.* The sound crippled her. A large rumble shook her loose and she fell to the ground. Lockwood and Taren lost their footing.

Naomi closed her eyes. Her magic moved violently within her. The scream became louder. It was her magic.

"Help us!" it rang out in her mind. *"She will take us from you. Keep us safe."*

"Who will take you?" Naomi tried to ask, but her magic was quick.

"She is here! Do not let us go away from you."

Naomi didn't understand what it wanted but agreed quickly. "Yes, please. Yes, I will protect you. I promise."

The scream subsided. A dull ringing left her dizzy. Within her head, the magic wrapped around her in a tight embrace.

"Wake."

Naomi opened her eyes, aware of the terror revealed to her by the magic. She was on the ground in the cave, the bands around her wrist snapped. She looked around. No one stood near her anymore. They had retreated behind her, waiting and watching.

The glow of the cave intensified, waves rolled over like ripples on water, but bright orange and flickering.

"Everstar . . ."

Naomi's attention turned to the voice coming from the edge. A woman surrounded by fire hovered before her. Every inch of her was in flame, fire wrapping her body with rich colors. Her hair moved out around her, waving from the intense heat.

Her face was just as unusual, with deep black eyes and a penetrating brow. Her voice was soft but echoed deep in every rock and vessel.

"You have come." The sound resonated around her. *"As you promised."*

Naomi's mind emptied of any rational thought.

"A Blood Promise is a powerful thing."

Finally, her voice returned. "Who—who are you?"

"I am Alene." Her beautiful, delicate arms reached up to the flame that danced around her. *"I have come to take you away."*

"Where?"

A half-turned smile crossed her thin, perfect lips. *"Your father took away the natural balance of the world with the creation of the medallions."* She moved fluidly around the wall of flame. *"But you are a creation he didn't intend. You are a secret weapon."*

Naomi didn't dare ask any more questions. She didn't want to hear anymore.

"I will consume your magic as my own, which will please my husband very much." An insane smile laced her mouth and Naomi knew she spoke of Sharrod. Her magic had been right to scream. She was about to die.

Alene's black eyes grew larger as she moved closer and closer to Naomi.

A growl sounded behind her, deep and angry. Naomi saw movement in her peripheral vision and turned to see Gurr stomping across the cave floor. A few guards tried to stop him, but he brushed them off like flies. His voice rang out in Naomi's mind.

"I will protect you till death."

Alene turned toward the troll, her fluid flames guiding her closer. *"The brave troll. Come to protect his princess."*

She spat a fireball at him, which struck him in the arm. He growled out and slapped the flame out with his other arm.

Alene turned back to Naomi. *"Little soldiers in a losing battle."* She snapped and another flame shot up near him.

"His soul is mine now. I hold all the souls you seek. I am the Keeper." Her tongue lashed out, spitting fire.

Naomi jumped away and scrambled to her feet.

Alene laughed and shot out more flame, her forked tongue moving in all directions.

Naomi narrowly dodged the searing attack. The licking flames began climbing up her cloak. She quickly ripped it off and watched the fabric rapidly burn, the magic snuffed out under the flames.

"You are lost, little Everstar. You are promised to me."

This time, when she spat out flame, a spark from her tongue landed on Naomi's hand and sizzled. The pain was unexpected; the sensation was hot and uncomfortable, but the energy behind it began to burrow in her skin, like a tick searching for cover.

Naomi acted fast and peeled it out with her fingernails. This was what Alene had planned. She was going to get to her magic from the inside.

She tried to run away, but one of Alene's long tendrils wrapped around her wrist.

Gurr, who had been watching everything, ran toward Alene.

"No, Gurr!" Naomi screamed. "She'll kill you!"

Gurr didn't stop. He picked up a massive stone from the cave floor and threw it directly at Alene. The rock melted away before it reached the floating goddess.

Alene whipped her long tendrils, striking him in the face. Fire ignited around his hairy head as blood began to seep from his mouth and nose. He screamed and grabbed at the flames, trying to pat it out, but the singe only intensified.

"'Til death," the mountain troll cried out in thoughts to Naomi, *"I promise."*

"No!" Naomi screamed, but her cry faltered. The tendril's heat increased as she tried to loosen its grip. "Don't hurt him, please."

Alene's eyes grew big and black. She shot a deliberate aim at Gurr. Little sparks spread all over his body. Gurr groaned, letting out a pain-filled scream as he sank to his knees and grabbed at his chest.

"Magic never hurt. I hurt. You have hurt me."

A large ball of fire engulfed the troll. His growling echoed louder and louder, swelling until, with a large poof, the troll was gone. Only a pile of ash remained, blowing away in the wind created by the heat.

"No!" Naomi cried, the struggle dying out of her. "No."

Guilt overwhelmed her, tightening her throat. She had introduced him to the magic.

The tendril around her increased in heat, drawing Naomi back to the moment. She struggled to get free.

"Magic is not yours to share."

Alene laughed, playing with her new toy. Her haunting black eyes penetrated Naomi, filled with curiosity. *"He will not have you. You are my prize. He wants to save you, but you are promised."*

Naomi struggled furiously. The tendril lifted her off the ground. Her burned body seared with pain. Sweat streamed down her back.

A throbbing pain grew in her head. She heard voices again, louder and louder, a strong scream coming from inside. The heat whipped around her, hollow voices creeping out.

CONJECTRIX

No, she thought. *NO, please magic, stay hidden. No! You will not get me!* The howling in her head grew stronger.

A voice cut through it, waking up her mind and heart.

"NAOMI!"

Reynolds' voice resounded around the walls. Naomi's heart reacted in a way she had never experienced, a swell overcoming her at his presence, tingling throughout her body.

Alene's eyes grew bigger, her grip tightening.

Naomi bent over in pain. A rush of fire wrapped around her completely, surrounding her with ripples of heat. The outside world no longer existed. All she could hear, feel, and see was the heat.

Bam! Something pushed her and her body jerked backward. Another blow came and the grip of the tendril loosened. She heard yelling and commotion. A scream rang out like an explosion. Another hit, the largest yet, jerked her body free. All the flame disappeared around her.

The wind whipped at her again and she went spinning. This time, nothing was holding her.

She was falling.

CHAPTER THIRTY
THE RIVER of Souls

Taren watched the hot wind sweep over Naomi and she vanished into the flame. The fiery enchantress had engulfed her prize and there was very little time to act. He had watched enough. It was now time for his knife to once more do what it was made for; the ancient blade that had sliced through Naomi's tender flesh would now again perform a greater duty.

The guards stared, mesmerized at the spectacle. With two quick blows, Taren sent both down to the cave floor with a thump. Only his father stood before him.

The sound of the falling men captured Lockwood's attention. At first he looked surprised, but then an intense stare of understanding overcame his face. He remained silent, withdrawing his knife.

"That is mine," Lockwood stated. "You have no right to it."

Taren didn't move a muscle. "You gave it to me, don't you remember?"

Lockwood laughed—a low, menacing sound. "The girl's magic has corrupted you. You would kill your own father for it, like that mindless brute sacrificing himself for it. You're no better than a troll."

"You asked me to lure her here—lure her to her death and give her to that monster."

"It is done!" Lockwood yelled. "Sharrod will have her whether you kill me or not. He has won!"

Taren twisted the knife in the air, almost dancing. "Sharrod is no match for her."

"She can't even fight Alene. She would never defeat Sharrod."

More guards moved in on the right, three of them coming up behind Lockwood, drawing their weapons as they watched the fight.

"She will never love you," Lockwood taunted. "She will never forgive you for what you have done."

Taren started forward, but Lockwood retreated near the guards. They circled around until Taren sliced one guard in the leg and he dropped to the floor. Lockwood forced the two remaining guards between him and his son.

A whizzing sound rushed by and both of the soldiers went down in a heap, wrapped together in a knot of ropes. Taren looked up to see the one person he'd known he would eventually meet again.

Reynolds stood on a ledge near an opening to the cavern. Taren wondered how much he had heard. If he suspected his feelings for Naomi . . .

But that didn't matter now. Lockwood was their common enemy. A brief nod from Reynolds confirmed he felt the same.

Taren didn't notice the axe until his father was inches away. He reared back just as the blade struck near his feet. His knife flew out of his hands.

"You're a traitor!" Lockwood yelled between his swings. "And Sharrod will know. You are as good as dead."

Reynolds leaped down, landing on the guards, who squirmed around in their binding of ropes, searching for a way out.

"Ah, the illusive Hawk." Lockwood swung at him before getting both men in his sight. "Always the troublemaker." Another swing. "Should have killed you when I had the chance."

Reynolds countered the blows with his sword. "And miss the fun?" He moved closer to Taren as he scuttled for his knife. "Where is she?"

Heart plummeting in his chest, Taren realized he had lost sight of her. "NAOMI!"

Alene turned toward them. Having successfully gathered her prize, she laughed, spitting fire out of her mouth. The flames singed all three men. Taren batted them out just in time to dodge another swing from Lockwood, whose axe now had a flaming blade.

Lockwood aimed at Reynolds, the hot axe slicing his arm, burning the skin inside and out.

He staggered to his knees but countered the next blow.

"Save her!" Reynolds shouted. "Taren! Save her!!"

Taren turned and saw Alene's tendrils pulling Naomi's golden hair from view. His magic was building close behind his fingertips. He shot a fireball at the flaming monster.

Alene laughed.

He tried again—a larger fireball, a searing fever behind the fury of his madness. It pounded her square in the chest. The impact jarred her, but she merely absorbed the fireball.

"You and I are one, magician," she mocked. *"You cannot hurt me."*

In desperation, Taren ran toward Alene with his knife warming in his hand, ready to be used for the last time.

In his peripheral vision, he saw his father being knocked down to the ground, unconscious.

Reynolds came running after him, but he didn't care. This would work, a sacrifice for a sacrifice.

CONJECTRIX

Alene laughed again and spat fire. A great fireball landed and spread out across the floor, blocking any passage. Reynolds halted, but Taren continued on through the wall of fire like a charging bull. He steadied his magic, readying for the impact, but he did not feel it at all.

Alene's laughter faded to a blistering anger, seeing someone untouched by her magic. Fireballs spread out everywhere. Chaos surrounded the cavern.

Taren moved forward with determination, reaching the end of the chasm. The knife felt hot in his hand, wanting to act. He jumped as far as he could at the fiery witch. Alene watched the magical blade sink deep into her chest.

She reacted violently, throwing Taren across the cavern. Flames heaved out rising waves, spreading up to the roof. Alene's black eyes found Taren clinging to the edge of the chasm, filled with a hunger to destroy him. Her fiery tendrils shot out to ensnare him—

But stopped.

Her breath faltered.

The brilliance of her flames began to die. Embers flicked out of her tendrils, shriveling the long tresses.

Alene screamed in horror. She tried to grab her knife, but her hand started to disintegrate. Her beauty crackled into tiny veins, her ethereal glory shriveling in ash. The tiniest cry escaped Alene's mouth before her entire body collapsed into a brilliant explosion of dust.

※　※　※

Reynolds watched, stunned, as the last of the blazing light vanished. The wall of flames holding him back disintegrated. There was nothing left of the dangerously beautiful queen of fire but a cloud of ash hovering over the river of lava flowing down the walls of the ravine.

Naomi. His breath left him.

He ran forward, searching. Where was she?

Near the ledge, he saw pale fingers hooked around a rock. Reynolds knelt down to see Taren trying to scramble to the top.

"Grab my hand!" He reached to help, but Taren resisted. "What happened? Where is Naomi?"

Reynolds extended his hand once more for him, but still Taren did not grab it. ". . . Gone," he muttered.

The words stung. It couldn't be true.

"Grab on!" Reynolds persisted. "We can find her!"

Taren craned his head to look behind him into the flowing river of lava. Without another word, he let go of the ledge.

"Taren!" Reynolds tried to snatch him, but it was too late. He watched in horror as Taren fell toward the red river and disappeared from view.

Before Reynolds could process what had happened, a shadow approached from behind. A single blow was driven to the back of his head, and everything went black.

❀　❀　❀

The wind took hold of Naomi as she twisted about in the air. It grabbed and pulled, tumbling her over and over.

The thickness of the air slowed her descent. As she twisted, her clothes billowed about, whipping her with their edges as the wind pulled out secrets.

The Conjectrix floated before her. Naomi reached out to grab it, touching it lightly with her fingertips, but in that instant, she hit the jagged rock below, knocking the wind out of her. She turned to see the Conjectrix rolling away across the rock, cracks clearly visible from the impact. She crawled over, trying to grasp it; its smooth surface flashed every image in its memories. It held Naomi's reflection before it shattered. Purple feathery streams escaped like its last breath before it burned out in a flash.

Her entrusted gift, the Conjectrix, was no more.

Naomi couldn't believe it.

Her astonishment was soon replaced with unimaginable horror as she realized where she was. She stood on an island of built-up lava flow. All around her in the steaming heat were myriads of souls, tortured and screaming. Like a sea of fire, they floated with wave upon wave of thick heat blowing them to unknown paths above and below.

"... *save us* ..."

"... *save us* ..."

They began to spiral around her, circling Naomi in a cyclone. A woman with hollowed-out eyes and a greedy expression emerged from the crowd, hands reaching, stretching—wanting something—something inside her. The Vivatera felt hot against her skin, her magic flaring around her fingertips.

The woman shrunk back, like a cat with its back up, waiting to attack.

More souls gathered. They could feel the magic, pulsating through Naomi with every heartbeat.

A moan resounded through the air. Faces moved in and out of the molten river, peering out and then disappearing again.

The face of a little boy caught Naomi's attention. He made eye contact, pleading in anguish before slipping away and vanishing. How many were here? How many were trapped?

And then a voice came back to her mind.

"You are mine."

Naomi turned, trying to find the single soul mixed with the others, but she only saw the gaunt, hollow expressions, the hunger in their eyes.

"You are mine."

Please, no. Naomi couldn't bear to look for Malindra, the beautiful woman who had raised her. She could not bear for her to be among these miserable souls. The magnitude of their predicament pressed down on her soul. The realization of her interference with the law of the elements crushed her spirit. There were thousands now surrounding her, looking at her with haunting wants, all gaunt and hungry for life.

The rock overhead rumbled. The souls noticed but did not move. They were too desperate, too hungry.

Another rumble knocked Naomi off her feet. One soul close to her seized the opportunity and reached out for her.

Naomi jumped back up, her magic shooting out like a shock of light. It spooked them back for a moment, but they soon inched in even closer.

A few rocks tumbled down in the river. The island was unstable, Naomi realized. If the cavern continued shaking, it would not last. She had to think fast. Her magic could protect her, but for how long? The souls were hungry for life and she possessed everything that could make them live again. They would swallow her soul and dispose of her remains in the river.

A screech echoed around. A few of the hungry souls scattered as a steady thumping moved closer and closer. The souls became braver, daring to touch her. Naomi's magic reacted once more in defense, but too many pushed forward.

Naomi attempted to fend off the souls one by one, but it was growing harder and harder.

Soon, a face stood out from the rest, the face she had feared most to see. Malindra.

She moved forward slowly, standing apart from the others. Her eyes were sunken and depressed, the same hunger eating at her soul as all the rest.

A scream bubbled out of Naomi's chest. It was the scream of the child she used to be, the scream she never dared make when she'd witnessed the murder of this person she loved so dearly.

With that, all the fight went out of her. She wanted to stay. Malindra would take care of her, would make her safe. She would never harm her.

Other souls moved away as the ghostly shape of Malindra drew near.

"Save us." Her voice echoed in Naomi's mind, the same voice she had last heard defending her, before it was silenced forever. *"Come home."*

Yes. This was where she needed to be. Everything else made little difference. She was finished. She had failed and would die here with the souls that needed her body and strength. *Yes*, she committed in her mind. *Yes, I will stay.*

A screech echoed around them and the souls retreated—all but Malindra, who stood before her, arms outstretched.

Suddenly, a shadow moved over her, snatching her from the edge— right away from her accepted fate.

Naomi flew high in the air. Large talons gripped her tight and tucked her deep against a large, scaly breast. Together they traveled through tightly molded caverns.

The fire eater screeched and turned sharply, diving fast toward a rock. A limp figure dangled there, inches from the lava flow. The beast snatched the body with its empty talon and continued its flight.

Up they went in a neat spiral through the top of the caldera. The brisk night air was refreshingly cool against Naomi's face. The dragon flew down the side of the mountain and along the ridgeline, descending to earth. Opening up its talons near a high rock, the fire eater released Naomi and its other captive, rolling them out in a soft tumble. It backed away, settling down into the dust.

Naomi caught her breath. The intense yellow eyes of the creature glowed down on her, filled with understanding and intelligence. He knew exactly who she was.

"We got you! I knew we would!"

Naomi sat up as she recognized Arie's large grin. He picked her up and swung her around. "I can't believe it! Are you okay?"

"How did you find me?"

Another figure moved closer out of the shadows. "With a little help from his friends." The voice was a girl's, not familiar, but similar to her own. "I'm Sera. I hear you're looking for me."

Naomi could not help herself. Emotion washed over her, like everything had been building up to this moment. She ran to her sister, grasped her in a tight embrace.

Sera cried into her shoulder. "I felt you kick, you know."

When Naomi finally pulled away, she turned to Arie. "But where is Reynolds?"

"Didn't we grab him?" Arie glanced at Sera, who then ran to the figure that lay lifeless near the edge of the precipice.

Naomi rushed to the body, turning him over as a cold horror washed through her. It wasn't Reynolds, but Taren. Blood covered his head and there were scratches all over his body. One leg had to be broken.

Naomi moved her hand to his heart. The beats had slowed. Ripping off a portion of her tattered sleeve, she covered his head wound, all the while moving her other hand over his heart.

"We need to get him to help," Sera spoke up. "We can fly him."

"Where?"

"To Linnonbury. To my—*our* mother."

Naomi let the words sink in before she spoke again. "I can't leave. I need to find Reynolds."

Arie put his hand on her shoulder. "I'll look. You go with Webster. He's stronger and faster. I'll search with Frieda around the mountain and meet you in a few days."

Sera kissed him. Naomi looked away, turning back to Taren. The bleeding from his head had slowed, but his heart was still weak. She knew what to do, but had to wonder—why? Taren had once tried to kill her. What he'd said to her and what she'd witnessed in the cavern didn't excuse him. Why was she saving him now?

Because she couldn't let him die.

Because it was the right thing to do.

"Come," Sera beckoned her to the fire eater. She placed Naomi directly behind her, grabbed two leather straps for steering the beast, and lifted up in the air, snatching both Taren and Arie up in the large talons.

The dragon released Arie on a nearby ledge.

Naomi watched him become a small speck and then disappear. A prayer rose in her heart as they sailed high on the wings of a dragon.

Find him. Keep him safe.

CHAPTER THIRTY-ONE
LINNONBURY

Light filtered through the clouds, showcasing the snow caps on the mountaintops as they drew near. The crisp air nipped at Naomi's bare skin as they descended.

The ride had been exhilarating at first—bareback on a dragon, flying higher than even the clouds, but her emotions held her in check, her worry overwhelming her enjoyment.

She took comfort in the dark night. The stars spoke to her, letting her know they were always there, watching her, protecting her. They whispered of dangers she could not see; of paths she should not take; and of perils to come.

But even with this distraction, every thought eventually turned back to Reynolds.

He had been there in the cave. She'd heard his voice yelling her name. Had he fallen like Taren, into the chasm of suffocating souls? The last time they were together, they'd fought. He'd left her alone. Could she ever apologize for what she'd said? A pang of intense fear hit her again at the thought of being without him, the thought of never getting to say goodbye.

CONJECTRIX

As the sunlight brightened her surroundings, tall mountains came into focus; mountains she had no memory of. Going from such intense heat to extreme cold made every muscle in Naomi's body contract. As they neared the ground, she couldn't help herself and pressed her chest next to the dragon for warmth. The Vivatera mirrored the heat next to the magical creature, sending a tingling throughout her body.

The tiny black and green dots began to take shape. They were homes in little villages, scattered in the depths of the mountains.

"Brace yourself!" Sera yelled through the wind. Naomi gripped tight while the creature dove down. Sera directed it to a clearing near a few of the small homes Naomi had seen from the sky.

The dragon hovered, releasing Taren from its claws, then twisted around before landing on the soft snow. A jolt of energy shook Naomi as they landed; the flight had made her feel weightless. Before she could climb down, Sera slid off the fire eater and ran toward where Taren had landed. A woman in a fur-lined hood exited one of the homes and rushed to meet her.

"Thank you," Naomi said to Webster, the fire eater who carried them there. She wasn't as graceful as Sera and fell clumsily down the back of the dragon.

Naomi rushed to the clearing and found fur-covered hoods filling the center. A man near Sera rushed to Naomi and took off his own cloak.

"Here, young miss." He placed it over her. The skins, already warmed from his body, felt wonderful next to Naomi's frozen skin.

Sera looked up, frantic, from Taren's side. "We need to warm him up. Take him to Tolks. I will bring Jeanus."

"Yes, my lady." A few men wrapped Taren in furs and hoisted him up, rushing him away.

Sera and Naomi watched them leave. "Where are they taking him?"

"His heart rate is slow," Sera explained as she guided Naomi across the snow-covered ground. "He has a few broken bones, but the bleeding has stopped. The men are taking him to Tolks, the medicine man." They began to wind up a trail on the mountain. "But Jeanus needs to know. I'll need an interpreter."

Jeanus. Naomi's hear fluttered with nerves. She remembered the old woman vividly, at the beginning of everything. Jeanus was Malindra's sister, with the same frame and ethereal likeness. She was blind to the real world, but could see the magical world. The Conjectrix had belonged to her.

Fear crept into the pit of Naomi's stomach. She would have to tell Jeanus the truth—that she had dropped her precious gift and shattered it.

They reached a small wooden hut, built in a circular shape with a stack of smoke billowing out the top.

Sera walked right in without knocking. "Jeanus, I've returned with a gift."

The warmth of the house greeted Naomi as she entered, draped with trinkets and fabric, burning candles and smells of deep lavender and honeysuckle. It smelled of home, Naomi thought. The cabin where she'd spent the first years of her life had looked and felt like this charming home. It was almost like the last few years were a dream and she had never left.

A staircase wrapped around walls of books that opened to the main floor. A figure with cotton white hair stood at the top of the stairs. "A sight for very sore eyes." She came to Naomi, encircling her in her arms. "Come, sit."

A fire blazed in the center of the room, surrounded by soft cushions.

CONJECTRIX

Naomi sat. A cup of hot tea was set in her hands, warm bread on the table next to her. She took a closer look at the room. All the lamps and oils that burned must be meant to help Jeanus' sight ignite with magic. The fine silks hanging about were made of a familiar material.

"Shadesilk," Naomi murmured.

"I made a very good friend of Spotswood Shadower," Jeanus informed her. "After Malindra acquired that lovely scarf you're wearing, I took it upon myself to get one of my own. It is a shame she never got to see this place. She would have rolled around in jealousy—"

Malindra. Naomi's color drained, remembering her guardian's face amongst all those wretched souls.

"What is it?" Sera asked sensing the change in her.

Naomi sipped her tea, avoiding the question. "How safe are we here? Spotswood said the Durundin was safe, but the army found us there."

Jeanus laughed, a musical sound. "You are not in Parbraven anymore. Linnonbury has magic of its own and is not affected by the decisions of man. It obeys other natural laws." She motioned to the food on the table. "Now, eat up before it gets cold."

Naomi took a bite of the bread, filling her mouth with such sweet butter and honey, she could hardly remember anything so wonderful.

"You were right to send her here," Jeanus spoke up, interrupting the silence.

"Who?" Sera inquired with her mouth full of bread.

"The little girl."

Naomi dropped her biscuit. Sera looked confused.

Jeanus smiled and patted her hand. "Miracles can happen in the strangest places."

So, it wasn't a dream. "Is she okay?"

Jeanus nodded. "You can meet her if you wish."

"Thank you." Naomi tried to smile, but couldn't help but remember how she'd seen the little girl in the first place—the Conjectrix that now lay broken at the bottom of a cavern.

Something in Jeanus' eyes gleamed, as if she already knew. "No worries, my sweet. Magic comes and goes in unexpected forms. I'm sure something will come along to help you in a different way."

"Sera?" Another voice called from the top of the stairs. "Sera? Is that—"

Something dropped. A woman clothed in dark green velvet stood at the top of the balcony, not seeming to notice the glass shattered on the floor. The same long golden curls flowed freely from her head; the same steely, green eyes and gentle freckles; the same small, willowy frame. It was like Naomi could look into a mirror of her future, of the woman she could become.

"Mother!" Sera hopped up and ran up to her.

Mother? A nervous feeling sank in the pit of Naomi's stomach.

Sera carefully guided her mother down the winding stairs.

Naomi's heart moved faster than ever before. Sera had said they would be bringing Taren to their mother, but in all the chaos she hadn't had time to properly prepare. She'd never had a mother, except for Malindra, who was everything a guardian should be. Looking down, she saw she was shaking.

"Naomi, this is Andriana, our mother."

Tears streaked down her face. Andriana moved her hand up to Naomi's face, gently wiping away her tears. "There is no mistaking you are mine."

They embraced. Naomi held tight, afraid if she let go the dream would end and she would be back to living alone without family. She had a mother. She had a father. At that single moment in time, everything felt complete.

❄   ❄   ❄

In a deep corner of the village, away from the main meeting places in the town, was a small yurt. Hand-carved, wooden wind chimes hung about, clattering against themselves. Sculpted icicle stars and patterned, spiraled glass were intermingled among them.

Naomi had asked Sera to accompany her on the visit. But now that she stood in front of the strange dwelling, she wasn't sure about the trip. She nearly turned away when a woman answered, light hair bouncing in curls down her back.

"Ah, yes. We thought you would come. I'm Genève. Won't you come in?"

Naomi's nerves raced around her body, but Sera pushed her in.

The yurt was dark but comfortable. A cozy fire had been lit in the center of the home, the warm scent of cedar exuding from the rich wooden walls.

"I am so glad to meet you." Genève grasped Naomi's hand and moved in to hold her. "I think it is truly miraculous what you have done."

"I only did what I thought was right."

A gentleman with a graying goatee and peppered hair walked toward them. "I'm Elian," he introduced himself with an outstretched hand. "Lottie is a pure joy to us and is getting stronger."

"May I see her?"

"Oh, yes," Genève answered, "she is anxious for company. I have not let her outside. The weather is much too cold right now."

"Come with me." Elian directed them to a curved room near the back. A small bed rested against a wall. Among the quilts and furs lay a girl. The moment Naomi entered, she sat up.

Naomi lost her breath. The memory of when she had first seen this girl in the Conjectrix returned so strongly it hurt to think of it.

"Come closer."

Naomi did as she asked and sat down on the bed. The girl smiled. "I just wanted to see you. I thought you might be an angel."

"An angel?"

"Yes. I was rescued by an angel."

Naomi liked the idea. "No, I'm real." She grabbed her little hand to prove it.

Lottie took it and squeezed it. "I did a really stupid thing and that lady knew it. I told her secrets and I promised I wouldn't. That lady was very nice at first, but then she cut my throat."

She lifted up her hair, exposing the bandaged wound around her neck. "I don't think she's going to give me the doll she promised."

Naomi's heart filled with grief at the innocent words. "Tell me about your companions. You were traveling with Landon and Katia. They are good friends of mine."

A big smile stretched across Lottie's face. "I knew they weren't married. It's hard to trick me."

"Really?" Naomi laughed. "Tell me about it."

Lottie filled her with all the details about the Travelers, meeting Landon and Katia, the journey through Davenport and down to the Salt Dunes—everything up until the Louving.

Lottie looked down at her hands. "I knew she was a fake."

"How?" Naomi asked.

"I know secrets when I touch people. Like you, Naomi. She wanted my blood. I remember the pain and then the light."

"The light?"

"Yes." She smiled. "From you. You lit the room up and made me warm all over. My neck started to feel better, but then I got really cold."

"Jeanus brought her to us shortly after." Genève entered, bringing some warm water from a kettle and filling the cup next to Lottie. "We've loved having her."

Lottie squeezed Naomi's hand tighter. "You hold no secrets. You are honest and live who you are. There are so many that don't."

"If I hid who I was, I wouldn't have saved you. But I'm so glad I did."

Lottie grinned. "Come see me again, please. You can help me get stronger."

Naomi agreed, and she and Sera left Lottie to rest in the care of Genève and Elian.

"One more stop," Sera told her as they walked toward the medicine hut.

Naomi's insides churned uncomfortably.

✿ ✿ ✿

The sun was setting behind the mountain, reflecting on the snow-caps and filling the valley with purples and pinks.

Just ahead was the medicine hut, located near the edge of Linnonbury by a deep canyon ledge. Tolks sat outside with his bare feet propped on a barrel. When he saw the two girls approaching, he quickly stood. He was a strange little man, shorter than ordinary, but not as small as a dwarf.

"Oh, good ladies, glad you could come. Nice to have another healer about."

Naomi smiled. "I can hardly say I'm a healer, but I hope I can help."

Tolks scratched his bald head. "Perhaps you can figure out why he's dying."

"Dying?" The news came as a shock. "But I thought he was getting better."

"I can't snap him out of it. It's like he's lost something—lost the will, if you please."

Naomi didn't like the sound of it. "Let me see him."

The smell of thick medicine permeated the old wood, filling her nostrils and lungs. Naomi coughed and cleared her throat, trying to get used to the smell.

"This way." Tolks led Naomi and Sera into a circular room, kept much warmer than the rest of the hut. A purplish light filtered near the ceiling where the heat from the sweating coals escaped to the outside.

Taren lay in the middle of the room on a cot with only a sheet around him, his hair wet with sweat. Naomi moved closer. His head was bandaged as well as his right arm. His chest rose and fell in quick movements, like he was in a fitful dream.

"Taren?" He did not move. She placed her hand on his. A burst of energy pulsed through her and his eyes opened.

He stared, not saying a word. After a moment, he moved his hand away, pain in his eyes. "Please, go."

"I want to talk."

"No." He turned his head away from her. "Please, go."

"I need to know what happened in Mount Ignis."

"Nothing." Taren closed his eyes again and remained silent.

"I thought a lot about what you said to me that night," she murmured. "I think . . . I *know* you're right. The magic needs to be whole . . ."

She trailed off. It was hard to articulate the words with him so unresponsive. "Do you hear me?"

Taren remained silent, his head turned, his eyes closed. Bracing herself, she took his hand again, this time not letting go.

Taren flinched. "Stop it, Naomi. Stop."

But at that moment, Naomi felt stronger than he was. Energy rushed through her. Under protest, she pushed her magic, searching. There must be a way.

BLACK!

A black fog blocked the entrance.

Her magic sent out spurts of energy, penetrating the shield, absorbing, swirling, and returning to the wall.

A deep voice resonated. *"You are not welcome here."*

"You cannot protect him from me." A hum of energy surrounded her, growing stronger with every breath.

The black wall began to lose its strength. Taren's magic was swirling around in a frenzy, protecting him—like a scared child.

"You cannot have him!" the magic screamed again.

Naomi, though terrified, calmed her magic. "You cannot claim him. He owes me his life. You have no power."

"You have no rights to a soul—"

Naomi spoke with authority. "You are wrong. I am the Protector of souls." A magic emerged that she had never experienced before—white and brilliant, spinning around in great streams. It targeted the great wall, the fibers penetrating the darkness and eating away his anger.

The black wall fell like pieces of shattered glass, but Naomi knew Taren's magic had life beyond this darkness. She could feel it swirling, like a tornado of energy hidden from view.

She cleared her mind. "There is no guilt, Taren. I forgive you."

Naomi reached out to the magic, caressing it with the tiniest of touches. A crashing sound, like breaking mirrors, sent vibrations

328

quaking down deep into the core of Taren's magic. The reaction was startling, but Naomi stood tall against it. The power rushed through her like wind, but she did not falter.

Taren's magic—the stain of his wasted self—huddled down on the ground, grabbing his knees, watching his reality break into pieces.

Sweet silence followed. Her energy calmed, the magic inside dancing peacefully up and down her skin. "I know it is because of you I survived. Please, let me help you now."

Taren didn't move. He looked so frightened—so scared and alone.

"Will you never know how loving magic can be?" Naomi whispered.

"I will not." His voice cracked like the magic around him.

He looked up at her now, taking in the glow of magic about her. "I am selfish. I will always be selfish."

Sadness overcame her. "I understand more now. I witnessed the souls with no relief. They need me to help rescue them from misery."

Taren grimaced.

"There is no other way. You're the one who told me that."

"You saved me. You forgive me." Taren's intense eyes held her gaze as he rose to his feet, looming over her. "I don't understand."

Naomi had no more hatred in her heart. Her anger slipped away, replaced with empathy.

Taren stepped closer. "I have seen the ugliness of people, and the dark side of the world, but you are light and truth. You are honest and good and pure. You are . . . the most beautiful thing I have ever seen.

"How could you forgive me? Stabbing you was the hardest thing I've ever done. All my hope that you would come back was placed in—" He lost his voice. Tears filled his eyes and he looked away, trying to control his emotions.

Naomi was speechless.

CONJECTRIX

Taren looked back, his eyes filled with an inconsolable sadness. "I will look at you," he stated, voice choked with emotion, "and with every glance I steal, you will know. No matter how this ends, at least you will know that I—that I did this all, because I-I love you, Naomi."

❀ ❀ ❀

The connection was lost. Naomi opened her eyes and released her hand from his.

"Naomi?" Sera moved behind her. "Are you okay?"

Naomi looked around. She was in the domed Yurt of the medicine hut, no longer in the magical realm. "Yes. I—" She lost focus when she saw Taren's real body again, broken and bruised. His eyes were open, lit with the same intense gaze in his eyes.

It was all true.

Something screeched outside the yurt. Sera grabbed Naomi's arm. "He's back."

Naomi rushed out the door to the sight of flapping wings. Sera hurried behind her, pulling on her fur. "It's Frieda!" She pointed at the blue creature sweeping in closer and closer.

Others came out of their homes to watch. The large blue dragon swept down and landed in a clearing. Both girls pulled up their hoods against the twilight wind.

Sera ran ahead of her. Arie's bright hair stood out against the dragon. Without thought, she threw her arms around him and held him as tight as she could.

But something was wrong. Naomi's pace slowed as Arie looked toward her.

"What's happened?" Sera pulled his face to her with her hands. "Where is Reynolds?"

Arie's eyes revealed everything. "I don't know."

Naomi's stomach pitted. "What do you mean?"

"I couldn't find him. I searched everywhere. We scoured the mountain range. I don't know what to tell you. He's gone."

Naomi put her hands to her mouth in shock. "If he fell in the mountain." Her heart pounded faster and faster. "If he fell in the river . . ."

No! she screamed inside. *No . . . no . . . NO!*

The weight of it consumed her and she fell to the ground.

❊　❊　❊

Traveling . . .

*　　Searching . . .*

Despair grew with every city, every town.

*　　　　　　　　　　　　The seaside, on a boat,*

*　　　　　　　　　　her friends, safe and together.*

A hillside.

Blue eyes among dark skin in sleeping trees,

Her sister sharpening arrows, worried.

*　　　　　　　　　　Traveling . . .*

*　　The little one, safe.*

*　　　　A lost sister in a band of dwarves and a prince.*

*　　　　　　Searching—find him—please.*

A stone floor

Hands in chains

Blood coming from his mouth.

*　　　　　　　A whip cracked!!*

A yell of pain!!

CONJECTRIX

"Speak!"

A harsh voice bellowed.

"Tell us where she is!"

Tears filled with anguished pain

Despair

And failure

"She is dead."

WHIP!

Naomi opened her eyes to find herself in her own bed. A warm fire flickered near a plate of fresh food, waiting for her to wake and eat. She looked around. The room was empty, except for a chair in the corner. Someone sat in it, the look in his eyes open with honesty it confused her.

She sat up, staring at him. "Why are you here?"

Taren didn't respond, just sat quietly watching.

"Are you here to triumph over Reynolds disappearance?"

"Of course not." His voice was kinder than she'd expected. "I came to make sure you were okay."

Naomi bit her lip. Now she was the one who was speechless.

Taren stood, walking over to her. "Look. I wanted to show you what you did for me. You healed me."

Hobbling over, he sat next to her on the bed. "You should eat something."

Naomi glanced at the plate. "I don't think I want any food right now."

Taren smiled. It was uncomfortable for Naomi to see. There had always been a secret behind any smile he gave, mischief, anger. But there was none of that now. He looked completely sincere.

"What are you thinking?" she blurted out.

332

"I'm concerned, that's all."

"About Reynolds?"

Taren's smile faltered. He covered it with a smirk. "About you."

Naomi shifted in her covers. "He's alive. I saw him in my dream. He thinks I'm dead."

"Are you sure?"

"Yes. He's bound in a cell somewhere. He's being tortured. He's in pain." Her voice cracked in her last words.

Taren placed his hand near hers, engulfing her with his warmth. "My father has him."

Naomi reeled back, staring at him in surprise. "How do you know?"

"The last time I saw him, we fought together. He told me to come after you, to save you. I took on the fire goddess. And he took on the guards and my father. I fell. He did not."

Naomi sat up and tried to get out of bed, but Taren stilled her. "This is good, Naomi."

"Good?" She stared at him incredulously. "How? If Sharrod thinks you're dead, then he will not pursue you. This is to our advantage."

Naomi's head fell. "Reynolds believes it. He thinks I'm dead. It's broken him. What if he does something stupid?"

"I've seen him do stupider things." With great effort, he stood again. "I should leave you."

Naomi stood next to him, holding his shoulders to support him. "Let me help you."

Taren grinned, then grimaced at the pain. Together they walked out the door and down the rounding stairs.

"Naomi, you need to know," he said between steps. "You have changed a part of me, but not everything. The darkness is gone, but I still don't think you should trust me. Or forgive me."

333

CONJECTRIX

Naomi stopped and looked him in the eye. "I have seen your good."

He lifted her chin and looked into her eyes. "That doesn't mean I am good."

Naomi saw it again; his heart had not changed. If possible, it had grown in his feeling toward her. She tried to look away, but he held her gaze.

"I will always help you," Taren said. "Whatever you ask of me, I will do. I am selfish. That will not change. I hope in time you will understand that."

Naomi let go of his shoulder and he disappeared into the night. She turned, seeing Arie and Sera standing behind her.

Arie shook his head. "Nothing's easy with you, is it?"

Sera slugged him in the arm. "Are you saying that what we have is easy?"

Arie rubbed his sore arm. "Of course not, especially with that punch."

Contrite now, Sera rubbed it better. "If it was easy, it wouldn't be as fun."

Naomi smiled at their affection, but it pained her as well. Walking outside, she watched Taren hobble back to his yurt.

A blanket was placed about her shoulders. Naomi looked up in surprise to see her mother.

"It's cold tonight," Andriana said. "The stars are always watching us, you know. They can guide us and lift us when we are in doubt. And these same stars are over Reynolds, wherever he is. I hope that gives you comfort. Do you understand?"

Naomi reached her arm around her mother and pressed into her. "If you believe in me, then I understand everything."

END OF
PART TWO

ACKNOWLEDGEMENTS

MY GREAT LOVE to my amazing family: Kevin, Mia, and Julia, mommy still loves you.

TREMENDOUS THANKS to my brilliant team at Xchyler for their undying faith in this project, especially Lissa Gilliland for returning to the adventure and being such a fan, Terri Wagner, Laurisa Reyes, McKenna Gardner, Dale Pease, Rachel Vasquez, and as always, Penny Freeman.

MY DEAREST APRECIATION to the Hong Kong Neily's. "Annette, I can't fully express how much your help meant to me during the first drafts of this story. You are truly amazing. And thank you, Brandon, for your enthusiasm for fantasy, and tremendous support from halfway around the world. We all will miss you terribly."

LOVES to my parents, and my many family and friends, for such wonderful support; specifically to Dave and Becka—the other Thomases, for moving back; Seth, Josh, and Adam and their amazing families; Becky, Sarah, Danny, and all of my favorite people from WJ93; Dr. Dave and his staff; the Blood Bankers; LTUE and everyone associated with it; the Oquirrh Writers Chapter; and again, to Benedict and Martin, for the Third; and Elbow, for getting me through my edit—"And if we only come this way but once, what a perfect waste of time."

ABOUT CANDACE J. THOMAS:

Candie started scripting parodies of plays at a young age and had dreams of becoming a playwright. This led to her studying Theater and Creative Writing at the University of Utah. She is the winner of the Diamond Award for Novel of the Year for VIVATERA, published by Xchyler Publishing, April 2013. She has also been featured in the fantasy anthology MOMENTS IN MILLENNIA. She is very proud of CONJECTRIX and is excited to continue the Vivatera Series.

When not writing, Candie loves anything that expands her imagination, especially if it's nerdy or geek-worthy. Her lifelong goal is to one day have a convincing British accent. She lives in Salt Lake City, Utah, with her husband, two girls, and tailless cat.

ABOUT XCHYLER PUBLISHING:

At The X, we pride ourselves in discovery and promotion of talented authors. Our anthology project produces three books a year in our specific areas of focus: fantasy, Steampunk, and paranormal. Held winter, spring/summer, and autumn, our short-story competitions result in published anthologies from which the authors receive royalties.

Additional themes include: *Mr. and Mrs. Myth* (Paranormal, fall 2014), *Out of This World* (Fantasy, winter 2015), and *Losers Weepers* (spring/summer 2015).

Visit www.xchylerpublishing.com/AnthologySubmissions for more information.

LOOK FOR THESE RELEASES FROM XCHYLER PUBLISHING IN 2014:

Around the World in 80 Days-themed steampunk anthology. May 2014

Tomorrow Wendell, an urban fantasy by R. M. Ridley. June 2014

On the Isle of Sound and Wonder, a Shakespearean steampunk rewrite by Alyson Grauer. July 2014

Black Sunrise, sequel to *Shadow of the Last Men* and second book in the Next Man Saga by J. M. Salyards. August 2014

Accidental Apprentice, a wizardry fantasy by Anika Arrington. September 2014

To learn more, visit www.xchylerpublishing.com

**Sneak Peek of R. M. Ridley's *Tomorrow Wendell*,
book I of the White Dragon Black series.**

Chapter One

Jonathan parked his old Lincoln, squeezed the steering wheel, and shook his head. Three months prior, he hadn't even heard of Apatedyne, or their nasty pyramid scheme. Today marked the fourth case, in as many weeks, involving that very con job.

Grabbing his doctor's bag of paraphernalia from beside him on the seat, he got out of the car and into the early November cold. The wind, like a coroner's scalpel, cut right through him. Entering through the glass front door of the five-story block of red brick got him out of the wind, but not significantly warmer.

The building owner thought it wasteful to heat a lobby only Jonathan used. The place would have been torn down by now except it had been deemed a historical building. The owner had never proven who instigated that crusade and Jonathan had worked hard to keep it that way.

Trusting the elevator to carry him, as much as he would a starving crocodile to ignore him, Jonathan started up the stairs. He figured if the elevator were ever upgraded, he would put on ten pounds by the end of the first week.

When he reached his floor, the third, he saw through the open door his newest secretary sitting at her desk. She was reading a gardening magazine. Jonathan thought it optimistic of the woman. He happened to know she lived on the fifth floor of an apartment building with a balcony not much bigger than the desk she sat behind.

"Hey . . . El . . . ?"

She looked up at his voice with a sigh. Her red curls fell back exposing her freckled face. "Alicia. Ah-lee-sha."

"Right, of course." Jonathan flashed her a broad smile. "Here's the invoice for today's case. She'll pay by check at the end of the week."

He opened the door to his personal office, but before swinging it closed, heard her ask, "I thought this was the same sort of job as the last one?"

"Yeah, it was—removing some hexes and compulsion spells from Apatedyne products."

He stepped farther into his office.

"It's just, well, it's less than you charged the last few."

Jonathan sighed.

All he wanted was to sit down, smoke, drink, and pretend his body wasn't eating itself up because of the magic he had performed all day.

Breaking down stubborn hexes and curses made for a tedious and trying job, but it didn't stop the craving to feed his addiction. Jonathan knew from experience that if he started drinking now, and drinking hard, he could get past the worst of the withdrawal.

He turned around and leaned on the doorframe.

"It is less," Jonathan admitted, "but the compulsion curses had used up a good bit of the woman's savings. She's a sixty-seven-year-old widow. What was I going to do?"

"I just wanted to make sure the figure was right, for the books."

"Oh. Let me see?" He leaned closer as she held up the ledger. "Yeah, that's right." He straightened up. "I'll be in my office . . . resting. If anyone comes in, I'm out working a case."

"Okay," she said with a small nod of her head.

Closing the door, Jonathan crossed to his desk, where he collapsed with a groan into the chair.

There was a term, ancient in its origin, that practitioners used for the way he felt: 'Bitten by the Dragon Black'. The dark side of using magic was how it turned to sink teeth deep inside and tear at you once the energy stopped flowing.

The yellowed blinds were drawn over the two windows, filling the room with a murky glow that highlighted the dust motes suspended in the unmoving air and draped the rest of the room in dark gauze.

Jonathan opened the bottom desk drawer and removed a bottle of bourbon, which he promptly used to fill his glass. He tossed back the liquor and then refilled it.

The burn of the alcohol didn't dull the pull of the addiction. He had worked too much magic for one drink to fully numb the withdrawal already digging through his skeleton to tear at his soul.

He glanced at the old clock ticking away above the door and couldn't believe when he saw it was only just three. He was bushed.

He couldn't argue that the Apatedyne jobs weren't good for a steady paycheck. However, both the work, and the company, were tiresome and annoying. Jonathan didn't feel like playing David to their Goliath, on the other hand, he couldn't allow them to continue their malicious con jobs in his city much longer.

New Hades may have been a cesspool, but that didn't mean everyone could just come to the city and dump their crap into the waters.

He dug out a cigarette and, resisting the urge to light it with a spark of magic, spun the wheel on his lighter.

The first drag sent nicotine flooding into his brain, easing neurons no longer infused by unearthly energy. Jonathan hoped to spend the rest of the day simply watching cigarette smoke float up into the cobwebs that festooned the ceiling.

As he sloshed bourbon into his glass for a third time, he heard the light, double rap on his office door. He refused to acknowledge the intrusion, but the door cracked open anyway. His secretary slipped her head in.

"What is it, Alice?"

The woman rolled her eyes. "There are some . . . gentlemen, here to see you."

"I told you to say—" Jonathan leaned back. "Fine, show them in."

She swung open the door and stood back. Behind her, three large figures loomed and Jonathan understood her hesitation over word choice.

The things that had come looking for him were not, strictly speaking, human. They had been, but once dead, the term doesn't really fit anymore. That goes double if death hasn't stopped them from making business calls.

All three wore cheap, grey suits that hung like water-logged flesh on them. They were well-preserved though. Hard to spot that they weren't still living. Jonathan was willing to bet they had been turned within a day of their demise.

"Cursed necromancers," Jonathan mumbled.

Zombies were the stock and trade of many practitioners, but since one had to use necromantic spells to accomplish the feat, Jonathan felt justified in cursing that particular lot.

All three of the animated corpses were over six foot and none of them lanky. Jonathan didn't know why they were always giants—it didn't matter if the corpse was four-foot-six or six-foot-four. A zombie's strength and resilience came from the magic.

"Everyone always thinks size matters," he muttered.

Although they didn't look like the sort of animated corpses used to deliver verbal messages, there was always the chance. Jonathan decided to take it, but not being a fool, he slid the top drawer of his desk open a few inches.

"What can I do for you boys?" He got up from his chair and used the motion to slide the desk drawer farther open.

For a moment, all three corpses just stood, unmoving, unblinking, unbreathing.

Zombies could do a lot, or hardly anything. It depended on the spells used when they were reanimated. With the proper rituals, a zombie could be anything from a chauffeur, a personal bodyguard, or even a nanny. Mostly though, they ended up being programmed for thuggery.

Jonathan figured the three in his doorway were just that after all—voiceless, single-thought, leg-breakers—then the middle one spoke.

"Apatedyne wants you to understand that it doesn't appreciate you affecting their profit margins by meddling in their business affairs."

"Really? Well, I suppose that makes sense, but you can tell your—"

Jonathan never got to finish his thought.

The two silent zombies came towards him in a flanking maneuver. They didn't moan, shuffle, or lurch as popular media often portrayed; the corpses came at him like heartburn after bad Mexican food.

Jonathan tossed the glass of bourbon at the zombie on his left as he dodged the wide swing of its hairy-knuckled fist. He kicked his chair out at the one on his right, scooped his Beretta out from the top drawer, and vaulted onto his desktop. An avalanche of books tumbled onto the floor.

He took less than a second to aim the nine-millimeter before taking the shot. Shooting zombies is considered ineffectual at best. They felt no pain, were animated with spells, and also, already quite dead. But that didn't mean a firearm couldn't be put to use against them.

The key was to target the appropriate body parts.

The report of the gun in the small room was thunderous and followed by shrill screams from the front office. Jonathan dropped the Beretta; he wouldn't get much use of it again in such a fight.

He slid off the front of his desk and ran headlong at the zombie in his doorway.

Hitting the body felt like tackling a hanging side of beef, but it did move, which is what Jonathan needed. The corpse toppled back and to the right, as its bullet-shattered kneecap gave way.

Jonathan scrambled over the chest of the creature and couldn't resist giving it a kick to the head.

He had managed to get one down for the count. Now, he just had to draw the other two out of his office; there were too many valuable volumes and rare texts in there.

Once in the front office, the ear piercing shriek emanating from behind his secretary's desk had become more strident. He tried to think of comforting words to tell her. He tried to think of comforting words to tell her, but 'shut the hell up' was the best he could come up with.

He spun around to look back at the other two zombies.

Both goons had clamored into the front office. Jonathan moved to his left, away from the strident screeches, and further into the room. He hoped to draw them further in with him. It also put him out of the reach of the one-legged corpse.

The two came at him, one stepping on its felled companion.

Jonathan took another step and reached blindly behind him. His hand felt the smooth wood of the coat rack and he grabbed it. He attempted to swing it up, only to find its weight awkward and uneven.

With a curse, he spared a glance to figure out what was wrong and saw a pink, fluffy coat dangling from one of the tines.

Taking out zombies could be done with relative ease, as long as you had access to a hot enough flame. Once started, the things went up like balsawood carvings. The tricky part was stopping them from bumbling about, setting the whole building, or yourself, on fire.

Jonathan shook the coat rack, trying to dislodge the coat his secretary had, for some ungodly reason, hung on it. He finally managed to get the article unhooked and swung it around, hoping to corral the corpses long enough to set them on fire.

The coat rack collided into the side of the brute and cracked. It didn't slow the creature. An upper cut lifted Jonathan into the air and he landed against the far wall. Jonathan found himself on the low bookcase, his face a raw ache, his back a single spasm. He had put up with enough.

"Screw this."

He had them as close as he could hope for, and at least one of them wouldn't be wandering about.

He brought up his right hand and rubbed his middle and ring finger together. He began to chant the words of power, of focus. After being hit by a ham hock of a fist, his jaw felt like rigor mortis was setting in, which made pronouncing the proto-Egyptian language of the spell tricky.

Luckily, it was a short invocation.

Jonathan felt his energy swell as though the earth itself were rising up through him, and reached further still. He tapped into the beyond and pulled the forgotten forward, through him.

He rode the White Dragon.

Sweat soaked into his clothing. His skin felt abraded with the heat.

He hated this spell.

His chest burned from the inside out, his heart pumped lava through his veins.

He hated necromancers.

As his mind spun through infinite harmonies, every molecule of his body danced violently.

The fire he had formed leapt from ethereal to physical. A flame that burned deep-orange engulfed his hand, its flickering edges sending swirls of black soot into the air.

Jonathan lashed out with his foot, catching the closest zombie on the chin and rocking it backward. Before it had a chance to close in again, he released the spell.

The flame rolled off Jonathan's hand, growing as it absorbed oxygen from the air around it.

He shivered with the sudden cold.

The summoned fire smashed into the closest zombie. It pushed the corpse backwards and lapped over it. The overspill ignited the bourbon soaked fabric of the second zombie. The room quickly smelt of melting polyester and overcooked ham.

Still, they came at him. One thing that had to be said for zombie employees, they literally couldn't quit.

Beyond the flames, Jonathan caught sight of his wide-eyed secretary as she bolted up from behind her desk.

"Hey, Alice, while you're up, grab the fire extinguisher from the hall would you?"

She looked at him, or the walking flames, and darted out the door.

"That-a-girl."

Jonathan relaxed a little. All he had to do now was keep them at arm's length and wait for his secretary to return.

He wished he had the coat rack. Without it, he was reliant on his feet. That was a good way to ruin a perfectly serviceable pair of shoes.

All three of the corpses were blazing pyres now. Flames licked at the ceiling, and charred the cheap rug. The heat trapped in the room caused his arm hairs to curl and his lips to crack.

"Any minute now . . . secretary."

He kicked the nearest zombie and hit its arm. The limb rocked backwards and just kept going—a flaming comet. Jonathan brought his knees to his chest and kicked out with both legs at the same time.

The zombie staggered back a few feet and then crumbled in on itself. Jonathan hastily beat at his trouser cuffs to extinguish the flames lapping up his legs.

He looked up and saw the other two had been almost completely emolliated as well. What he didn't see . . . was his secretary.

With a sigh, Jonathan slipped off the bookshelf.

Skirting the pile of burning bones, he went to the front door to look about.

There was no sign of the woman.

The fire extinguisher remained clipped to the wall. With a groan, he retrieved it, returned to his office, and sprayed down the flames that had found fuel for their appetites beyond the corpse flesh.

The office smelled like charred meat, burned bone, and, oddly, sour milk. The ceiling had a large scorch mark and the rug was ruined. Jonathan put down the fire extinguisher. He stepped over the pile of smoldering ash and entered his office. He closed the door, righted his chair, and sat back down behind his desk.

"I hate necromancers," he said, pouring himself a fresh drink. "They never consider the second-hand damage."

Chapter Two

The office, the next day, was thick with a fug that went beyond just the cigarette smoke trapped in the small room. The smell of bourbon clung to the blue-grey air, but it was his own fermenting emotions that thickened the enclosed space.

Frustration draped the walls, and Jonathan couldn't deny the guilt that clung there as well.

The Apatedyne situation really needed to be handled on a level beyond simply freeing those affected by cursed products; like the widow yesterday. He saw little choice but to stop this company from operating in New Hades before their business went further than a few people being rooked of their savings. Preferably before more corpses walked through his door.

He had to admit he wasn't enthused with the idea of another corporation adding him to their black list. Jonathan knew firsthand how difficult it was to force a company into a position where they decided to back off. They had their own practitioners. They had money. Industry, as a rule, didn't sleep.

Still, he thought, *if not me, then who?*

Sitting back and fixing the mess afterwards—for a fee—made him no better than Apatedyne and Jonathan knew it. He just wasn't as young as he used to be. Tilting at windmills hurt more than it had in the past.

He needed to find a method which would be effective, and hopefully, not drawn out. A prolonged siege wasn't what he considered a good time. Devising ingenious ways to trip them up could be fun, however.

If he got his imagination going on this one, it might motivate him to act. Needing to get his synapses fired up, he reached for his cigarette case when a pounding on his outer office door resounded through the office.

Jonathan paused. His hand hovered over the silver case as he waited for his secretary to answer the door.

The pounding came again and reminded him he no longer had a secretary.

He couldn't be blamed for forgetting; she had only left the day before. When she had failed to get the fire extinguisher, Jonathan had hoped she had simply decided to grab a breath of fresh air.

He had to accept that he'd lost yet another secretary.

The hand assaulting his door didn't seem to be doing so in anger and so Jonathan assumed it wasn't another attempt to dissuade him from meddling in company affairs.

As he got up, Jonathan realized the nature of the knocking belonged not to someone who wanted in but someone who *needed* in.

He opened the door separating the offices and the stagnant air escaped with the speed of a diesel truck backfiring. Through the frosted glass of the front office door, he saw the person turn away.

Jonathan slowed.

But the dark blob of a hand rose again. With a groan, Jonathan took the last few steps and swung open the door.

In the hall towered a lean man. His true height Jonathan couldn't approximate from the way his shoulders rolled forward over his chest.

A wide-brimmed hat, squashed on hair that looked like a pile of straw, seemed designed to obscure the man's identity.

Jonathan might have been worried about that if wasn't for the other unmistakable oddity; the lower portion of the pallid face was spotted with tiny wads of tissue paper, most with a crimson center.

"Mr. Alvey?" queried the man with a voice possibly unused in the last decade.

"That's what the door says."

"You are, though, right? You're Alvey, the private investigator?"

Jonathan reached up to the top of the open door with his fingers and studied the man's face.

Resisting the urge to flick the pieces of tissue from the stranger's jawline, he wondered why they always asked that question. What sort of sacrament made them want to hear him speak those specific words?

"Yes, I'm Jonathan Alvey. I guess you'd better come in."

Jonathan stepped back, allowing the man he tried desperately not to think of as Lurch to enter.

The man slipped the hat from his head and walked in. Jonathan swung the door closed and marched past his guest into his office.

In the short time the door between the rooms had been open, a reasonable portion of the accumulated smog had dissipated. Jonathan felt somehow vulnerable without it.

He sat behind his desk and waited for his latest client to accomplish the feat of settling himself into a chair. Once the glum man was seated, with leg twitching and finger tapping the crown of the hat in his hands, Jonathan reached once more for his smokes.

Opening the silver case, Jonathan made sure he could actually see the man's reflection in its smooth exterior as he withdrew a cigarette. Having satisfied one curiosity, Jonathan extended the case towards his guest.

Perhaps, Jonathan thought to himself, *it's the haunted look in his bloodshot eyes that makes me think he's glum.*

The man's square jaw swung slightly from side to side. "No, I quit—" he started to say. But then suddenly, and vehemently, he proclaimed, "Oh, what the hell does it matter now?"

351

He leaned out and grasped the case long enough to slide a cigarette from it. Jonathan put the case back on the desk, relieved that the man had been able to touch silver. Made the odds better that he was human.

He lit his cigarette then slid the lighter to the scarecrow across the desk. Jonathan took one deep drag. "So, how is it you've come to be in my office this evening, Mister . . . ?"

"It's my life," the man blurted out.

"Come again?"

"My life," the man croaked. "I'm here for my life."

"Someone stole your life savings?" Jonathan tried to hook one single barb into the wriggling fish of this man's conversational gambit.

"No." He took a deep drag and Jonathan watched the tip burn bright and hot.

"Why don't you start at the beginning, Mister . . . ?"

The man moved his mouth oddly. To Jonathan, it looked as though he was trying to tie a cherry stem—only this stem fought back.

After a minute, he vaulted out of the chair.

Just as Jonathan became convinced he'd have to ram a stick between this guy's teeth while dialing nine-one-one, his potential client landed back in the chair.

He had produced a small card from his back pocket, which he smacked down on the desktop with one long arm before dropping back into the seat.

Jonathan leaned over to investigate the item before he considered touching it. It looked quite familiar and, as the protective wards tattooed like a necklace around the base of his neck were not flaring up, Jonathan reached out and slid it closer.

Made of stiff paper with an inked outline; it called to Jonathan's mind the title card which popped up between scenes in silent movies.

Inside the simple, yet elegant, border were six words. They did wonders to clarify his client's statement.

Printed in a simple font was the phrase: 'You will die in three days.'

Jonathan looked up from the card to the man across the desk from him. No hint of amusement tugged at the man's tight lips. No humor danced in the wide, brown eyes. Truth be told, Jonathan only saw the hazard signs of someone breaking under the burden of stress.

Whether the statement was threat or prediction, his client seemed to believe the validity of those six words.

"All right, Mister—what *is* your name?"

"Uh . . . Courtney," the man wiped a long-fingered hand over his face. "Wendell. Wendell Courtney."

"Okay, Wendell, is there anyone you know of who might have a reason—any reason at all—to want to hurt you, or even just scare you?"

The head slowly went from one side to another. A single flake of crimson-dotted tissue paper floated towards the floor.

"Are any of your friends pranksters?" Jonathan asked, looking for a nice, normal reason for this man to be in possession of such a card.

Once more, the ponderous turning of the head one way and then the other.

"All right, Wendell, I think you had better start at the beginning. Take your time and let's see what there is to make of this."

When his client didn't speak, seeming once more to have forgotten how to form words, Jonathan began to despair of having any patience left.

He wished he had thought earlier to call for an order of Singapore noodles from The Lucky Monkey restaurant across the street. Accepting it would be a while before he got to eat, Jonathan pulled out the bottle of bourbon from his desk drawer.

He filled his glass, took a coffee cup that didn't appear to be dirty, and sloshed some of the bourbon into it as well. The mug he slid towards Wendell.

The gaunt man didn't hesitate over the liquor. He took the cup, gulped back a slug, and did a damn fine impression of a consumptive cat ridding itself of an aggressive fur-ball. However, he took another drink and, eyes watering, began to speak.

"The card—I got it at an antiques shop. A machine, see? That's what unnerved me at first. I've always found the things quaint, a memento of a different era. But now . . ."

Wendell took another drink, but before Jonathan had a chance to interject one of the questions already swimming in his not yet sufficiently bourbon-soaked mind, the man went on.

"I ran out of the shop, and when I got to my car, I found the card still clutched in my hand. I tossed it onto the passenger seat and drove home quickly. I'd calmed down a fair amount by the time I'd driven back to my house."

Wendell turned the mug ceaselessly in his hands.

"I still thought then that I was being silly, see? I mean, I told myself, who knows when the machine had been filled, or by whom, or even what for? I was foolish enough to tell myself it probably wasn't even a *real* antique but a movie prop that the bastard in the store hoped to pass off as an original."

Wendell gave a weak, deprecating laugh and then drained the last of the bourbon. Jonathan thought about refilling the mug, but at the rate his client seemed prepared to suck it back, he'd never get a coherent story if he obliged every time it emptied.

"It wasn't until a few hours later that I read the morning paper."

Jonathan flicked his eyes to the folded paper on the far corner of his desk.

354

"And then I began to really freak out."

Jonathan had grabbed the paper from off of the bus stop bench outside his building. It had already been well-read before he had gotten it and now it had a felted look.

He had skimmed through most of it as he did every morning. He liked to make sure it contained no news that actually impacted his life, such as new by-laws, price hikes in the cost of gas or tobacco, graves that had been displaced or bodies disinterred over the night—the standard stuff.

Jonathon couldn't bring anything to mind from what he had read, that would, in any way, connect to the card before him and his client's ramblings.

"I was born on the fourteenth of September." Wendell informed Jonathan as though understanding his thoughts.

With the same reluctance he once had for putting his hand into his grandmother's purse, knowing she stored her not-yet-ready-to-be-discarded tissues and her hard candies made sticky by spilt perfume, Jonathan picked up the paper and found the horoscopes.

He quickly scanned until he came to Virgo and read what it had to say.

This week will be good for most Virgo's. Mercury is in the ascension. Use this week to forge a new friendship. Be wary of lending money to family during the month. If you were born on the fourteenth of September, this will be your last week in this life cycle.

He laid the paper aside.

Wendell's eyes, devoid of emotion, looked past him. Jonathan felt he should say something. He had no idea what though. 'Do you like long walks on the beach?' didn't seem appropriate.

Wendell spared him.

355

"I got quite unnerved. I confess I drank a bit, then." Wendell glanced to the mug he'd placed on the corner of the desk.

With a sigh, Jonathan leaned out and poured a measured amount of the bourbon into it. He topped off his own glass and then pointedly put the bottle away in the desk drawer.

Wendell took the mug, wrapping around its sides fingers long enough to verge on being tentacles.

Jonathan knew this could all still be a set-up. A well-placed bribe gets the paper to print a certain line in the horoscopes. Cue the actor carrying a printed card with hopes of playing the assigned role well enough to earn a few hundred bucks. A half decent actor could manage the body language and facial deadpan.

Jonathan had no problem thinking of people who would actually bother.

Apatedyne was obviously the first to leap to his mind. It seemed a little out of their style, however. His second guess came quick on the heels of the first.

There resided in the city a certain Welshman named Owen Braith Davies, who had long been a thorn in his side—and to be fair, vice versa. Davies hadn't made a move in their on-going chess game for several weeks now.

If it was a con, Jonathan had no problem playing it out a bit longer. He had no pressing cases. He could do so long enough to spot the reason for the diversion and turn it around on the perpetrator.

It was always good to know one's enemies and how they thought.

However, if this guy was being straight with him, then Jonathan had to admit his interest was piqued. In truth, Jonathan thought if it was a con, it was being played on Mr. Wendell Courtney.

Still, he was a private investigator—somewhere he even had a license to prove it—and a job was a job. He could use the money. It would be nice to earn on a job not involving cleaning up after Apatedyne, especially if his last secretary did find her way back to the office. He owed her a few days' pay.

"Okay, Mr. Courtney," Jonathan said. "I'm willing to take on your case and look into who's doing this to you." He opened up his cigarette case.

"No, you don't *understand*," Wendell nearly wailed. "Damn! He said you'd take me seriously."

"I am," Jonathan replied calmly, fishing out another smoke. "Wait. Who said?" He straightened up. The cigarette broke half way out of the case. "Shit," he mumbled.

Taking out another cigarette and lighting it, Jonathan asked. "Who, Wendell? Who told you I would be able to help?"

Here we go, Jonathan thought, *now we come to it.*

"The policeman," Wendell explained.

Jonathan took a drink. He dragged deeply on his smoke, and then dove in. "A policeman?"

"Yes. I went to the police before coming to you. See, I thought—like you seem to be thinking, though you're wrong, I assure you—some*one* was messing with me, maybe actually threatening me."

Wendell grew progressively more animated the longer he talked.

"I went to the police and they basically laughed me out of the station. It was humiliating and scary. I didn't know what to do next. Then, one of them from inside came out and stood near me.

"While he lit his cigarette, he said into his cupped hand that I should seek you out. When I asked him what he meant, the officer took out his cell phone, and though he acted as if he spoke to someone on the other end, what he said was directed at me, see?"

Wendell took a drink and Jonathan held his tongue waiting for his client to finish the whole tale.

"He said that you, Mr. Alvey, were the only person in New Hades who could or would help me. He said where I could find you and that you would believe me."

"Yeah, I think I know who you're talking about."

Jonathan remembered his father's body on the ground, the blood pooling into the carpet around it, the knife handle sticky in his grip. He remembered the looks on the cop's faces and how the cuffs had dug into his wrists. The trial, the questions, the sentencing—he remembered every second of it.

He also remembered the one cop who had shown the slightest sympathy towards his plight: a man by the name of Lamont Bonham.

As time went by, Jonathan had sent certain clients to Bonham, knowing he was an honest and open-minded cop. And over time, if Bonham came across people whose trouble couldn't be handled by mundane means, he would direct them towards Jonathan.

"So . . ." Jonathan began, but before he could assemble a conceivable response to all he'd been told, Wendell jumped up.

"Wait! There's also this. I found it in my closet after being at the police station. I had tied to convince myself that everything happening to me indicated I *did* need the help of a professional when remembered I had it."

Jonathan bit back the remark that Wendell should have chosen the professionals with the white coats and padded rooms. There remained a possibility these occurrences *were* paranormal in nature. A well-phrased curse could mess with a person in such a way.

The curse would carry no actual potential for harm, but it could mess things up. If someone would go through the effort of hexing a person in an attempt to kill them, they wouldn't bother tacking on a warning spell first. *Unless*, Jonathan told himself, *they were truly twisted.*

Wendell had gained his feet and loomed over Jonathan's desk, a cross between Quasimodo and an NBA player. He pulled a large black orb from his coat pocket. Instinctively, Jonathan brought his ring and index fingers together and began an incantation.

Then he saw, on the side of the globe, a white circle with the number eight on it. Jonathan forced down the energy he had summoned. What Wendell had produced from his coat pocket was a 'Magic 8-Ball'.

Dry-mouthed and sweating, Jonathan fought back the desire to finish the incantation.

The need to perform the magic consumed him. His body vibrated and every particle within called out with the necessity to use.

Jonathan downed a mouthful of bourbon in an attempt to gain control of his addiction. If Wendell noticed any of Jonathan's struggles, he made no show of it.

"You try it first," Wendell insisted, setting the novelty item down on the desktop.

Jonathan thought he could predict the outcome of the exercise but wanted to play it out anyway.

Picking up the 8-Ball, Jonathan turned his hand and looked at the little, circular plastic viewing window at the bottom. 'Answer uncertain' floated in the window.

He turned it away and shook it hard before turning to look at it again. This time Jonathan read, 'Signs point to yes'. Turning the orb a third time, he looked to Wendell and read the dour acceptance on his face.

Jonathan concentrated. He cleared his head and thought of a question. Only one question came to his mind. Thinking only of it, he turned the Magic 8-Ball over and looked at the answer.

In context, the result could be considered a bit unsettling, but Jonathan already believed Wendell's answers would be worse. The answer to the question, 'When will Wendell Courtney die?'—the only question he really could ask—floated up.

'Outlook not so good'.

Jonathan set the oversized pool ball on his desktop.

"All right, Wendell. Show me."

The man nodded and reached out for the thing as though it was a severed head. He shook it and turned it so Jonathan could see it.

Jonathan would have liked to say he was surprised by what he read, but he'd be lying.

'You will die soon' was the message printed on the tiny card floating in front of the plastic window.

Wendell didn't bother checking what the outcome had been. Jonathan guessed he'd already spent a few horrible hours turning the ball over, and over, and over.

Wendell shook the ball and held it for Jonathan to read once more. Jonathan had to admit, he had just become more intrigued. The message had changed. It remained just as grim and definite, but the words were different.

If this was a hex, curse, or spell, it was a complex one.

Now, instead of 'You will die soon,' the small clear circle revealed the words 'Outlook is death'.

To make the novelty item display one dreadful message over and over when Wendell touched it would require a tricky, but attainable, curse for a proficient practitioner. Different messages on the same theme changed the game significantly.

"I kept at this for over an hour. It was like watching my own train wreck. I couldn't stop even though I felt nauseated with each turn. I was gripping the thing so hard my fingers turned white. Every time I turned it over, it predicted my death. The words changed sometimes but never the message."

"All right, Wendell, I believe something's going on. I'm going to look into this. I want to check out this thing," he said, pointing to the orb, "and I want to go to that antiques store."

Wendell looked relieved for the first time since he'd entered Jonathan's office. He placed the ball on the desk and sank back into the chair, not looking at cursed object again. "Could I impose on you for another cigarette?"

"Yeah." Jonathan said and slid the case towards Wendell without sitting down. He was, for the moment, not interested in Wendell. Jonathan knew he still needed to get more information from his client, foremost being what the hell had actually happened at the antique store, but it could wait.

He also hoped Wendell could become settled enough by that point to tell him clearly about the excursion. In the meantime, Jonathan would be remiss if he didn't check out the Magic 8-Ball for any lingering spells or hex marks.

He perched on the edge of his desk, picked up the ball, and slowly turned the item in his hands. At every slight irregularity in the smooth surface of the black plastic, Jonathan stopped to examine it. He would run his fingers over the mark, bring the toy under the light of his desk lamp to inspect it, and wouldn't move on until absolutely certain it was just a scuff or scratch.

It took some time, but finally Jonathan convinced himself that no hex mark or spell symbol had been carved on the item.

The next thing he wanted to do was test the thing for residual magic. However, he wasn't sure it would be a good idea to perform magic, even the most subtle and benign of spells, in front of Wendell at that point.

Wendell seemed to have reached a place, mentally, where he could be content to just sit back and allow Jonathan to take over.

He gazed absent-mindedly out the window on the far wall and, though his fingers still loosely clawed at his pant leg, his foot had stopped its staccato twitch. His eyes had lost some of their haggard appearance.

Jonathan considered it a good enough condition to be able to leave the man alone. What he wanted to do would only take a moment at any rate.

"Wendell, I'm just going to step into the next room. I'll be right back."

Wendell nodded and, slowly turning away from the window, looked at Jonathan. "That's fine—if you think it will help." He then looked back out at the grey sky.

With a nod, Jonathan stepped into the front office. He set the Magic 8-Ball on the desk he kept for the secretaries he never could keep.

From his pocket, Jonathan took a small, wooden container. He dipped a finger into the ivory powder within and smeared an almost undetectable layer of it on the black orb. Jonathan then spat lightly on the 8-Ball.

He brought the ring and middle fingers of his right hand together and rubbed them together. In a voice, hardly more than a whisper, he spoke in Latin. A luminous white aura formed around his fingers.

The spell came fast. The energy he had suppressed just moments before leapt into him, his very flesh eager to perform even a simple spell. As the magic flowed, he felt the need that always resided inside his bones relent a little.

He placed his hand above the ball and, with a small effort of will, caused the white glow to fall away from his flesh and onto the orb.

Jonathan watched the white luminosity as it coated the black plastic. He kept his gaze firmly on the spell light and not the item it almost obscured. After a while, when nothing else had happened, Jonathan shook his head slightly.

He brought his two fingers together once again and started to chant. The cadence of this spell differed completely from the previous. Jonathan spoke the Ojibwa words quickly. Despite their rapid movement, a grey powder began to gather on those same two digits.

Once the powder became thick enough to obscure the details of his fingers, Jonathan stopped summoning. He tapped his left hand lightly on the back of his right, depositing the powder over the eight ball.

Nothing happened.

There were other spells he could use, less effective castings but still viable.

He wanted to use them, despite their limitations. He yearned to cast just for the feeling of purpose and power. Use, simply to bask in the feeling. Allow the energy to flow through him, to unshackle himself from the constant self-control. Soak in it and relieve the aching mental fortitude that bore down on him every moment he denied that which dwelled in him.

Jonathan closed his eyes. He gasped and expelled his breaths like a beached fish. He dug his nails into the flesh of his palms to stop his fingers from moving.

He had to be stronger than his hunger. Using would consume him eventually, but not today. Not this time.

Squeezing his hands tighter, Jonathan forced himself to speak the word to cancel the current spells. He cursed softly and sighed.

Not only had he found no hex marks on the damn toy, there appeared to be no evidence of *any* magical tampering at all.

Jonathan walked back into his office, leaving the thing where it was.

As soon as he sat down behind his desk, he took a drink to fortify his resistance and lit another smoke.

It took a moment for Wendell to get around to noticing that Jonathan had returned.

"All right, Wendell, this card." Jonathan picked up the first thing that his client had given him and tapped the edge of it against his desktop. "Tell me again where you got it."

"It came from a machine . . . one of those fortuneteller booths," Wendell added when Jonathan drew in a deep steadying breath.

"You mean the coin operated 'Zoltan' things from, like, the thirties?"

"Yes—yes! Only this one wasn't a 'Zoltan'. I don't remember just what it was called, but it featured an old woman inside the booth, not a man. She had a scarf on her head, and a shawl, and tarot cards spread out before her."

"We *are* talking about a mannequin, or animatronics, or whatever here, right?"

Wendell sighed his answer. "Yes."

Jonathan decided he'd better only ask questions when absolutely necessary. He feared Wendell still mentally teetered too close to the edge to be sidetracked or distracted. Some people just couldn't handle their brushes with the mystical.

"Okay, sorry. Go on."

"I was on my way to my dentist's appointment. I always try to get there ten minutes early so I can relax and get myself in the right state of mind, you see. But the office had moved quite recently and, as this was my first time there, I had misgauged the time it would take to get to the new building. Consequently, I arrived twenty minutes early for my appointment, not the ten I had planned for."

Jonathan wondered if Wendell had a medium setting.

First, he hadn't told Jonathan anything. The conversation had been only slightly above the grunt and point level. Now, Mr. Courtney had given into pointless yammering that Jonathan thought unlikely to hold any significant meaning to the issue of his death threats.

"Finding myself so early," Wendell continued, oblivious to Jonathan's opinion regarding his speech, "I wondered what I should do with the extra time, when I spotted the antique store two doors away.

"Being as I like to peruse antique shops, I thought it a perfect solution, see? I even had the thought that I could make a habit out of treating myself to a trip to that store after my appointments with the dentist.

"The owner had seemed nice enough and though the shop felt cluttered, it appeared reasonably clean. The contents of the store were the usual compilation of curio's, crap, and collectables. But I was drawn to the . . ." Wendell actually gave a shudder before bringing himself to say, ". . . the fortune machine, as soon as I laid my eyes on it.

"I had always loved them and found them fascinating, you see. I checked the asking price and though more than I could manage, it was, from my experience with such things, rather cheaply priced."

Jonathan lit another cigarette from the dying embers of the previous and tried to will his client to get to the salient point of his rant.

"I asked the owner if it worked and he looked up from the counter at me with a look of puzzlement. He had been concentrating on a crossword, I believe, and it took him a moment to comprehend what I had asked.

"But once he understood to what my question pertained, he said to me, quite affably, that it did indeed work before lowering his head and once more resuming his scribbling on the paper.

"And so, with this reassurance, I took a coin from my pocket. It cost only a nickel, see, and I figured what the devil. Well, they do say you shouldn't tempt fate or the devil, don't they, Mr. Alvey?"

"Yes. Yes, I believe people do say that."

"Well, once my nickel clanked into the bowels of the machine, the head of the doll began to move back and forth slowly—as though reading the cards spread out before it. After a moment of this, the head looked up and the hand reached down, as though sliding the card to me personally. That damn card you now hold."

They both looked at the card Jonathan still toyed with. He placed it flat on the desk and motioned for the man to continue.

"That very card was what came out of the little slot of the machine. I read it and, at the time, thought it a joke.

"I glanced back at the owner of the place to share the jest he had set up but he could not have cared less about me. I looked again at the card and it was as you see it. I left then, swiftly, and went directly to my car.

"I drove home and tried to calm myself. I didn't even know why it had affected me so. Perhaps, on some level, I knew it was more than a prank, even then. Knew it to be what it is."

"What is the address of this place, Mr. Courtney? I want to go check out this machine. It's possible it's been tampered with."

Wendell got a confused and hurt look on his face and Jonathan back-peddled to explain just what he meant.

"I'm not talking about the owner, or someone else, putting in these cards, Wendell, although I will check into that as well. I think the horoscope and the eight ball prove there is more to this than a simple card swipe. No, the tampering I am speaking of is, well, more esoteric in nature."

"You really—you do that? It's real?"

"At this point, Wendell, are you doubting there is something unnatural about what is happening?"

After a moment, Wendell replied he did not. He looked down at his shoes and went on to say, "No. I guess as much as I might like to hear you say otherwise, Mr. Alvey, well, I guess I know better."

"Okay. I'm going to go visit this machine. You are going to go home and relax. I know that sounds insane, but run yourself a nice warm bath and soak in it."

Jonathan slid a small notepad and pen across the cluttered desk so his client could give him the address. "Every time you start thinking about what's happened, I want you to picture, in your mind, an acorn."

Wendell's head came up.

"It's a meditation technique I find helpful to those who have never done it before." Jonathan explained, "You think of nothing but an acorn, Wendell. Then, slowly, get more and more intricate in your vision of the acorn—see the cap, the ridges in the side of the nut, the rich color striations."

When Wendell nodded that he understood, Jonathan reemphasized, "Try to do as I say. Home. Relax. Take that bath and I'll call you as soon as I've done what I can." And then Jonathan felt he had better add, "With what we have. Deal?"

"Sure," Wendell agreed amiably enough. "Yeah. I'll try the bath and even the nut thing. I'll *try*."

"Good. Don't worry, Wendell, we'll get to the bottom of this. And hey—in the mean time you could always live wild, you know, since you're not going to die for three days yet."

"Um . . . right. Thank you, Mr. Alvey."

Jonathan nodded and escorted his client out.

Chapter Three

Jonathan thought about what he would need to test the fortune-teller machine for a curse, or its like.

He wouldn't be able to use the methods he had for the Magic 8-Ball. He disliked drawing up and casting from the innate power within like he had before . . .

That wasn't true. The truth was he *did* like it—liked it too much. Anyway he could avoid triggering that craving was the wise man's way to go and Jonathan hated playing the fool.

Performing magic, Riding the White Dragon, made your bones feel like they were sweating and soaked your brain in colors that had no name. The comedown, Bitten by the Dragon Black, when you stopped using, would make a heroin addict look like a teetotaler.

You couldn't have one without the other. Which is why the symbol to mark a practitioner was called the White Dragon Black. The Chinese called the symbol a *taijitu*, better known as a ying-yang symbol, but without the center dots. The symbol was far older than the Chinese use of it. Anthropologists had found the image in Etruscan art from the fourth century B.C. It had served as a way for practioners to know each other and mark safe havens for centuries before that.

Jonathan knew he was a functioning junkie. To remain so, he didn't like to push his luck, not if he could avoid it.

He tried using his own energy when there was no other choice. What he'd just done for Wendell's magical ball had required a small amount of energy dispersal, but even that had still left him downing another glass of bourbon to counter the yearning and jittering deep within.

Jonathan filled his glass, lit a smoke, and sat down.

There was other reason he couldn't use the same method on the fortuneteller machine—it wasn't exactly subtle. Jonathan adhered to the unspoken rule to hide the truth of the world, from the world. He had to think of a substance to place on the machine that would perform the same test without overtly drawing attention

It also had to be something that wouldn't damage the machine, should it prove, like the Magic 8-Ball, to be magic free.

If it did appear to be cursed, Jonathan would deal with that problem, even if it ended up being destructive and obvious. Some things were more important than the issues they caused.

He leaned back in his chair, sipped from his glass, and drew long drags from his cigarette while staring at nothing.

Had there been anyone there to observe him, they might have concluded that he couldn't care less about his client's problems. It would be easy to think, in fact, that he had lied to Wendell about doing anything for him. However, in his mind, Jonathan scrambled about like a rat in a maze made of cheese and garbage.

He combined and recombined ingredients to find a way to test the fortune machine discreetly. Such mental exercise also helped to distance himself from the effects the magic usage had wrought.

Jonathan never tried to go dead, straight out, cold turkey, even when using magic was unnecessary, but he had a feeling his new client would make his chance of controlled usage a laughable effort.

Jonathan focused on creating the perfect mixture: a substance that would require little expenditure of his own power. He needed a concoction that relied mostly on the active energies and magical properties of the ingredients themselves, but would still reveal any paranormal tampering.

Slowly the right combination fit together in his mind. Knowing that he wouldn't conceive of a mixture that would cover every possible application of esoteric influence, he had targeted the most logical spells, and curses, that a practitioner would employ.

Jonathan had found, in his own history of interacting with this sort of thing, that there were just certain ways a practitioner did and did not make things happen.

Someone might have used an incantation whose residual magical energy wouldn't show up with his final formulated concoction, but the odds were so low that he couldn't allow himself to worry about it.

If he was honest, Jonathan still thought the whole thing a prank—that someone, somehow, had played this out on poor Wendell. He just couldn't figure out why. At this point, he had no idea *how,* either.

Whoever had targeted his client had to be using magic. There should have been something for Jonathan to pick up on.

Suddenly, his mind supplied the last ingredient needed to make a paste that would turn different colors as it reacted to each residual energy left by an incantation or conjuring.

Jonathan wouldn't bother making much of the mixture since the very nature of the concoction would inherently make its effectiveness last only a few hours. No use wasting the ingredients on something that would shortly be good for nothing, except possibly masking bleach spots on dark natural fibers.

Jonathan got up and opened the only other door in the office, revealing his own little apothecary.

Stored in the large closet were glass jars, small boxes, hanging plant material, cork plugged bottles filled with various liquids, and assorted writing materials, on shelves lining the walls .

On the back of the door, among other paraphernalia, hung his shoulder holster. The gun currently lay in his desk drawer, but he almost never left the office without it, so he took a moment to put strap the thing on before collecting together the ingredients he needed.

After he'd gathered everything required, Jonathan carried the tray to his desk and, shoving a few papers out of the way, set it down. He got to work using a mortar and pestle to crush herbs, minerals, and other organic materials.

Occasionally, as he added an ingredient, he would chant in languages—most of them obscure and quite dead—to activate certain properties inherent in the substance or call on the innate power of the herbs.

His brow began to bead as he fought against the urge to summon up his own energies. Jonathan fought his addiction and concentrated on the making the paste.

He knew the mixture was a success when it suddenly congealed into a waxy substance. It also turned the color of green one expects from the blood of overgrown frogs or bloated lawyers.

Jonathan went to search the front office desk for a suitable container. He knew that one of the secretaries no longer in his employ had to have left something he could use.

Sure enough, at the back of a bottom drawer, he found a small circular container of lip balm with only half the yellow waxy substance left inside. The label said something about bees, but Jonathan didn't care what it had been, just that its former product would be a great cover for his potion.

Jonathan took the lip balm into his miniscule, and admittedly grungy, washroom behind the secretary desk. He turned the hot water tap on, placed the container in the sink, and walked back to his office.

He took the tray of ingredients back to the closet and put each jar, box, and herb back in its place. The closet looked a disaster, but Jonathan knew where everything was, give or take the odd item.

The walls shuddered and the industrial clanking of old steel pipes choking on their own load filled the air.

Jonathan took in another portion of the bourbon and finally wandered back to the washroom. He put his finger under the stream of water and, taking it back out, returned to his office to get a smoke.

He leaned on the washroom doorframe, smoking, until a particularly loud and disturbing rattle came from the wall behind the sink. For a full five seconds following the clattering, nothing came out of the spigot. Then, water sputtered and spurted forth.

Steam began to curl around the tap and Jonathan stuck the rubber stopper over the drain hole and allowed the sink to fill.

He tossed the cigarette butt into the toilet, where it died with a hiss, and grabbed a pen off the front desk. He used the end of the pen to hold the lip balm container under the hot water slowly filling the sink.

The room began to fill with the cloying, sweet scent of honey. Jonathan hoped the container would clean out quickly, but in the end, he had to use the tip of the pen to dig lingering blobs of wax out of the bottom.

Then, to be certain there was no remaining residue, he carefully washed out the container with soap and rinsed it under fresh running water.

Jonathan brought the now clean container to the mortar and pestle and scooped two fingers worth of the substance into it.

It in no way resembled anything that anyone would want to put on their lips, but Jonathan didn't expect the owner of the store to ask to borrow his lip balm anyway.

He didn't plan on engaging the owner at all, really, until after he had already used the paste. According to Wendell's account of the owner, he wouldn't be spending much time observing Jonathan, either.

For more of R. M. Ridley's *Tomorrow Wendell*,
watch for its release in June 2014.

34482160R00231